GOSPEL PRISM

In memory of Marie Colvin

GOSPEL PRISM

GERALD WEAVER

LONDON WALL PUBLISHING

Published by London Wall Publishing

200 Aldersgate Street
London
EC1A 4HD

www.londonwallpublishing.com

ISBN 978-0-9929943-3-4

The great thing is for life to be seen through a prism. . . . In other words, life must be divided up in our consciousness into its simplest elements, as if into the seven primary colors, and each element must be studied separately.

—Anton Chekhov

One must write as one should live, for one's own sake and for that of some kindred spirits.

—Johann Wolfgang Von Goethe

Choosing forms of worship from poetic tales…

—William Blake

Be on the side of the angels. Be a prism.

—James Joyce

CONTENTS

PREFACE

I did not write this book.

Books are peculiar things. The reactions that some people often have to the odd book here or there can be quite casually extreme. Sometimes a book is banned or burned, or the author may be pilloried, or a *fatwa* may be called down upon him. Or what may be worse, depending upon your point of view, the book or one of its characters may become the object of worship for some more highly enlightened people. Since most individuals can only fully have faith in a thing that they cannot see or sense, entire congregations may spring up around a book that its truest believers have not even read.

Each one of these many things may even happen to a single book, as has already happened to this very book, perhaps owing to its unusual status as both the first book and the last book. In fact, if you are not reading this book on a screen at this moment you are reading a calcified fossil, a frozen relic from only a particular point in its evolving life. If you are reading it on a screen, it is not the same as the previous time you had read it nor will it be the same as the next time you or anyone else reads it. This book is always in a state of passing into its next form and exists as a living and changing document in a place where one may only access it electronically. In that way it is the first book. A book nowadays is a more ephemeral, or perhaps a more chimerical, thing than it once was.

But in another way this is the last book, one that subsumes many other books. It is also one that has been read and which you are reading mysteriously even before its final publication and which has come to be quite well known before it was ever read by the general public. Much of what seems to be this book may be based merely upon surmise or conjecture. The only copy of this book to have escaped into the world prior to this more general publication was an author's galley that had been pierced entirely through by a shotgun slug, leaving behind it a hole big enough to put a thumb and two fingers through. The consequent and quite literal holes in each page of the narrative have made the story all that much more difficult to follow and at the same time just that much more likely to be stead-fastly revered or to be hated and feared as only such books can be. In other words, this is a book that was holy even before it was written and it has also as equally been unwritten.

Even that careful explanation is misleading. It was written, partly unwritten, then leaked, and then it entered its viral stage. It got out into the world and was read. Even then it was changed by those readings and by various electronic cuttings and pastings and redis-tributions. It is also a book that is acutely aware that it is being read and still being written and unwritten at the same time, as it is also aware of its spiritual and historical import.

There is an author. I am not he. We have different names, as you will see. I merely represent the author. I am his lawyer. It does explain how that hole came to be in the first copy of the original manuscript. As I held it in my hands on one of my other journeys of legal repre-sentation, some person who was perhaps a disgruntled former client took a shot at me with that shotgun which was loaded with a lead slug, and that slug missed me and passed through the book.

Every man, woman or child deserves representation. I should not be held accountable for what that man or author says or writes or unwrites. My name is on this book, but the moralists and theocrats bent on punishing the author should not look to me. I especially hope to avoid those fawning and devoted souls traveling this way in search of the author from the incipient centers of worship to which this book has given rise, in many far flung places such as Coventry and Florianopolis and Madhya Pradesh.

The true author of this book is safely away where few may reach him. He is certainly beyond the kind of contact sought by those spiritual seekers who devotedly would like to expedite or preclude spiritual contact by making more worldly approaches on the writer. The author is physically beyond reach and can be literally found in a United States federal prison.

What some devoutly revere as this book's spiritual mysteries may be taken as gospel or as dangerous heresy. Or they may not. It is a book, simply put. Books are what they are. And we see things and read books as through a prism. In classrooms and living rooms across the globe, an agnostic or an atheist may be heard to strenuously argue, "But the Bible is just a book." Similar arguments may be raised against other holy books. But they all are too ironic, by half. A book is the Bible.

The best thing about being a lawyer is that by exposure it is a continuing adult education of a distinctly liberal arts nature. I have learned disparate and useful facts about a myriad of subjects, from the operation of copyright law in the communications field to the operation of brothels in Prague, from government regulations (and conspiracies) to the darkest maunderings of the criminal heart. My experience teaches me that this book is a spiritual detective story as it is also a mystical journey for its writer, one that may have a great reward for its readers.

In each one of its twelve chapters there is a distinct divine revelation or insight which Christian found or through which he lived, a spiritual truth, each of which may be considered one of the sort of "twelve disciples of truth" that are contained in this book and are why it has become a new book of devotion for its growing flock of the faithful. These new believers trust that this book, *Gospel Prism*, is the guide to the new spiritual age which we are entering in the beginning of this millennium. Some of them are Catholics and Protestants. Many are Muslim or Jewish or of other faiths. You may make it your task to recognize each transcendent verity and to better understand its source. You may become one of the believers. Or you may not. And that may not be dependent upon how well you read this book, or even whether or not you read it at all.

Finding divine revelation in the words in a book is not all that easy, nor may we all be able to do it, especially in the actual reading. The numbers of people who believe in it and those who read it and believe in it are largely different.

Apparently, faith in life is one thing and faith in literature is another.

I place this book and its twelve divine insights before you, as it was placed before me. Much of it will be in the first person, but you must never doubt that I am not the "I" that begins, places gaps in, and continues the narrative that you are about to read. I cannot even tell you all that much about the author.

You may seek every quality of the writer's mind where it lives, in his words. You may seek his inspirations where you may find your own, in your heart.

LEPANTO ROAD DOGS

I had determined that Philly Ray would aid me on my quest. And he would do so for love.

Little Philly Ray Sanchez had something in the dusky corner of his swarthy heart that was gleaming white. It was as completely separated from anything else that he had ever experienced in his nasty, young and brutish life as it was as totally different from all that was part of his apprehensive and volatile personality. He contemplated this snowy presence inside of himself and it brought him in touch with the ineffable other. It appeared as phlegmatic and as smooth and as abundant as he was garrulous and flawed and meager. And it had arisen from an understanding that he had only acquired since he had come to prison. On the outside, growing up on the corners and in the alleys of a South Bronx neighborhood in New York City, the name of which he had no desire to recall, he had learned to overcome the limitations dictated by his diminutive stature by simply being quicker, quicker to anger, quicker to figure something out, quicker to make a comment, quicker to cross the line from anger into violence. He was a small earthquake of a young man and had survived and even prospered in the street-corner drug trade that had ground up and destroyed more young men like him than prison ever could. This new and pale silvery apprehension of his had only become possible because prison had made him more contemplative.

1

He had truly turned his attention for the first time inward, to find that he might contain inside himself something different, something that he could not have expected to find and certainly not find inside of himself. This luminous soft white space inside of Philly Ray had a name, and it was Belinda Hahner.

I had been dropped into prison from a height that Little Philly would have never recognized. I had roamed among corporate board rooms, legal conferences, the finest educational institutions, foreign countries, sophisticated salons, fine homes and elegant bedrooms, before I had found myself in this restricted place. I had kept my head down for several months before I allowed my background to become known and before I began to help other inmates with their problems, legal and otherwise. So I came to be known for knowing certain things that were beyond the understanding of most of these men and this would be where I would start with young Philly Ray. I became known in the prison for having a more sophisticated understanding of the world and life and women and literature and government and art and medicine and the law. I was looked upon as jailhouse lawyer but also as a kind of a professor or a statesmen or a sage, to some extent because I had been well-educated and I had been plucked out the upper echelons of society and plunged into the subculture of American prison life. But mostly it was because of the chopsticks.

Only a couple of months after I had arrived on the inside of this minimum security prison, it had occurred that it was the annual Chinese food take-out day, which was looked upon by the general population as a kind of Christmas and Thanksgiving rolled into one. Chinese take-out food was cordon bleu to these men who faced a drab daily diet. Once a year, inmates were given the opportunity to use their commissary accounts to order from the take-out menu of the local Chinese restaurant. The trip to the restaurant was made by a quick work release detail conducted by a handful of trusted inmates and I had made a point of asking those inmates to be sure that my order would come back with a pair of disposable chopsticks of the kind with which I had almost always eaten Chinese food. It almost caused a prison riot.

The inmate delivery men had spread the word of what I had done, and when I started in on my kung pao chicken and my beef with broccoli using my chopsticks almost every other prisoner in my cell block was compelled to watch me. The crowd and the excitement were akin to that caused only by a particularly good prison movie on the television in the common room. There were shouting and high fives and pointing and exclamations of disbelief. Small shoving matches broke out on the periphery. None of these mostly urban youths had ever seen anyone other than an Asian person on television manipulate chopsticks to pick up his food and place it in his mouth. Soon I was grandstanding, using my chopsticks to pick up individual half peanuts covered in sauce and waving them in the air to loud whoops of approval and chanted lines from the refrains of popular musical songs. I used them left handed. I used them to cut the chicken. I picked up two pieces of broccoli at once. From that point on, I was an international man of mystery to my fellow inmates.

And I did not ever take this to mean I was to act in any way differently than anyone else. I had read *Coriolanus*. Shakespeare had shown me what the people will do to someone who makes no secret that he believes himself to be better than they are, even when that is actually the case and even when he has done nothing but a crucial service and had been a benefit to everyone else. I kept to myself and was demonstrably humble and I took on the most physically

3

demanding and least in-demand job in the place, that of landscaping, which not only included snow removal in the winter but also was the only job that was a full eight hour work day. And I did not make an effort to move on to a better, more cushioned job assignment, as had everyone else who had started out in landscaping. I was then given a kind of favorable treatment by most everyone in the place. And I had also, in another way and in a story later for this book, obtained the kind of necessary protection from the kind of inmates who will hold it against another and take it out on him simply because he did receive favorable treatment. I was soon the inmate to whom many of the others would go on all other more worldly questions, including legal questions and questions of what might be considered trivia in the salons and boardrooms and law offices I had once frequented. It was also considered that I might know a thing or two about women, because the small handful of women who came to visit me were all well-scrubbed and college educated and attractive. And this is indeed how Little Philly Ray would come to see me.

I was the one man on the inside who could probably tell Ray Sanchez what he most desired to know about his pale and snowy first love. He had only just seen her for a short time during a trip he had made on a prison work release program excursion to nearby London, Kentucky. On the work details in this prison, inmates were often loaned out to various non-profit organizations and projects seeking free and skilled labor. Most often, these projects were for performing renovations or demolitions or even working at fairs and fundraisers for churches and community groups.

Some work release programs were very regular and well established, such as the regular prison detail that worked for the United States Forestry Service. Those men truly worked eight-hour days and left the prison for the entire time to go into the nearby Daniel Boone National Forest as part of a Forest Ranger work team. Those inmates earned a roughly one fourth of the regular minimum wage and also actually worked for that. Prison makes a show of requiring that all inmates have jobs inside the facility but very few are anything more than make-work jobs and all of them pay only pennies an hour. They are not at all like real work, so most inmates prefer them over Forest Service work. For such an inmate, then, one with a job inside the prison, an actual trip outside the prison on a short-term work detail was a much-sought-after small vacation from the sameness of the place and it was a somewhat restricted, hands-off visit to all that the outside world represents.

Such a trip could be to clean up a stream and to rebuild its banks and improve its structure for a local chapter of a conservation organization. Or inmates could completely renovate an entire nearby church shelter for battered women. They could even man the booths at the local Apple Blossom Fair for a civic or business organization. And humanity being what it often compassionately and generously is, the sponsors of these outings could see that they would become opportunities for the genuine excitement and simple joys that are afforded by everyday life, to be visited upon a small group of men who had been suffering the deprivations thereof. A ride on a four-wheel drive all-terrain vehicle for an incarcerated man working on that stream for the conservation organization could strike him and stick in his memory in such a way as if it were actually a gondola ride down the Grand Canal in Venice. Or the taste of a funnel cake served at the fair would seem like a meal at a four-star restaurant to a man subsisting on prison food. And to young Ray Sanchez, meeting and watching Belinda Hahner at the renovation of the Lepanto Church Shelter for Women was at once a washing away of all the malice and deceit and idle gambling and dark double dealings and the dodging of missiles and blows and all the hundreds of outward dangers and concerns that had occupied his life up to that point. It was at the same time a symphony of sublime feelings that seemed at once so overwhelming and new and impossible to understand or to resist. He had been emptied out and refilled in some respects. In other words, he was the perfect candidate to assist me on my particular quest.

After all, I had received the word of God directly from the alluring female Christ who had entered my cell one mystical night. It was as jarring an experience for me at the time as it is perhaps to read about now. That visit is most appropriately the subject of its own descriptive episode and which follows this one, which is for now focused on my quest. She had told me something almost fantastic. I had understood it to be of such critical importance to mankind that I had to begin to spread the story. I believe I had understood her divine Word to be that no man could ever explain God to another. I felt moved or compelled to explain this to people. I had to become the evangelist of the impossibility and the inherent failure, of evangelism. Such an enterprise had to start somewhere. And in this case it started with some small items that are as inconsequential as they are necessary to an understanding of this story.

Prison was not my first trip into the demimonde. I did indeed know other things about the seamy side of life. I knew things that Little Philly wanted to know. I knew things that he could have never guessed. And I knew them without being told.

I knew that to young Belinda, Philly was as exotic and as romantic a figure in her personal mythology as she was in his. I had never met the woman but I had seen her and had known her in many other forms and impersonations throughout my life and in my reading. There is a broad demographical swath that runs on a southwest to northeast slant through the east of North America, from Georgia to Maine, along the Appalachian Mountains. The people in this broad stripe of the United States tend to be white and Protestant and descended from English or Scottish ancestors who arrived there after the original colonization of the North American coast. There are enclaves of exactly this narrow demographic description in some of the upper-class reserves of the United States, in New England and New York and the Middle Atlantic. And though there is a vast gulf that separates these two groups in terms of wealth and its appurtenances, particularly education, they are very similar in many ways. In both of these white Protestant worlds, one poor and one wealthy but both containing people largely of English descent, there is a lot of changing of partners and divorce and petty squabbling over money, and in many ways each individual is subject to greater dangers within his or her family than outside of it.

I did not have to know or even to have personally seen the subject of Philly Ray's transformative obsession to have known several things about her with certainty. She was slightly overweight, and this was as much due to the fact that she had a problem with her self-image as it was because she had already become a mother at a very early age. Her own mother never cared much for her or for Belinda's siblings, the two or three other children she had born along with Belinda and who had likely been fathered by different men. In fact for Belinda, the word "father" probably had a fluid and somewhat dark definition and had been applied to more than one man in her childhood, at least one of whom at some point or another had laid hands upon her in a way no real father ought. She was also no stranger to disease and alcoholism or drug abuse. And she knew what it meant to live in a kind of low-key and constant fear and also to live like a vagabond on the couches of friends and relatives. She was no stranger to the government and knew things that more privileged and well-educated young adults would never learn about the local governmental offices of child protective services, welfare, social services and the police. Some of her closest relatives, or perhaps even she herself, had been incarcerated at one point or another. I could surmise that she had sought the thing she had never known in the places she would unlikely ever find it and had accepted it in its counterfeit forms from real pigs of married men and derelict neurasthenic little boys. Love had always eluded her because she was not ever sure what it really was or that she deserved it.

Philly Ray was also one of those prisoners the rest already seem to know because there was always a bit of a buzz around him, even in a place populated by counterfeiters, bank robbers, international smugglers, murderers, organized crime bosses and other colorful characters. What I had previously described as his quickness was in some quarters interpreted as a kind of mental or emotional instability that can be as protective in such a place as courage or resolve can be. I knew him only by this reputation and by observation myself, until one day when I came upon him in the bathroom, just having emerged from the shower, towel wrapped around his waist as he was shaving and looking in the mirror. I was also a prisoner whom he and other inmates had noticed, for the chopsticks and more. So it was not an unusual thing for each of us to drop the prison protocol of keeping out of each other's business and to speak to one another briefly and directly.

"Are those what I think they are?" I said as I looked at two round smooth scars of a shade slightly lighter than the rest of his dark tan skin which were located halfway up his back on the right side.

"Where I got shot?" he said.

"That is what I thought."

And as he continued shaving and looking in the mirror he slowly turned toward his left and lifted up his left arm and under it were similar raised and smooth and lighter marks but that were roughly the size and shape of the outline of a paper clip.

"Those are where I got stabbed," he added, "Got a couple more of each under this towel somewhere. Got 'em all, standing on the street corner."

"I assume you were not just waiting for the bus."

"I was doing what you know I was doing. It was my corner. Everyone else wanted it too. I was making several thousand dollars a night, standing on that corner, selling drugs. A lot of people wanted to take it from me. I will have to fight to get it back, when I get out."

"So much for the supposed deterrent effect of prison," I said.

"You think I give a shit about prison?" he asked. "I risked being killed every second I was standing on that corner. That did not 'deter' me. I made more in a week that I could have made in a year in any square job. For that kind of money, it was worth the risk. Prison don't mean shit compared to that kind of money."

I walked out of the bathroom. That conversation had reached the limit permitted by various other prison protocols regarding personal space, bathroom behavior, and initial discussions. Had I stayed any longer, he would have started to wonder about me in ways that would not have served my specific purpose.

Part of the favorable treatment accorded me for being well educated, well-traveled, and well-read while also keeping myself down at the level of the rest of the general population was that such treatment also was given to me by the authorities of the prison. I had humbly worked my way up through landscape department from cutting grass and tending the grounds to being permitted to drive the truck. And on the work release program details I was often assigned as the driver of the large van that shuttled the inmates to and from the work sites. It put me in touch with the prison administrator who was in charge of selecting which inmates went on the work release detail, and sometimes I could make a suggestion as to which prisoner or prisoners should be included. I was planning to make just such a request.

Little Philly Ray Sanchez would become my road dog. In the prison patois, a road dog is a very important and rare and precious type of inmate friend. A dog is loyal, above all. And a road dog is loyal on the road or in the road or in the most difficult and dire circumstances. In a place where everyone gives each other a great deal of personal space, physically and metaphysically, in a place where no one stands up from his meal without signaling those around him that he is about to get up and that such a movement is not to be misconstrued as a possibly aggressive act, men do not form a bond very easily or very quickly. But when they do it exceeds what might be expected, and loyalty becomes the sole virtue and true road dogs will stand up for one another when it is fruitless or when it is wrong.

I had planned to begin my work at the same London, Kentucky, church at which the pale white subject of Ray's passion was a volunteer and which was a regular customer of the prison work release program. There was a detail coming up which was fairly straightforward. It would present several opportunities for detours and free time as it was largely a matter of making certain deliveries for the church. The deliveries would require myself and one other person and would take only a few hours even though we would be allotted a full work day. So there would be plenty of other time, time for my sacred mission.

Philly had seen Belinda only once before, for a few moments at a job site where he and other prisoners had been working to help renovate the inside rooms of the church shelter for women. She had brought them food for lunch. She was pleasant looking, slightly shorter than medium height, with fair skin that was smooth and full on her rounded face and on her rather full arms. What could be discerned from her body in her clothes was that it was at best a comfortable body, not particularly shapely and certainly not svelte. Her eyes were a cool gray-blue and had that same kind of glimmering paleness that every other part of her seemed to emanate, including her short blonde hair which was cut rather plainly to the length of her chin. She had worn loose blue jeans and a gray sweater. To every individual man she had ever encountered on the outside she had been unprepossessing but sweet and not a first choice but one not to be overlooked either. In short, to Little Philly she appeared to be a luminous goddess.

To any man suffering the deprivations of prison, she would had to have been a profusion of feminine delights, smiles and postures and scents and tones of voice that all would have been wonderful reminders of the women from whom each been separated. But to Philly Ray Sanchez she had been the first woman he had ever seen. There had been no other. Whatever he had known in the past had sloughed off of his impression of what was feminine as if it had

11

been the water drops that fall from a wet umbrella that is shaken. There was something just so soft and yielding and open about her, something that he had never encountered in any of the women he had known. There was not the slightest hint of brass or of assertiveness or of some complicated connections to brothers or family or even to the church. She was an island of ultimate femininity over which a man could be a governor. And she was so unaccountably fair-skinned.

She had smiled at him. There was something extra in that smile. It was possibility. It was not sassy or flirty or dismissive, as had been the smiles he had known back in his neighborhood. Nor was it perfunctory or merely polite, as had been the smiles of women and other people that he had encountered when he had occasionally been in the society of middle-class white folks in America. It was a light and it was an opening. And it had lingered. Nor had she given that smile to any other man on that job. It had become for Philly one of Wordsworth's stops in time, which he kept inside of himself and from which he could draw spiritual sustenance simply be recalling it. And he recalled it often. He could have had no idea in the world what was on the other side of that smile at that moment.

What Belinda had seen and had thought at that moment could not possibly have been dreamed by Ray, even at his most outrageous reveries. She had been struck by the masculinity of the dark and kinetic stranger, by something about him that was mysterious and unknown. And she had lost most of her customary insecurity in looking at him because his status as a prisoner was the source of a kind of sympathy. She was not as afraid of him as she had always been with other men. She had allowed herself to be open. She had looked at him at first not as a man but as a poor inmate who was suffering from his incarceration. And when he had looked back at her with eyes that no man had ever focused on her, eyes that were neither haughty nor mean nor possessing of a kind of detached and common hunger, but that were admiring and humble and just the slightest bit surprised, she suddenly felt in the middle of her spine that he was a man and more than just an inmate. And all that mystery and dark and kinetic masculinity suddenly entered her heart through those eyes that were so direct and which seemed to be interested in her and not just in something about her. So she looked back at him with a look that itself was direct and open and then modest but receptive. And then, finally, there had been a flicker of something else, a kind of apprehensive yearning.

So at the moment their looks and her smile ended he was smitten and could not believe the possibility which had just seemed to present itself to him, one like no other he had ever had. He simply could not believe it. He could only hope. And for her it became a sort of gentle litany of questions, all aimed at herself. She wondered if he had been disappointed by her blankness and failure to react or if she had seemed to him not to be paying attention. She wondered why she had not been more friendly and engaging and whether would he think it was because she might be condescending to him because he was a convict. She hoped she had not offended him.

I had surmised all of these things in an instant because I had been there. But neither of them could ever have had any idea what the other might have been thinking. So it was all left to me as a set of tools with which to recruit Philly Ray on my blessed mission. And I took up that task not long after our discussion of the failure of prison or threat of death to be deterrents to truly lucrative criminal activity. I was in the prison yard on a weekend afternoon when there was no one else walking about. I had just seen him walking toward his building and I stopped him and greeted him. Without too many preliminaries, I asked him, "How would you like to go on another work release job to that church?"

"When?" he said. I was getting used to answers that were questions.

"It will be in a few weeks. My plan is to do some things that are a bit off of the prescribed duties of the detail, and I will require your complicity and assistance. There will be that much freedom in the job. And it will be a two-man detail, just you and I."

"I don't know about breaking no rules. I don't want to stay here no longer than I got to."

"Wait until you have heard what I am planning. I can not only get you to see the lovely Ms. Belinda Hahner, I can help you to get her to fall in love with you. I can get you fifty Belindas."

"I don't know about fifty. Two might be nice, but one is probably enough."

"Better than that, I can do. Even better than having her merely fall in love with you, I can teach you how to get her to let you be her governor, how to get her to completely surrender to you."

With this my new friend became quiet and contemplative. No such idea had ever occurred to him, not even as a possibility. Yet when I uttered it he became convinced that such a thing might be possible, that I might be able to help deliver to him what he desired most and in a way that he had never imagined possessing any woman. He was running over in his mind those few moments in her presence that he had contemplated before, many times before. And this time he was subjecting the whole episode to a new possible interpretation. He was coming under the grip of a different kind of feeling, one that would give him the courage to risk a great deal more than an extended stay on the inside. His wonder and his dreaming had in those minutes of listening to me turned into something that had quite a much stronger hold on his imagination. He had begun to anticipate. He was in for the duration and in for the detours I was planning.

"I will need your full cooperation in this matter," I began. "It is a mission of critical importance to the entire world. I have had a divine visitation, and such a thing cannot be meaningful if I hold it merely to myself. I must begin to spread the new gospel and I cannot fail. We cannot fail. There will be times when we will be assailed and there will be obstacles. But on the other side of those obstacles will be a new world. There are so many wrongs to be righted, grievances to be redressed, abuses to be done away with, and duties to be performed. The beautiful female Christ has personally and directly talked to me, and I must not keep her words to myself. You must help me to spread this new gospel."

"I just hope when we are on this so-called sacred mission that your holy vision includes the memory of your promise to me that you will help me to get this woman to surrender to me," he said.

"It is all part and parcel of the same thing, I believe. If you will be my acolyte in all things, you will learn this as well as some other truths."

"I'd like something a little more certain."

"And I shall produce it."

At that moment we were interrupted by toilet paper man. He had just walked up to us. Toilet paper man was a slightly built, Caucasian, soft-spoken man of around fifty years old and slightly taller than average height. He was bald on the top of his head and he compensated for that by growing the hair on one side of his head very long and combing it over his bald pate, which is a practice far more common outside of prison than inside. He had a slow drawling way of speaking that in America is known as country. His combed-over hair was neither gray nor brown but in between. There was something about him that was spectral. He could often be around the premises, and no one would have noticed him. He could also often be found in the yard, walking around, talking to himself and reading very obscure small publications of the far right wing of American politics. And often but not always, a small tailing of toilet paper could be seen trailing out of one or the other of his pant legs.

All of this is to say that he was the one inmate of whom every single other prisoner was rightly afraid, which made it a rather tense moment when Little Philly Ray, agitated by his contemplation of my promises and insights and by the meditation upon his moments, past and prospective, with the lovely Belinda, suddenly blurted out, "Toilet paper man, what the hell is up with the goddamn toilet paper?"

I quickly contemplated a premature end to my nascent evangelical career, when surprisingly toilet paper man calmly answered in his country voice, "I wrap it around my body every morning to protect me from thermonuclear waves."

"Can you believe that Ray?" I responded, with alacrity and no small degree of relief, "not knowing about the thermonuclear waves? What a knucklehead."

As both that moment and toilet paper man passed beyond us, I shot Philly a remonstrative glance, and he reminded me that I had promised him something more certain. So I produced for him a bit of doggerel I had once written. And I told him that what had been true four hundred years ago was still true, that the romantic heart of a woman was susceptible to poetry. In any other place on the outside or at any other time within this baleful enclosure, handing this young man a poem of love for the object of his affection would have met with a scoff or something worse. As it was, Little Philly was rapt as he read the poem.

BELINDA
She shines before me
Like the first love of youth,
Brilliant as rain, and smoother
Than moonlight on snow.

I lean forward to give
A weeping kiss upon the light;
And the sound of the morning,
My heart now returning.

My eyes can hardly see her
And my mind has always known
That I cannot catch the shining
Of her small and winning moon.

I burn with fire to touch an angel,
Thick with desire to reach a star,
So close upon the flying dream
To grasp with hands of smoke and tar.
How to take the kind perfection
And hold it to my dusky breast?

"Do you think this will work?" he asked, then he added, "Never mind; I know it will. What else you got for me?"

"All in good time, my young squire, all in good time," I said, knowing well that he now saw me as some kind of magician who truly might be able to help him to become the governor of his Belinda.

He was also more strangely at home now in prison. I had thought before at quite some length that this enterprise on which I was about to embark required that I have an acolyte or a votary but that it was essential that he possess a name equal to the import of the mission. I wanted him to have an appellation that at once would indicate the profound significance of this sublime undertaking, one that suited the new order of my life since my divine visitation. And certainly none of the many combinations of my new friend's current name would suffice. This new revelation about the heart of my young companion settled the question for me.

"I shall call you Fabrizio del Dongo," I pronounced, "after the Stendahl hero who fell in love with a beautiful young woman whom he chanced to see while he was imprisoned and then for whom prison had become transformed to the one place he most wanted to be. And I like the name. I like its appropriately Latinate derivation. What say you, Fabrizio?"

"You can call me anything you want. Not so sure about the 'del Dongo' part. You just be sure that you help me get what you promised."

"I will do much more than that."

Now that I had brought my powers of persuasion to bear on my Fabrizio and had convinced him to ride forth with me and to assist me, all I had to do was to inform him of the day and hour when we were to take to the road. And I told him to make whatever arrangements for this adventure that he saw fit, while I made my own preparations. Apparently, Fabrizio decided that one provision he had needed to make in the interim was to get a jailhouse tattoo of a cartoon parrot on his upper arm in order to impress his intended. I was not so sure that it made sense for an assistant to a prophet to be adorned by such a thing or even that it would have the effect he desired. But I decided that it must be a sign, the meaning of which would become clear to me at the appropriate time.

And so we set forth on the appointed day and thus would begin the story of the ingenuity that was displayed in pursuing our quest and other events as outlandish as they are true. We took ourselves to the administrative office in order to be processed out of the prison for the work day and I was given the keys to the van. Once on the road, I began to tell Fabrizio in depth about my celestial visitation and exactly what had been divinely revealed to me and how I had been deeply affected by it all and how I was planning to spread the new good word. I cannot say if I was surprised or not surprised at the acceptance with which my votary took all this startling and dramatic and original revelation. He was even amenable to my restrictions.

"We may plunge our arms up to the elbow in religious discussions and disputations and theological discussions of the most sublime nature. But I must warn you, Fabrizio, to remember that you are not the one who has received the divine visitation, nor are you well versed in the nuances of theology. In all the other matters of our interaction with the great unwashed masses you may take your part. But you must not involve yourself directly in my evangelical pursuits or in the matters of high spirituality."

"You can count on that, Christian. I ain't interested in these picky discussions of what is holy or what is not. I never even thought about it. I was raised Catholic. Just tell me one more thing about how to get Belinda to want me," he added.

"Kiss them on their scars, I always say."

"What the hell is that supposed to mean?"

"Every woman in the world has some mark upon her that she does not like," I said. "Many times it is actually a scar or a stretch mark or a wart. Other times it is a crooked nose or an odd laugh or a thick waist or a skinny neck or a squeaky voice. It can be almost anything. But it plagues her. It becomes a focus of all her insecurity about how she appears to men. But you and I have the advantage of being in prison and knowing that for us all women are beautiful and they are all beautiful all over. We would no longer turn away a woman for having a lisp or an overbite or a scar than we would turn down a beer or a steak or a vacation with our children or any of the other things of which we are currently deprived. So we have no problem kissing a woman on her scar, so to speak. What I am telling you is that which you must do, and that it will pay a large dividend if you love her exactly where she is most insecure."

"But what if she really is perfect?" Fabrizio asked, half in a reverie.

"There is not a single woman in the world who is completely satisfied with her posterior, even the perfect ones."

This took a while to sink in. But as with any other truth, my statement allowed Fabrizio to realize what he had already always known but could not have seen unless and until I had told him.

"Genius," he muttered under his breath.

And it was in this mode of deep contemplation that we arrived at the church. Our job was simply to park the van and to take on the management of a rented truck and to load that truck with tables and chairs that were to be used for a church benefit later that evening at a community hall. We were met at the church by the deacon, a man in his seventies. He was thin and tall and still had all of his hair, which was white. And he still had some sparkle in his blue eyes.

"I have directly heard the word of Jesus," I frankly told him.

"Amen, brother."

"No, Jesus has literally come to me."

"As he does to all men who are honest and true and who seek him."

"No, she came to me in prison. She was a beautiful mixed-race woman. She was not a prostitute. She told me that the Pope must choose toilet paper and interpret the Bible, all with the same human mind."

"Amen, brother."

Later, as Fabrizio and I were loading the truck, I said to him, "I think that went well. I believe we have made an excellent start."

"Amen," said Fabrizio, "and when do I get to see Belinda?"

"All of this will happen in good time, my young squire."

When we had loaded the tables and had no more to our assignment but to deliver them to the community hall and set them up, would we then return to the church and report the job that day as finished. All of this would leave us an additional four or five hours to do with as we pleased. It is difficult to explain what this means to men who normally have no such choice or such freedom. But it is perhaps the way in which all men should look at the small choices and freedoms which they are provided by every day. It was my intention to begin my proselytizing immediately, to get my feet wet at the job of conversion. I was full of zeal and passion and the light of a skeptical faith. These four or five hours were like an emerald or a tiger or a solar eclipse. They were rare and precious and they were

21

matched by the profundity of the enterprise with which I intended to fill them.

"I say we head over to McDonald's and get some French fries and a double cheeseburger," was the suggestion which came from my companion.

"My dear Fabrizio, I do not think that you grasp the magnitude of our undertaking here. This is a very long process and one that history and faith will record as having started here, today, with you and me. It is hardly the time to be thinking about the all too common fare that is sold at your standard American fast food restaurant."

"It has been two long years since I have had good French fries and a good burger."

"Men who have been given such a sacred mission do not concern themselves with food, my young friend. The spirit is their sustenance."

"McDonald's fries are the best in the world. They are one of life's simple pleasures, and the simple pleasures are the best."

"Have you never heard the story of Rodrigo Diaz de Vivar?"

"Was he from the South Bronx?"

"Rodrigo Diaz de Vivar lived in Spain in the eleventh century. It was a time when Spain had been ruled for three hundred and fifty years by the Moors, the Muslims from North Africa. It was also a time when the rest of Europe was in the Dark Ages. The Moors had brought to Spain schools and universities and religious tolerance and museums and math and science and the rule of law and many other good things. The people of Spain lived in relatively civilized security while the rest of Europe lived as serfs in huts and in fear of feudal wars and disease and where the Catholic Church permitted no variance from the faith. But Rodrigo Diaz de Vivar knew that there was one thing about this relative prosperity and peace in Spain that he did not like."

"It was probably that cheeseburgers and French fries had not been invented yet."

"No, it was that the Moors were foreign invaders. So Rodrigo Diaz de Vivar set out to expel the Moors from Spain. It was a very unpopular idea at the time. The Moors had improved Spain, as I have said. And they were also the power and the authority. So to fight them was to stand in stark rebellion and to take a stand against all the good they had done. And in 1092, Rodrigo Diaz de Vivar began that long quest with the siege of Valencia, which he eventually won. He had been a professional soldier and had even fought for a time in the service of the Moors. They had an Arabic name for him which was Al Sayed. It literally means, 'the man.' The Spaniards later borrowed from this and called him El Cid."

"We saw that movie in the TV room last year."

"The point is that the Moors were eventually expelled from Spain. It happened in 1492, exactly four hundred years after Rodrigo Diaz de Vivar had begun the process. What had once been a completely unpopular idea, taken up by one man, later became the status quo. It was such a massive undertaking that it took a long time. But it started with one idea and one man, on a day much like today and a mission much like the one I have sought your assistance to undertake."

"And it took four hundred years, which is about as long as it feels like it has been since I have had a milkshake and an apple pie. When was the last time you had one of their milkshakes?"

Our lives are odd combinations of fate and choice, with one or the other seeming to come to the fore at different times. As Fabrizio and I were on our way to the fast food restaurant we drove past a different kind of church, the kind of church that neither Rodrigo Diaz de Vivar nor the first nine hundred years of his descendants would ever recognize as a church. It was one of those institutions of what can only be called the American religion. It even assiduously avoided referring to itself as a church on its sign on the street, calling itself instead a Christian Community. It was one of the end points on the journey, I pointed out to Fabrizio, that had begun with the very beginning of the Protestant Reformation and which had accelerated and diversified in the United States in the early nineteenth century with the founding of the Mormon Church, the Jehovah's Witnesses, the Seventh Day Adventists, and the Pentecostal Church, and which had partly arrived at this building and all the others like it. It was, strictly speaking, a non-denominational Christian place for gatherings of the sort that were once held only in revival tents but now had become quite respectable and which drew its membership from lapsed Catholics, Lutherans, Methodists, and all of the other Christian denominations.

We ate our fast food feast like men having their last meal. We savored every bite, and for us it was breakfast, lunch, and dinner. Every dash of salt, every drop of ketchup, every bite of beef and potato and bun, every sip of a milkshake was a celebration for each of us. It was an appropriate way to stoke our fires for the grave and weighty mission that was ahead of us.

After lunch we drove back over to the Christian Community, parked the van, and went into the main building. We walked through a short entry hall and into the main room. The room was the shape of a half circle, and along the straight edge, in the middle, a stage stuck out into the rest of the room. On the stage were a few chairs and a speaker's stand. The rest of the half-round room was lined with rows of theater chairs in concentric semicircles. There were two aisles running to the stage from the back in such a way that the seats were divided into sections that each represented a third of the seating capacity. The ceiling was high and gradually rose to be at the highest point just over the stage, so that the space resembled half of a round tent. The walls were blank.

"This ain't no church," Fabrizio said in a modulated but exclamatory voice, knowing full well that he did not want his surprise and disdain to be overheard.

"We must take things as we find them, my friend. And have we not agreed that you would not engage in theological discussion?"

"If I say it looks like a damn high school auditorium, is that being less theological?"

"I suppose so; certainly so. But look, over there are some of the parishioners. May I call them that? I have no idea. But let us go talk to them."

As I had said, there was a time when meetings such as this of Christians occurred in tents and were called revivals. I had supposed that the architecture of this place paid homage to that past. Those meetings, from the early nineteenth century through the twentieth century in America, took place in rural venues in the South and Midwest parts of the United States and they were attended largely by the rural poor and the less educated. The passion and spectacle of the spiritual revival and of the conversions and of the healings that were portrayed must have been an exciting counterpoint to the poverty and the banality of daily life for those people, as if it were the best kind of traveling show to arrive in the small towns as well as being a religious convocation. Late in the twentieth century, television and particularly television evangelism allowed these kinds of gatherings to become more commonly accepted and institutional and permanent. But it was only very late in the twentieth century and in the early twenty- first century that their demographics had begun to change. Some of these institutional and non-denominational Christian communities had become quite suburban and middle class and were populated by doctors and business executives who had drifted away from the organized sects of their fathers and mothers and had later returned to Christianity, but in this form.

It was such a group that we approached now, although it was not exactly as suburban as I have described, since this part of Kentucky was a small town that was in a rural setting. But still, it was clear these ten or twelve individuals were the burghers and the tradesmen and housewives and professionals of their town. I decided that I had little time to lose.

"I am here to tell you that Jesus has come to me personally."

"As to us all, my friend, as to us all," the apparent elder answered me. He was a very fit man of around fifty five years of age, handsome and well dressed, with perfectly cut gray hair.

"No. I mean that she walked up to me and sat down and had a conversation with me. She was a beautiful mixed-race woman. She looked like a movie star and told me that we have to be suspicious of all words, even and especially the word of God, because words are limited in and of themselves and by the human minds that form and then hear them."

"Baby Jesus came to me and told me that my Aunt Judy was in Heaven and was happy and doing fine," chimed in a heavy-set matron in her forties, with curly brown hair and wearing a floral print loosely fitting dress. "He came to me in my room, too. And I was amazed that as a baby he could speak so well."

"And," added a very austere-looking, tall young man, exceptionally slender, blond, and dressed in slacks and a short-sleeve dress shirt, "Jesus came to me, looking like my late father. And he told me that my skin would clear up and that if I gave my life to him I would find safety from the bullies and the thugs."

"I am not sure you understand," I demurred. "This actually was Jesus who came to me. And we had a real conversation. And she said that if we have ever lost our keys we can never be certain of anything and that the minds of our cats were more likely to know Chinese Algebra than we are to know the will of God."

"God bless you, son," chimed in the handsome, gray-haired elder. "Jesus moves in mysterious ways. His will be done. And we have all had him enter our lives. Perhaps you would like to come to our service once or twice and consider joining our community. You might want to talk to Jeff Cole. Jesus spoke to him from his car radio and told him of his wife's infidelity. And Melinda Sherman saw crucified Jesus on a telephone pole and he told her to join the Navy. We have all had Jesus enter our lives in some way or other."

"This is all a little bit confusing to me," I said. "I will take you up on that offer to possibly attend one of your services. But in the meantime we have to leave. Thank you very much."

"God bless you," came back to me in more or less of a chorus.

"That went well," said Fabrizio.

I was shaking my head and looking down as the two of us left the building and I was contemplating all that had happened. In fact, I was still looking down and lost in contemplation when we got to the truck and suddenly I felt myself being given a forcible shove that pushed me with some speed toward the truck so that I rammed into it with great force. As I more or less bounced off it, I heard a voice say, "God bless you."

It was not any of the same voices that I had heard inside of the building, and that same phrase, this time in another voice, punctuated the next blow which landed on me, a punch in the side. I was trying to ascertain who my attackers were and where my assistant was, as more blows began to rain down on me, each one accompanied by the same phrase. I struggled to get my hands and arms up to protect my face and head and I put my back against the truck to prevent any more blows from behind, where I could not see them coming. I am a good size and made several failed attempts to strike back at my attackers, and that was enough to cause them to step away a bit and to turn their blows into words.

I did not recognize either of them. They had not been inside when we had met the parishioners and had our discussion. They were younger than those people and seemed to be in their late teens. They were dressed like teenagers at least, in jeans pants and jerseys. Both were smaller than I. And the words that had replaced the blows now were no longer blessings, but threats. Most of this I do not remember very well, as my mind was still in a state of surprise, and I was having difficulty making the transition from contemplating the sacred to confronting the violently profane. But I do recall that they seem to be accusing me of a kind of blasphemy, a rural American version of the accusation, tinged with bigotry. They yelled at me for saying that "Our Lord was a . . ." and here they used an epithet I will not repeat in this volume and which has been used in derogation of Americans from Africa and of African descent from the first days when Africans were forcibly apprehended and brought to North America in slave ships.

"No, you do not understand," I feebly added, not entirely having recovered my mind from the theological concerns which had been occupying it, "she was of mixed race."

"You saying Jesus was a bitch?" shouted the meaner one, the one who had struck me first from behind.

By this time a small crowd had gathered, and the boys then fled. And after they left, the small crowd dispersed, but none of the indi- viduals that had been in that crowd had stopped to check on my well-being. Only Fabrizio remained. It was to him that I addressed my remarks.

"Why didn't you come to my assistance there? Aren't you sup- posed to be my road dog?"

"I am, but you had told me not to involve myself in any theolog- ical discussions."

"That was not a theological discussion," I countered. "That was a mugging."

"If they had tried to rob you, it would have been a mugging. If they had just called you a jerk or a punk and had attacked you, that would have been a mugging. But they sounded sort of theological to me."

"I am not so sure of that. They were just a couple of violent and mean-spirited bigots, with anger management issues."

"Wait a minute. Aren't you the one who told me that it was a theological point of view when I said that building was specifically not a church, but it was not theological for me just to say that it looked like a high school auditorium? Those punks were making a point about your opinion of Jesus. I had to stay out of it."

Just then we were approached by an apparently Middle Eastern man who had been walking toward us from a commercial van that was labeled on the side for a company called The Original Rug Merchants. The back of the van was open and a couple of younger men were in the process of having pulled a rug out of it and were walking into the building with the rug. The man who approached us walked right up to me and introduced himself as Benyamin Hamete. I shook his hand and introduced myself. He was shorter than average, stocky, with curly black hair and what seemed to be a constant five o'clock shadow. He was about forty and not bad looking. There was also something about him that was thoughtful and sensitive and somewhat melancholic and wise. It was in his eyes. And then he turned and said, "And you must be Fabrizio," much to the surprise of both of us.

"I have read the book," he added. "Over here, let me show you." And he held out his left arm and hand toward us with the palm up in what must have been a desert signal for peace and an invitation. At the same time he held up out his right arm and hand toward the truck with the palm sideways and inward. This broad gesture was at once gentle and gracious to the extent of almost being comical. We followed him to the truck, and he reached into the cabin of the truck and opened a compartment and pulled out an electronic device as wide and as long and as thin as those two palms of his, had they been held open and side by side. It was a small hand-held computer comprised almost entirely of a screen. He deftly touched the screen, and in a few strokes of his fingers it illuminated itself, and he handed it to me.

"There," he said.

"What the hell is this?" Fabrizio intoned.

I could not read it either but I knew enough to know that it was a text of some book on the screen and that it was in Arabic. I also knew immediately that Mr. Hamete meant to tell us that the Arabic text on the screen was my book, this book, the book you are reading. I was puzzled by this more than anything.

So, I asked, "Is this really my book?"

"Wait a minute," Fabrizio interjected, "if you think we are going to buy some junk about these chicken scratches being the book about us, then you really are the original rug merchant."

"This is it, honestly," Mr. Hamete insisted, "it is why I was able to recognize you, from reading this. It tells your story, or at least up to this point. It talks about how you set out to spread the word that was given to you when Mohammed came to you in your cell."

"See," said Fabrizio, "I told you it was not our book."

"It is not as simple as all that, my good friend," I said. "I have heard that there may be more than one version of this book out there. Even though it is my story, the story of my spiritual journey, it seems that at least a few other authors have attempted to write their own versions of the things that have happened. In fact, I may later refer to one or two of those books myself in order to refresh my memory of some of the events as I rewrite this book. And there will have been books about this book. And I have no doubt that there are also translations. This particular translation seems to put me in a more dangerous place than in the prison where we currently reside. It attempts to place me squarely in the ranks of those who have taken Mohammed out of his own context, something I would never do. He is entirely for another book, his own book. This book cannot have any reference to that book."

"But I thought you were the El Cid. What should you worry about a few Moors?" Fabrizio interrupted.

"I guess you are right," I answered him. "I knew from the beginning that there would be resistance to my mission and that it would be significant. But that is a problem that is not yet in front of us. I am more puzzled about what these Christian Community kids have just done."

"I believe that the young men who accosted you had read your book, or they just may have heard about it. I do not think it had anything to do with this church of the Christian Community," Benyamin said.

"That's no church," Fabrizio chimed in and I gave him a sidelong glance.

"You really do not know about all that has been happening on the internet, do you?" asked Mr. Hamete.

"No," I said, "we are not allowed access to the world wide web. We are only allowed to watch a communal television, and the prison library gets some newspapers. Some of us have contraband radios. And just recently the library was given a few very old computers that are not able to be connected to the internet. I use one to write."

"Then you and Fabrizio cannot know what has become of *Gospel Prism*. It will be a long story. How much time do you have?"

"Not much time is left today. We have a truck that is full of tables and chairs that we have to take to the community center and set up. Then we have to get back to the church, the real church," I said, casting an eye toward Fabrizio, "in order to check in with them and return the truck. And then we have to return to the prison by 4 p.m. But tomorrow we may have some time. We have to come back out and pick up the truck and go get the chairs and tables and bring them back to the church. That should not take all day."

"Then I could meet the two of you for lunch tomorrow at that McDonald's down the road," Hamete said, "after you have picked up the chairs and tables and are on the way back to the church, the other church."

"We will be there," I said, and our new friend got back to his work and turned to go help his workers, who were taking the last rug into the Christian Community building.

Fabrizio and I got back into the truck and drove to the hall at the community center and unloaded it and set up the tables and chairs and then got back into the truck and returned the truck to the church. During that time that ensued, a conversation occurred that involved several shrewd things that were said to me by Little Philly Ray Sanchez, also known as Fabrizio, which related to what had already happened in our adventure and in connection with our holy and evangelical mission and the pursuit of the fair Belinda Hahner, along with other events of this, our true story.

"I guess, after your fight in the parking lot, that the rule against me engaging in philosophical discussions is now out the window," he began.

"Philosophical discussions were never proscribed, Fabrizio, only theological ones. And even then I asked only that you not involve yourself in theological discussions in which I was engaged with third parties."

"That was not much of a party back there. I had a real party one time, after I had made a huge street-corner haul one week. There must have been some word of mouth among the white boys or something, because business at my corner was double or triple what it normally had been, and the increase was all these kids from the suburbs. I sold a ton of drugs and made a load of money. You know how the story goes with that kind of money. When it is easy to make a lot of it and make it very fast, you kind of spend it the same way. I rented out a warehouse. I hired a salsa band and a rhythm and blues group and got several kegs of beer and a fully loaded bar. We hauled in couches and chairs and put posters on the wall. And I gradually brought out some of the 'product' that I had not sold. That party lasted two days. It was famous. Let me tell you this: All my cats was geeked."

"In any event," I said, "you and I may enter into any kind of conversation, theological or philosophical. I only ask that you be circumspect about entering into a theological conversation I am having with another individual or individuals."

"Should I be circumspect or whatever, even if those individuals are expressing their theological points of view with their fists?"

"I would think such would not be a time for circumspection, but for prompt action. In fact, that is one of the main reasons that I recruited you for this divine mission. It was to help me face just these types of obstacles."

"But you and me, we can talk religion?"

"Certainly," I said.

"Have you ever seen a vampire movie?"

"I have seen a few," I said with some confusion.

"Well, let's just say that you see a vampire in real life . . ."

"They do not exist."

"We are having a discussion, not making decisions."

"Okay, if I were to see a vampire in real life . . ."

"Would you run into that building at that Christian Community, or would you run into a Catholic church or some other church that was more like a real church?"

"Well, as vampires are merely legendary creatures, and the legend has it that they may be hurt with holy water and crucifixes and may not stand on holy ground, if I were to believe I had come face to face with a vampire I suppose that I would have to assume that the rest of the legend is true. So I would look for a Catholic church, yes."

"That is exactly my point. You would not run into a place that looked exactly like a high school auditorium."

"We are not talking about vampires. We are talking about Jesus. And she came to me in a prison cell. If Jesus can be found in a prison cell . . ."

"That's exactly my point, too," he interrupted.

"I don't see."

"Have you ever seen those movies where there are demons, or exorcisms or the Devil himself?"

"Fabrizio, I am alarmed at how much of your knowledge comes only from movies. But yes, for the sake of discussion, I have seen those movies."

"Well, sometimes in those movies, the guy is not a believer. He has lost his faith in God or whatever. But as soon as he sees the Devil, he immediately knows there is a God. What did you say? He would assume that the rest of the legend is true. If there is a Devil, then there must be a God."

"My good friend, I see where you are going with this. Since Jesus has revealed herself to me, then I must assume that there is a Devil," I concluded.

"And, dude, that Devil is the one behind all these troubles. He sent those two kids. He might have possessed them. And when things are not generally going our way, you can count on it that he has had a hand in it. You need to watch more movies."

"I will keep this in mind, although I would assume that all this would have been part of the revelation that was brought to me in my cell that night and not just something you say you have seen in some movies. I will remain skeptical."

"You see, I am more valuable than you expected. Now, can you help me out with this taking control of sweet Belinda, if we ever see her. You told me about the value of poetry and you gave me a poem. You also told me kiss her on her scars, which she may or may not have but which will be her backside in any event. I want to know at least one other thing."

"You must live in her imagination."

"What the hell is that supposed to mean?"

"Women are creatures of their imaginations. They are like Italians in that regard. We must appeal to those imaginations first. Think of writing a book or telling a good story, like the story about your party, for instance. Or even just think of putting on your party. You just don't blurt it out, or rush it. You think about it. You subject it to a plan. And you make sure that every part of it is good. That is the way you have to approach a woman. You plan how your first impression will be made and received. You put on your performance. And then you get out. You really give her something to think about and then you give her time and space to do that thinking. And you approach every subsequent meeting in the same way. Give her something dazzling and then get out of the way. She will not fall in love with you. She will fall in love with what she imagines about you. And all those other guys who are hanging around her, they will just be like the wallpaper or the chairs. You will be like some movie she saw and really liked."

"Man, that is gold you just gave me. I have been a chair more than a few times while the girl I wanted was dreaming about some guy she barely knew. Where do you get this stuff?"

"Oh, Fabrizio, I do not know how to begin. My life seems to have culminated in this divine visitation that I have had and all that was revealed to me and all that I must get out into the world. But I have lived a long and full life before this time and I have been a student of all that I have seen and heard. I am happy to share what I have learned in this regard."

"You are right about this much at least," Fabrizio, opined, "you are certainly an evangelist. I recognize the truths as soon as you say them to me."

By this time, we had returned with the truck to the Lepanto Church, and all we had left to do was to return the keys to the church deacon, get him to sign the form that said we had performed our work release duty, get back into the van and make it back to the prison by 4 p.m. We had enough time to do all that, with a little to spare. As we walked into the church offices we were greeted by none other than Ms. Belinda Hahner, doing her volunteer work for the church that day as a temporary receptionist. I saw her blush as we entered the reception room, but young Mr. del Dongo was too beside himself to notice. The rising tide of passion in him had risen to well above his ears, but his own blushing was disguised beneath his dark skin. This was certainly an advantage, one of which he was unaware. When Ms. Hahner got up and left the room to go get the church deacon, I suggested to my young charge that after she returned might be the time to hand her the poem. This he quickly and quietly did immediately after she came back into the room and sat down at the desk.

The deacon was right behind her and as he spoke to me Fabrizio more or less hid behind me. Belinda read the poem. She blushed even more.

"I want you to know," the deacon said, "that I am so glad that the prison has sent to me a man who has had Jesus enter his life. I took the liberty of calling them today and telling them how pleased we are and that we would appreciate it if the two of you were to be sent here on future work release projects."

"Well, I am certain at least that young Mr. Fabrizio del Dongo and I will be returning tomorrow, on the second day of this particular detail. We have been assigned already."

"That is good. I will see you tomorrow, then."

We said farewell and turned to go out the door. We walked into the parking lot and found the prison van. As we were getting into the van we heard a small voice and we looked up. It was the subject of Fabrizio's dreams and fantasies and plans for the future. She had followed us out. She spoke to my young friend in a sweet and soft voice.

"Thank you, Mr. del Dongo, for the poem."

"I'm gland you like it. I will kiss you on your ass," was Fabrizio's hurried and somewhat incongruous answer. Then he said, "Look," and he pulled up his short shirt sleeve to reveal the cartoon parrot.

"Oh, I own a parrot," she said in something that was between a squeal and a whisper.

"Good afternoon, Ms. Hahner," I said, in order to ease the charged and awkward mood and to say something more or less on behalf of my now stunned and silent assistant. "Perhaps we will see you when we return tomorrow."

Fabrizio remained somewhat stunned most of the way back to the prison. Then he spoke up.

"What stupid things to say, 'gland to see you,' and, 'I will kiss you on your ass.' Damn it."

"Actually, Fabrizio, you said, 'I'm gland you like it,' but I would not worry about that. I think it was one of those wonderful Freudian slips. And I am sure she will either overlook it or understand it as such. And I believe she liked the idea of you kissing her on her fundament."

"I am not sure what a Freudian slip-up is, but I wish I could take it back."

"I guarantee you, young friend, that those few minutes of seeing you were not like any few minutes she has ever spent with any other man. I do believe that you have placed yourself in her imagination."

"I doubt that she will even be there tomorrow."

"I had thought that your parrot tattoo would be a sign. Did you see her smile as you showed it to her and she told you she owned a parrot?"

"I don't remember much of anything. Did she really smile?"

"Yes, she did. You made a very good first impression."

We arrived at the prison, parked the van, and went to be processed back into the facility. At the desk that afternoon was Lieutenant Rutabaga, at least that is what I always called him because he turned that color of purple whenever he lost his temper and started yelling, which was something he did quite regularly. I have no idea what his real name was. As it turned out, when we were being processed Fabrizio came forward and stood too close to me and to the desk as I was being signed back into the facility. Normally he would have known not to do this because he had been on a few work details. And there was a sign on the wall that clearly stated: "Only one inmate at a time is to advance beyond this line." The line on the floor was several feet in front of the desk.

"What the hell is wrong with you, inmate?" shouted the Lieutenant, turning that distinctive purple. "Can't you read the sign?"

"You can't hold that against me," offered Fabrizio. "I'm deliterate."

"You got a hell of a nerve," Rutabaga said, simmering. And turning to me he asked, "What the hell does that mean? Does he mean he is illiterate?"

"I think it does mean that and perhaps more," I ventured. "I think it means that not only can he not read, he has the quality of making those around him less literate as well, sort of like television or deconstructive literary criticism."

"That's enough of your smart-ass crap," the officer capped off the conversation.

We were processed back inside without any further mishaps and we made our way to the mess hall. Fabrizio was still pensive, even as his friends came up to him and were asking him about his day "on the outside." He looked at me as if we shared a secret, and I nodded to him as if to say that I would see him tomorrow.

Not much of note happened on the next day of our adventures until such time as we met with Mr. Hamete at the McDonald's restaurant, after we had gone to the church and picked up the truck and had gone to the community center and had loaded the chairs and tables. When we had stopped by the church that morning, Belinda had not been in evidence, and this put my assistant into a quiet and contemplative mood. We walked into the restaurant and went to the corner, where Mr. Hamete was sitting with his portable computer screen device.

"I am glad you both could make it," he said as we were shaking hands.

"We're glad to be here. And thank you for seeing us," I answered.

"I will be glad when I get something to eat here," was Fabrizio's contribution.

"This will be of interest to you, as well, Fabrizio," added Mr. Hamete, "as you will see that you are as famous as your friend."

After some more preliminary discussion, Benyamin Hamete started out by showing us what he had shown us the day before, an electronic book that purported to be a version of *Gospel Prism*, only in Arabic. I asked him to read us a translation of what was written in that version of the book and what was read back to me in English was really quite close to the various versions which you and other readers are reading and have read and will read here. There were differences in style that can be attributed to the translation, mostly such that in the Arabic the prose was considerably more florid and the characters were more likely to be described by the occasional epithet, and by that I mean the Homeric usage as a descriptive additive to a name and not the more pejorative and secondary meaning, which is a derisive nickname. Fabrizio was often referred to as "the droll Fabrizio" or "the slow of understanding Fabrizio." I could not help but note that Benyamin Hamete himself was often called, "wily" or "cunning." And that should have given me notice of what was to occur later in this text. There were also differences of substance, but these could also be attributable to translation as well or to cultural differences such as the visitation being made by the prophet and not by Christ. While this bothered me in a way that was attributable to my concerns about my personal safety, in terms of what the book might mean to those who read it in this form, it seemed to be closer to what had actually happened. And it is with this difference that Mr. Hamete began his explanation.

"I am guessing that what you do not know is that your book has gone viral. It has spawned copies and versions and translations. There are various and disparate congregations of people in different pockets of most of the countries in the world who meet on a regular basis to share their understanding of this book and to base their lives on it as a holy guide for living. I could say that it has generated a kind of faith, albeit one that contains its own skepticism. In certain Muslim populations it has begun what can only be called an analogy to your own Christian Protestant Reformation."

"Great," interrupted Fabrizio, "that means we will soon be seeing mosques that look like high school auditoriums."

"And I am not so sure that would be a bad thing," Ben Hamete responded. "It might be a step forward for women's rights, among other things."

"Other than this campaign for the dignity of Moorish women," I asked, "what else has come of all this?"

"A great deal, it seems. As I said, there are *Gospel Prism*-ers everywhere. In some cases they have led entire movements in the secular world. In Greece and Portugal there has been a political movement which has successfully cut healthcare costs. Based on your visitation and the discussions you and the Christ had about death, this "dignity in death" movement has pointed out that it makes little sense that one-quarter of all healthcare costs are attributable to expenses incurred in the last year of life. Now in those countries, rather than spending astronomical sums to keep terminally ill people alive, those people are placed into hospice care. The success of these changes has encouraged the *Gospel Prism*-ers in this country, and a significant dignity in death movement is picking up momentum here in the United States."

"It is not right to call these people *Prism*-ers. Each of us is a prism," I said. "That is sort of the point."

"There is no controlling the word once it is out. I think that is also the point," added Hamete. And turning to Fabrizio, he said,

"And you should know, Fabrizio, that *Prism*-ers in Mexico and other Latin American countries have cited you and your example to argue that prison sentences and even the threat of death do little to combat illegal drug sales, because the economic incentives are far too compelling. And now for the first time the foreign ministers of some of these countries are calling upon the United States to decriminalize drug use because the intended deterrents clearly do not work, and the only effective solution is to reduce the economic incentives."

"Glad I could do something for those prisoners. Now, if we could only get something to eat," was droll Fabrizio's comment.

"I have to say that I am troubled by a certain aspect of this," I said. "You can call it the death of intellectual property. A wise man once said that there once was a time when books were written by men of letters and read by the public. This, he said, was followed by a time when books were written by the public and read by nobody. Now it seems to me that the public is the book, and nobody is a man of letters. A book or any other product of a human's mind is instantaneously transmitted around the globe, translated, copied, modified. It is a fluid thing, indeed, and it is impossible to be the author of such a thing or to have ownership of it."

"Intellectual property," Hamete said, "was always a fiction, a mere legal construct anyway. No one can own an idea once it is released. The law tried to project and then to protect an ownership right. But imagine five thousand years ago. Imagine if the inventor of the wheel had tried to patent it. The instant it was seen, it became public property. There would have been no way to keep people from making and using wheels. You should be glad. Getting the story out has never been as easy. And controlling the story or how it was read was never simple, or even possible."

By this time, it was getting late. And Ben Hamete had said a great many other things that I do not include here. It had been a long discussion and one piece of information that Mr. Hamete had made sure was imparted was that there was a congregation of *Gospel Prism*-ers here in London, Kentucky. And he gave us the name of the place where they met, which I seemed almost to recognize. I told Fabrizio that we had better take the truck and the chairs and tables within it back to the Lepanto Church. To this he offered no objection.

"What if Belinda is not there?" were the first words out of his mouth, once we had climbed into the cabin of the truck. "I was so stupid yesterday. She will be staying away from the church. I am sure."

"She will be there," I assured him.

"I don't know," he said. "Sometimes you are so right. Obviously your experience and your learning are beyond me. Then there are times when you are being an evangelist, when you say that the word of the Lord is that you cannot trust the word of the Lord and that He is really a She, that I actually think you have lost your mind. And then I fear that I should not believe a word you say. And even then, on the other hand, when you are at your most crazy sometimes you make the most sense. I hope you are right on this one."

After we arrived at the church and we began to put the chairs and the tables back into their storage, Belinda Hahner, who was indeed volunteering at the church that afternoon, took it upon herself to supervise us. She stood near the front of the church and watched as we took these things out of the truck and carried them into the storage space. Fabrizio kept his head down and worked very earnestly, only occasionally glancing in her direction. I kept my eyes on her. I could see the way she kept her eyes downcast, the way her feet played at the ground, the plaintive way that her hands moved in front of her waist as if she were saying a kind of a prayer, a prayer of feminine openness and willingness. But my young friend did not notice any of these things, nor could he have interpreted them if he had.

At the end of the job he simply got inside the van and left it to me to go inside and get the deacon to sign our forms. And when I did that Ms. Hahner followed me inside, and when I turned to leave she followed me out. Then she handed me a slip of paper.

"Will you give this to Mr. del Dongo, please, I mean, to Mr. Sanchez."

She had obviously read the work release forms and had likely done as much other homework that she could. It was not surprising to me that the piece of paper she had handed me for Fabrizio had written on it her address. Fabrizio was hungry for what news I could give him about the conversation I had with the object of his affection and he desperately wanted to know what the slip of paper was. I gave it to him. He could not keep from smiling and moving about in his seat, as we started to drive out of the parking lot and onto the road.

"What is it?" he asked. "What does it say?"

"I think you know, Fabrizio, that it is the young lady's address and that she expects you to write her a letter. She expects to respond to it and to begin a correspondence. I imagine that you will have to learn to read and to write now."

"You were right," he said, almost under his breath. "You were right about all of it. I can see why you are the one who got the divine visitation. You know what to do. You just know."

"Why, thank you, my friend, and I know what we are going to do right now. We are going to pull over and go into that building right there. It is the place where Ben Hamete told us that the local devotees of our book congregate. I thought it sounded familiar when he said it. We have been driving right by it to get to and from the prison. There, the van is parked. Let's go inside."

So it was that I entered the West Central Kentucky Hillbilly Garden and Square Dance Club with the intention of speaking as a preacher to the converted, which is never a very painful experience and which I figured would finally be the jump start to my evangelical career, which had sort of been spinning its wheels. I had found it very difficult to convince the deacon of the Lepanto Church or the people of the Christian Community that my experience of Jesus was literally the only one since the original Gospels or even that it was unique in any way. It had seemed that all manner of Jesus characters were now wandering the American landscape, and each one of them was barely crucified and seemingly born permanently resurrected. I was looking forward to conversing with people who knew what I meant, people who had read this book and who believed in it. I was pleased to see that we had walked into a good-sized meeting room, and that there were about thirty people in it.

"Friends," I began to address the group, "I have come here to share with you my experience. I am the one to whom She came. Jesus let me smell her hair. She spoke to me about the Pope's toilet paper. She looked like Halle Berry. She revealed to me that the ways of the Lord are like poetry and Chinese Algebra."

At this point, Fabrizio was waving his arms and trying to get my attention, but I continued.

"I am onto the scent of Jesus. She told me that the proper study of God is to study our own humanity. And I am pretty sure she turned into a bear . . ."

This time, Fabrizio grabbed me by the arm and started to walk me briskly back out the door toward the car.

"It's them two kids from the parking lot at the Christian Community," he said to me at just about the time that it registered in my consciousness that I had indeed seen them in that group of people inside, the group of people which was now following us out the door and onto the street. Soon we were running and dodging the projectiles that were being thrown at us: books, coffee mugs, rocks, anything handy. We barely got to the van just ahead of this mob and got into it and locked it. They began to beat on the van with their hands and just about anything they could find. Soon they had cracked the windshield, had broken a headlight, and had put several small dents in the body of the vehicle. And then we were able to pull away.

"I think this means that Mr. Benyamin Hamete was having a little fun with us," I said. "I also believe that he actually rewrote that version of *Gospel Prism* in Arabic that he showed us. It was just another of the many permutations of this veracious and august history but it was distinctly his own. I think it means that we have to take everything he said with a grain of salt and assume that it is as likely to be untrue as it is to be correct."

"Isn't that your point, in general?" Fabrizio queried. "And anyway, I think you are wrong. That guy was the Devil, pure and simple."

"What makes you say that?"

"He was in McDonald's and he did not want to eat. And he did not let me eat."

"I am not sure you are making a theological argument."

"Do you want a theological argument? Here is one. I think this evangelical mission or whatever you want to call it is as likely to be a misadventure as an adventure and that no one sees things exactly as you see them. Besides, even if Hamete is telling the truth or not telling the truth, I think we can assume that the word is getting out there. And what is happening to it is what always happens to words. And there is not much that your personal evangelism can do to add to that or to change it."

"You know," it had just occurred to me to say, "you are right. Mr. Hamete is just a single part of the soon to be celebrated concatenation of authors and editors and translators who will take you, Fabrizio, and me and all the others in this story and will make sure that we all live for unnumbered centuries for the spiritual edification and delight and general pastime of our fellow men."

We then drove the rest of the way to the prison in silence. I was concerned now with the more worldly matter of explaining what had happened to the van. I had no good ideas. And sure enough, Lieutenant Rutabaga was on duty. No sooner had we pulled up than he had looked out the window and had come out to the parking lot and had begun to turn his customary shade as he began to yell.

"What the hell did you do to the van? You damn idiots. You will pay for this. I will see that you each get put into the hole." The hole was prison jargon for solitary confinement. It was at this point that Little Philly Ray Sanchez spoke.

"You know, Lieutenant, how I cannot read? Well, I had to go to the bathroom very bad and at a stop light I got out of the van and ran into an establishment to go to the bathroom. Because I can't read, I did not know that I had run into the London chapter of Black Like Us. I accidentally incited a riot and they chased me back to the van. We barely got away with our lives."

"You mean, the blacks did this?" the Lieutenant asked. "It figures. Okay, then, we will just have to file an insurance claim. Get inside and I will process you later myself. You probably have to still go to the bathroom."

There was not another work detail on the immediate schedule. And despite how we had dodged the Rutabaga bullet I was fairly sure that I was not going to be allowed to be heading up any work details soon. Prison, well, was prison and it was our life. It did not allow for any kind of transition from the excitement of the last couple of days. It just closed down around us. I spoke several times to Philly Ray about his letter writing and what should be said and I also pitched in with the reading and writing lessons he began to take at the library. Then one day he was not around anymore.

The prison rumor mill is something that is about as credible as any other rumor mill. It is often as wrong as it is right. When it is wrong it contains elements of the truth and when it is right there are always flaws in the story. But in prison it is always taken as gospel. There is never any counterpoint. Information is hard to come by, so any scrap of information becomes accepted as the local truth.

The story was that Little Philly Ray Sanchez had gone over the wall, which is not at all difficult to do in a federal minimum-security prison. I remember that on the day it was supposed to have happened there was a count of the inmates that had come up short. We had to be formally recounted. And though I am sure that there are out there coarse and ill-bred pretenders who have taken up their computers and have had the audacity to try to write their separate accounts of all that has transpired here, and that those accounts may differ, my true and honest story is that the word on the inside was that the federal marshals had found him several days later, "shacked up with some local white woman."

Such was the end of my ingenious personal evangelical career. It had stretched itself out at length in a bed and had fainted dead away. It gave up the ghost. It died. And food being what it is, as well as sleep and drink and friendship and work being what they are, my life went on. And in such ways the world often gives us cause to forget.

Yet, within this story, in this chapter, we have been exposed to the second insight, or revelation, second of the dozen insights by which so many devoted people are now living their lives. You may or may not have guessed it, and it will surely be revealed to you later if you continue to read this book. But at this point, I was not even sure of it. I did not know if it was something to do with my message or the way in which it had been received, and I suspected that it might have been something more to do with the relationship between Fabrizio and me. The first divine revelation appears to have been about what is the truly the Lord's intent for how we must delicately apprehend our beliefs and then how we must gently apply those beliefs to the world. Now I believe that this second insight lies somewhere in the way in which the evangelism of the Lepanto road dogs added to that first revelation by the examples of the way in which it succeeded and in the way it had not. It demonstrated a refinement to the first insight that will assist with the understanding of the rest of the journey and perhaps with life itself. And now this is the story of how I received that first insight.

DOWN FROM THE TOWER

The woman walking down the hallway of the cell block toward my cell at 3.30 a.m. had certainly been Jesus Christ herself because she clearly was not a prostitute.

Seeing a woman walking down a cell block at three thirty in the morning at Manchester, Kentucky, minimum-security Federal Prison for men is not as completely unusual as one might think. Such appearances by women were not all that rare, but those feminine visitations had always been made by local escorts, who had been well paid to break into the camp by one or the other of our white-collar criminals. These men were generally serving very short sentences for some financial malfeasances that had deprived thousands of people of their retirement funds and inheritances and savings and food money, but these men of course had not really hurt anybody. So they were given short sentences in minimum-security facilities. And those ladies of the evening whom they would hire would always have a certain insouciance about them, a casual and seeming disregard for the effect that they knew their appearance had on men who had long been deprived of feminine company, coupled with a ready lack of surprise for any prison guard who might discover their presence.

But this particular woman was not like that at all. She seemed to belong here, as much as was possible for a stunning beauty of an unidentifiable mix of the races. She had a swaying, almost hypnotic

51

walk that let you see her considerable but not overbearing curves even beneath the blue business suit she was wearing. She had large, brown doe eyes that at once communicated intelligence, depth, passion, wisdom, playfulness, and that unmistakably preternatural knowing grace that you would expect only in a prophet or the messiah.

She walked straight into my cell and made herself right at home, sitting in my desk chair. I sat up in my bed and looked at her. She had a soft and smoothly rounded face with perfect features, those larger-than-life eyes, slightly full lips, a pert, faintly wide straight nose and the kind of honey-brown skin that looks like it is in a photograph that has been digitally perfected. She was wearing a navy-blue, light wool, twill designer business suit with a knee-length skirt that had a short slit in the back, and an off-white blouse and a pair of blue pumps. Her figure was straight out of a men's magazine from the time when American men wore hats and smoked cigarettes and listened to jazz music and remembered how they had once fought to prevent the world from being overrun by fascist imperialism and mass murderers. The fact that her abundant body was almost concealed under that business suit made it all that much more appealing, in the way that a foot of newly fallen snow makes the rolling hills of a golf course seem much more beautiful. Her dark brown hair was medium short with that relaxed curled texture of a woman who perhaps had just one grandparent with African roots, and it was cropped around her face like a softly curling halo.

"I am not a lady of the evening," she intoned.

"I know," I answered, "You are Jesus H. Christ herself."

Perhaps I should add at this point that it may not have been the first time I had been certain that a woman was some kind of messiah nor may it be the last. But in those previous cases it seemed there were circumstances involving dark sexual tensions and dreams of finding a different heaven through a path that D. H. Lawrence might have taken, or James Joyce. There was nothing like that in this case, or maybe not too much of it. There was certainly that unmistakable mix of spirituality and the feminine. Some questions at this point were whether or not she was going to sleep with me or if she was going to impart her divine wisdom upon me or if I was going to have to wade through the wisdom part in order to get to that other part.

It is widely and incorrectly shown in the popular media that when a man enters a jail or a prison that one of the more seasoned inhabitants turns to him and asks him, "What are you in for?" This actually almost never happens. It is in fact a violation of the etiquette of the incarcerated. It is considered the equivalent of asking any stranger, "What vile criminal act did you actually commit?" It would be asking that question of a person who has spent almost the entire time up to that point strenuously denying that he had ever done anything remotely close to that of which he had been accused. And it would be asking him in a place where the relative severities of different crimes are deeply understood and actually play a role in forming a sort of a hierarchy of the prison and play a role in helping to create the various identities of the individuals who people it. It is asking a person to give a first and permanent impression of himself in a place from which he will not soon be departing.

It makes just as much sense that such a question should be asked out in the real world, in the everyday life of civil society, as if for instance if one attendee at an after-school parent meeting were to turn to another, or if one patron at a bakery were to turn to another, or if a mother were to look at her toddler and ask, "Why are you here?" In prison the question is only ever asked when two prisoners have learned to trust one another and have become friends. And even then the answer is always the same, and it is also exactly the same as the answer that may honestly be given out in the real world: "I am here through no fault of my own."

This Jesus was not about to explain her reasons for being where she was. Nor was she going to ask for mine. But there were many distinct spiritual mysteries that I hoped she would help to unravel over time, and more than a few of them were under that suit. This is a detective story and it is also my spiritual journey. And this was just the first step. People have turned to God or to Jesus or to any other deity for just the sort of answers that I knew I was about to learn through this divine intervention. I was going to be given a chance here to hear the word of God and maybe to learn a great deal more than that from this divine young woman.

She turned her head downward and to the side slowly and in a catlike manner, then she looked up and directly into my eyes and with a playful smile she said, "I bet I know what issue you would like to discuss."

"And what might that be?" I asked, my heart beating faster.

"You want to know what kind of toilet paper the Pope uses."

There could be no question that this was exactly what I wanted to know at that instant. But I could not tell if this certainty arrived in my mind at the same time as her statement or if it had been a question that I always had wanted answered. Still, I needed to know.

"Yes," I said, "I want to know, because his choice is infallible."

"The more important thing to know," she said, "perhaps is simply that he needs to use toilet paper. His Holiness the Pope must defecate as each and every one of us must and then he must deal with the aftermath. The same mind that knows God's will on matters such as birth control and on what exactly must be done during a Mass for the dead who are in purgatory and how to perform the extreme unction for all terminally ill individuals also must decide on whether or not he personally should use the thick and soft toilet paper or the thinner kind that requires him to use more sheets or the quilted toilet paper."

"But does the decision to use which toilet paper come to the Pope in the same way as divine revelation shows him God's will, say, on the issue of the ordination of women?" I asked. "In other words, is it the word of God?"

"I am sure it is not the same," she said. "But that word and that revelation come to his human mind and to the same human mind that also must make the toilet paper decision."

This all made me think of something along the lines of a parable. There are millions of men and women in the United States of America just like my friend, Carl Cartwright, who is a lawyer in Moline, Illinois. He is a member of one of this country's many non-denominational or evangelical churches. He does not need the Pope or any other intercessor in order for the spirit of the Lord to enter him. Dozens of his fellow congregation members come to him because he is a lawyer and a church member and they trust him. In fact, one woman came to him some time ago seeking to divorce her husband who had beaten her repeatedly and who had restricted her to the home and who prohibited her from having any friends or seeing her family. This same husband had taken over the family finances, which were in part derived from her income earned as a waitress at a truck stop on Interstate 80, and he made wide use of the funds for drinking and gambling and whoring. And if he had even the slightest inkling of dissension on the part of his wife he would strike her.

The spirit of the Lord had entered Carl Cartwright on many occasions, usually when he was on his knees. So he got on his knees in his office and invited this client to get on her knees with him. And together they prayed, and as the spirit of the Lord entered Carl, he told his client to think of her children and to ask herself whether or not she believed that the Lord was communicating to her at that moment the message, and that the message was that divorce was a sin and that it would permanently scar her children. She felt the spirit move within her and she knew that Carl was correct. And she knew that she would go home and endure, because that is what God wanted her to do. She turned to Carl to thank him, but he was gone. He had run to the men's room with a severe case of diarrhea. The eggs he'd had for breakfast had not agreed with him.

My discussion with Jesus had mysteriously required me to be reminded of this story, and I asked her, "What does the word of God have to do with pooping?"

"Everything," she said, "that we do is human. Just think of what you have said. You used the term, 'word,' but which word? Or let me put it to you in this way. In what language does the word of God arrive?"

"I assume English. Everyone has to speak English. They speak English to me when I go to Italy and to Germany and to Spain. You are speaking English."

"Let's set aside the question of language for a second, even though it might make the most sense if God spoke French. The word itself must be spoken and must be heard by humans. Think of what a word is," she added. "We use words for laws, for human laws. But if words did not have limitations we would not need to have courts. We would not have thousands of briefs and decisions and precedents which set out to determine the meaning of the words in certain statutes and in certain other precedents. Think of the words that are in this book you are writing of this experience, or that you have written and that you will write. Thousands of people have already written thousands of interpretations of those words. Some say they are holy. Others say they are heresy.

"But perhaps it is the law that is the best example," she continued. "The law is where we seek and strive for clarity of scope, so that men and women do not stray from the law. But have you ever read a legal document? Is anything more confusing? And how is it that the words of these legal statutes are decided in a case going one way by an honest judge and going in exactly the other direction by another honest judge? There are as many interpretations of the law as there are men and women. And what if this law, these words which come to us in plain English, had been translated from Latin, which had been translated from Greek and Aramaic? Would we not have the opinions of the various translators with which to contend?"

"That is why I prefer Carl Cartwright's method," I finally was able to add. "He just knows. The spirit of the Lord enters him, and he knows. There are no words."

"There are no words until he speaks them," she responded. "And then they are words, formed in a human mind and communicated to another human mind which must hear and understand them. Have you ever read *Middlemarch*?"

"Why, yes," I said.

"Do you know that there are more words written about that book than there are words in that book? There are countless books about that book."

"In fact there are more books about books than there are books about anything else," she said. "A word is a strange thing. It is evasive and it is divisive and it tends to proliferate. It is like a ball of mercury on a plate. The more you try to corral it, the more likely it is to divide and multiply. That makes it a curious place in which to try to find God."

"I find God everywhere: in the sunset, in the streams of the mountains, in a charitable gesture, in the Bible, in a child's laugh," I said.

"And you apprehend those things with human eyes, human ears, human senses, and with a human heart," she answered, "and describe them with human words."

At this point I was able to anticipate what many of the millions of readers of this book would for many years dispute and discuss and believe and for which some would kill and die. I was ready to become one with Jesus, and she was very attractive.

"So the miracle of God that is closest to you, in fact the only one with which you have direct experience, is yourself, is your own humanity. You are the only thing on which you actually have your hands, so to speak. So," she asked, rather omnisciently, "what happened in the end of that Carl Cartwright story you were just thinking about?"

Carl had come back into the room in a decided hurry. His client looked up and asked him where he had gone and why he had returned so quickly. His answer was strained and it was quick and almost rude in a way that surprised this penitent woman, who was still on her knees. He practically barked at her, telling her that he had felt the need to run to the men's room and that he had been certain that he had the key to the building's men's room in his pocket but that he had found out it was not there when he got to the men's room door. He was about to burst. Then she told him that she thought she had seen some keys on the table by the couch. And sure enough, on this table was the key ring on which the men's room key was strung.

"But he had been absolutely certain that the keys were in his pants," my divine guest added, "just as he had been certain that the spirit of the Lord had entered him and just as he had been certain what that spirit had communicated to him and at about the same time as he was attacked by his malady. So in other words, let he who has never been certain he knew where his keys were but later found out he was mistaken cast the first stone. That we may not ever be so certain is the hallmark of our humanity, in the same way that even the most exacting words are easy to misconstrue and are often inapplicable to each and every case. The certainty of words and the certainty of our apprehension of them is always suspect. So it is best to take them for what they are, fall back on your humanity and embrace the uncertainty."

"I am certainly glad that you are Jesus," I stated, "because if anyone else were to say such a thing it might be heresy."

"Or in your case, reporting it will be blasphemy," she pointed out to me. "And so is what you are thinking about right now."

All male prisoners, in the popular mind, are supposed to be incredibly sexually charged because they have been deprived of intercourse with women. In fact this may be true for only the most rudimentary men. For those who live at that elemental level, this deprivation gives rise to the sexual predation that is a part of the popular and partly accurate myth of prisons. These brutal prisoners force other weaker inmates to take the place of women. What actually occurs in such cases is quite different from sex and in most ways is the opposite of the shared intimacy that sex is. These elemental urges are as much or more aggressive than they are sexual. What these brutal men miss, and the frustration they are expressing, is not exactly the desire to share intimacy with a person for whom they feel affection.

Most men in prison, the ones who actually miss having sex with a woman, are far different from what is most popularized in the fictions about prison. What these more humane men feel is a kind of awe for what was once familiar and enjoyable and they feel an uncertainty about how it all once worked. They feel it like anyone who feels a deep and aching and long-unsatisfied hunger. Like any man on the verge of starvation, one of them cannot swallow down a six-course Italian meal with antipasto, pasta, bread, wine, vegetables, fish, meat and dessert. In prison, a woman becomes a distant goddess. Sex becomes an impossibly deep and extensive approach to that ideal. A man's hunger for her may only approach her on the edges. That is all he can digest. And that is all he can imagine being able to digest. So he hungers for hearing the gentle timbre of a woman's voice as she laughs, for seeing the odd and unique cant of her hip as she stands at rest, for relying on the way in which she may be more willing to believe and to trust, for the sight of her dancing in a way that is more graceful than a man or for touching her smooth skin.

"I said that I know what you are thinking, Christian," said my sublime and alluring mixed-race Jesus girl.

Seven hundred years after Dante wrote *The Divine Comedy*, most of the names of the people that he placed permanently in Hell are of little meaning to us unless we are scholars of medieval Italy. We need the footnotes in order to understand his Hell a little better. Seven hundred years from now, readers of this book will take the dated facts and references that are in it directly into their minds without even reading, perhaps through micro-computer transceivers placed in their contact lenses. They will not need any reference material to understand what I mean when I write that this Jesus looked exactly like Halle Berry, the American movie star of this period, even though they will not really know what a movie was because they will have never seen one. They will simply see her in the book as it enters their minds and they will understand from that vision exactly what I mean when I say that through this entire conversation I occasionally thought not of the spirit of the Lord entering me but something more along the lines of the opposite.

But as I have said, for a man who is deprived of a woman, a woman becomes divine. Paradoxically, this woman already was divine, which is how she knew exactly what I was thinking.

She smiled as she said, "Okay. All right. I will let you smell my hair."

We both stood up. I could barely step in her direction. I could barely breathe. I was out of practice and I did not know how I would react or if I would do something wrong. My approach to this divine female was one of utter uncertainty. So she moved gently closer to me until my head was next to hers and only a few centimeters away. I closed my eyes, and the feeling I had was one of overwhelming sexual transport. It may have been that it would be the only kind of sex I was able to have at that point. She was a symphony of scents that are a synonym for music. I could smell just a little bit of the peach shampoo with which she had washed her hair that morning. There was also some hint of a perfume, a kind of jasmine perhaps. I could also smell the insinuation of something that was just a bit more piquant. It was her warmth and her skin. And there was a soft under scent of something with a bit of musk in it, something of her womanhood. It was, in a moment, much more sex than I was able to manage at that particular point.

"You are going to catch Hell for this being in your book, you know," she laughed lightly. "And it is not by any means the first time that such desires have been crossed, that passions have been mixed, that the divine has melded with the concupiscent. And this makes perfect sense. Romantic love is a passion for the other, for someone who is completely other than you. But it is also a passion for the ways in which your self is improved, a passion for a self you prefer to be."

"Well, I have to say, I think I just experienced that kind of confusion or whatever," I mumbled, as I wondered what might be next.

"Yes. And this can take many forms," she said. "The poetry of John Donne was at one time the poetry of earthly passion and later became the poetry of passionate devotion. And there are conversions and reversions and inversions of this passionate and spiritual combination throughout the poetry of Emily Dickinson."

"Do you read poetry?" I asked.

"I read it all the time. All manner of sincerely terrible poetry comes over my transom regularly," she answered, "so to speak. But I only re-read what pleases me and what is beautiful, which is really the same thing. But poetry is important. There is poetry in that sunset you mention and in the child's laugh and in the charitable gesture. And in them too is a beauty that enters you immediately and which pleases you. That is how you can feel their value. They are the exact opposite of the legal words. The notion of a human understanding the divine is necessarily paradoxical, so poetry is useful as poetic words express paradox. They do not strive to be understood or to limit their interpretation. And from them one cannot fashion a code of law or a religious creed. But in them there is some of God, in the only way a human can glimpse, by hints."

"But we were talking about passion," I said. "I was confused by passion. I am confused by passion."

"And there are many kinds of passions," she answered. "You may call them vapors or passions or humors or appetites. Your friend,

Carl Cartwright, was caught by a kind of vapor. It forced him to be rude his client. Humans are uncertain creatures and we are also subject to unfathomable passions."

Indeed, I thought. I had been onto the scent of Jesus, and when it was over the memory of it was strong. It is such a strong memory that I could not tell if it ever really happened, only that I am certain that it did, like many strong memories.

"This irony you are now sensing is one of the hallmarks of the human mind," she added, "the certainty that accompanies things of which we are not really certain. It is we who are the crown of God's creation, and this is our unfortunate keystone. Plus, our most transcendental humors can give birth to our most beastly acts. Once we step away from the knowledge that we are often certain that our keys are in our pants when they are really on the table, and once we forget that, no matter how holy or righteous we strive to be, we are still tied to the toilet at least once a day, and once we fail to remember that sometimes our uncertain judgment is swayed by our human vapors and humors, then we fail our duty to God. Among all of the most miraculous creations, we are the only one to which we truly have access. It is our divine duty to strive to know ourselves first, to make sense of our experience. We need to be careful not to exceed our grasp, as well. Have you ever tried to teach Chinese Algebra to your cat?"

"I have, in fact," I said, remembering with certainty the entire episode. "I had done my best. And I made sure to show her that all the variables are in Chinese characters and that there are no Arabic numerals and that the equations are read down to up and that they then go right to left and that everything could be changed at an instant with a smile and a nod, just to keep outsiders confused."

"Did your cat understand it?"

"I do not think so. I am not sure."

"But how do you know," she asked, "that your cat might not have long since understood it and was really trying to teach it to you? And how can this uncertainty go away, when we are thinking of God and not a cat? It is one thing to wonder about God, to worship God, to pray to God, to try to aspire to a godly life. It is another thing entirely to speak with certainty that one knows the word of God or the will of God and to believe that other people should understand it in the same way. But though these two sets of things are very different, it is most important to remember that they both are very human. In every word ever written, no matter what the subject, there is a great deal of human art."

"I know this is almost beside the point, since this book I am writing has already been out in the public and that it will change as it continues to be read, but," I said, "I just have to ask. For whom are your words meant?"

"That is a question that misses the point," she answered. "The words are yours, not mine. They are what you hear. And then you report them as you think you heard them. You feel certain, but you cannot be certain. And some other deep humor or vapor of yours may be at work as you write them. The words are unable to approach the sublime nature of what you call God. And they will undoubtedly be subject to numerous interpretations. The instant you heard me, this all became yours. It all became human. And when it is read it will be another step further away and it will still be human."

"I guess you mean to say that when the time comes you want to be truly heard," I stated, "you will be understood by everyone, without the possibility of misinterpretation."

"That makes the most sense, doesn't it?" she asked, rhetorically.

"Yes, it seems that any truly divine truth would arrive within us all," I added, "and simply be known for certain."

"As an 'author,' I would be of a completely different magnitude," she added, with a smile at once beautiful and terrifying and very alluring.

"Book" was the nickname of one of the prisoners at Manchester. His name was really Bookman or Bookerton or something else like that, but everyone called him Book. Book was the boss of the general population. Book was a bully. He was a very big and muscular American man of African descent. He was loud and pushy. He seemed to rule the television room and the weight room with monarchical authority. He had sycophants and followers, men who would figuratively shout back, "Amen," upon many of his pronouncements. Almost all of the white prisoners feared him because his ghetto status was something they did not understand and because they assumed that all the black prisoners stood behind him. A majority of the Latin and black prisoners also feared him. No one crossed him.

But there was a certain small elite who knew how to read Book, or any other of the lesser prison bullies like him. They could be black or Latin or even white. They were always the quiet ones, the watchful, thoughtful men whom life and prison had not so much hardened as educated. One of them was my friend Stanley. Stanley was a compact black man from a neighborhood in my home town, one that I knew was very hard.

I had more than a passing knowledge of his neighborhood and I knew some of the people he knew, and that was enough to start a conversation and to begin as much of a friendship as could occur between a white and a black man in a prison. Stanley almost never spoke. But he was very intelligent and thoughtful. One day, after about a month of almost silent understanding between the two of us, we were standing in the compound when the convocation of the prison's black Muslims passed us on the way to prayers, Stanley turned to me and smiled for what may have been the first time I had ever seen, and said, "You know, that shit is all about 'Hate whitey,' nothing more."

Very few white inmates were aware that Stanley played no part in the Book congregation. No one was more aware of it than Book. My own understanding came on an evening when Stanley came to my cell, bleeding from a knife wound. He came to me because he knew that I had leatherworking needles and he knew that whatever I did would not be spread among the population of black prisoners. Under his calm direction and using a curved needle and some dental floss, I stitched shut the three inch wound in his side. No one but I ever knew, at least not until I just wrote this sentence. If an inmate was found wounded like that, the prison authorities would assume he knew who wounded him. He was then placed in an impossible position. If he were to tell them who wounded him he would be considered a "rat," and his word and his continued well-being would become things upon which the remainder of us would place little faith. If he did not tell he would be violating the rules and could be thrown into solitary confinement and lose whatever time good behavior could have had taken off his sentence. He could even be charged with obstruction of justice and have his sentence lengthened. Stanley was more concerned about getting away with not saying anything than he was about dying.

Six months after I had stitched Stanley's wound with dental floss and a leatherwork needle there was an accident in the weight room. One of the prison's minor bullies, one of the acolytes of Book, had been working out all alone and he slipped while lifting a heavily loaded barbell, and it fell and crushed his sternum. He was hurt so badly that he was transported to a prison hospital facility, and we never saw him again. No one knew anything about it but I knew it had not been an accident. I had accurately surveyed the prison power equations. I was certain of one thing. Everyone believed that Book was the man in our prison most to be feared, but I think that Book himself and perhaps a few of his lieutenants knew that this was not the truth.

I had no idea how much time had passed during this discussion with my late-night distaff messiah. It could have been a few minutes and it could have been a few days. But I sensed for the first time that this interview might be coming to an end. It is a strange and incongruent notion, to be confronted by the limitless and to have a limited time. It seemed like a paradox, similar to the idea of the "word" of God. I reasoned that I should make use of what time I might have left.

"So, please just give me a little kiss," I said. "I am no longer afraid."

"It might kill you," she smiled devilishly as she spoke. "But there is no need to fear death, nor is there any reason. Like all fear, fear of death is irrational. There is something to fear in what may lead up to death-illness, injury, loss of capacity, abandonment. But in death itself there is less to fear than there is in life, or in sleep. It is simply the transition from what is, from life.

"We should think of food and sex less than we think of death," she said. "And we should not fear it, but simply know at all times that this life of ours may at any instant be overtaken by its only certainty. Death is the best sauce and the most important spice in the dish of life. It makes it more savory than any other thing could ever do for life. The constant attentiveness to his own death can enrich the life of an impoverished man more than the application of riches can. And in this nature itself provides the direction. We need not prepare for death. It takes us as being prepared, whenever it takes us. There is never a need to prepare."

"But what about after death," I asked, "is there life after death?"

"The issue here is again what it always is," she answered, "words, and the uncertainty of what we may think we know. You chose to use the word 'life.' We may be certain that we do not keep our bodies as they are and therefore we would not be living the life we know. It is something else. Whatever it is, it is not life as we live it here and now. And we do know what it will be like after death. We cannot be certain."

"But people have faith, and that is a kind of certainty," I interjected, hoping that she would reward me for this good question.

"Certainty is like taking too violently and desperately a grasp of something. We risk destroying what we grasp," she said. "Even if we grasp a virtue too tightly and rigorously, we risk using it in a way or in a situation that is not virtuous. Honesty is a virtue. But who has not destroyed an evening, a gathering, a friend by holding too tightly to an honest truth? Who has not stayed too long on a course toward destruction of self and others for having too strong a grasp on hope? And hope is also a virtue. Those who have wielded their goodness and virtue as a sword have injured as with a sword."

She continued, "You have read in the Bible that I have said that men should not kill and that if they do they will risk judgment. And I have said we should do good to those that hate us. And I have said that true justice is found not in life but through God. And I have said you need to love your enemy and that he who will pick up the sword will die by it. And yet if a known killer were about to murder a child, and that child's parent had the means to stop that murder by killing that known killer, he or she would certainly do it."

"Damn right," I said.

"But it might be argued that I have taught that it is wrong to kill anyone," she answered, "even your enemy, particularly your enemy, and that you and your child will have your reward not in this world but in the next. If you do this good to your enemy you may convert him to the way of God and may add one more person to the roll of heaven. I would say that this is the strongest reading of what I have said, and perhaps the only true reading of it."

"So, let the child be killed?" I asked.

"Yes, and find your justice not in this world, but in the next," she answered.

"Well, that seems a little extreme."

"Exactly," she continued, "the kind of faith it would take to not kill the murderer in that instance and to await and to seek your divine reward elsewhere than in this world would be very extreme. That kind of faith is always extreme. It is something that is grasped a bit too desperately and too fiercely. Though many will profess that they have that kind of faith, almost no one does have it. And that does not make them wrong or bad. It makes them human. Doubt is our birthright and our gift from God.

"Hold everything you believe," she said, "and particularly everything you read and believe, as you would hold a child or a bird, firmly but gently and carefully. What is important to know about this message that I bring you is that it is already generally known. Everyone is aware of his or her doubt, and this doubt is exactly why they would stop that killer and not seek reward in the next world. But they think that they can forget that doubt in other cases. Many of them would argue that it is hypocritical to profess faith and to have doubt. It is really the other way around."

The television room is one of those places in a prison that is ineluctably tribal. Sometimes the ethos is that the show that is already being watched just stays on the set. Other times it is that the program to be watched is determined by a kind of majority rule that is not set out by a vote but by the majority of the clamor. An inmate or a group can attempt to stake out a program to watch by posting notice of their intention. And an inmate or a group can commandeer the television by intimidation and by threats. And as in any tribe, sometimes the decision is made by an actual test of strength.

But real crime shows are watched by consensus. If there is a show on with a televised helicopter shot of a white sports utility vehicle driving down the interstate being chased by several police cruisers, it is a safe bet that almost everyone will be there to watch it. So it was a big event several months back when a Russian court had sentenced the Muslim commander of a large famous terrorist organization that had taken credit for a string of suicide/murder bombings at Russian oil facilities, shopping malls, and government buildings. The Russian judge explained that he was well aware that the crimes had been committed by young men who had gone to their deaths with complete faith that they would be worshipped as martyrs and would find great reward after life. Because of that understanding, an entirely new punishment had been devised.

It seemed that the terrorist chief had been forced by the local Russian authorities to undergo an involuntary sex change operation, replete with hormone injections and a genital reconfiguration and the installation of breast enhancements, and was being paraded in a summer sun dress on a television program that was a Russian version of a dating reality television show. When it was announced that on this show the honor of "her" hand in marriage would be the subject of a competition between a dozen hardened and loathsome characters hand-picked from the worst prisons in all of Mother Russia, the gleeful and boisterous outbreak in our television room was so great that several guards had to come to the television room.

These inmates were by all measures the greatest practical experts in the field of crimes and punishments. They immediately knew the truth and the inevitability of what would only become evident to the rest of the world over the next couple of years. Because of this new punishment, the activities of this terrorist group in Russia would soon come to a complete stop.

"We have read your book," was what the Russian judge had said. "We treat our pets better than you treat your women."

My divine nocturnal visitor somehow had made me recall these incidents, sort of as parables. This particular memory was triggered by what she had said about gripping faith or anything too tightly, by ignoring uncertainty and by the limitations of words. Faith can be a weakness as much as a strength. And the word can be read by many people in different ways. I had only ever been taught to think that faith was always a strength and never a weakness. It was one of my father's favorite smaller topics, after baseball and the American legal system. He would read some article in the newspaper and he would comment upon the power of the faith of one of the persons in the article. He would wax eloquently on the power of faith to perform miracles and to heal and to effect great events, even where that faith might have been misplaced. He always spoke about it with the complete reverential awe that could only have been available to him as an agnostic.

I was getting less and less tired at the time when I really should have been getting sleep during this divine visitation. I was energized by all that had been said to me and revealed to me. I was filled with the fire to start to make use of what had been revealed to me in order to set the world straight. I had become my own peculiar version of an evangelical Christian. The hot mixed-race girl Christ had come to me and had reconstituted his words in a way that were new and different but which were exactly consonant with what I have always known from the Bible. This was an electrifying understanding, one that was practically bursting out of me. And I really wanted her at that moment.

"I know what you are thinking," she said, without the slightest trace of irony. "It is far easier for men of conscience to agree upon what is good and what is just than it is for them to agree upon the nature of God. What is more vain than to try to relegate God to our human understandings, feelings, virtues?" she continued by asking. "Because we truly cannot stretch our comprehension so far as to reach Heaven, we have tried to bring the Deity down to our words, our creeds, our institutions and corruptions. When we say that God is angry or that he loves or that he is wise, we lodge him down on the ground where we are and we confine his sublime feelings to words that describe our own. God alone can interpret herself. There is one thing that seems to me to be common in almost all ancient and current and modern religions," she continued, "and that is that God is and has an incomprehensible power."

I had been dying to bring this divine woman down to my own corruptions. That much had been certain. But this was a warning. My passions had been misplaced, and now I was deeply moved in a single different way and by a single different thing. And it was this great revelation that all revelation should be suspect and that the communication of a revelation is doubly so. This was not something that I ought to keep to myself. I had been indeed onto the scent of this divine woman Jesus. I felt deeply moved to spread this new gospel. As was always the case, my visitor sensed this.

She stood up and revealed herself in a completely new light. Though she had skin the color of brown honey, there was something suddenly wild and white and northern about her, as if she had stepped out of the untamed landscapes of the north or west of England. She was like Emily Brontë's Catherine Earnshaw, or more like Thomas Hardy's Eustacia Vye. There was something fiercely beautiful about her that would have had the exact same effect upon a primitive man or an ancient pagan as it had upon me, the effect of something like a forest fire or a night storm or of something of the ancient darkness and sinister depth of the sea. At that moment it would have been easy to picture her with a spear or a bow in her hand and wearing either a skin or a helmet. And suddenly it made perfect sense to me how the world could simply rest in the hands of such a being and how the world could be as it is, with some individuals being excessively favored and others cursed, with all its perverse justice and impossible problems, with the uneven pattern of blows and caresses we must bear.

"Beware your own vanity," she intoned. "When you seek to use this revelation in order to exalt yourself, you will be humbled. You need to remember your friend, Stanley, and emulate him. The truth is humbling. Keep it to yourself and grasp it gently. Do not try to be like Book. Do not think it gives you power over others."

"How can that be?" I murmured, not bearing to look too long or too directly at her, while at the same time being physically unable to turn away.

"You shall learn. You shall see. It is all part of this book you are living and writing. Both the folly of your vanity and the answers you seek are being revealed to you. And you may not be able to see or find all of them. You will have to re-read what you wrote and re-write what you have read. You will have to write and to read more. This is just the first revelation. There will be a new one with each new chapter of your journey. You must endeavor to understand each one and to see how each new revelation is connected to each of the previous ones. And in the end you will be answerable to me for your understanding of the lot of them, at sort of your personal judgment day," she said as she stood in the new light of a dawning day.

That awesome aspect she had just shown me had then tempered into a kind of casual insouciance, and she added archly, "You think you have a duty to distribute your acquired wisdom to the general public?"

"Yes, I think you could say that."

"It is not really a duty. It is really something you think you deserve, something more along the lines of a privilege or a right. You wanted me, and that was a vapor. This evangelical desire is another one and no less passionate or wrong. Since the first man wrote the first word and since the first man told his neighbor that he had a line on the will of the divine, it has been the same. I will tell you what each of you has believed you have had: *Du droit qu'un esprit ferme et vaste en ses desseins a sur l'esprit grossier des vulgaires humaines.*"

She flashed her movie star smile and left, but this I understood. I knew enough French. And I knew why perhaps it is that God does speak French. She had said that I thought I had the right that an enlightened soul always feels, that it has the privilege to educate the masses, not a duty but a right.

But for me it was much more than that. There was so much I needed to tell the world about these teachings, about our humanity being the one miracle of creation which we are at risk of losing if we move beyond it, about the certainty of uncertainty and of little else, about my new Christ and her words. My mixed desires had become entirely a spiritual desire.

It was clear to me now from all that she had said that all of life is a kind of prison. We all serve a sentence. We all have our freedoms extremely limited. We all cannot do what we really want to do. We have not done anything to deserve these limitations, this sentence. None of us is really guilty.

The only crime is art.

So if I was going to be serving this sentence, I was not going to be one of the countless who are serving through no fault of their own. I was going to deserve being here. I was going to commit art.

It was now the morning and time for the 5 p.m. count. In federal prison, they have five daily "counts," when the prisoners are counted by the guards, who are called "hacks." There is a count at 5 a.m., 4 p.m., 9 p.m., midnight, and 3 a.m. The largest gap between counts is during the day, when everyone is at his prison job. The most counts are at night, when the things that should be prevented are likely to occur. Every inmate has to be in his cell and visible during each count. At night the hacks shine a flashlight into the cells and check to see if each inmate is in his bed. When the count is over, if it does not add up correctly it is done over the second time with each man standing at a kind of rough attention and stating his full name and federal inmate number. This is because in a regular count one man may be simply counted for another. The formal count reveals exactly who is missing or out of place.

This regular count that morning was interrupted. There was a general commotion of the rare and good-natured variety that would allow the count to be interrupted, delayed and restarted but without the formality and the imminence of a standing count. A

75

large black bear had wandered onto the grounds. The hacks did not want to move from building to building to do the count. And everyone was curious to see what would happen with the bear, so we all had run to the windows. It was a magnificent creature, perhaps five hundred pounds, very large for a black bear in eastern North America. He was nosing around on the walkways and exercise yard and taking his time about it. Inmates were shouting at one another. It was one of those odd communal or tribal events, like a prison movie, or crime news, masculine and lively and pertinent, only this time it really was rather primeval. Bears in the eastern part of North America normally stay away from people. But this old boar had learned which humans to fear and which not to fear in his twenty-something years in these woods. He had acquired a graceful nonchalance that must have only been natural and which had dated back to the time when his ancestors knew of no other animal that could kill them. He looked into the buildings and dug up some contraband that inmates had buried on the grounds, which caused even more shouting. He roared and bellowed back at the shouting. He knocked over some chairs and scratched his back against a fence. He made the hair on the back of the neck of every guard and prisoner stand on its end. And then he wandered back into the woods.

Such had been the way in which I was delivered the first spiritual insight. The faithful already know it, as surely as they recognized the second revelation as it has been described in the first chapter.

THE RABBI

The Mafia guys arrived at and settled into our prison the same way they always have arrived at and settled into every other prison in the country at every other time, by order of rank. It is exactly the same way that Allied soldiers arrived at German prisoner of war camps in World War II. Although the Germans had systematically murdered millions of innocent civilians simply for being Jewish or gypsies or homosexuals or political opponents or merely mentally challenged, and even though they had murdered tens of millions more captured Russian soldiers, they treated the French and American and English and Canadian soldiers and sailors and airmen in German prisoner of war camps in a way that was not nearly so murderous. In fact, survival rates of Allied prisoners in German prisoner of war camps were roughly close to ninety-five percent, which was unlike the less than fifty percent who were able to survive the prisoner of war camps of the Japanese, whose own genocidal ways are less remembered in the West because they tended to murder masses of people who were not white. The Germans allowed a certain order among the prisoners in their camps and that was according to the rank of the prisoners, as was also provided by the Geneva Convention. So the prisoners of war in German camps fell in and organized themselves with their commander being the highest-ranking officer at the prison, no matter if he was Canadian or English or French or

American or an airman or a sailor or a soldier. Those ranks were recognized across services, across international boundaries and across languages.

So it was with the mob guys, the O. C. guys, the mafia men, the Italians. They all called their business on the outside "our thing," and whether or not they were from Boston or Cleveland or New York they knew exactly where they fit once they got inside. And they did have a decent place in which to fit when they got to prison, which made it a lot easier on them than it was on everyone else. O. C. stands for organized crime, and even though the various mafia organizations are a lot less organized than they once were, it was clear to the observant eye what their organization was in prison and how they all fit into the hierarchy. At the top of the pyramid in our prison was Big Frank. He had not been a boss of a crime family on the outside but he had been an underboss or a direct assistant to a boss. He was in his late fifties. Then under him there were two men in their late forties, each named Angelo, one called Big Angelo and the other called Little Angelo, although no one would ever call him that to his face. They had been captains in their gangs; they had run their own groups of crews. Under them were what I called "some guys named Tony," and they tended to be thirty to forty years old and were "made" men on the outside, and each had a small crew of a handful of men. And under them were the young guys, the soldiers, the regular wise guys, the ones who made up the crews. These younger men invariably spent their time in the weight room in prison and were inordinately concerned with their personal appearance. They also did not seem to be all that smart. So it was apparent that a certain intelligence or cunning was required to move up the ranks, to become a Frank or an Angelo or one of the men named Tony.

I may be engaging in a stereotype, albeit a benign one, when I also say that I was always surprised when I met a Jewish man in prison. I was constantly tempted to say to him, "So, what's a nice boy like you doing in a place like this?" or, "Does your mother know you're here?" This was a temptation to which I usually yielded, and I was always met with a wry confession, almost an admission that it was somehow more embarrassing to be Jewish and a convict than it was to be a criminal gentile. I guess I was less surprised to learn that most of the dozen or so Jewish men in the prison were there on white-collar crime convictions. There was still the occasional drug dealer among what was simply known in the prison as "the community." But most of the Jewish men were there because they were "gonif," or due to some kind of fraud or embezzlement. And even though they did not have a distinct hierarchy like the mob guys did, they also formed a group and they too had a leader. Since he had actually been a rabbi on the outside and still was one, he was simply known to guards and inmates alike as the Rabbi. He had been convicted of defrauding the Amish, selling bogus debentures to the Plain Folk. And while there were men inside who were more feared by the other inmates than the Rabbi was, he was the prisoner that caused the guards the most concern.

There has always been a kind of a thing that is between the Jews and the Italians. It may not be merely facile to say that this thing is the Mediterranean Sea, because that may also be an apt metaphor. It is certainly a metaphysical space which can be easily and quickly traversed in a way that makes each seem close to the other, but it can also be a stormy connection. This same thing also exists in the space between the heart of every individual Italian and that of every individual Jew, and it would not be incorrect to call it a broad affinity or sympathy that also contains within it a strain of antipathy. It is almost as if the totality of their shared history is quietly and secretly incorporated into each of their sensibilities. Both peoples speak with their hands and are bright and volatile and personable and have a love of family. And both have a respect for hard work and intelligence and the value of money. But somewhere inside of each is the unconscious memory of the destruction of the temple of Jerusalem in 70 A.D., and of Masada.

So it also was in our prison. One day out on the yard, in the corner where the bocce court was located and where the older gentlemen of Italian descent would congregate, there was an interesting conversation which I was able to overhear for a reason that will be evident later.

"You know, Frank, what this place needs is a few more amenities. You know what I mean? It is all right as these places go, but we could make it a lot better," Big Angelo began the conversation. He always had an unlit cigar in his hand or in his mouth, and his voice had a grating quality, as if the sound of it were being ground up before it came out of his mouth. He was a tall man and rather heavily built, with wavy black hair, a pockmarked face, a large nose, and large facial features. He had an expansive way of speaking and of acting that was ingratiating.

"What were you thinking, Ange?" asked Big Frank. Frank was not as tall as this particular Angelo, but he was barrel-chested and thick through the middle. He had brown hair that was thinning and it was clear that in his youth he had been a handsome man. And while he was clearly very reserved, he also had a kind of knowing and ironic tone to his voice and a similar spark in his eye. He had a way of asking a question as if he knew what the answer was going to be.

"I was thinking," Big Angelo answered, "about the Jews. I think we can talk to the Rabbi."

"I don't like dealing with the Jews," added Little Angelo, "unless it is to hire one as a defense attorney. They always exact some hidden extra tax." Little Angelo was small and thin and had a sharp aquiline nose and piercing brown eyes. His cunning and his ruthlessness were never far from the surface. His hair was prematurely graying and his tone of voice was always just a little inciting. And "tax" was a term that they used to refer to a payment that was based on some kind of assigned and not inherent value. For instance if a member of one crew had wrongly assaulted or insulted the captain of another crew, when that first crew paid the second crew for a service or a shipment they were then required to pay a little more than was the norm. That difference was the tax, for the wrong they had inflicted.

"You know," Frank added, "we have been dealing with them since before any of us had been born."

"Yeah, and it has always cost us extra," Little Angelo intoned.

"These simple country knuckleheads at this prison are afraid of him," Big Angelo continued, referring to the Rabbi. "It is like they think he has some magical powers. The whole Jewish thing is a huge mystery to the Kentucky crackers who run this place."

"I think something happened at some point," Frank said, "that put the fear in them."

"I heard it was something they did to him," said Little Angelo, "and he turned it into some kind of example of religious persecution. Important people made complaints to Congress and to the Bureau of Prisons and all kinds of hell rained down on these local people. There was already a presumption that they are all bigots in this part of the country anyway. It was a perfect move on his part, very shrewd."

"It must have put the fear of God into their inbred hearts," laughed Big Angelo. "But what I do know is this. Not only are they afraid of him but he gets stuff shipped in here directly to him under some kind of kosher label. And the guards won't even go near those shipments, and the warden would not let them even if they wanted to. All we would need to do would be to come to some kind of arrangement with the Rabbi."

"Whatever that arrangement would be," Little Angelo commented, "would be one that they would not stick to in the same way we would. They would always be increasing their end. You can count on that."

"There is usually a way to nail them down," Big Angelo added. "We just have to figure out what that would be. And of course, we would have to arrange to sit down with the Rabbi and begin the negotiation."

"Even that will cost us," was Little Angelo's comment.

"We could invite him to sit with us for dinner or we could ask him to come to our meeting room," Big Angelo said.

The meeting room to which he referred was the prison chapel room. The young wise guys had all been directed to sign up for Catholic services and had all been volunteered for duty to maintain and care for the prison chapel. Once a week a local priest came and conducted Catholic Mass. All the mob guys attended. And several other times a week they had access to the chapel for religious and other reasons because they were overwhelmingly in the majority among the inmates who had volunteered to maintain it. And during those times when there were not services business was conducted within the organized crime group that was in the prison. It was their room essentially, their meeting room. The other Christian denominations within the prison also used that room, but only once a week. The Muslims had use of it too once a week. Jewish services were conducted by the Rabbi, but in a separate room, one that was also attached to a separate kitchen, which was their kosher kitchen.

Those rooms for "the community" were even in a separate building along with a couple of the cell blocks at the far end of the complex. The chapel was in the main building with the administrative offices, the commissary, the mess hall and the library.

"The Rabbi may make a deal with us," Frank finally intervened in the dialogue. "He may negotiate with us. He may even play a game of bocce with us. But he will not come to our place of worship. And he most certainly will never break bread with us. He will not eat our food or drink with us or even use the same plates and utensils we use."

"And we are supposed to trust someone who won't break bread with us?" asked Little Angelo in what was more of a statement than a question. "That shows he has nothing but contempt for us, the weasel."

"But, Ange, we have never exactly loved them either," Big Angelo said, with a smile. "We both grew up in Brooklyn. We knew plenty of Jewish guys and we never were very friendly with any of them. And then there is the whole historical thing. They got a reason to have a chip on their shoulder."

"We still sit down and eat with someone we make a deal with," Little Angelo answered, "even if we do not like them or do not trust them. We don't act like we are holier than everybody else. But they do."

"Maybe they are just more honest than we are," said Frank. "We have broken bread with people we intended to be not very nice to later, and with people for whom we have had nothing but contempt. The bigger point here is that none of us trust them. But we have also always been able to make deals with people we do not trust. We will set up a meeting."

My own experience with these men was an interesting one. Oddly, it was also one for which my family and I were grateful. When I came into this prison I had arrived the same way everyone else did, with a target on my back, figuratively and literally. New prisoners are taken into the compound wearing a dark green coverall. Everyone else is wearing khaki shirts and pants. There is no chance to be anonymous or to blend into the general population before you are fingered as a new guy. This is a stark exclamation point to the psychology of being placed into a totally alien and potentially dangerous setting without any understanding whatsoever of what is expected or what to expect. The only thing that I or anyone else might know is to trust no one. I was first placed into a cell with a Colombian gentleman who spoke no English. What I soon found out was that cells were assigned by seniority, so I had been put into the least favorable cell. The rumor was that my cellmate had escaped a longer sentence in a maximum-security facility by providing evidence against a Colombian drug cartel. In other words, no one in the joint wanted to be standing too close to him at any time.

For the first three days straight I kept to myself and remained alert. And for three nights in a row I did not sleep.

In order to get fitted with the standard issue khakis I had to pay a visit to the prison tailor. I did this on the second day. The tailor's name was Rocco, and he had actually been born and raised in Italy and had moved to New York City as an adult and had worked as a tailor and saved his money until one day he owned his own tailor shop. He had made it a lucrative business. It became much more profitable when he was later known for being the tailor to the Mafia stars, including the famous New York City boss who always appeared in court wearing immaculately tailored Italian suits at the many trials in which the government failed to convict him. Because of that, Rocco had been very much in demand and not just among the O.C. guys but with other wealthy Italian-American men and even among the Wall Street set. He had turned a blind eye when one or two of his clients asked to use his phone. They had assumed it would not be tapped. They also had assumed that since Rocco made numerous phone calls to family and friends in Italy that one more call here and there would not stand out. But the phone line was eventually tapped. And Rocco's consent to use the phone was taken as his role in a conspiracy to import heroin from the Mediterranean.

When I met him he was on the last two years of a five-year sentence. Rocco was innocent, and by that I mean it was his nature. He was almost child-like in his sweet manner and his unassuming demeanor. He was like a kindly younger uncle, one who always had a treat for the kids and a smile for the women. He was a small man and slight of build with a dark handsome look that was also boyish despite his salt and pepper hair. He spoke with very broken English and would lapse into Italian without thinking. While he was measuring my inseam and my waist he would mutter in Italian. Every once in a while I would throw some of my limited Italian at him, and he asked me where I had learned it. I told him that my mother was Sicilian and that her immigrant mother had been my nanny when I was a toddler because my mother had worked then. Up until I was five years old I had spoken both English and Italian. He asked me about my work, and I told him that I had worked in Washington. And I gave him a tip. It was his job to measure and to hem and adjust the waists on the khaki pants. He refused the two packs of cigarettes I gave him as a tip. Neither of us smoked, but in a place where there is no currency certain things come to fill the void, and, as much of a cliché as it is, cigarettes are currency in prison. Eventually he took the tip because I had insisted. He probably knew by my insistence that I had not been lying about being half Sicilian.

It was on the fourth day, two days after I had seen Rocco and one day after he had given me my finished khaki clothes and after three sleepless nights, that Big Frank posted himself on the bench right outside of the mess hall as I was leaving it from lunch. He did not say anything to me. He simply gestured toward the spot next to him on the bench. I sat down. His first words to me were that he had heard from Rocco that my mother was Sicilian. And what followed this was a fifteen-minute conversation about my family, my work, my home, all about me and nothing about him. I knew enough to know that it was not a conversation at all but was a quiz. There were no direct questions. I made a point of not seeming too eager to answer what were not really questions. But I let enough comments drop and made enough references to assure him of what he was seeking to know, and that was if I really was what Rocco had reported.

He concluded the conversation by literally dismissing me. "You can go now," he said, "and you can start to get some sleep at night. Now that you have been seen talking with me no one here will mess with you."

He took that even further, one day in the visiting room. He had seen me there many times with different visitors and had done nothing, but on the first visit that my mother made he got up and walked over to us. He put his hand on my shoulder and looked at my mother and he told her that he knew that she must be worried but that she must not ever worry anymore because he was personally going to protect me. Then he walked away. Nothing else, no other thing at all, no assurance I could have made would have had any effect whatsoever on the magnitude of her worrying. But this did. It was like they had communicated much more than was said and that they passed that information to each other on some silent wavelength of the *Mezzogiorno*.

So I became like a pet, an auxiliary, an "of counsel" to this group of men, most of whom had at some point or another been extortionists, thieves, pimps, drug kingpins, loan sharks, and even murderers. Rocco and I were not in the organization but we were allowed near it. I was sometimes included and consulted but only in an ancillary way. My opinion mattered but it was almost never sought directly on any issue that related directly to what they called among themselves "our thing." It was at once exciting and frightening and provocative and familial. As with the other inmates, I was often called upon by them to speak on matters that lent themselves to my education and experience, both of which were somewhat beyond these men, who were very street smart. Even then I knew not to venture an opinion that was too much at variance with the general understanding that they all had. So I would often be asked to discuss an instance in which I knew a specific way in which the government was corrupt or that politicians were motivated by money or that there was still an upper-class bias against Americans of Italian descent. And I was no longer afraid of what might happen to me within the larger group of prison residents. I was figuratively behind a kind of shield, and it was assumed among the general population that I was connected in some way to the mob. Those previous fears were now replaced by one fear, and that was that a favor would be asked of me or of my family, because such a request is not normally refused, and in a very important way I was already indebted.

One way in which I was called upon to help, although I did not know it at the time, was when Big Frank engaged me in a long conversation about the history of Judaism, particularly in Italy and in relation to the Catholic Church. I had not known it, but he was doing his homework.

The Rabbi was in a short time approached by Big Angelo to come and sit down with Big Frank and some of his men. The Rabbi brought with him the one member of the prison Jewish community who might have had a few things in common with my new friends and whom they might respect, Leonard Lubatich, the bank robber, a man who actually walked into banks with a gun and held them up. He was quite young and tall and soft-spoken and nice-looking, with dark wavy hair. He was attractive and unassuming, both in ways which I gather helped him in his profession.

"What have you been hearing on the yard?" the Rabbi asked Big Frank, by way of greeting. "I hear you want to talk to me, that you might want to enter into an agreement with me."

"Have a seat, Rabbi," Frank said quietly, and the Rabbi and Lubatich took seats on the bench and the chair next to the bocce courts. The Rabbi looked like he actually might have been Little Angelo's cousin. He was a small, wiry man with sandy brown hair, light brown eyes and sharp features. He was more fair skinned than Little Angelo or any of the Italians. And while little Angelo was reserved and calm but would become sharp or active in an instant, like a snake striking, the Rabbi was mercurial and kinetic and then at critical moments would lapse into a calm and distant demeanor. He was hard to read in that way and he knew it.

"I don't know what to say, Frank," he began, "you being a big man in New York and I being a nobody from Philadelphia. You are an important part of a big organization, and I am just a single person. I don't know what you could want with me."

Frank only smiled at the Rabbi, who continued.

"I will thank you for your attention and for this honor of being asked to sit down and talk to you but I don't know what I can possibly do for you. So if you will permit, I will be on my way."

"Hold on a moment, Rabbi, please. We are all in a tight spot here,"

Frank said, "in prison. And we both know that it is much harder on those who love us than it is on us. Our families suffer more from us being in prison than we do in here. I am sure that you know what I am talking about."

The Rabbi paused for several moments before he answered, "So, do you have some kind of way to help my family? Is that what you are suggesting?"

"That is exactly what I mean. I am certain that you have always been a good provider for your family and I know it must hurt that you are prevented from being that now. I think there might be a way for you to continue to provide for them, even from inside here."

The Rabbi put on his quiet look for a minute. Then he said, "I am not sure that our differences don't prevent us from working together like that. For two thousand years, your church has persecuted my tribe. Your people have spat upon my people. There is a lot of history here to overcome. And I am not sure you and I can overcome all of that."

"I understand that you are Sephardic," Frank said. "And when Ferdinand and Isabella banned the Jews from Spain, what did the Sephardim do?"

"Many of them became marranos, or conversos, and were forced to pretend to become Catholics. The rest had to flee Spain for their lives," the Rabbi answered as a matter of fact, but his eyes showed some surprise.

"And where did they go?" Frank asked, but only rhetorically. "They went to North Africa and to Italy, where there had already been Jewish communities since the time of the Romans. Many of them went to the town of my ancestors, Naples, where they lived in peace and where they were only persecuted by the French and the Spanish when each of them had ruled Naples for a short time, but never by the Italians. There have been synagogues in Naples for five hundred years."

"Italy is the home of the Roman Catholic Church," the Rabbi countered, "and they invented the Inquisition, which was used against my people for hundreds of years as an instrument of torture and persecution."

"We Italians did not make the most of that. The Spanish did. We are a much more ancient and sophisticated race. Christianity came to Rome long after civilization had taken root there, and the Romans took it and put their own brand on it. We have always had a unique relationship to our faith, one that you may or may not understand. Tell him Angelo."

"Religion is good," answered Big Angelo, "for the women."

"I am aware of that opinion," the Rabbi answered, "and it is one that I cannot say I fully understand. I will have a hard time disassociating you from the Catholic Church quite as easily as you seem to say you can do for yourselves. And the Church was complicit in the Holocaust, as I am sure you know, as you seem to be a student of history."

"Again, I am going to remind you of how that was all different in Italy," Frank added, "as I am sure you know as well. Italy was an ally of Nazi Germany starting in 1936 and still did not engage in the systematic mass murder of its Jews at that time. Nothing much like that happened until Germany occupied Italy and ran that country from 1943 until 1945. And even then, when the Germans tried to carry out their mass murder, the Italians actively and passively resisted, and as a result fewer than ten percent of the Jews in Italy were killed. I do not have to remind you that the story was much different in Poland, or the Ukraine, or even in France for that matter."

At this point, the Rabbi went into one of his quiet phases. Frank glanced over at me briefly, and his glance was followed by the Rabbi, who then continued to look down. I was amazed at the retention that Frank had. We'd had only one conversation in which I had told him the things he so clearly remembered now. It was obviously a trait that had helped him to rise to the top in a business where nothing at all is ever written or recorded.

"So what is it that you have in mind?" the Rabbi eventually asked.

"We are interested in that kosher shipment that you get every couple weeks or so. I would like to be a part of it every once in a while for the next year. And I would like to compensate you for that privilege, say to the tune of three thousand dollars," Frank said with a look of expectation, one that I had seen before, the one in which he appears to know what the answer will be.

"You know that I cannot do that, Frank. That would violate any number of the tenets of my faith, the faith of my fathers. I would have no way of knowing what would be coming in your part of the shipments, and it might be something that could contaminate the whole cargo."

"We both know that the things I would bring in would not mix with your part of the shipments and we also know that you could easily perform a ritual cleansing afterwards. And we could multiply that figure I mentioned by three and multiply that product again by three."

At this point Lubatich interjected himself into the conversation in a way that none of the men on Frank's side of the conversation would have ever considered. "Are you out of your mind? Twenty-seven thousand dollars. It would be worth much more than that to you, something more like sixty thousand dollars. Or you could pay six thousand dollars for every shipment you want to make."

The Rabbi spoke, "I could not do it for sixty thousand dollars nor for six thousand dollars a shipment. My young friend is impetuous and he does not have the privilege and the duty that I have of being a caretaker of the faith. Not even if you were to pay six or nine or twelve or thirty-six thousand dollars a shipment. I simply could not set out to break the laws of our faith and then hope to cleanse my sin with a ritual. What starts out in bad faith cannot become good."

"Then we will have to leave it at that, then," said Frank. "And please do not take any of this the wrong way. I do not mean to ever impugn your faith. I just have a more worldly approach to my own faith and to life in general. And thank you for taking the time to sit down and talk to me."

The Rabbi got up to leave, turned as if he were going to say one more thing, paused and then turned away again and walked out of our presence. After he had left, Frank turned and looked at Little Angelo. These men all had a way of communicating entire sentences with a look. I imagine that men had been condemned to death on little more than a glance such as this. But this particular look was a question.

"I think he wants to drive up the price," Little Angelo offered. Frank looked at Big Angelo.

"This may be a job for Tony P. and his crew. They would get him to come around," Big Angelo stated.

"I think you make a good point, each of you," Frank said. "Tony P. and his crew might be able to intimidate him, and we also may be able to get the Rabbi to come to terms at a much higher price." Then he turned to me and surprised me by asking, "What do you think?"

"Jewish people are not only of a different faith," I said, "they have a completely different relationship to their faith. We can stop going to church and still be Italians. But a Jew who leaves his faith has also turned his back on his people and his culture. It is a faith that became a people, and the people and the faith are indissoluble. And in order to be a rabbi the Rabbi has had to immerse himself in the faith and his culture. He has literally given his life to study and to observance and to a people. He is a man of faith in a way that we are not used to seeing. I don't think he can be brought into any arrangement that might conflict with his faith."

"The way I see it," Frank said, "you have all said pretty much the same thing."

We sat there for some time, trying to think of what Frank could have meant by that comment.

"It is the hardest thing in the world to live a life of faith," he said, "and the critical phrase there is 'in the world.' It may be possible to live a life of faith in a monastery or if in some other way you are not 'in the world,' such as if you are insane or are extremely simple-minded. Hell, it is hard enough to live life in the world alone, without faith. But mixing a life in the world with a life in faith may be more dangerous than living without faith or living in a monastery. Faith can create what seem to be miracles; it can be the foundation of great feats of courage or perseverance. But it can also lead an entire congregation of a so-called church to drink poisonous fruit juice in some South American jungle, or to that Inquisition we were just talking about, or to a group of fanatics flying a plane into a building and killing thousands of people.

"Here is another example," he continued. "Let's say some maniac killer is standing over your children with a meat cleaver, and you have a gun in your hand." Frank turned to me as he asked, "What would a real Christian do? What would a man do who was a true believer and a true follower of the words of Christ?"

"He would do nothing," I answered, "because he would know that killing is always wrong and that he must love his enemy. He would know that his reward and the rewards for his children would be in Heaven, where they all would be reunited. He would also know that his example of love and forgiveness and sacrifice might be the example that would bring his enemy into the faith, so that would be a net gain, one more Christian in Heaven."

I was puzzled for an instant as to why that question had been directed to me. Initially, I had assumed that it was because I would be the one in the group most likely to have actually read the Bible and to have considered what was in it. But then it occurred to me that this man who seemed to simply know things that others did not know might have actually have read this book you are now reading and had also read of just this same discussion in an earlier part of the book.

Frank went on, "Yet almost every Christian man or woman alive would shoot the maniac before he could kill the children. And each of them would be able to find justification for it somewhere in the Bible, in the Old Testament perhaps. But he would be making an entirely worldly decision on worldly grounds and would only later be trying to find some religious justification for it. He would not gamble the life of his children on his faith. There are a few who might do that but very few indeed. We all arrive at and live in the same world. Faiths are different and are arrived at in different ways and are not at all universal.

"This is the way in which you are all right," he continued. "To say that the Jewish faith and the Jewish people are inseparable is to posit a very worldly basis for the strength of their faith. To send Tony P. and his crew after the Rabbi would be to inflict the world on him in such a negative way that he would have to make the worldly decision to save himself. And to say he has a price is to say he will succumb to worldly incentives, just as likely as he would like to escape worldly difficulties. You may have all noticed that when he refused the deal he did so each time at a specific price. He never once said that he would not do it for 'all the money in the world,' or not for a 'trillion dollars.' Those phrases would have meant he had no price at all. But he left the prospect open.

"And perhaps the greatness of Italian culture is that we are very worldly and have been for a very long time, since the Romans took over the Western world and in a sense created it as we know it," he continued. "And the Romans stayed in charge through the birth of the Church in Rome and its expansion throughout Europe, which generated Christianity as we know it. Italians were in charge through the Renaissance, during which we brought light of civilization back to Europe and the world. The Florentines and the Venetians and the Genovese and the Romans were at that point the flowers of civilization, and for them it was even then the second time around. What people could be more worldly than we are?

"And our friend, the Rabbi, is also a very worldly man. He is obviously a student of the world," Frank said, as he smiled. "His Amish victims will tell you that he has larceny in his heart. And even though he may call it something more innocent, it would still admittedly be a desire to make money. Even his special brand of his faith has conferred upon him a title and position that clearly has its worldly benefits. But perhaps the most important thing to know is that the Jewish faith is in fact the one most inextricably linked to the world, since it is inseparable from its people; its worldliness is woven into it, culturally, ethnically, and socially. The Rabbi's faith is one of his strengths but it is also his blind spot. We have no such blind spots.

Bring me that other Tony. What is his name? Tony G., the kid from our thing in Philly. I want to see what he knows."

I was not completely conversant on the roles of each of the men named Tony. I was told later that the Tony P. to whom they had referred first was a "Shylock," which meant he was a loan shark, a lender of last resort on the street, a man who made personal loans at outrageously high rates of interest, charged on a weekly basis. The men of his crew were all enforcers, men who took measures to see that this interest was paid and that the loans were repaid. They were brutal, ruthless men. Big Angelo's solution to the problem would have been to have Tony P. and his crew beat an agreement out of the Rabbi. I was told that Tony G., the one from Philadelphia, the one Frank had just mentioned, had been an expert at credit card fraud and at bogus stock deals and that he had operated what were called boiler rooms that made calls to bump up the price of some penny stock that he would then dump at a profit. He was clearly at a different level of sophistication than Tony P. While we waited for Tony G., Big Frank gave us some more of the benefit of his thinking.

"I don't want to use Tony P., because a man who is intimidated into an arrangement does not want to stay in the arrangement. He remains a risky proposition. You can never know if he will set you up or run on you. We don't want to put the Rabbi in that position. He is too smart. We also don't want to negotiate. Whatever may be the Rabbi's eventual price, it will be higher than we want to pay."

At that point, a rather rotund and jovial young man walked up. He had curly black hair and a round pleasant face. He looked as if he was always about to make a joke or to laugh at one, but within that was the spark of some intellect. He was about thirty or thirty-five years old.

"You want to talk to me, Frank?" asked Tony G.

"Yes," said Frank, "I want to know what you know about the Rabbi."

"You mean when he was on the outside?"

"Yes."

"Well, he started out completely legitimate, they say, as a financial planner or an investment adviser or a stock broker or something like that. Then he got behind, started to lose money. In order to keep up his successful image in the community he started robbing Peter to pay Paul. He shifted money around and was hoping to make it up with future profits and stay legitimate. But by then he had learned the value of keeping two sets of books. His operation became a total sham. Someone got wind of it and blew the whistle on him. When he was busted by the cops he had just sold some fake bonds to a bunch of elders of an Amish church out in Lancaster County, Pennsylvania. The press had a field day with that. His wife left him. He still has some very important friends, and his daughter stuck with him. She is the one who puts together the kosher packages and sends them here. I think her name is Jessica."

"You got to be kidding me," Big Angelo interrupted, "Jessica Rabbi, for Christ sake?"

"Actually their last name is . . ." Tony G. started to say, but was interrupted again, this time by Big Frank.

"I think we all know his last name is not Rabbi. Thanks a lot, Tony. When is your bit up?"

"In twenty-five months."

"You want to move to New York? When you get out, you look me up."

"Thanks. I will give that some serious thought," Tony G. said and then he left.

"Angelo," Big Frank directed his question to Little Angelo, "what is the name of that kid you got on one of your crews, the kid who runs the pros out of that cathouse in Bay Ridge?"

"That would be handsome Geno," Angelo said, "one of boys in the crew of Tony B. He has gifts, that kid. But he has a problem keeping his hands off of the merchandise. What are you figuring?"

"I figure we are dealing with the wrong member of the Rabbi's family. Get the word to this Geno. He is taking a trip to Philadelphia."

Some days later, after lunch, I was talking to Big Angelo out in the yard by the bocce courts. We were alone. He was telling me a story about his waste disposal business and how he had been damaged by the actions of one of his suppliers. I told him that I thought he had had very good grounds for a law suit. He took the unlit cigar stub out of his mouth and said to me, in his gravelly voice, "Kid, I never had to sue nobody for nothing." I realized in an instant that this was the appeal of the mob. This was why mob movies and Mafia television shows have been popular. It is because they have access to a kind of tribal justice, one that acts with more speed and efficiency than our legal system. It is not the romance of crime that is the sole attraction of those films and programs. People are also attracted to the idea of a justice that is quick and effective.

I took the opportunity to ask him about handsome Geno.

"That kid, Geno," Big Angelo said, "is a piece of work. Let me tell you. When he was in high school, there was a teacher who was very active in the New York City gay and lesbian community. She was like the chairman of one of their committees. Even though she was a dyke, she was an attractive woman. Well, by about halfway through Geno's senior year she was riding on the back of his motorcycle to have lunchtime trysts with him and get this at his parents' apartment. Both his parents worked. When they eventually found out about it, there was a big blow-up, the teacher got fired, and he was expelled. And she went back to girls.

"Then there was the time when he first started to work for us," he said. "It was some other wise guy's bachelor party, and they had hired some hookers to entertain the guy. And while they were there, these girls decided to offer a discount rate for the other guys at the party, you know, because they were already there. Geno did not participate. He has some principle, something about not paying for it. Well, it's about two in the morning, and one of the girls walks into the room and points at Geno and she says, 'Him, I will do for free.' And the legend of handsome Geno was born. When he is introduced now his friends say, 'This is Geno. He cures lesbians, and hookers fall in love with him.' It is also rumored that he is well endowed. Let's just say that Geno has never had a problem with women. And that may be the problem. Since he took over Little Angelo's house in the Bay Ridge neighborhood of Brooklyn they have been able to recruit more girls and better girls, and their profits have gone way up. But they have had to put another guy on the job, just to keep the girls off Geno."

About five weeks after the initial meeting the Rabbi requested another sit-down with Frank. He again brought Lenny Lubatich with him, and this time it was a negotiation. Lenny started off with the negotiating. The Rabbi sat quietly, looking at his hands on his lap.

"You said something about six thousand dollars per shipment," Lenny said, "but we are thinking more along the lines of thirty-six thousand dollars per shipment."

Big Frank let Little Angelo provide the answer. "That seems a little steep. And you know that we are not interested in negotiation per single shipment. That might mean we would have to come back to this negotiation over and over again. We want the right to participate in any shipment for the period of a year. And for that we are willing to pay you thirty-six thousand dollars, which is an increase on our previous offer of twenty-seven."

"No," Lenny said, "that is still way too low."

"Then it looks like we will not be able to make an agreement," Angelo concluded.

"That's right," said Lenny.

Then, without leaning forward or raising his voice or making a point of intervening, Big Frank spoke quietly, "I think we all know why we are here. Something has happened to the shipments. They are no longer arriving. You gentlemen are trying to sell us something you no longer have and you still want to charge an exorbitant price for it. Something has gone wrong on the other end of your shipments, or else you would not be sitting here."

Lubatich was silent. We were all silent. The Rabbi, however, had now looked up from his hands on his lap and was observing Frank.

Frank continued, "Something has gone wrong with your daughter, Rabbi, and we both know it. You are no longer in touch with her. In fact, what you probably also know is that she is in a hotel in Atlantic City right now, consorting with some gentile guy."

"Then she is damned for it," the Rabbi said. "My own flesh and blood. I had feared something like this. At every point that my life has come into contact with the goyim it has been a tragedy. If a Jew does wrong to a Christian, there is hell to pay. Yet you foul our lives over and over, as with my daughter, and as with this so-called negotiation. I have no use for the lot of you, except perhaps to bait fish with."

"Those are very proud words, Rabbi," Frank said, "but what would you say if I told you we could bring your daughter back to you, bring her back to Philadelphia and make everything the way it used to be? What would you say to that?"

"I would say that I should have figured as much. Then, if you do that, then we will make your deal. You may take part in our shipments for the next twelve months, for a fee of thirty-six thousand dollars."

"The time for that deal has passed, Rabbi."

"What, you are not a man of your word, you, the great leader of your organization? I will have you live up to your word."

"This is coming from a man who was going to take my money for a service he could not deliver. Come on now, Rabbi. We will take part in your deliveries for as long as I say and we will not pay you a dime for it. You will let us do it and we will let you have your daughter back."

"But your word . . . is the word of a Christian worth nothing?"

"I am about as much of a Christian as you are a rabbi. But tell me, Rabbi, because I do not want to go any further if you are not comfortable with this. I need to know if you are willing to go forward with our deal. You get your daughter back, and we get access to your shipments. What do you say?"

"What do you want me to say? Do you want me to say I am happy with that? Then I am content."

"Good. And one more thing: we get the use of your kitchen and side room on Christmas day, the entire day."

"Is that it? Is that all? Now that you have taken your pound of flesh, are you finished?"

"I would say that we are finished. We know how to get in touch with your daughter. Once she has returned we will contact her in order for us to begin adding to your shipments. Thank you for your time and for your consideration."

With that the Rabbi and Lubatich got up and walked away from us.

Big Frank then addressed Little Angelo. "Make sure that kid Geno brings her back to Philly. Also make sure that he has been making digital video recordings of all the fun they have been having in Atlantic City. I want some insurance on these shipments. And tell him that he will have to be the contact on the shipments. He will go to Philly every two weeks, and she will get to see him then. That ought to keep her happy."

"Sure thing, boss," Little Angelo said, "My crew is happy to help out on this thing."

The most immediate and obvious result of this negotiation to me was to be seen and smelled in the cigar stubs that Big Angelo always had in his hand or in his mouth. They were no longer the dark, cheap cigars that could be bought at the prison commissary. They were a rich aromatic cigar with a lighter brown color. They were from Cuba, by way of New York and Philadelphia. Not only were they prison contraband, they were contraband in the entire United States. There were other small changes, some in the clothes of Big Frank and his friends. At one point, I saw Frank in a pair of shorts.

I asked Big Angelo, "What are those scars all over Frank's legs?"

"Oh, those," he said, "are from some car trouble he had one time."

"Car trouble?"

"Yeah, the trouble was that when he turned on his car that time, it caught fire. And then it blew up, but not before he got out of it."

But perhaps the biggest and most obvious change from my perspective was dinner that Christmas. Christmas dinner was always considered a big deal for the inmates because there was the promise of a piece of steak for dinner. It really made it into Christmas for all of them, because the food was so generally bad that a medium cut of a decent steak was a bonus for everyone. I had been invited to Frank's Christmas dinner. So I made a sort of synergy out of it by offering to go to the prison dinner first and getting a steak and then turning it over to the toughest guy on my cell block for nothing and by telling him it was no real sacrifice for me because I was going to eat with the mob guys. That was a two for one for me because he was grateful to get the extra steak and he was proud to be a friend of a guy who was such a good friend of Frank. When he thanked me, I laughed and told him, "Just so I can tell people later that I gave you my meat when we were locked up together."

Then I hurried to the building at the end of the facility, the one with the kosher kitchen and side room. When I walked in even I was surprised to see what was happening. The young wise guys were doing some of the cooking and preparing and setting the table. Big Angelo was doing the main culinary duties and was directing the rest of the cooking and preparing. The table was set for Big Frank, the two men named Angelo, the several men named Tony, Rocco and me. No one else was to be eating. Big Frank sat at the head of the table, and Little Angelo at the other end. Big Angelo was moving around, but his seat was next to Big Frank. My seat was also next to Frank, on his left, and Rocco and the men named Tony were mixed in at the other seats.

It was an archetypal Italian feast, with about seven or eight courses. The first course was a Caesar salad with anchovies and parmesan cheese and croutons and bleu cheese dressing and vinegar and oil. There were the antipasti: prosciutto with melons, various cheeses, and olives. This was followed by shrimp, although everyone called it shrimp scampi, which I found curious since to Italians that was redundant. Perhaps it was a nod to their mixed culture, to use each name in each language for the one thing. There was a *braesola*, a Venetian dish of browned steak wrapped around a *bel paese* cheese with spices and stewed in a tomato sauce. There were various pastas. The main course was rabbit Bolognese, which was rabbit with carrots and onions and basil, in a white wine sauce with Romano cheese. There was enough Tuscan *vino nobile* for everyone, and espresso after dinner. And there were several pastries for dessert, along with some *zabaglione* and of course the Cuban cigars. It was not only the very best meal I ever had in prison, it may have been the best meal I had ever eaten. It was a tour de force of Italian cuisine.

There were plenty of jokes about "Rabbi Bolognese," and there was some general discussion of the negotiations that led up to what had allowed the Christmas dinner to be possible. There was also a lot of general Christmas cheer, many stories about "our thing," and plenty of questions to me about my life in Washington and among the Protestant upper classes. Later, amid the cigar smoke, I asked Frank about how he knew what to do with the Rabbi.

"You know the story," he answered, "of Abraham and Isaac, the one where he goes to kill his son in a human sacrifice because his God has asked him to do it? No one likes that story. But it is in there for a reason. And it is the same reason that no one likes it. It is an impossible story, just plain impossible. What is faith next to the love we bear for our children? Can a God we neither see nor hear compare to our own child? There are some people who may sacrifice their own lives for their faith. There are even some who will sacrifice their families along with themselves. But it is hard to imagine the parent who could decide to continue to live, knowing that he had murdered his own child for his religion. And who could want such a religion? The story is in the Old Testament, to set the bar very high for the Jewish faith, to establish their God as capricious and demanding and to let them know that there should be no limit to their commitment. But it is impossible. The Jews are like a secret society, and so is 'our thing,' but if we were to include sacrificing our children to our thing, we would not last a minute. That is why family is off limits and completely separate for us."

"I knew," Frank continued, "that the Rabbi is no Abraham, because almost no man is and because he is just as clearly as much a man of the world as you or I are. He sold stocks and bonds. He rose to a position in the community. He lost a wife and he loves a daughter. These things are of the world. None of what happened is surprising. The only thing that would have been surprising would have been if he had held onto his faith in the face of sacrificing the one family member he had left."

"But damn, Frank," I said, "you left him nothing when you said you would not pay him."

"Oh, we will pay him. But it will be as we see fit. And I had to let him know that I knew what was the value of his initial objection, that we both knew. I had to put that to bed."

"You know, Frank," I added, "because of this meal, this kitchen is no longer kosher."

"We have already established what that is really worth," he said. "Weren't you listening to what I just said?"

Then he said in a voice loud enough to be heard by everyone, addressing Big Angelo, who was standing at the stove, "Hey, Ange, our friend here says we just made this kitchen not kosher anymore."

Big Angelo laughed and he called back, "The hell with them. Let them use their Jew magic to protect it."

The phrase "Jew magic" caught the attention of Little Angelo, who asked me from his end of the table, "In just what ways have we contaminated this kitchen, and what is the magic that Angelo is talking about?"

The room was quiet as I answered, "The very first thing we ate had cheese and anchovies in it. Cheese and all dairy products must be completely separated from the meat. That means they keep separate pans and dishes and utensils. We have definitely messed all that up. And we brought ham into the kitchen, and ham is strictly forbidden under any circumstances."

"Prosciutto ain't just ham, kid," Big Angelo said loudly over his shoulder as he was standing at the stove. "It is the Cadillac of ham. It is just ham the same what that Sophia Loren is just a woman."

"Well, even so, that alone has made this kitchen unusable by an observant Jewish person," I added. "And then we had the shrimp. They may eat nothing from the sea that has neither fin nor scale."

"No wonder they got no cuisine," said Big Angelo, laughing. "You got your Italian restaurants, French restaurants, Chinese restaurants; you even got your Mexican restaurants. But there are no Jewish restaurants. And what is funny about that is you see Jews all the time out eating, especially at Chinese restaurants. But you still got no Jewish restaurants."

"I am also pretty sure that rabbit is not kosher," I added. "And I think even when they handle cheese separately that most cheeses are not kosher. And whatever other meat or beef we have eaten is probably not kosher since these animals must be slaughtered in a certain kind of way in order to be kosher. Our wine may not be kosher. And the meat, I think, has to be cooked in such a way that there is no blood. And I am pretty sure that all the food, no matter what, is not kosher because it was not prepared by a Jewish person."

"You hear that, Ange," Frank said to Big Angelo, "the least kosher thing in here is you."

"But tell me about the magic," Little Angelo said to me.

"I don't know about magic," I answered, "but since he is a rabbi, he could do whatever is necessary to return this kitchen to kosher status. I am not sure exactly what that would entail, but he might replace all the utensils and plates or whatever. At the very least he will perform some ritual that will cleanse and will bless the kitchen and all that is in it."

"But the prosciutto," Little Angelo asked, "that is always not kosher, right?"

"Right," I said. And with that Little Angelo had a strip of prosciutto in his hand and he was on his knees under the sink, where he stuck a piece of prosciutto up under and behind the sink basin, where it would never be seen. Then he scrambled up onto the counter and stood up and put a piece on the top of the cabinets, where it could not be seen. He taped one under a chair, then he thought better of it. He said that would be too easy to find, and if it was found they would know to look other places. He also congratulated himself on using the prosciutto and "not the shrimp scampi, because it would smell. The prosciutto will just age nicely." All in all, he found about half a dozen places in which they all figured it would never occur to anyone to look.

"That will fix him," he said.

"Jew magic," Big Angelo added, "done in by fine Italian cuisine."

Frank turned to me and said quietly, "In other words, it is the hardest thing to honestly live a life of faith in the world. I know that this is one of the divine lessons in that book of yours, the one in which all of this is written. I think that your beautiful female Jesus had called them spiritual revelations or the twelve disciples of truth or the Christian insights or something like that. I have just given you the third one, and I think you may have recognized it. I also have already read what you have yet to learn about your journey. It will be a pilgrimage for you, one that will see you experience the insights and then will see you learn them by observation, one that in a way will take you to Hell and back, and a journey in which it will seem that you may be possessed, and later on it will be one in which you will be required to learn to read people as you read a book, and one in which you will learn yourself and others in ways that will give you and your readers and followers spiritual sustenance.

"You didn't think I knew about that book," he smiled and continued. "None of these guys know. So don't worry about that. But I know. Hell, I even know about the sequel. And I want to thank you for not using our real names, Christian. That was good, kid. That was the right and the smart thing to do."

I had been correct earlier. He had read the book. He even seemed to understand the spiritual insights more clearly than I seemingly had, perhaps because he apparently had already read to the end of the book.

"How could I use your real names, Frank?" I responded. "No one would believe them. They are too farfetched. Like I said, no one would believe them."

MR. RIMMON'S
NEIGHBORHOODS

About half of the way through the length of my bit, I was given access to the dark room at the prison. Similar to the way in which the British refer to the parts of their bodies as bits, inmates in America refer to the part of their lives that is spent on the inside as a bit. And being in prison itself is referred to as being "on the inside" or as being "down." The prison dark room was a double relic, a vestige of the time before prisons became just huge warehouses of humanity and when prison bureaucrats were still thinking toward vocational rehabilitation, and also harkening back to a time when photographs and movies were recorded onto film, and those films were developed into prints, and therefore a dark room could still be vocational. I had been interested in old black and white photography and photographic development in college and still knew my way around a dark room. I myself am a vestige of a time when an Ansel Adams or a Dorothea Lange was still possible and when graphic art was done by artists and not by computers. I was given the chance to teach a small class in photography and development, an exercise at that point in time which could have no longer been considered vocational but merely aesthetic or perhaps historical.

I had access to the dark room even when I was not teaching my class of three or four inmates and it was to there that I often would retreat to read a book or to just be alone. It was where I would often go to avoid the three great scourges of prison: violence, dissipation, and boredom. At this particular moment I was taking time to unpack and store some new photographic material when I noticed a peculiar thing. The photographic paper had always come in folders that were marked with graphic designs of various animals. I took it to mean that the man who owned the company was a fan of large four-legged predators because the leopard, the wolf, and the lion were the three figures that marked the three sizes of the paper. The sheaf of photographic paper which I held in my hand at that particular moment had been the only one that was emblazoned with the sign of a black bear. I considered this emblem to be another kind of sign, one relating to my nocturnal and divine visitation, and one perhaps pointing to what was going to be my fourth divine insight. So I was curious. I opened the folder and took out each piece of paper to examine it individually. I was not too surprised to find that one of these sheets of paper was about fifteen times as thick as a regular piece of paper. In fact, it was not paper at all. What I held in my hand was a white, razor-thin computer screen which apparently also housed its processor and other computer elements. When I touched the screen, it whirred to life and showed me an internet browser that was set to a page at which I could begin to search the internet.

There is no such interface with the outside world that is permitted by the prison authorities. If there were, it would be less like prison, too much less. And worse, criminal enterprises could be continued by inmates who could then communicate by electronic mail with their conspirators outside of prison. The existence of this particular electronic portal to the outside world and the sign that had led me to it had to have been a part of my divine election, another signpost on the path to enlightenment. But I was less amazed by that than I was in awe of the prospect of accessing the internet. I was almost overcome by the intensity of two great urges related to that. I desperately wanted to access some form electronic mail program, so that I could contact my loved ones. And I had an overwhelming curiosity to learn about what was out there that pertained to this book. If I could make contact with my family I could lessen the impact of my absence. And I wanted to know what was happening to this book, to see if I could better direct its progress through the world. I did not have much time to do either of these things. So after I spent about thirty or forty minutes fruitlessly trying to find pornography I began to search for an electronic mail program. I did not have much success with either of those enterprises. As a matter of fact, every single search I mounted ended with frustration. I knew enough about using the internet to know that this is by no means uncommon but it soon became apparent that this device was an electronic portal that was very circumscribed in its ability to move about on the internet. I realized that this machine was in some way another part of the guidance toward the fourth of the divine revelations with which I was to have been blessed.

It was leading me, and in no way would I be allowed to control it beyond what it wanted to show me. So I typed the name of this book into the search line, and it took me to one site which was apparently the official or divine version of *Gospel Prism*. In fact, I was able to skim over the very introduction and three chapters which you have just read. I opened the fourth chapter and I was also surprised to see the three and a half paragraphs that you have just read of this chapter.

I then began to read about what is in Mr. Rimmon's neighborhoods just exactly as you are reading it now, with a few slight differences that are to be found in a purely electronic medium. It was, after all, a website, and so for those differences I here offer explanations and descriptions or else I just forge ahead and allow you to figure it out.

What I was reading and looking at and walking toward was a large town by a river. It was not really a neighborhood but a small city comprised of nine neighborhoods. Just across the river was the first neighborhood of this town. I crossed the river and entered the first development, which looked not unlike many an American suburban neighborhood. The first thing that I noticed was at the first house I encountered. A man was mowing the lawn. The lawn was already perfectly manicured, and the landscaping of the home was also perfect. Every tulip was in bloom, and even the roses lacked insects and imperfections. It was then that I noticed the mailbox, and on it was written the name Dan Quayle. And surely, the man mowing the lawn was the former Vice President of the United States.

"How long have you been mowing that lawn?" I asked.

"It seems like an eternity," he answered.

"Well," I added, "it may be time to stop. The lawn looks very nice. I don't know how much more you can do to improve it."

"I don't know, either," he said, and he stood there looking rather blankly.

"Do you think you could get me a glass of water?" I asked. "It seems awfully warm here for some reason."

"It is always like that," he said.

He turned to walk down the walkway toward the front door of the house and opened it. I had followed him. The inside was some vision out of a story by Jorge Borges. It was a normal-size living room but it contained literally many tens of thousands of people, yet they all fit. Many had the same blank look on their faces that I had seen on Mr. Quayle's. Several thousands of them were watching television. A few thousand of these people were reading Harry Potter books and novels by Stephen King. The television shows that were being watched were invariably of the type known as reality television. There was a buzz of conversations, and these conversations were all about what was on the television or what had been said or what someone was doing. I stood there, and in what felt to me like a few minutes they watched hours of a show called *American Idol* and a show called *Dancing with the Stars* and other shows that began with the phrase "Real Housewives." It was a scene that was at once unbelievable and fantastic and mind-numbing and dull. And I had the feeling of standing out in a way that was intangible. I was beginning to sense a kind of low-level antipathy flowing toward me from almost every direction of the house.

"These are my voters," Mr. Quayle said to me. "They all voted for me. You may want to leave soon. You think you are better than they are. They might figure that out in a few hours."

"Thanks," I said. "And how do you know that?"

"I don't think I like you either and maybe for that same reason," he said.

"May I ask," I said, "a question or two? Where is this place? What is it?"

"I don't know," he said. "I really don't know."

"Is your former boss here, the first President Bush?" I asked.

"I don't think he is in town at all," he answered, "but his son is here somewhere, in one of the other neighborhoods. But this is the nicest neighborhood."

I was still thirsty, and it was still rather warm, so I walked across the lawn and arrived at the house next door and knocked on that door. It was answered by a tall, thin, attractive, young, blonde woman who looked very familiar to me. She was Paris Hilton. I just asked her if I could come in for a drink of water, and she answered that I could. So I stepped inside and as I did so I was confronted again by that phenomenon of thousands of people keeping company with one another in a space that could not have held more than a dozen people. They were chatting away amiably and they were all young women and all of them were very much like Ms. Hilton, thin and attractive.

As I began the process of wading through this throng in order to get to the kitchen I was aware of the fact that it might be a pleasurable process, but it was not. Every single one of them upon closer examination was not all that attractive. Each was wearing too much make-up and had bleached blonde hair. As far as I could tell they all had been the subject of some kind of plastic surgery. Many had surgically altered breasts and capped teeth. And they were all ignoring me and were talking with one another about various clubs and cocktails and beauty treatments and men. Mostly they were talking about men. I looked at Paris, as if I were about to ask a question.

"They are the Miss America contestants" she said. "I know: they're hot."

I too was hot, and thirsty, and finally I reached the kitchen and walked into it. It was practically empty, except for two people, a younger man and an older matronly woman, each dressed in clothes that belonged to the early nineteenth century and to England. They were Mr. Collins and Mrs. Bennet, and they were discussing why Mrs. Bennet's daughter Elizabeth had not accepted Mr. Collins' proposal of marriage.

"And as I had tried to assure her, Mrs. Bennet," said Mr. Collins, "that it was with complete and utter felicitations of those, her interests, and those of her excellent parents, as well as those of my magnificent benefactor, the Lady Catherine DeBourg, that I did propose to her to make her the companion of the remainder of my life at the time, and for the reasons related to the violent nature of my affection as well as for the reasons that it was the right thing for a clergyman to set the example of matrimony in his parish, and that I was reasonably certain that it would add an order of magnitude to the quantity of my happiness."

At this point in the conversation I had taken my glass of water, had drunk most of it, and was leaving the room. I was forging a path through the thousands of Miss America contestants that were cluttering the living room and within a minute or so that seemed like hours I had passed through the front door and onto the lawn. I began to walk down the road. Soon I came to a nice, sturdy home built of oak and stone in the style of England in the seventeenth century. In the front yard was a moderately tall man with long brown hair, about fifty years old, with the kind of beard and mustache that used to be called a Van Dyke. He was dressed peculiarly for the heat in a dark blue velvet coat with ermine trim. He looked every bit like a picture I had once seen of Charles the First, King of England, who has a way of appearing in memoirs.

I tried to think of what he might have in common with Paris Hilton and Dan Quayle, the Miss Americas, Mr. Collins and Mrs. Bennet, and the fans of Harry Potter, Stephen King and American reality television. Then I remembered how he had foolishly relied on the reputed divine right of kings to try to get away with grossly offending all the congregants of both the high church and the low church, and to think that he could run roughshod over both his own Parliament and the entire kingdom of Scotland. He had also terribly bungled the handling of the English Civil War. And when he had been executed by the forces of Parliament he had appeared for all intents and purposes to have been uncharacteristically brave, but his bravery had been merely a matter of being simple. Much like the sea captain in a story by Joseph Conrad, called *Typhoon*, who had "just enough imagination to carry him through each successive day, and no more," this king's intellectual stupor in the face of adversity had seemed to be a calm bravery.

At this point I had begun to recognize a pattern and I was curious to see just who was thronging the house of this once-powerful king who had foolishly lost his kingdom, not to an invading army but to his own subjects. I walked straight up to the door and opened it. On the inside were many different kinds of people doing many different kinds of things. A visual inspection offered no clues. I am a student of the accents of spoken English, so I decided to listen carefully for a few minutes.

I can even tell the difference between an accent from the northern part of the American Midwest and the accent of the lower Midwest. People from Minnesota lengthen their vowels and put a slight tone into them, while a Kansas accent is flatter. I can tell the different accents within the major regions of England and I can identify the difference between the nasal tones of an Australian accent and the equally nasal South African English, which is more clipped and crisper. I know that the American English that is spoken in New Orleans is slightly more like what is spoken in Brooklyn, New York, than it is like what is spoken anywhere else in the American South. And I know that in Mississippi a single vowel and single syllable word can be stretched to two syllables. I have much less of a facility for French but I can tell the strong difference between what is spoken in France and the flatter and less musical version of the same language that is spoken in Quebec.

It did not take me very long at all to determine that the living room and other rooms in the home of Charles I were literally filled with practically the entire population of Canada.

I left that house and by this point I was at the end of the neighborhood and as I looked at the computer screen in my hand I saw an icon on it that read, "Ask Emma Bovary," and within it was a box that read, "click here." So I clicked on it and I was immediately into a "live chat" with Emma Bovary.

Me: Is this really a neighborhood for intellecutally challenged people and is it some kind of fantastical punishment?

EmBovary: Yes, pilgrim, it is, on both counts.

Me: Then is it some kind of modern version of a sort of Hell of the future.

EmBovary: No, it just is Hell or more correctly it is the outer suburb of Hell, the part that is reserved for people who are not all that thoughtful.

Me: But first of all, some of these people are still alive on earth and also, why does Hell punish unintelligent people?

EmBovary: There is no present, past, or future in the mind of God. And if there is an eternity there cannot be an end or even a beginning. There can only be an eternity. Alive and dead are distinctions that do not exist in eternity. The first reasons for dull people being here are practical. There are simply too many of them for them to be among the elect.

They would not know the difference, either way. Wherever they were would be a bland version of that place, and there can be no bland Heaven. As far as the spiritual reasons are concerned, what is your prison mantra?

Me: It is "self-improvement."

EmBovary: And that is true of life as well. So they fail. There may be another reason they are here, which you will discover later.

Me: What about the mentally challenged, people with Down Syndrome and other natural impairments?

EmBovary: They are in Heaven. They are complete innocents. And occasionally, God is politically correct.

Me: Okay. May I ask then what you are doing here? My impression of you is that you simply were one of those cases of having too much life inside of you, too much freedom, too much spirit, and too much heart. People like that, like you, do not fit well into the world and eventually become destroyed by its restrictions.

EmBovary: That may be true. I am the smartest person in this part of the place, which is why I was given this job. But in the final judgment, as it were, based on the things I had done I was found to be pretty stupid.

Me: Let's see. You married the wrong man. Then you fell in love with another wrong man and then fell in love again with yet another mistake of a man. And of course to the extent that you did not waste your wealth, you let it be taken from you. None of that was particularly bright, especially given that you had a responsibility as a mother.

EmBovary: That about sums it up.

Me: Where are the virtuous pagans? Are they here?

EmBovary: Why would anyone who had been virtuous be here?

Me: You mean Plato, Virgil, Job, Aristotle, Jonah, Epicurus, they are all somewhere else?

EmBovary: They are not here.

Me: What does the next neighborhood hold?

EmBovary: It contains the irritating people. It is a worse neighborhood.

I entered this next neighborhood by crossing a small bridge over a stream. The first things I noticed were the insects. There were mosquitos and flies in abundance. There were also sand fleas and gnats. The air was not exactly thick with them. They were just enough in evidence to be very annoying. I must have had the benefit of some kind of metaphysical insect repellent. None of them landed on me. The second thing I noticed was Woody Allen. He was there to greet me.

"It's a heck of time to learn I have an immortal soul," he said, "after I have died. And if I had known I was going in this direction, I might have gotten some more out of it. My seventh grade teacher, Mrs. Dombrowski, always said I would end up here. I wonder if she was also right about patent leather shoes and mayonnaise."

"So, is Natalie Portman also here?" was my first question.

"Yes, she lives in a house with Pete Rose and everyone who ever kissed a pet on the mouth," he answered. "They spend all their time watching that television show, *Jersey Shore*. When the two of them go out they engage in dramatically public displays of excessive affection."

I noticed that as he spoke the flies and other bugs did not stay away from him in the same way they avoided me. His normally nervous facial tics and verbal idiosyncrasies were punctuated and exaggerated by gnats landing on the edges of his eyes and mosquitoes flying in and out of his mouth. I don't know why it had not occurred to me earlier, but this seemed like it should have always been the natural state of affairs for him. There had always been a small, nervous, and noxious buzzing near him. And this was certainly the case as he made his way through the neighborhood, showing me the sights, his head in a small cloud of flying insects. And in yet another development within this story, one that is as equally outlandish as it is important to the plot, this Woody Allen would occasionally and temporarily transmogrify into Sarah Jessica Parker. And again this seemed like it always should have been the natural state of affairs with him. He, I mean she, still had that same overly talkative and obsessive way of being self-referential and psychologically insightful, while at the same time reminding me fondly of New York City while also making me wish the place would fall off of the map. The primary difference between these two people after one of these changes was that she was significantly harder on the eyes.

"So this is what they meant when they said my films would make me immortal," he deadpanned. "If I had known, I would have dressed for the occasion."

I noticed that the houses in this second neighborhood had the quality of seeming to occasionally evanesce, at once giving me an insight into, and the insects access to, the inhabitants. I had seen all the people who had ever kissed their pets on the mouth, seemingly crammed into the home with the startlingly diminutive and anxiously self-conscious young actress and the equally startlingly un-self-conscious and magnificent baseball player. The next home I saw was clearly housing anyone who had ever had anything to do with National Public Radio. The most insects seemed to be hovering around the guy who had invented those musical segues that form as the transitions between stories. There was another home, the contents of which were Lord Byron and all of the rap singers who ever existed. Byron somehow seemed to be one of them, and they were not aware of the ways in which he was different, although he was. Across the street Tom Sawyer lived with all the men who had ever given a name to their penis. And they lived next to Madonna and Lady Gaga and every person who had ever invented an internet meme or had used that word in a sentence or even knew its definition.

"You will note," said Sarah who had just been Woody, "that this neighborhood development is as populous and as crowded as the previous one."

I just had to ask, "What about all the black people who ever gave their child a made-up name that does not exist in traditional English?"

"They are not here," she said. "God is either not a racist or else he is an underachiever."

Standing in the next yard and apparently discussing the *Twilight* movie series were Benjamin Franklin, General George McClellan, and Thomas Jefferson. They were surrounded by thousands of people doing yoga when suddenly a house coalesced around them. We then walked past a large empty tract, and I looked at it inquisitively.

"It is not a house," my guide mentioned. "It is a poem, *The Waste Land*, perhaps you have heard of it."

"Is T. S. Eliot here?" I asked.

"Of course," was the answer Woody or Sarah gave me. "He lives with Gwyneth Paltrow and with your former father-in-law, Carl Brewster, and the three of them all live with all the people who have owned more than three cats at one time or have ever worn flip-flop sandals into a restaurant."

There were many other streets and many other homes and more gnats and flies, and I was getting tired, and my senses were being overloaded.

"I know. I know. I know," Woody said, looking at me. "It's like bad television. It's like California. It's like the Republican Convention or a dinner party in Manhattan. I will get you out of here. I know a short cut. It is always valuable in life to know a short cut, and how far to sit away from the television, and where to get good Chinese food."

And we turned down a long, empty road to where there were no houses, and on either side of the road there were people just milling around in the spaces on either side, more people than there were to be found in the rest of the neighborhood. And just as we were nearing the end of this road and the end of the neighborhood, I asked him the identity of those places that were on either side of that road. He told me that he wasn't certain but that he thought on one side was Argentina and on the other was Japan, but he was not sure which was which. I asked him one last question. I wanted to know where the people who had been guilty of the sin of lust were. His answer was that they were here and there and everywhere, same as in the upper world, and that if lust were a sin then so was breathing and love and getting parking tickets, and that maybe lust is only a sin if and when it is satisfied.

We had come to a large, sweeping grass meadow, and I had been left on my own. I finally came upon a person whom I had recognized from a news story I had just read recently. She was a young mother who had been driving in her car with her two-year-old child when the car had run out of gas on the road. She had walked down the road to get gas, and when she returned the child was gone. It turned out later that the child was all right. Some older children had come along and had let the two-year-old out of his car seat and out of the car and had been playing with him. Then they had just left, and the two-year-old was found later, wandering down the road. Just as I was about to ask this woman a question about where I had now found myself, a piano fell out of the sky and landed on her and crushed her. It was like scene out of the animated cartoons I had watched as a child, the ones that still possessed the genius of knowing that violence can be terribly funny.

I was very much in need of the "ask Emma Bovary" icon, but that screen was no longer available to me. And there was no new Woody Allen corresponding to this third neighborhood. Apparently, there had been some negligence in providing for guidance here. In fact, the entire landscape appeared as if it had been subject to some negligence. There were no neat lawns as I had seen in the first two neighborhoods and no houses. It was just windswept grassland, gone to seed and empty. There was also an absence of the teeming crowds of people that I had earlier witnessed. Occasionally off in the distance I would notice someone wandering. And as often as not, the same violently humorous event would befall each of them. A piano or a safe or a large farm animal would come hurtling down from above and land on someone. The place was dangerous, and oddly dangerous at that, in its emptiness. Then I saw an anomaly. Each person I had seen in this place had been alone, but now two men were walking more or less in my direction, and I hastened to place myself in their way and I hailed them. They told me that they were Admiral Kimmel and General Short and that they were on their way "to hear the appeal" of their case. They had been the United States Navy and Army commanders at Pearl Harbor in December of 1941. They either had been made to be scapegoats or had been terribly negligent. I did not tell them what I had known and had heard about the mind of God having no past, present, or future but at all times knowing all things. In such a system there can be no appeals.

I turned to my screen and found a "help" icon and I clicked on it. I got a screen that said "error." I tried this several times, only to continue to get the error screen, and then finally I was directed to another website, which told me that this particular help website was no longer operating and it also inquired as to whether or not I wanted to purchase the domain name. After several more efforts I just stopped trying.

Then I saw a most remarkable thing. It was a person walking directly toward me with the apparent intent of speaking directly to me. It was the first very direct thing to happen in this third place. And it was perhaps the most critically important and the most unbelievable and irrelevant part of this entire story. What was clear to me was that this person was Hamlet, Prince of Denmark.

I asked him if this place was for the punishment of people who had been damagingly negligent. I told him that I assumed that he was in this place because he had thrust his sword through the arras rather negligently, having indeed not checked to see if it really had been King Claudius hiding behind it as he had assumed. I also said that I had felt that his treatment of Ophelia and of the great love she had shown for him had been rather negligent. And I told him that I had felt that he had approached the whole matter of the duel that had eventually led to his death in a rather negligent manner.

In coming to the matter of his responses, I am somewhat at a loss. I had received a visitation from the sublime and alluring Christ woman and I have been reporting that visit and what was said in it in a way that is utterly consonant with what can only be described as a kind of a gospel, truthfully and honestly and without any judgment as to any elements that may seem fantastical or heretical. But as I have tried to relate the words of this Dane I found that they were always receding from me as if they were cannonballs launched over the horizon, noteworthy and unmistakable in their report but rapidly escaping my view. From what I can remember, I am sure that he told me that this third area, which was not really a neighborhood, was indeed for the dangerously negligent but that he was not really in it himself since he had free range of the entire Hellish city as well as of the other two places for the dead. He seemed to tell me that I was also mistaken in assuming that he had died as a result of that famous duel and concomitant poisoning and that Ophelia had died from her apparent suicide. I believe he also told me that this partic- ular place for the negligent was one from which I could not soon depart, if I were to depart at all, and that he had come here to help direct me on to the fourth neighborhood as he was sort of a utility man for all such troubles. He showed me to a cave, which I assumed was also a tunnel, and told me that the only way out and to the next place was to travel through it.

Then, before I set foot in the tunnel and as a way of farewell he seemed to be saying that I should never confuse negligence with a conscious refusal to do a thing and that this was somehow related to how he could not be contained by Hell or by death or any of its places. And then what I seem to recall him saying receded even further from me, and all that was left me was an uncertain vision of him, either posited in me by his words or arrived at independently. And in that vision he was sailing a ship on uncharted seas with his eyes on the horizon. And in the boat with him was Ophelia.

At the other end of the tunnel was the fourth neighborhood. It was bright and warm and very clean and suburban. It was at this point in my journey already my favorite place. There were no flying insects, and it was not too hot. It was clear that every house and street and light and sidewalk had been well and honestly constructed. There was something about it that was just too correct. It was like a small, plastic, perfect Christmas model train display neighborhood only it was the regular size with flawless landscaping and beautiful homes. The sun was shining brightly. There was a pleasant breeze. Standing right there as I emerged from the tunnel and entered the neighborhood was Bill Clinton, the former President of the United States. He was wearing a dark blue suit with a white shirt and a gray tie and black dress shoes. His hair was also gray. He was looking like he did when he was in one of those phases in which he had put on weight. He had on electric-pink socks. I had met him before, twice, so I was aware of his openness and his engaging intellect. He was simply a man who inspired much in those who were in his company, and one of those things was a kind of forthrightness.

"Is this where the gluttons are?" I asked.

"Gluttony is not a sin," he said.

"Then this place is for people who have committed sodomy?" I suggested.

"No," he answered. "Love in all its many forms is never a sin either."

"Then what is the story with the pink socks?" I asked.

"I learned a long time ago," he said, "that it is better for people to be looking at what is on your feet than what is in your hands."

"So then this neighborhood is for the deceivers?"

"Actually, in some sense," he answered, "the opposite is true. This neighborhood is for people who have caused pain, loss, or damage on purpose."

"I assume from that and from your presence that would include adulterers," I added.

"Only the ones who have confessed to their spouses or partners or who let themselves get caught or who have lied to their liaisons. The men and women who have managed to spread their love around honestly and have never caused pain are not to be found here."

"But aren't you alive on earth right now?" I asked.

"*Dinanzi a me non fuor cose create se non etterne,*" he said, "*e io etterna duro.*"

I took this Italian sentence to mean that God had created only eternal things which endure eternally with no end or beginning. This was more or less the same explanation that had been given to me by the Emma Bovary chatroom person.

"So, you speak Italian, then?" I asked.

"You should not at all be surprised that Italian is being spoken in Hell," he went on, "and not because there are more Italians here than other people. There are not. It just makes sense, and in the same way that if you hear French being spoken you might be in Heaven."

I was not going to be distracted by the pink socks. So I asked another question.

"But your presence here as a living person being due to the fact that all things are eternal and without beginning or end is not exactly the case with you, is it?"

"Actually, you are right in that my case is different," he said. "Sometimes when I am called upon to do some work down here a demon is sent to the world to inhabit my body and to control it until such time as I am able to return."

"I guess that explains a few things," I commented. "And I can see how your adultery might have caused pain, loss and damage," I continued. "But it does not seem as if you had allowed it to become known on purpose, especially since it damaged your legacy."

"Do you know the Freudian apothegm, that there is no such thing as a mistake?" the former President asked. "Well, even though that may not ever be exactly or entirely true, it is perhaps most true in the case of adulterers who get caught. They, I mean we, usually secretly intend to get caught. It is always more or less on purpose. Let me give you another example. Sometimes a woman will have an affair and then she will feel terrible about it and will then tell her husband about it and she will do so in the name of honesty. It will hurt her spouse and will cause him a loss. Again, revealing the affair is a way of forcing the issue. And it causes much more pain and hurt than just first admitting that something is not right in the marriage. This particular neighborhood is full of souls who took that indirect and hurtful path to honesty."

"And what," I asked, "is the punishment of this place?"

"There is no depth," was his answer. "Everything is exactly as it seems. The place is utterly devoid of irony or ambiguity or unseen meaning. Everyone here is forced to exist on the surface."

"I am wondering," I began to ask, "that causing loss, even by a Freudian slip, might be judged so harshly."

"You know," Clinton said, "Emily Dickinson once wrote a poem about having lost a golden coin in the sand and having looked for it and having found enough change in other coins to be worth the value of that coin."

"I know the poem," I said, "and she makes it clear that finding the equal value in other change in the sand is not enough to ameliorate the specificity of that particular loss. All loss is specific and from that there can be no recompense. She says that for a person who causes such loss . . ."

"I believe she said, 'No consolation beneath the sun may find.' And that truth is not only a poetical one, it is a theological one and a practical one as well," Clinton added, "for here I am. Here we all are."

I was not at all surprised that this man who spent a lifetime in policy and politics would still be thoughtful enough to know his Dickinson. And it was even less surprising to discover that than it was to find out that her poems were somewhat dispositive on matters of the afterlife.

I was not and am not the kind of person to not know a singular opportunity when one is before me. I was standing in the presence of a soul who had been the most powerful man in the world. And while many other men had also been President, among that group who were in office for the several terms before and after him he was the most uniquely intelligent and much the most deeply thoughtful. That alone would set him apart even within that exceptionally elite group. But he was also perhaps the most astute politician of his age and rarely is that singular skill also to be found in conjunction with such depth of scope or intimate understanding of the innumerable issues of public policy that confront a great nation. Historically, he had enacted the North American Free Trade Agreement, he had created a rare federal budget surplus and he had presided over the greatest eight-year period of peacetime expansion in the history of the United States. He was like an American Augustus. There were a million important things he could tell me. It was the opportunity of a lifetime.

"So, I just have to know," I began. "Did you sleep with Pamela Harriman?"

"Why do you want to know that?" he asked, showing me that famous twinkle in his eye that had always been one of his trademarks. "Did you?"

"No, no, no. But I had met her once."

"I know," he said.

"At the time I was only twenty-eight years old," I said, "and she was sixty-three years old, and I was incapable of seeing her in that way. I saw her as being a respectable older lady and no more. I was interested in her history such as I knew it at the time, which was that she had married the son of Winston Churchill and had lived at 10 Downing Street during World War II. I had a conversation with her about it and about Charles Lindbergh. I had asked her about him because Winston Churchill had given her his personal copy of Lindbergh's book, which I had seen was in her library, and it had a personal note in it to Churchill from Lindbergh. The Prime Minister must have liked his daughter-in-law very much, to have given her something so significant and so personal."

"Well, if she was too old for you when did you decide that she might not have been too old for me? When did you formulate this question?"

"When you later appointed her to be Ambassador to France," I answered. "And by that time I had read that she had been romantically linked with many rich and powerful men and that the American media mogul Charles Paley had called her the greatest courtesan of her century. It made me recall how in my brief conversation with her she had been so attentive and engaging and had made me feel like I had been the only man in what had been a very crowded room. I realized much later that I had merely been too callow to have recognized those qualities as being part of what must have been her magnetic sex appeal. When you made her the Ambassador several years later, I realized that you probably had met her at about the same time that I had. And even though you would have been separated from her by the gulf of years equivalent to a quarter century, or almost as much as she was older than I, I figured that your idea of just who might be sexually appealing differed from mine both by degree and in kind."

"So, you are now asking me if I might have had sexual relations with a woman so much older than I that perhaps she had known the great Winston Churchill intimately."

"Thanks for answering my question," I added. "And who is in the next neighborhood, and what is it about? Does it house the people who are guilty of the sins of avarice or anger?"

"Neither of those is a sin itself, particularly not greed, which is rather unavoidably natural and part of the fabric of our most affirmative impulses. This is only somewhat less true of anger, which can generate acts of great courage and self-sacrifice. Impulse is much less important than effect in the infernal calculation of who lands here among the shades of Hell. You may want to hurry through that next neighborhood. It is rather boring. And one more thing, Christian: you need to know that the twelfth and final insight will clarify what you may or may not understand about this fourth revelation."

And with those words I took my leave of Bill Clinton, stuck in his neighborhood of living always on the surface, deprived of a good joke or a double meaning or an innuendo, and where he would spend eternity trying unsuccessfully to explain to his neighbors that the definition of sexual relations could not be defined by sexual contact and that the definition was dependent upon the meaning of the word "is."

I found myself quickly on the small bridge crossing over into the fifth neighborhood. It was very urban in nature, quite crowded and gritty. The streets were busy and thronging with people seemingly on their way to somewhere but actually keeping a sharp eye on those around them. It was not unlike parts of New York City. More precisely, it was exactly like Brooklyn and not the Brooklyn of Walt Whitman that always comes to my mind through the music of his poetry, with its flood tides and ample hills and its teeming crowds of working men and women from all nations. It was more the Brooklyn of Big Frank and Little Angelo and Big Angelo and some of the guys named Tony, with its huge apartment buildings, its street-corner panhandlers and con artists, its grime and graffiti, its gangs and its street art and the assault on the eyes that passes for urban style and fashion. This neighborhood was similar to Brooklyn in another important way. There was a great deal of noise. But as I listened only slightly more closely, what I had thought was only noise was actually sort of a street symphony of very bad music, much of it being street-corner rap music, with some of it being country music or European pop songs. There was even a smattering here and there of the sounds of what have been called poetry slams. Bad rhymes abounded and with a forceful sincerity that was meant to ascribe passion to words where there had been little applied thought and only slightly more honest passion. On every corner there was some street musician or group of musicians, each with a donation cup or hat or guitar case.

I was again reminded of Whitman, who was not immune to creating a bad rhyme here or there but whose own expression was full of his more difficult pleasures and his more honestly effusive passion. On crossing the Brooklyn Ferry, Whitman had made note of certain dark patches and had made note of the evil in all hearts. And while I know he was perhaps attempting to make another confession of a darkness that was indicative of his own desired universality, I could not help but see this infernal Brooklyn as having been predicted or seen by him. The dark had thrown its patches all over this place, and there among its citizens was something that was palpably greedy, shallow, sly, and cowardly.

One of these street-corner denizens was dressed rather differently than the other persons in the poetry slam in which he was participating. He was wearing a shirt and doublet and hose and boots. His tan linen shirt was embroidered in blue and gold braids. And for the reader who does not know a doublet, it is merely a kind of second shirt that goes over the first and is usually longer and more open than the shirt under it. His was pale green and it was pleated in the back to give the effect of a tapered build. His hose were like a pair of thick gray tights and they were tucked into his boots, which were brown and worn-out leather. He wore a brimless red cap. And he was very white. In a room full only of Caucasians he would have seemed white. On the streets of this Hellish Brooklyn, where all the hues of brown were evident on the faces of its people, he truly stood out like a fly on a wedding cake but in reverse. If this group in which he was had been a basketball team, he would have to have been the coach. His different look and dress surely would have drawn comment in any place other than here or on the streets of New York City.

The poetry jam was in full progress, and the words of it came to me in a way that I will faithfully and accurately report here, but which one of the many redactors and amenders and contributors to this electronic book may well find susceptible to improvement. In most cases I could not identify the speaker except when it was this harlequin-clad snowball of a man. All of it was shouted with the same urgency with which important secrets are divulged to large crowds, such as when a building must be evacuated or a people are being warned of an approaching tornado. There was also a lot of bobbing up and down and waving of hands that were forced into finger formations that do not accompany some useful act or grip.

"The bling I wear is not a fraud. Call that bitch my bodyguard."

"Five hundred for the dicky cap on my head, gotta hustle to pay my overhead."

"If you know exactly what I'm gonna do, I'm gonna give the bizness to you."

"At Rouen, doomed and burned her there. Where are the snows of yesteryear?" said my man in the gray hose.

"I don't write shit 'cause I don't got time, so I bleed my mouth to pop this rhyme."

"She ain't never had a love like mine. I never seen an ass like hers."

It had occurred to me that this last line was not even a rhyme when I suddenly noticed that the very white man had lapsed into French, and it surely seemed his native language, "*Ou elles sont, ne de c'est an. Mais où sont des neiges d'antan?*" Then someone else spoke again.

"Come and meet me in the bathroom stall and show me why you deserve to have it all."

"Workin' wit da police, actin' like you know me, you be nothing but fake, Homie."

At this moment, my staring at him had caught the attention of the man whose French I had just translated to mean something along the lines of, "Where have they gone, and nor this year. Where are the snows of yesteryear?"

"That last line seems somewhat familiar to me," I said to him.

"Yes, part of it was stolen from 'Put On,' by Young Jeezy, but no one ever bothers to complain about that manner of borrowing here. We are all thieves."

"*Mais bien sûr,*" I observed, "but I was talking about your line, the 'snows of yesteryear' line."

"I am called François Villon," he said, as he swept off his hat and bowed, "and I am at your service as your guide."

"But weren't you some kind of poet or something and not a thief?"

"All poets are thieves. You know that. I was also a thief of the other kind. I robbed a church of some gold it had no right to have. And I stole a few other things here and there in France in the fifteenth century. Walk this way, *s'il vous plaît*, and I will get you to the next neighborhood."

"What you said about poets being thieves, does that mean they are all here?"

"The people here are real thieves. And as it is the place that it is, they are also victims of theft and on a daily basis. You may note that a place that employs what might be called 'the justice poetic' is unlikely to be harsh on poets. No, there is a certain license permitted to writers or else you might be here on a rather more permanent basis. Only the more obvious plagiarists, like Judith Miller, are here."

As we walked down the sidewalk, in the crowd I saw Bernie Madoff, and he was walking with Fagin. They were in rapt conversation and had their hands in each other's pockets. They apparently had more in common than just having stolen some measure of the goodwill of their people. I saw John D. Rockefeller and Andrew Carnegie, and each were being hounded by well over two hundred small pickpockets. Moll Flanders was walking with Doris Payne, the daughter of a West Virginia coal miner whose successful career as an international jewel thief was advanced simply with a certain charm and misdirection and occurred entirely during the business hours of jewelry stores and in the presence of sales personnel. There was also a huge high-rise that apparently housed the nation of Greece. Then we saw a man in desert garb.

"That must be Ali Baba," I joked, "and where are the other forty thieves?"

"*Mon Dieu!*" François shouted. "I have been trying to catch that *voleur* here forever." And he took off on a dead run. I followed him for several blocks before I became quite fatigued. I had to be careful not to bump into anyone, since that is the dream opportunity of any pickpocket. Soon Mr. Villon also tired of his chase and returned to me, and together we sat on a park bench while we both caught our breath. He was muttering in both French and English in between hard breathing, and it was not easy for me to understand what he said. I could only catch snippets, and the words and phrases I heard were: "testament," "lifted whole cloth," "*hadith*," "gospel," "Persian," "plagiarism," and the one word that immediately caused me the greatest concern, "prophet."

"Listen, François," I said, "there is a lawyer who is the one person that the public knows as being somewhat responsible for this book, and his safety and well-being are as important to me as my own. I do not know how much you know about lawyers, but a good one who cares about your case and who is conscientious is as rare as a comet or AB negative blood or getting free food in a Chinese restaurant. I do not want to see mine harmed by what I fear may be read of what you are going to report to me here and now."

"Are you worried, *mon ami*," he replied, "that I will tell you that the prophet Mohammed is here?"

"Hell, yeah!"

Following that, he laughed in that light and pleasant and ironic way that comes so easily only to the French and he said, "No, no, no, I do not believe that man who consistently escapes me is Mohammed or that the prophet is even here. I think that the fellow I see here but have never been able to confirm is gentleman of the name of Zayd Ibn Hadith. And he supposedly collected the memories, scraps of paper and other testimony both written and unwritten that were supposedly the word of God as related to the prophet and assembled them into the Koran. It is my opinion that the entire thing was plainly stolen from existing texts."

"I have to tell you that I am only barely comforted by the way that this story differs from the one I had feared would have to appear in this book."

"And I must say to you that if a living man has been selected to travel to Hell and back, there is only one way he can possibly report that journey. He must tell the story with dash and éclat and in a way that is without any hint of fear, my friend."

"If I were to tell this tale fearlessly it would cast a shade upon its credibility. It is the truth of it that will inspire anger and hatred in a way that fiction never could."

"*C'est un siècle tardif.*"

"This age is more belated than you can know."

Suddenly we were interrupted by an Italian man, who was thin and aristocratic and who looked anxious. He asked François for a light for his cigarette. There was a lot of smoking in this place. The man got his light and with a backward wave of hand thanked us and gave us farewell.

"That was Eduardo de Valfierno, the man behind the theft of the *Mona Lisa*. He hired a worker at the Louvre, another Italian named Vincenzo Peruggia, to walk out with the painting and to bring it to Florence. Peruggia was later caught and arrested, then jailed, and in classic Italian fashion he was then hailed as a patriot and released after only a year. But by that time de Valfierno had been able to have the painting copied. He kept the original. The copy is back in the Louvre. He and I have a sort of mutual admiration society down here. I may be the only one to whom he will talk."

"Speaking of the Italians," I said, "I would suspect that the mafia guys are here in force. I also noticed that one of the differences between this place and the real Brooklyn is that there are no police on the streets here. That made me think that mafia must like this place."

"Actually, that is part of their punishment. They cannot get out on the street, where they know there are no cops. They are stuck in those large Irish pubs you see on every corner, being forced to eat what the Irish think passes for food, listening to Irish music and having only pale and thick Irish girls at whom to make passes."

"So, they did get it right on that television show, *The Sopranos*."

"I have never seen it."

"Neither have I," I said, "but the mob guys in prison talk about it all the time."

"I have to take you to the subway, right over there, and put you on the train to the next neighborhood, the one for the heretics."

And before long I found myself on the subway train to heresy. It was crowded. It contained mostly men, many of whom had accents from the American South. More than a few of them were African Americans. Many of the white men had the kind of haircuts you usually find on Republican Presidential candidates in the United States, every hair swept back and neatly in place and giving the impression of being like that found on a mannequin. The suits they were wearing were also just as uniform and as uniformly conservative. Many of them had that look in their eyes that was perfected by the great actor Burt Lancaster, the look of being happily transfixed on an object slightly above the horizon and as far away, as if having caught a glimpse of a gleaming city on a hill and being slightly giddy from the vision. There was an occasional woman in the group, and each looked like a country club matron from Mississippi, redolent with hair spray, jewelry, and each slathered in as much evidently faux charm as she was in make-up. As is often the case on the subway, I was so intent upon the fascinating side show right next to me that I had not noticed the three-ring circus in some of the other cars, where there were many men who were wearing miters. The headgear of so many popes and patriarchs and cardinals could only mean one of two things. Everyone was either going to get off at the next stop or no one but I was ever going to get off.

This subway was actually the sixth neighborhood in itself, and as soon as I made that discovery I recognized one of the men as being Jimmy Swaggart. And another was Jim Bakker. I also saw Joyce Meyer and Garner Ted Armstrong and Reverend Ike and James Jones. There was a small, well-dressed crowd of men sitting around Joseph Smith. They were all here. If you have ever seen a man or a woman on television holding his or her head in his or her hands and claiming that he was having a vision of a person in Peoria having a troubled son or daughter and needing the guidance of faith and who could find that guidance by calling this person's ministry and pledging a contribution, then that television evangelist was on this train. If you have ever seen a man holding his hand to the television studio camera in such a way that it would appear on a television screen as roughly the size of a human hand and have heard that man asking the faithful to hold their own hands to the television screen in order to receive the spirit of Jesus, then that man was on the train. If you had ever seen a minister who had never been ordained preaching some unrecognized gospel in an abandoned storefront in a ghetto neighborhood, then that man or woman was right there on the same train with Pope Alexander VI, who had appointed the seventeen-year-old brother of his mistress to be a cardinal and who had ordered more than a handful of murders and, with Pope Gregory IX, who had initiated the Inquisition.

The one thing they all had in common was that they could not have possibly believed they would end up on that train. That they figured that this would never happen was exactly why they were there. There were no skeptics or doubters on that train, only those who had been absolutely certain they knew there was no such thing as divine justice. It was only with that kind of negative certainty that they could have made use of the faith of the poor, the feeble-minded, the desperate, the disillusioned, the old, and the emotionally infirm in order to finance their own private jets, wardrobes, expensive vacations, visits with prostitutes, mansions, and opulent lifestyles. Even a skeptic or an agnostic might at one point wonder what the divine retribution for such acts might be. Had even I thought for a second to hold my hand up before that camera, I would have been just a little bit afraid that the sword of the archangel Gabriel might have cut it off right there and then. And I have no idea what an archangel is or what one might resemble.

I was at once touched by the irony of my own position, having been given this insight and having received my visitation and now putting it down in words for others to receive. And while it may be said that faith in the world and faith in literature may not be one in the same or that they may, I make no effort to remove any of this from the human sphere. It seems to me that if one were to be literally filled with the spirit of the Lord that such an occurrence would be plainly impossible to put into words, and that trying to do so would immediately reduce the experience or perhaps even kill it entirely.

Such evidences as these evangelists professed would surely be too weighty and ponderous for the tongue. The fact that these men and women were able to ramble on at great length about such things without the slightest lightness of grasp or of any sense of the ineluctable poetry required by such a telling was quite proof enough that they were speaking of something that was quite dead in their hearts already, as a wise German man once said would the only possible way they could possibly speak of such things.

And as it was on this train now, there was no flock to fleece. The train began to slow down, and an announcer's voice came on and said, "The next stop is abuse of power. Please be careful exiting the train."

We slowly pulled into the station. I expected it to look like any other drab subway station in New York or Paris or London or Boston. Instead it looked like one of the finest of the extraordinary stations on the Moscow Subway Circle Line, such as the Komsomolskaya Station with its baroque chandeliers and soaring granite arches and marble floor and vaulted ceilings with ornate mosaic tiles. These "people's palaces" had been built as demonstrations of Communist dedication to the masses and as a way to provide a daily reminder to those masses of the immense and impersonal superiority of socialism. The same thing spoke to me here in this station, of the overwhelming and monolithic power of state authority and the almost total insignificance of any individual, though that individual might be the only one armed with the truth or the only innocent one.

Upon alighting from the train, it was apparent that I was the only person getting off or who had considered disembarking or who might ever get off at any station. The station for which each other commuter was waiting in order to get off was far beyond the end of the line in eternity. I walked through the station, at each step feeling smaller and less significant simply by virtue of observing the architecture or by simply being near it, a feeling similar to that which gets standing amid the buildings of official Washington, DC, or perhaps looking at Disney World from a distance, or looking at Albert Speer's drawings for a new Berlin. This overarching Stalinist edifice expressed to me the kind of power that speaks for the entire state. But it was also the expression of one person, the one who with that power behind him or her, and who had decided upon its design.

I had lived in an efficiency apartment in a very poor part of town once in my modest youth and I will never forget the experience of turning the light on in that apartment, to be met with the fleeting hints of innumerable insects scurrying as rapidly as possible to escape the illuminating report of my apartment's feeble lamp. I would have to say that they were cockroaches, but the preceding three hundred million years of evolution had conferred upon them the stealth and speed that simply put them beyond my examination. Such was the scene when I emerged from the subway onto the platform and into the one neighborhood that finally struck me as utterly like my childhood conception of Hell. This dark and blackened and fiery topography was rendered to appear almost as if it were liquid by the darting and scuttling and whizzing and dashing and running about of hundreds of thousands of prosecuting attorneys, members of the legislative branches, judges, social workers, and other government or official functionaries. I would have to say that they too appeared to be cockroaches, but the preceding three hundred million years of evolution had conferred upon them the stealth and speed that simply put them beyond my examination.

But every once in a while one would become still enough for me to see more clearly and in much the way that a lifeless emperor moth is made to be more observable by the efforts of a lepidopterist. Only in each of these particular cases the object was pinned down by something quite different than what a butterfly collector might use, and that difference was only in degree and not in kind. Each time this pinning was done by the external male organ of copulation that was attached to some hideous demon. Above the plain, thousands of them flew. They were huge, dark, scaly, winged creatures, so hideous and full of death that these words cannot possibly reproduce even the sensation of their image. I do not have the unforgiving and discordant words that would be fitting for that miserable hole, nor can the vitality of my conception withstand the heat and weight and dark that bore down on me as well as on that place and all that was in it. All such possible representation is limited, in both writing and in reading these descriptions, by it being made in the same language with which one must greet one's mother or child. And in each case and on each ground-bound soul, the point of entry for the demon was the fundament of the sufferer, who would then be pinioned upon that blackening soil through his body and out his mouth by each demon's barbed organ. And each such rapine capture was accompanied by sounds that made the infernally horrible music of the neighborhood for thieves seem like a symphony by Bach.

It was also in this way that I was able to occasionally recognize one of the abusers of power. At one point I recognized the face of a woman I had seen in a picture that had accompanied an article in a newspaper that had chronicled the case in which the woman pictured had been a twenty- three-year-old social worker at the Children and Youth Services Office of Memphis, Tennessee. She had ordered a child to be removed from the home of her parents and she had charged the parents with child abuse, only for the authorities to find out two years later, and after that child had died in a foster home, that the frequent bruises that had been reported on the child had not been caused by beatings but by an obscure form of leukemia more common to Americans of African descent. The child's parents had been doctors, and it had been they who had diligently taken their child to the hospital where the bruises were reported. The removal of the child from their care may have prevented the further conscientious care on the part of the parents that perhaps would have actually effected a discovery of the disease.

It is a universal truth that is always acknowledged in prison that any inmate in possession of intellect and education wants desperately to be the jailhouse lawyer. However little-known the feelings or views of such a man may be, in the minds of his fellow prisoners, he is the very man to help them with their appeals and other cases. Being such a man, I have come into direct contact with the cases of more innocent men and more overly punished men than ought to trouble any man's nightly attempts at sleep. The Assistant United States Attorney who had prosecuted one of those cases stood in front of me at that moment, not impaled and not screaming. He was in his mid-thirties and was a thin and animated African American man of medium height and skin tone.

"I am here to take you to the next two neighborhoods," he said, and we began to walk together down to the other end of the platform.

"You are Thomas Nutley," I said, "and you were the prosecutor in the case of young Webster Long, who is locked up with me in Manchester."

"I don't pay too much attention to any of my old cases."

"You must surely remember this one," I added, "because the man was clearly innocent. He was twenty years old. He lived with his mother. He went to church with her every Sunday and he held down two jobs. He had an older half-brother who did not live with Webster and his mother and who had been under police surveillance. When this older half-brother discovered that he had been watched conducting a drug deal, he quickly ducked into his mother's home and when he emerged he was arrested. But he had nothing on him that was incriminating at that moment. So the police got a warrant and searched the house and they found a gun and the some drugs in the back of one of the drawers in the bureau of Webster's room. Webster had not been at home at the time. But he was arrested later."

"Is that what he told you?"

"No, that is what I read in his pre-sentencing report, which was filed after his plea bargain. It was the part of it that was the statement of the police. They had said that it was their later and considered opinion that Webster was innocent and that the drugs and gun had been planted there by his half-brother. You had gone ahead with the prosecution despite that."

"So, he should have fought it."

"I told him that he should have," I said, "but he told me that you had charged him with the gun charge and the drug charge, and that each one carried with it a five-year mandatory minimum sentence. And since you offered to drop the gun charge in a plea deal, he took the five years rather than face the possibility of ten. He also said to me, 'When the federal government is after you, you have no choice,' which was a sentiment I am sure you know is common among poor and uneducated defendants who are represented by overworked public defenders."

"My raises and promotions were determined by the numbers of total years in sentences I was able to have imposed in any given year.

Those five years helped me get a raise. The job of determining his innocence was the court's. It was not mine."

"To how many criminal witnesses have you granted immunity from prosecution?"

"I have done that for hundreds of men and women, because they were of use to me in other cases."

"So, by your own authority, you were deciding to put certain guilty people back on the street at the same time you were also putting innocent ones in prison."

"Look around," he said as he paused, "and you will see this place is full of my colleagues. That kind of power can only be abused."

"Speaking of your colleagues, I have to ask, are you wearing some kind of demon repellent or something? You are not being assaulted by demons."

"They found," he rather wistfully said, "that I enjoyed it too much when they tried it the first time. Since then my punishment has been to watch it happen to the others."

"That is only fitting." I said. "And since the abuses of power perpetrated by everyone in this place include fraud, violence, and treachery, I can only wonder what awaits me to discover in the last two neighborhoods."

"Well, we are there now," he answered, "so you do not need to wonder anymore."

We had merely walked to the end of the platform. We were standing in front of a small building, which along with the subway platform was the only structure within view. I realized that this realm of the abusers of power had not been a landscape that I would have been able traverse as I had the other neighborhoods. Mr. Nutley opened the door for me, and I walked in and he closed it behind me and remained outside.

On the inside was a medium-size room with a low ceiling, lit by some whale oil lamps and a fireplace. There were two other doors across the room from where I stood. The room was paneled and had wainscoting. There were a few chairs and a table, and sitting in one of the chairs was a man, roughly in his fifties, with gray hair that was thinning very much in the front. He had cold steel-blue eyes. He was wearing dark-colored and well-worn clothes that seemed a bit loose on him and which dated to the era of the oil lamp. There was a look on his face that was one that everyone has seen many times or has imagined he or she has seen. It was the look on the face of an actor who is waiting to see if he got a role or the look of a job applicant wanting to know if he had been hired or the look of a writer who was waiting to see if her book would be published. But there was another look beneath this one, which emerged from it as in a palimpsest. It was reminiscent of the faraway gaze of the evangelists. But it was much more intent, less light-headed and more engrossed. There was a curious and stern set to his jaw. He held in his hands a book and he held it as if it were a treasure, slightly closer to himself and a little more tightly than would be expected. And his hands were literally ink-stained.

"I come here for the ink," he said as he looked up at me. "Between the best and worst there are many degrees. That is right to say. But the best and the worst differ in only one thing, and that is in the object of their love. This place is less unlike the other one than you might expect. In each place, eternity is in love with the productions of time. And everything that is possible to believe is an image of truth."

It seemed to me that actually listening to William Blake was neither less inspiring nor more confusing than it was to consistently re-read all that he had written. But I found that I suddenly rather understood more about where I was and what was going on than I had before, though I did not know why. I had been given the power to envision things I could not normally see or know. I knew that Blake, like Hamlet, was not of this place even though he was one of its guides. I knew that the two doors that stood facing me were the last two regions of Hell, and that behind the first door were the souls of individuals who had caused others to go to their deaths, but had done so through mistakes that they had made in the objects of their love. Behind the second door were spirits who had simply intended to commit the murders that they had committed.

Standing in front of the first door, I had a vision. In that vision an American soldier lay dead in the surf of some Pacific island that had been held by the Imperial Japanese Army in World War II. He had been part of the Allied forces that had landed and fought in order to forcibly repel the spread of their empire of murder, rape, and destruction. He had died almost immediately after he had disembarked from his landing craft and before he had been able to do much in his part of the effort. His youth was evident. As in a short story by Anton Chekhov, I could also see the life he had not lived, the one with a wife and children. It was the life he might have led had it not been taken from him so soon on that beach. I saw that his death was not held on anyone's account. His blood was not on the hands of his commanders or of his country's leaders. He had been sent on his deadly mission by a people and its leaders and indeed by his own family, all of whom loved liberty and life and peace and who felt the call to defend those things for their own country and for others when it had been so clearly and profoundly threatened by the march of a military imperialism that had left in its wake millions of murdered Chinese people, tens of thousands of prostituted Korean women, and the subjugation of tens of millions of other east Asians.

Lying face down in the surf, this soldier was speaking to me. He told me that he was the standard by which all here had been measured and that for a man such as he to be sent to his death for the love of some things less than life and peace and liberty was a terrible sin, almost the worst. He told me that the proper measure for a leader was whether or not he would send his own children on such a mission. And then I had another vision, and it was not one I alone have had. It was one that was not missed by too many people anywhere, because it has been much publicized.

"Unknown Author Finds Obama in Hell," was one of the headlines that appeared after this book first went viral on the internet. There had been a great deal of commotion surrounding this fact which I had discovered. I indeed found President Obama behind that first door, in what might be called the eighth neighborhood. He was there with several presidents, more kings than can be enumerated, many prime ministers, many of the popes who were not to be found on the heresy train and countless other leaders. The space behind the door was no more than the size of a wardrobe and it was enclosed behind a glass panel. This closet had many shelves, and between adjacent shelves were some ladders and slides that might permit movement up and down in what was essentially a large cupboard. Each of the persons in it was very tiny, giving the glass-covered closet the look of a terrarium or an ant farm. A miniscule George W. Bush was joined by an even more diminutive Benjamin Disraeli and a minute Charlemagne and a pocket-sized Jefferson Davis and a microscopic Julius Caesar and a very compact Joshua and an infinitesimal Napoleon and a miniature Lyndon Johnson.

It was also as if this "ant farm" were being kept in the refrigerator. All of the lethargic movements of its inhabitants were typified by a lack of exuberance. There was little if any enthusiasm or even any vigor. Occasionally one of them would take a chute to the next lower level, but none of them ever seemed to climb one of the ladders. The bottom-heavy tendency of such a circumstance was alleviated by an ingenious device, built into the side of the cabinet, which simply scooped up a few souls off the lowest shelf and took them by conveyor belt to deposit them on the top shelf. There they were, trudging and maundering through an eternity of virtual lifelessness. It made the demons that flew over the tortured souls on the infernal countryside beyond the walls of this building on the platform seem like welcome diversions.

At one point I saw the teeny Barack Obama look up at me and begin to speak. I could not hear him at first, but my new visionary command told me of a button I could push to magnify his voice.

"The American people . . . elected me on a platform . . . of hope and of change . . . and although I changed . . . very little in a manner . . . that might have justified any . . . hope that I would . . . put an end to . . . our costly foreign . . ." he had been saying just at the moment I had released the button and could no longer hear him. While it was clear that his manner of speaking meant that he had determined that he had an eternity to express his thoughts, I did not have that much time. In fact, it had been occurring to me that perhaps I had been here too long and that conceivably I had even missed a count in the prison and was now the object of a search. My own internal time piece had been telling me that I had been at it for half of a full day and that the earth had indeed turned halfway round and that I would find myself at the same time of night when I might emerge as had been the time of day when I had arrived.

I closed this first door and I opened the second. Behind this second door was the innermost Hell. I stepped through the door and onto a balcony that overlooked a large nightclub. The club was well appointed and not garish. The music was pleasant and not cacophonous. It was well lit, and no one was smoking. The atmosphere was generally conducive to warmth and geniality. There was a groaning board larded with shrimp, steaks, scallops, veal, caviar, pasta, cooked fresh vegetables, risotto, cheeses from Italy and Holland, fresh fruit, every French dessert ever devised, and much more. The champagne and cocktails seemed to flow freely. And among the crowd were murderers and mass murderers. I could see Jack the Ripper and Adolf Hitler sharing a laugh and some drinks with Genghis Khan and Osama bin Laden. Ted Bundy was stood on a chair and was playing charades with what seemed to be the German military commanders of the invasion of Russia. Talaat Pasha was playing backgammon with Joseph Stalin. Ilse Koch, the witch of Buchenwald, sat and chatted with "Bloody" Queen Mary, and with Mary she seemed to be vying for the attention of Idi Amin. In fact, the possibility for amorous dalliance was so palpable as to make this place no less like any other nightclub on the face of the earth. There also seemed to be any number of young and fresh alternative potential mates for all of the murderers and mass murderers. My visionary sight permitted me to know that most of these lovely young men and women were really demons in disguise. But I also knew that the souls in this part of Hell could not see that.

There was something else, though, that kept these gorgeous youths out of the hands of true inhabitants of this particular neighborhood. A kind of banal inertness or lack of animation lay at a fundamental level below the whole scene, despite the clink of glasses, the sound of occasional laughter, and the ineluctable dance beat of the music. This was even more evident when I noticed that there were weapons just lying on the bars and tables. Just as easily as Genghis Khan could have snatched a gaggle of young women and attempted to have resumed his earthly mission to populate Asia and Europe with his descendants, he or Tamerlane could have picked up a sword and begun collecting severed heads that would serve to compose another grisly tower of skulls, like the many each had left across the Asian steppe. Hitler or Talaat could have shot a few people just because they might have looked Jewish or Armenian. Yet nothing like this happened. So I closed this door and I turned to William Blake.

"Why don't the people in this part of Hell do what they did on earth, given that the possibilities are available to them?" I asked him.

"That is a frequently asked question," he said. "I only answer questions that are so infrequently asked that they may never be asked but once, if at all."

"Okay," I continued, "why are fictional and actual and historical people mixed in together throughout Hell?"

"Again, I cannot answer that," he said. "I must refer you to the frequently asked questions link on the website."

"Do you mean there is a FAQ page for Hell?"

"The truth can never be told as to be understood, and not believed."

The FAQ page for Hell was as trivial and outrageous as it was absolutely true and essential to this part of the story. It turns out that whenever a new murderer or mass murderer arrives at this last stop, he or she does engage in killing. But all it does is make everyone sick, and soon enough the new arrival is included among the violently ill. Eternity, as Blake had intimated, is in love with the productions of time. But his meaning of the phrase "in love" contained many

152

ironies. It seems that even an enterprise as fulfilling and rewarding as killing people in large numbers not only loses its luster over time, but in the term of eternity takes on a flavor that is so distinct from its original tang as to be its anathema. And according to the FAQ page, since Hell is for the mind of all humanity it would make no less sense for Macbeth to be there as it would for any man's ex-wife to be there. Her emotional range and nuance may encompass no more than that of a scorpion or a spider, but Macbeth has a personal and distinct human meaning to hundreds of millions who may understand his murderous courage.

And the other reason, at which the EmBovary chat person had only hinted, that intellectually challenged people are nominally in Hell is that they make much of the rest of it possible. It also turns out that if you had voted for Hillary Clinton you get a kind of pardon from going to Hell and get to go to Purgatory. And you get points for reading the books of Christopher Hitchens.

I was stunned by the fact that I alone on earth now knew Hell and its inhabitants. This in some way had to be the fourth insight or revelation. But I could not be sure; nor could I even know completely what it might have meant or how to apply it to my life, although perhaps this is clear to the discerning reader.

Before I put away the white, razor-thin computer screen which apparently also housed its processor and other computer elements, it had one more webpage to show me. It was simply a video of my celestial visitor, the resplendent Christ of my personal salvation. This time she was wearing a low-cut, calf-length, bodice-style, black lace designer evening dress, which contained its own attached under slip that was the color of her skin and which was strapless and only knee-length. She wore black sheer stockings and black high heels. The décolletage of the dress was rimmed by a black ribbon that came to a subtle bow at her cleavage, with the ends of the bow delicately draping. Through the floral-designed black lace, one could see the skin-colored slip but also the actual skin of her arms and shoulders and upper calves. The effect of the entire presentation was that her magnificent form appeared to be covered only by the lace and then only so long as one did not give even the slightest tug to that slender ribbon in the front. The complete appearance was that she was on her way to a heavenly party. I was relieved she had not appeared in my cell in that fashion.

Her demeanor was one that put me in mind of the way that Dostoevsky had described Alyosha, who was the youngest of *The Brothers Karamazov*. She emanated a powerful innocent allure and a celestial beneficence in such a way that one could have no doubt that were she to take a walk through any town she would quickly and perpetually draw a crowd of admiring children and wild animals. It was clearly apparent to me that she was quite simply the Lamb of God, if also a stunningly beautiful fashion model.

"I hope that you have recognized that the first divine insight which was communicated to you by me was about how to personally approach your certainty. The next one you also learned in person and with a friend when you tried to communicate your belief to others. The third one you directly observed in the actions of those who would manipulate the beliefs of others. This fourth revelation was the strangest and most amazing of all and it was experienced only by you. It is now inside of you and is yours alone. Stay with that," she said, "and I will see you later." She blew me a kiss, and the screen turned off.

I then emerged from the dark room, only to find that the earth had not turned on its axis one half of a revolution. It had only turned, in longitudinal terms, a single minute.

THESE DARK MILLS

It would be a sad and obvious overstatement to say that when I had arrived at earth from Hell I had taken with me some part of that evil miasma or to assert that my character or perhaps my soul had been palled by a dark patch thrown down upon me while I had been in that infernal deep. Such a notion could only be a cliché of the kind unlikely to be found in this book. In fact, my character and personality were still governed by the same general intellectual considerations and warm emotional responses as had ever been at work in me. I had the same impulses to consider in my life as I had long lived it: to embrace the world as much for the problems that it brings as for the joys which it evokes, to treat all with equanimity and to withhold my judgment as long as possible, to see the wonders of everything in the smallest thing and to spread out my goodwill with only hope (and no expectation) of returns. An entirely different set of rules, however, was being observed by the demon which had returned to earth in command of my body and which had left me back there in Hell with Bill Clinton.

It is again at another point in this book where there will be some general confusion pertaining to the use of the personal pronoun in the first person, singular. The "I" who speaks at the beginning of this book, in the introduction, is not I. Legally, he is my representative. I also have not infrequently spoken or considered the word "I," without a certain degree of natural ambivalence or even confusion. And of course, whenever I overhear the same word actually spoken by myself or by another, I am inherently aware of all its abounding ironies, both intended and unintended. But this again is another matter.

I will be speaking not as I am. In the following few phrases of this chapter I will speak, but as the demon I had the misfortune to have had commandeer my body. I had not flown to earth with just a part of Hell in me. It was all of it inside of me, and with very little spare room. This condition was not all that much unlike what is inside of each person that I saw then in that prison or ever had seen in the outside world. That condition was where I would start my demonic enterprises, what I had planned to do, with the commonality of that thing that is, and is not, at the center of each man or woman.

Nature struck me first upon my arrival, in all of its transcendent wonder. Nature is always in evidence, and one may access it immediately. This alone would inspire man or demon to worship. It also contains a recondite, ineffable, and hermetic power which we may only surmise and which is even more inspiring. It is that part which is more often confused with the gods. I came to nature at this location, as I had in each other instance I have found myself before it, in awe of it and with a warm and familiar understanding of the beauty of my part in it.

The Manchester prison complex rests in a stretch of ancient earth that rolls up the North American continent from northern Georgia through the states of the eastern quarter of the United States, all the way to Maine and beyond. It is Appalachia, and the appreciation of it has dwindled since it was first discovered by European settlers. At that early time it stood as an almost impenetrable barrier to the vast central and western expanses of the continent. It was more habitable to the original Native Americans than to the majority of the settlers from England and Scotland, for whom it was to remain largely a place over which to pass. A smaller number of those early pioneers settled there. They then did not much change or develop beyond the manners and customs of that first early time. Progress and successive immigrants to America from other lands seemed not to have lodged there, which has led to the connotation of Appalachian as being somewhat less or something backward. But that is really just another part of both its accessible and its secret beauty. It has a mysterious friction to time that seems to arrest any who have stayed there.

The Appalachian Mountains stand like no other place on the continent, as some middle ground in the spiritual geography of the land mass. They are not as hospitable as the rolling fields of the Great Plains or the cozy valleys and coves and hills of the eastern, southern or far western part of the continent. And they are not as difficult or as demanding or as forbidding of large settlement as are the deserts and stark mountain promontories of the greater western part of the land. They are not easy or close as is waking life or the lowlands. Nor are they as other or as foreign as the Rocky Mountains or the true subconscious. They are a halfway point, like a dream.

This dream quality is always apparent in the clouded hills, as one sees each more distant ridge slightly more shrouded than the one before it. The mind grasps the rolling quality of these mountains green in such a way that makes them seem almost as familiar as the curves and rises of the female body in recline. They seem like they can be touched by simply reaching out in a way that is never felt in the forbidding Rockies. There is in every direction a verdant fecundity that springs forth where there is also the dearth of human development, which this smaller set of mountains has scarcely permitted. Bear and deer and raccoon and bobcat and trout and hawk and hog and turkey do not have to be seen in order for one to know that they teem in the foothills and elevations and the hollows where the pines and oaks and spruce and maple and laurel and rhododendron grow. All this warmth and light and life does not change them from being mountains and at once able to obscure and then suddenly release brutal high-elevation storms and bitter cold snaps, pouring rains, and mudslides, and the precipitous and sometimes hardened actions of the clans of men whose families have lived in them for generations. It is a place I cannot help but love.

Prison is a closed and restricted system that does not allow for observation of all of the complex and evident elements of that part of nature which is human nature, but this terrarium aspect makes it an excellent instrument by which to gain various narrower views into its deeper and less accessible places. Perhaps one can see less broadly but occasionally more deeply into the inhabitants of a place where numbers of men are tightly confined by a rough and unforgiving authority and are rigidly restricted and where they are kept without women, real work, or freedom from associating with those they would normally avoid. Seeing deeply and delving deeply was the way in which I had planned to evoke all the glory of their own truer nature for these men in this hermetic system. That they were in prison was only going to make that effort more beautifully focused as well as making it more easily done. One only had to hear what I could hear but which was inaudible to others to know the truth of that. This was the sound of grown men, tough men, hard men who had faced and who had dealt death, hearing them silently and secretly crying in the bathroom stalls and prison beds because they missed their wives or children or because they were torn by the passions of regret or remorse. Though no one else could hear it, I could hear it. To me it was the background music of the prison and it was playing all the time.

There lay inside of each of these men a blank. Within this blank was an opening. And below that opening could be found essences of what might bear many names. These could be called utter freedom, or the indestructible will, or sorrow, or anger, or the self-negating power of love, or the imagination. Or one such essence could just be a simple and different version on a theme of a question, such as, "What or who will I be today or at this instant?" All the rest of what would constitute each one of these men his character, his personality, his image of himself was merely bright Christmas paper wrapping to be triumphantly torn off. Inside is where the presents and the toys lay.

In fact these things are tyrannies, these coverings. It has been said that few men realize that their lives, characters, capabilities, and boldness are only an expression of their belief in the safety of their surroundings and that their confidence and courage and their very emotions and principles and thoughts belong to the crowd, to society which blandly believes in the irresistibility of its institutions and morals. Though it prevents a man from seeing what is at his core, that bland faith also actually oppresses the natural freedom into which each man is certainly born. He becomes imprisoned by family, by love, by school and work, by getting along in civil society, by god and church, by reason and faith, by friendship, by virtue, by hope, by anything that keeps his attention outward and which guides his decisions to be made with a view to what is on the outside. Refreshingly, these men in this prison already knew how they might react, when all that had been their outside world had been changed, and they had been thrust into a heightened situation in which few if any of the old rules might apply. Since they had been bounded up in the nutshell of a prison cell, they had been forced to take a longer gaze into the infinite space that was within each of them. And all of their previous lives which had led them to prison were unified by the way in which they were also different from others who might never come to find themselves in this place. They had always been a bit freer on the inside and they more closely sensed and resisted the oppressive nature of all that is not who they are.

In these verdant hills and on this loamy soil and beneath this engendering sun I would begin my project of unwrapping. There is no word for the marriage of love and hate with which I would approach this task unless that word is the one word, love. The coverings, the tyrannies, the supporting institutions, the personalities and the characters, the civil society, this paradise on the surface of things, all this to me is bane. The more I see how they facilitate spiritual imprisonment the more they are a torment to me. But I love them as well for the way in which they cover men's inner packages, with a certain pretty appeal, preserving what is inside from being casually used and also falling aside and coming off at so easy a tugging. And I love what is inside for having been hidden and penned up, for being so much more like the nature that surrounds the prison than the society that is within it, and mostly for having the possibilities which can best be called bottomless. The wings of flies, to wanton boys, are not the subject of much debate. The tenuous serenity of these inmates would be as was once written, as the fish is to the osprey, who takes it by sovereignty of nature.

I did not know before I had arrived where I might begin to find a suitable starting point for my play of love and enmity. But I found that I already had in this prison a very good friend who loved me. There was also another man there who was considered most highly, the very first man of the joint. And then there were also the men of faith. There is birth in fire, as any forest man will say. And upon defeat in war the greatest civilizations had been built. I would give them all a new kind of creation.

Victor Fuoco was the first man of Manchester prison by virtue of the way in which he had fulfilled the highest requirements of the ethos of the place. It did not hurt either that he was Italian. Even though he was not a mafia man he had been given the respect that inmates so often give to the members of that particular penal fiefdom, and to the other prisoners he was immediately associated with their virtues, namely of having that particular kind of honor within his criminal calling and being absolutely dedicated to his compatriots in crime. Men arrive at a minimum-security prison in a number of ways. The first way is to be convicted of a lesser crime which is also one's first offense and to receive a short sentence. Each of these two things make a such prisoner a low risk for flight or for causing trouble and he is seen almost as a regular citizen who just wants to do his two or three years and get back to his life. The second most common way to be assigned is to have cooperated with the government on the prosecution of one's criminal associates and to have had a long sentence converted to a shorter one, sometimes permanently and other times contingent upon continued cooperation. A "rat" is the name each of these men was given, and they did all they could to conceal their cooperation and avoid that epithet, because everyone else in prison had been put there by a rat or by rats. Vic Fuoco arrived in the minimum-security penitentiary by the third way, by the long and hard route. He had been charged and prosecuted and had kept his mouth shut and had not cooperated, and the result was that he had received a twenty-year sentence behind the razor wire in a much darker and far more dangerous facility. He had done most of his bit and with the most assured yet unknowable difficulty and determination. He had kept himself out of trouble and had at each possible turn in the process been assigned to a prison with successively lower-security requirements. He had only to finish out his last two years at this place. The previous years had been his martyrdom, and this was his beatification.

There is no such thing as faith. Except in the hearts and minds of the innocent children or the mentally impaired or the delusional, it may only be arrived at after a certain amount of calculation or almost by mistake. This calculation is even more evident in the case of the religious conversions of inmates. That calculation will often be toward better treatment by the authority or keeping in mind that for an individual a membership in a religious group might polish off some of the rough patches that are on every man's surface and that sometimes just catch another man the wrong way. It was simply a bit safer, all around, to be part of a religious organization inside. Though tried and true, there was something just a little bit tired or hackneyed about becoming a Christian while one was down, as well as something about it that was a little soft. Becoming a Muslim, however, had a bit more of an edge and considerably more novelty. It was also largely a black thing. And it required the prison to make accommodations as it did for the Jews but not the Christians, such as opening the mess hall after dark on Ramadan. Becoming a Muslim was more of a statement than becoming a born-again Christian. There were several types of men in the small Muslim group at Manchester, running from the gentler ones who took to it for almost Christian reasons to the more militant ones who wanted to show, as one inmate had pointed out, that they were not too fond of the white man.

It turned out that I had a very good friend inside, named John. He was one of the college-educated men, as were many of the white-collar criminals, but he also always had had one foot in the demimonde before he came inside. That made him less of the tourist in here than the white-collar convicts were. He had been a marijuana grower and had been about as much of a potent threat to the fabric of American society as any other farmer. It also meant he was not as dangerous or threatening as the men who actually had carried guns and had actively made numerous or large-scale drug deals. He and I had the same sort of frame of reference for seeing prison and we were able talk to one another about shared interests in reading and philosophy and politics and the problems with our families and we could do so in the same language. He had lived with a woman who was not his wife but with whom he had a son and who was his partner. Her name was Eva, and she possessed that casual, handsome, direct, and youthful beauty and charm which almost always fit better and occur more often among the women of America. She was short and thin, but strong and well formed, with long straight brown hair and a face that was pleasant and good-looking. That she could work a hammer or the jack of a car was as evident as the fact that she would look good in a dress, whenever she saw fit to wear one. She and the boy were regular visitors since they lived near the prison.

There are roles in prison and they are populated. Vic Fuoco was deeply respected. He did not command the respect that Big Frank commanded within his organized crime group as a substance of its very functioning, but the respect Vic was given came freely and was more widely spread even if it was less reliable. He was nominally grouped among the small set of men who had been members of motorcycle clubs on the outside, the bikers. They were a more loosely formed criminal group than the mafia men and they were not given quite as wide a berth by the majority black prison population, but they were given one. Vic could only nominally have been included in that group because he had actually been in a motorcycle gang. But he had a calm and low-key charisma and an openness and fairness to his character that was in strong contrast to the hard-edged, dangerous and racist elements of the biker guys. These qualities of his were clearly what had likely helped him get along inside of the harder prisons, where violence and betrayal lurked in every open space. He was also probably aided by the fact that these qualities seemed to accompany a fair-minded and honest resoluteness that was almost palpable in his presence. In the way that most bikers made you fear them because they were a bit crazy, he made you fear him because he was not. Their wildness was always subject to interpretation and most of the time it was bluster or marketing, only occasionally and unexpectedly erupting into very real trouble. With Vic it was obvious that very real trouble would only come when it was merited, and then there would be nothing blustery or unexpected about it.

True and honest friendships do spring up in prison. They are not related to sexual predation or to the temporary realignment of sexual preferences. Casual friendships simply do not exist, as men give each other a great deal of personal and emotional space. But strong friendships will occur. Vic had one close friendship, with an inmate named Darren. And like all relationships in or out of prison, even strong same-sex friendships between heterosexuals, the connections often spring from elements of the heart that are apparently not all that different from what will make a man and a woman ineffably like one another. Darren Jones was Vic's great friend inside, and to my infernal vision that was a very unlikely pairing. It was obvious to me that Darren was a card-carrying member of the Devil's party and not at all cast from the same mold as Victor Fuoco. Vic was drawn to him because he was taller, in better shape, good-looking, gregarious, and humorous. He was on the surface in every way preferable to Vic himself, who was plain, short, stocky, simple, grizzled, and somewhat dour. It was even rumored that Darren was having at it with the female hack who was in charge of the prison commissary where he worked. That added to his luster.

What were deeper than luster were the things he tried to absorb from Vic by association with him. And it worked. Darren was given a bit more respect and latitude within the general population because he was Vic's best friend. Darren was tall, with black hair and blue eyes, and he was one of the men whose build clearly showed that he lifted weights regularly. He was also not very bright, and for such a man to open his mouth a lot in prison would have presented him with a number of problems from which his apparent strength and size would not necessarily have protected him. But he became even more mercurial because he was often accompanied by the taciturn, resolute, and noble Victor, who enjoyed hearing Darren hold forth almost as much as he appreciated that he was the phenomenon's principal foundation.

It was a beautifully hateful and tormenting sight, these two souls befriending one another across the space of their difference, secure in one another's companionship, each enjoying their share of the attachment, each recognizing a gain from it. I did not envy it as the men in the prison might. I was drawn to it because it was another beautiful wrapping that covered and oppressed freedom and veracity. I did not know why this tyranny of friendship should deny each man or any other prisoners of knowledge, of the knowledge of the truth. I would excite the situation, drive minds with a desire to know. My only concern was that the beauty of what I had planned seemed to extend beyond the bounds of my charter and to encroach upon that of the other realm. After all, what sin can it be for men to gain knowledge?

I began by giving some legal advice to a biker, who soon took enough of an interest in me to discover that I could draw pictures with some representational accuracy. He brought me a picture of an eagle and asked if I could draw it to look larger and change its pose slightly. I did this for him, and it was not long before I noticed that same eagle in brown and white leather stitched on to the back of a leather vest that another biker had made in the leatherworking shop. Soon I was receiving other requests from bikers. I was asked to draw animals and cartoon characters and motorcycles that would end up on jailhouse tattoos. I was also asked to look at photographs of women, girlfriends of the men, in which they were fully clothed and it was requested that I draw larger versions of these pictures in which the women would be naked. Knowing full well how these were being used, I approached the projects with some flair. I was then asked to join the evening activities in the leather shop, where I largely just drew pictures and became a kind of curiosity to these men. It was there that I noticed Jimmy, who was clearly on the fringe of the biker group. It was as if he had been permitted to be there, but no one really wanted to have anything to do with him. He always winced slightly every time Vic showed up or was mentioned. And he reacted more negatively to Darren's name or presence.

It was unlikely that anyone would volunteer to explain anything to me as an outsider about these reactions, and it would have gone beyond what is expected generally in prison and particularly in this subset of inmates for me to have asked a direct question about them.

The path to take presented itself when a prisoner who was never referred to by anything other than his prison sobriquet, "Spike," mentioned a legal issue he had, related to divorce. The approaching end of any married prisoner's bit is always apprehended by strongly mixed emotions. On the one hand, he is glad about his impending freedom. On the other hand, almost all suits for divorce, and there are many, are served on prisoners just before they are released. It occurs to the wife that she does not want either a convict or this particular convict returning into what had become her sane and quiet home after he had left. Or as was more often the case, the wife would have found another man almost immediately after the initial incarceration and had kept up the façade of visits and everything else right up to the time when she could no longer conceal her change of heart. My tendered advice to Spike helped him to maintain a relationship with his son, who many years later would profit from that relationship by getting a jump start on his own life of crime before falling to a hail of Mexican gunfire in, of all places, Traverse City, Michigan.

My decision to accept his offer of a jailhouse tattoo in barter for the legal advice was even more entertaining than it was fun, since the tattoo I was putting on this body was of a heart emblazoned with the name of the wife who would soon divorce its owner. I just smiled when Spike had repeatedly warned me that it is wisest only to tattoo the names of blood relations onto one's shoulder. A cordon of lookouts had to have been organized in order to give advance warning in the event that a hack might approach. It was, of course, the kind of low-level duty that would draw Jimmy as one of its participants, giving him a sense of belonging and keeping another from having to help Spike and therefore have Spike owe him a favor. Spike and his on-site assistant were impressed that I showed no sign of pain or even anything more serious than a mild bemusement as he tattooed me with a crude apparatus consisting of a sharpened electric guitar string, a cocktail straw, a tiny electrical motor extracted from an old cassette tape player, and some India ink that had been smuggled into the prison. I was quickly becoming one of Spike's new pals and from this association I had learned that Jimmy's reactions were due to the fact that Darren always mercilessly tortured Jimmy for having cooperated in the prosecution of another criminal.

Jimmy was marked by this in his own way, and his release was likely to be quite different than any of the other bikers. They knew this, and that is why they let him alone. He was as a ghost to them, more or less. So there was no need to torture him. Darren had not let the sun rise and set at its sweet and inoffensive pace over this thing. He sought to solicit matters that had been rightly hidden. He had not thought of only what concerned him as a prisoner. He had dreamed of other worlds, where creatures live in a state where all things are revealed. He had begun the delving. And it would engender the fall of Victor Fuoco.

I knew that Jimmy would not accept my help unless he thought it would cost him. The prison system is just too dependent upon barter, and no one under any circumstance ever would want to owe or be owed. So this service had to be bartered and then it would also take on the added gleam of letting my fool also become my wallet.

"I can help you, you know," I said to him the next day, "for a price."

"Really? With what?" he asked, as he looked at me with that combination of inquisitiveness and guarded respect that would be granted to me for all the reasons that I was a social curiosity to all the other bikers in the leather shop.

"I can help you with your Darren problem."

"What is the price?"

"I want you to give me a carton of cigarettes, your commissary privileges for a month, and your daughter has to put one of her girlfriends on my visiting list so that I can feel her up when your family brings her to visit."

"Man, you are a sick bastard. And that is a high price," he said and hesitated. "But you can take care of it for me, can't you?"

"We both know it. That is why I can charge so much."

After he had paid and I had significantly changed the view that some of the other prisoners had of me, I told him the simple plan one day at dinner in the mess hall.

"Here," I said, just handing him a glass of ice tea, "walk by Darren and spill this all over his tray. Make sure you ruin his meal and get some on him. I will take care of the rest."

So Jimmy did it. And Darren jumped up and yelled, "You goddamn rat! Shit! I can't believe we let this rat bastard walk around like this!"

There was a general cessation of talking, and long and silent looks of disapproval and surprise were leveled toward Darren. Comity and decorum are required in a prison mess hall, where all men prefer that the atmosphere be sedate. Issues are simply not dealt with in the full view of the general population and the guards. Where all these men are gathered together there is too much potential for an altercation to become sectarian, to involve factions and to become a general fracas that will bring down the armed and organized might of the prison government upon everyone. That is why each man will carefully knock on the table, as a way of serving notice before he gets up with his tray after a meal. Even the suggestion of a confrontation is to be avoided. But Darren was not finished.

"What are you looking at, you bunch of rats?" he said loudly and pointedly as he glared at everyone looking at him.

Jimmy had long since slipped out of the room. The situation was not yet volatile but Darren was in a bit of a spot. The black inmates never liked him much. His garrulousness was not considered cool, and there was too much swagger in his walk. It was Victor, whose silent alignment was already protecting Darren, who spoke from his seat across from him, loud enough for most of us to hear.

"I am sure it was an accident," he said. "It happens all the time. There is no need to get too upset. It's Jimmy anyway."

That took the eyes off of Darren, and it also put Vic in the place of taking responsibility for him, which he was capable of doing. He had more than enough personal prison capital for that.

After a few days of not being seen, Jimmy finally caught up to me in the hallway outside the prison chapel room, where I had been on other business, which I will relate later. He was very nervous and agitated as he spoke to me.

"Well, that did not turn out as you planned. Everything is worse, much worse. You messed up. I can't believe it. Shit. Look what you did to me now. What am I going to do? I tell you what I am going to do. I am going to tell. I am going to tell Darren and Vic that you put me up to it as part of your plan to do something to hurt Darren. Then I will tell the office that you are fomenting discord."

My answer to him was one that certainly surprised him and would have even more greatly surprised any other inmate who might have witnessed it. It involved an action no one would have expected from me, but which may have been just a little bit familiar to Jimmy from almost any quarter. I picked him up and hurled him against the wall. His back hit the painted cinder block concrete about seven feet above the floor and he fell, dazed and aching to the floor. Then I walked over to him and stood over him.

"It is not over, you idiot," I told him, as I glared at him. "It was going to all happen according to plan, but you just pissed me off. Now it is going to cost you much more. I want three cartons of cigarettes. And that fat girl you brought in to the visiting room for me is not going to cut it. She wanted it to happen. Now, you have to bring that cute niece I know you have."

This was all done in the frame that is farthest from anger. Nor was I angling for the cute niece in particular. And, of course, smoking meant nothing at all to me. I had just been terribly bored by the entire process, and it was time to do something fine-looking in order to keep my own attention. And it was part of my plan. I did not even have to have any exceptional or devilish vision to have figured it all out already. There were four or five men in this prison who could have applied themselves and could have put it all together. Darren's protests had been too much.

The next morning, on my way into the 11 a.m. lunch in the mess hall, I saw the long line of men waiting outside the door of the prison library next to it. There were half a dozen inside, gathered around one of the books that contain the synopsis of federal appeals cases and the texts of appeals court orders, books called federal reporters. The men were reading a case, and the ones in line outside were waiting their turns to also read it. As these men went from the library and into the mess hall there was a growing low level din. Eyes were again turned toward Darren and Victor. It seems that an inmate, not a prisoner who had any particular interest in the issues but just a bright one and a curious one and one who knew how to do legal research and had been doing some on his own case, had found an index card in his cell that had on it a citation to a case. He had naturally looked it up. The case was a discussion of the calculation of the reduction of a sentence for a specific level of cooperation with the government prosecutors, the prosecution of some unknown person in some high-level security prison, and the cooperation of Darren Jones.

What happened in the mind of Victor Fuoco may be surmised. He stood up that afternoon, at the 4 p.m. dinner, and addressed the assembled inmates in what had been the first such speech given in the memory of any present. It was a heartfelt expression of the bond of natural friendship that fixed his lot firmly with his consort and which spelled the doom of every understanding of every value that he had exemplified and had brought to this prison after serving the previous eighteen years of his sentence.

I had been in that hallway outside the prison chapel because, while I had been working on the education of Victor and all those who had once respected him, I had also been working on my Muslim escapade. I had simply befriended Abdullah, who was quartered on my cell block. It was not too much of an obstacle. He had been incarcerated under the name given to him at his birth, in Cleveland, Ohio, which was Ronald Fuller. There was a time in America when the Anglo-Saxon custom of referring to the first name as the Christian name used to be observed, preserving the intention of identifying as a Christian a person whose second or family name had descended from the pagan past. As sure as I was that I had known a few pagan fullers in sixth-century England, I was even surer that Abdullah had also gone to church many times with his grandmother and mother. He looked and walked and talked like, and was as open and as kind as, any Christian soul that ever was. He wore a Muslim *kufi* on his head and went to prayer five times a day with his Muslim brothers, but the way he carried his Koran was exactly as he had held his Bible as a child. That I was white would not have occurred to him for an instant as a reason to decline or to demur when I had asked to join him at the next meeting. He only cared that I seemed earnest.

The rest of the hard cases at those meetings were not as open. They gave me the "die white man" looks, not knowing that I loved their hate. They even appeared to not be surprised that I took to the learning of their *salah*, their prayer, and of all the rituals and ablutions pertaining to it, so quickly and so well that it might have been noticed that I already knew them. Within only a few meetings it was obvious that I already knew the material better than any of their group. I stayed quiet during the first discussions of the passages, the *ayats* and the *suras*, of their book. But when I did finally speak, I supported the readings and passages from the book with my understanding of the *hadith*, the supporting law, and it was evident from then on that I was the best Muslim in the group. I even undertook to help teach a prison class in African American history that focused on the suppression of that history in the traditional study of ancient history. I expounded upon how the fact the word Nubian in ancient Egyptian actually had the connotation of meaning something along the lines of "the old country." This was true. I said that this meant Cleopatra probably did not look like Elizabeth Taylor and was actually a strong black woman. This was not true; she had really been a Greek. And I had uncovered that much of what had been taught about the ancient Greeks being first in so many Western things had actually been their way of emulating the Egyptians, who were therefore the real font of our civilization. The primitive Greeks had always been obsessed by Egyptian civilization; this is true. And throughout the day, every day, among the population, I was able to guide my congregation with what can only be called my singular facility for being able to quote scripture to my own purposes.

I had wormed my way into their group. And I had more or less taken it over. From the start, there was always the kind of resentment as is to be expected when the white man becomes involved in what is essentially a black man's game. And game became an operative phrase. I took up basketball and softball, prison games that were dominated by young black men. Their domination took on a social aspect, and since the color line is rarely if ever crossed in prison, even the fit and athletic young white men avoided competing. And this body I had inhabited was well past its athletic prime. But I knew how to train it, not by attempt or by practice but by demonic devotion to success. Instead of practicing shooting the basketball, I practiced making shots. I would only stop taking a shot after I had made it twenty-five times in a row. I drove this body to a laser focus and never allowed it to settle into just practicing. And I swung the three softball bats at a time as practice, always emulating a home run swing. Soon I was the only white man in the prison basketball league and one of the only white men on a prison softball team. I could nail the outside shot and hit the home run. Soon the resentment of my having entered the black and Muslim worlds at prison gave way to the pride and acceptance that any minority might feel when a member of the majority undertakes to verify and validate the enterprises of that minority. I had prevailed upon their better natures and I had begun to appeal to their appreciation of my superiority of understanding in the area of this particular faith.

Ramadan brought my spiritual leadership of this group to its apotheosis. I had been called upon to work with the prison authority to ensure use of the kitchen and mess hall after dark and for the first time for them was able to make sure that all the food that was prepared was *hallal*, or according to the dietary laws of Islam. I provided the recipes for traditional Arab meals. I planned the daily special prayers, or *tarawih*, and laid out lessons for each day. I presided over the charity drive for donations to the local children's center. I made sure that the Koran was being read straight through by some member of the congregation at every time of the day, so that the words of the prophet could be heard by the faithful and the infidel alike at any time of the day. I had given the small Muslim community a real presence in the prison. More converts had come over to the faith. Christians, Jews, and non-believers in the prison and among the guards and staff began to take an interest in the details of the religion. Books had been brought into the prison that helped explain the faith. What had once been a small and slightly disorganized band of men working to believe had become a large and growing and organized and happy and recognized mosque of which I was the *imam*.

All religion is politics. This was best understood by each of the men who stood at the beginning of each of the great faiths. Whether those men were the apostle Paul or the Emperor Constantine, or Abraham or Rabbi Akiva, or Abu Bakr or the caliph Umar, much of the growth of their faiths had been dependent upon the personal appeal and political work of the individuals involved. There had been only one man within the early group of Muslims at Manchester, one of the early hard cases, Mubassir, the observer, who had withheld from me any part of his acceptance or affection. At the very beginning, Mubassir had wanted what he thought was this condescending white man to just go away. In the end he was quite happy to have witnessed the success that I had brought his community, yet he was the only one who had not yet fallen entirely into the fold. A small part of him was still concerned. Every congregant was happy for the new success of the prison Muslim mission. It is likely that his remaining concern arose from an instinct he had that this triumph had arisen politically from a single source.

Eid approached, and this traditional end-of-Ramadan holiday in the prison was to be acknowledged by special prayers, by the traditional forgiveness of the transgressions of others, by a large meal and a communal celebration. In what was singular in this or any other such prison event, the celebration was open to all, and many attended, including the warden and some staff. My intimacy with all things subterranean and my uncanny senses allowed me to foresee an event I might have had to otherwise manufacture in order to close out the festivities with the pyrotechnics that would prove so useful to my purposes. At the end of celebration, I addressed the assembly. After I had said what might have been expected, I began to speak the unexpected.

"We are all here blessed in ways no other men have ever known. Under this sky, upon this earth, in this prison, we are about to receive the divine light and in such a way as has not been seen nor heard since a Ramadan some fourteen centuries past. No words, no feelings, no ideas may begin to express what you will find here today in your hearts. I have been called and I have heard. And so shall you. A final revelation has occurred. The mountain has come to me, and I have taken the word. And you shall hear as well. The foundations of heaven have been shaken, and we here now will take its revelation. Just feel it."

And so began the intraplate earthquake that I knew would arrive, centered directly below the ground on which we stood and on which we now stood quite uneasily. It was almost a 6.3 on the Richter scale, which would even get the attention of earthquake-savvy Californians. This far into the eastern half of the continent, it was the kind of thing that had occurred in no one's memory. In fact, most of these men would not even be able to independently identify it as an earthquake. The windows rattled. Pictures fell off the wall. Utensils and glasses shook and slid off of the tables. Anything standing was tossed back and forth several inches to either side. The very building shook. And there was a glorious audible rumbling. Men were stricken. They fell on their faces and were sore afraid. And when they lifted up their eyes they saw no man, save only me. No one could speak. It had lasted a full thirty or forty seconds, after which I had more than the attention of everyone.

"Arise and be not afraid. It has been written. This sign is to tell us where to find heaven or hell. They are in us. Not in some place we can't see or never will. Allah is here. We do not need to be on our knees to find him. His power lies in our bodies and in our immortal will. He is in your heart and in mine. We need not ever again get down on our supplicated knees. We need never again doubt his power so much that we need to bow and sue for grace. His heavenly power is in each of us. And in each of us, this celestial power simply cannot and will not fail. Through this experience of this great event and in souls no less great than those of old, we will form a more successful hope and wage a more forceful war to win the world to our faith through the understanding that all we need to do is look inside our hearts to know the message of the truth."

"After all," I said, speaking more clearly and loudly with each phrase, "the human heart and human mind is its own place, in which we can make a heaven or a hell. What is Mecca compared to that? And consult your heart and mind and ask: Which will work best on our friends and neighbors here and at home? To tell them of this final revealed truth, that God is alive in each man's heart and that we may all find Him in our studies and in our dreams? Or must we say that our God is so limited that he may only be approached by ablutions and obsequies and by desert pilgrimages and in repetitious sayings in a language no one here speaks? What does your own heart tell you? Do you feel you must envy some cleric in some mosque in some other country for having a better path to Allah? Allah has made us free, and free we will be. We will never need to bow and scrape again to some authority that seeks to place itself between our hearts and the divine revelation that we know is in our hearts. Each believer is his own *imam*."

I had a minute and a half to finish, before I knew that the one large significant aftershock would arrive. I made myself about three inches taller, a degree or two of lighter skin and I placed my voice in a stentorian register no man had heard before. "That we were created and brought forth upon this earth is a strange idea. Is it not? Who here remembers this happening? We know no other time than right now, no other place than right here. We are self-created, self-taught by our own immortal inner fire. We are our own heaven. And our power is our own. Our own hearts and souls will teach us by proof that we are equal to the task. We need not ever gather again, or go to our knees, or utter other men's languages. We may go forth each alone and do our own will for the good of God."

And as I began to finish, the sound of rumblings deep and subterranean murmurs echoed my words, and my height rose again as did my voice, "You need nothing more than this. You know what you know, simply put. I will say not one more word about it. The rest is up to you." And the earth shook again with a strong force but slightly less than before and instantly a bit more familiar to the men. They stood agape, waited it out. I walked away, and returned to form.

It would be fair to say that there were no more meetings, that this was the end of the Muslim community in that prison. They did not gather again. Surely, as these current inmates were gradually released and as new prisoners began to replace them, a new smattering of souls would piece together the same sort of ramshackle little group that had sufficed before. But even that gathering would never be looked upon as the same as the assemblage I had entered that first day. The prison would always have a material and physical memory of the events of that Eid.

My friend John, it seemed, loved Christian, in whose body I was operating for the reasons that I was slightly more of many things he already was, intelligent, sensitive, well read, arch, passionate, insightful, attractive. He also loved me because of the things which he had in greater abundance, warmth, compassion, humility, and a kind of openness. I was now another matter entirely. There was a nothing inside of me. And that was everything.

John loved his Eva with as much of the ambivalence that is possible and ineluctable. Though he was sophisticated enough to be far more aware of its two edges than most men, he still thought it unnatural of him that her visits slightly oppressed him, that her love constrained him and that her own ambivalence crawled under his skin. And none of this was on the surface. They were thoughtful and sensitive souls, never more so than when with each other. And that was fairly often, since Eva and the son lived close to the prison. As a friend, I had been introduced at a visit, and Eva and I had passed some words. I also watched the two of them closely when they were together in the visiting room or on the yard outside of it. And, of course, I heard about her all the time, from him. It gave me what might have been called the drop on her.

It had been agreed that I would go to the house to help her and the boy on some skilled labors, the next time that I was able to leave the place on a prison work detail. She was quite capable of the handiwork required to manage a home but she had not been trained for things like plumbing and electricity. She had made certain and considerable efforts at her church to create the possibility of such a prison work detail being requested, so I could get out to take them. It was set. On the assigned day, I ran the men to the church and then went to the trailer where Eva was, while the boy was at school. I took a look at the plumbing problem under the bathroom sink and quickly did that work. I rewired the electrical outlet by the kitchen sink and installed a ground surge protector. And I re-built a favorite chair and added some finished carpentry work. This devil's work was never done in so quick a fashion and soon I was seated at the kitchen table with Eva, sipping the organic green tea she had offered me.

"So, tell me," she asked, "how is John really?"

"He is a special breed of cat, your husband," I said.

"He is not my husband."

"Well actually, he more or less is," I said as she nodded. "He loves you greatly, and I believe that is the weight that bears down on him the most. He feels that he has let you and the boy down. It has taken a piece out of him. It creates a strange backspin. The more he loves you, the more it hurts him."

She settled into this thought for a while. I studied her fine strong hands, ones that had always been such honest and useful tools but which had never seen the inside of a fine glove nor had ever picked up a salad fork at a four-star restaurant, as they went about her table, straightening a napkin, absently pushing a spoon, putting her hair behind her ear. No make-up covered a single part of her face. It was open and lined and care-worn. It was also strong and alive and expressive. I watched it wax and wane and change phase as she became pensive and then a little bit mournful and then distracted. There was a flash of something else there. It was a light, the kind of luminance that shines out from under a concern, a kind of escaping beam that could illuminate something unseen before. Her eyes were large, larger than most, certainly so for woman of her small size. One could see the whites of them at most times entirely around her green pupils, giving them a certain substantial plangent power. They would cloud and flash and wander and reflect. In short, she was like a discovered heap of nitrous powder, stored up for some rumored medieval battle, laid fit for a spark, to suddenly blaze up and inflame the air.

And out from every deeper part of her being came shooting darts of what can only be called desire, the desire to be elsewhere, to do something else and to be someone other than who it was she was constrained to be. These darts were not seen by her, and I am certain she was unaware that they were flying from her like water drops from a big, wet, shaking dog. I have seen this desire. In a way, I am it. Even my words cannot unpack its meaning. It may be said that is also the desire to not be, or to be not. It is best left for each to know on his or her own. Eva's was there, pouring as from a spring, and it was beautiful. The darts were finding their mark.

"But what of you?" I asked. "Are you holding up well? Having the boy in your care must be both rewarding and distracting."

"He is like my life," she said.

"I am certain. You pour yourself into him. I have no doubt. That must be a great comfort. It is a great thing indeed. Is it not? The more you give to a child like that, the more you feel inside, the more is poured back into you. The boy may dawdle and tarry and bolt and gambol, and for several minutes just plain ignore you. But as you look at him you know that he is able to do all those things because you give him the foundation for it. Even when he does not hug you or let you know he loves you, you are filled with the joy of being able to love him and to fulfill that love for him. You only wish you had more to give. There is nothing in the world quite like a mother."

She stopped moving entirely for a minute. She fixed her eyes on me.

"That's the thing, isn't it?" I continued. "You have so much to give. You spend what you have to give on wrangling with teachers, driving the car, making breakfast, washing clothes. It actually only barely touches the capacity of your heart. Oh sure, there are times when it seems a chore, when it seems to wear you down. But those are rare instances when you allow yourself to feel sorry for yourself. The larger issue is that you want to do so much more for your child. There is no limit to what you would do. And that is a large, aching, almost impossible to bear kind of love."

"How do you know all this?" she asked.

"How could I not know it? It is nothing more than common sense, to me. It only requires eyes to see and ears to hear and a mind and heart to sift through it all. I tell you this. I also know that your capacity to love your child and your husband is overwhelming, but that it is only partially being tapped. There is so much more inside of you than anyone can know."

"That's not just common sense," she said. "You are not like any other man I have ever met. Who are you? John has told me that you are well traveled and that you have read many books and that you are highly educated. But I thought that meant you would be an elitist. I guess with a certain kind of man, advantages like that can make one less of a snob."

"I have had a great many of what you could call broadening experiences, such as you mentioned. But I have also had experiences which you could consider deep. I have been at the very top and at the very bottom. I have been dealt blows and I have given my fair share of pain. I have been exalted and I have been damned. All of these experiences have taken my naturally insightful spirit and have polished it into a lens through which I see things other men just plain miss. My profound appreciation of you, for instance, springs not from anything callow or unseasoned but from their opposites."

"Oh, I am just a woman, trying to do her best."

"You are doing more than could be expected. You are doing exceptionally well. But you are hardly doing all of which you are capable. What you have is strength and depth of character, and the goodness to make correct use of it. You are exactly the woman any man would want with him when the wolf is at the door. That may be the best and most appealing thing about you, but it is not the most beautiful."

"What do you mean?"

"I mean that there is a vast landscape of potential inside of you. It is in the combination of your expansive mind and your questing heart. It is an inner topography of vast plains and stark promontories, of swift and deep rivers and arid deserts, of immense marshes and secluded glens, of rolling hills and jungle thickets, of box canyons and huge forests. It is an inner countryside that spreads out beyond the horizon of what could be any man's ability to understand or to explore. It is jammed full of more life than any man could fully appreciate. And above all, there are no boundaries."

"I can't catch my breath," she said as she reached across the table and put her fingers gently on the top of my hand. "Right now, I am having such strange and wrong feelings."

"There is never anything wrong about any feelings. They are just part of your nature, and nature is never wrong. It just is. Nor are these feelings strange. I am sure that if you think about it, this feeling that you are having now has always been there in some form or another. It is only now that you associate it with me at all and that is only because I have shown you that I have eyes to see it."

"But John would think they were wrong."

"I do not know what John would think. Nor do you. And what is thinking, but a thing you and I each do? Be in charge of your thoughts, or at least of their issue. If you do that, what anyone else might think is not your matter."

"Are you trying to seduce me?"

"That is the first flat note you have sounded all day. We are well past that, you and I. And it does not do you justice. You are far more than that. You are anyone you want to be, at any moment and in any way. And that will be true for every moment to come. You are free, absolutely free. What do you think I have been saying about you? Have I been saying that you are a slave, fettered to something that you think is imposed upon you from the outside, from some conventional notion of love and fidelity, chained to something you think someone else might think? Any shackles you think are on you have been fastened there by yourself, by your own mind. You are a lambent flame. Fire is free. What it is you have inside you is indomitable, and it is anything you want it to be, and it is yours alone."

"I am sorry," she said.

"No, you are not. You are relieved. You are making an apology where you should be giving thanks. I have merely told you what you already have always known in your heart. You can learn to live in the wild free space we both know you are inside. It is always the case that you are not who you think you are. And knowing that is a great gift and a secret."

"I know you are right. You seem to know everything. Do you know what I want right now?"

"Of course I do. You have so much as told me. And I saw it in your green eyes many moments ago. You understand the vast expanses of yourself, and your motherhood has taught you the greatest joy of it. You want to give yourself to me. And I am not talking about sex. You want to celebrate the indomitable nature of your will by negating it. You want to surrender everything to me and let me take you in ways you suspect you might have always wanted to be taken but never really knew that you would love as much as you are certain now that you would. You want me to show you all of those locations of your inner landscape and you want to explore each one of them. You want to be shown all the various women that you can be. You want to be made to fill each role in the harem and will know that all along you are just doing what you always wanted to do."

"This is unreal. I have never wanted anything more in my life. I want to be every woman that you have ever desired, yes. And I want to do all the things you have ever wanted any woman to do for you, even the dirty ones, especially the dirty ones. I want to know the hidden places inside of you too. Oh, God . . ."

"Not quite," I said.

"What do you mean?

"Never mind. What you have said and what I have shown you are infinite. We cannot contain it in an afternoon or perhaps even in a lifetime. It is a thing of incomparable beauty. And it is something that two people can never really share. We have come as close to sharing it today as possible. It is that for which I came here and I need never ask any more of you. And you know from all that we have already discussed that you and I have already done all this. You have given me yourself in all the dirty and holy ways. You have done it in the only place that matters. And that is on the inside of you."

"But you have to give me something. I am aching. I have never wanted a man like this."

"Take off your clothes."

And with that she looked down and slowly stood up. She unbuttoned her blouse and slid it off of her shoulders. They were as sweet as the breath of morning and as lively as the song of the earliest birds. She put the blouse on the table and began to step out of her pants. It was like a change of the season, when the sun warms the fragrant and fertile earth and trees and herbs and flowers spring to life. She continued until she was before me, naked. She was the moon in all its phases, in the mild summer evening of a dream. All the celestial wonders of the firmament were in her form. The light that shone from her was a substitute for a sonata. Nature was in her every sinew and in each soft sound and in her scent, which was intoxicating.

"Thank you," I said. "You have paid me for my attentions. And you have given me more than you know. I am only heartened to know that perhaps I have given you something as well. Perhaps I have given you yourself, in a way. But now I must leave."

And that is what I did. When I returned to the prison, I told John that I had taken care of the bathroom plumbing and the kitchen wiring and had fixed the chair. I also told him that I had a cup of tea with Eva, and that she was still doing her best to make ends meet. It was tough on her, I told him, not having him around. But, I said, I was sure he would make it up to her. I smiled, but the smile was for me. I knew that no words, no gesture, no effort, no amount of love, could ever buy him even the unsettled calm which he had owned the day before.

There are, to these several tales, some postscripts. Victor Fuoco came to me one day soon after his speech in the mess hall. He calmly told me that he had figured out that I had to have been the one who had found the case that everyone had felt the need to read on that day, because I was the only one that was smart enough to have done that and to have set it up that way. He had not known about the rest of the plan. He told me that "it was all right" that I had done that. I spoke no words. But I did note to myself that had the issue not been the truth itself and had the action been some foul affront, this visit from him would have to have been calculated as one intended in a significantly more threatening nature. As it was, it was a loose and empty shell of such a thing.

John was struck by the piquant nature of all his subsequent visits from Eva and indeed by the whole of what was to be his remaining relationship with her. He was so touched by it that it commanded his attention and he could think of little else. He wrote a story about one visit, which very aptly described his newer and deeper ambivalences. And that story was published in a magazine. He also was to say many years later that Eva had claimed that during that visit I had tried to sleep with her, a comment that never merited a response. As they were never married, the eventual and fairly rapid dissolution of their relationship could not have been called a divorce. They parted amicably and shared the custody of the boy. And John almost immediately became enmeshed in a similar and more lasting relationship with a woman who was also a writer, one who was one of the three or four more esteemed authors in the literary genre that can only be called books about Native American fornicating.

Mubassir may have been correct in maintaining some reservations about the fact that the growth and success of the Muslim community in the prison had been generated from a single source. But not a single person at that final revelation had been more deeply affected by it than he had. As a matter of fact, afterward and because of it he made a point of reading this book you are now reading and had read the part about a kind of a Muslim Protestant Reformation. And after his release he became the charismatic leader of an anti-clerical Muslim mosque that grew so rapidly and spread so fast that it became a very significant sect in the United States and in Europe. It has the largest population of members who are ethnically not from the traditional Muslim lands. What prayers are said there are spoken in the language of the country where the congregation meets. And in the United States they often meet in mosques where people wear their shoes and which look a bit like high school auditoriums. It was the second instance and the second major world faith in which the primary Protestant saint, or the patron saint of Protestants, had originally been Satan.

And that is who I am and why I was not to be found by your author when he was in Hell, which is to where I am returned now and at the same time have returned him to you. And I returned for the simple and most obvious reason. And that is that every time I undertake such enterprises as these among the men, I am plagued by the distressing irony that it often seems that I am really doing the work of my empyreal counterpart. If you do not laugh at my departure, you will not long be a virgin.

TWEET MAN

I just had to celebrate myself. I assumed that every atom of me was good as belonging to me again. No longer had I the imposition of meekly observing what was happening to my body while it had been requisitioned and expended to some infernal purpose. The smell of my own breath, the sound of my own voice, the very beating of my heart . . . I was in love with it. After all of what had just happened, it was sublime just to be me, myself.

And I struggled to understand what could possibly have been the meaning of what had been revealed to me by what had been my demonic possession. It had changed me certainly. And it had given me incomparable insight into the bottomless source of power of any individual soul and into the infinite potential for each soul to be completely changed as if it were of no substance at all. I had seemed to be shown that the two were one and the same. That sameness was a critical element as well to another part of the vision, because in some way it seemed my infernal possessor had surmised correctly about the nature of the work he had been doing. What had entered me and had possessed me has attained some godly results, and that seemed to be much the same as being in the spirit of the Lord. I knew it would become clearer to me as I made progress on my journey, and I knew to expect another celestial visit soon. At this point, I was somewhat puzzled as to how I might apply this fifth insight to my life and to my stay in prison. I was less confused as to how it had changed my stay and my position in this place.

The collapse of the Muslim community at the prison was seen in some quarters as a religious victory for the Christians. My role in that event had also changed the way in which I had been seen in the prison. I had gone from being known as an inmate under the protection of the mafia guys who was also very down to earth for a college-educated man and who had kept his head down and treated everyone with respect and was respected in return, to being far too high profile for what is generally safe and is conducive to finishing out one's sentence peacefully. My understanding of my need to take a lower profile was perfectly consonant with the joy I felt at being back to myself, to act on my own thoughts and feelings. It was time to be utterly unaccompanied, and I took to reading and exercise and being alone with myself with a relish that was unconstrained. Fortunately, personal space in prison is a sacred right. The personal space that is granted in prison is a much larger space than it is in the world, physically extending to several body widths and spiritually lending itself to complete privacy. It was only ever violated by the very rare inmate aggression or by a guard. So it was easy for me get away from the other inmates simply as a matter of form. The hacks would be another matter. And one in particular had decided to take a very Christian interest in me.

In this part of Kentucky the local stores and outlets of the major American sporting goods retail corporations are known to sell winter gloves with six fingers. It is also said that for many of the locals tails are not just vestigial bones contained within the pelvis but are articulated appendages. Such understandings helped the inmates of this prison mentally and emotionally marshal themselves while under the armed authority of their government as staffed by the local men and women. Oddly, appendages became the favored metaphor for the cauldron of incest and inbreeding that was assumed to be part of the social fabric of this part of country. It was even said that tasting blood on her son's most tender appurtenance would be the most likely way by which a Manchester mother would be able to tell if her daughter had begun her cycle. Such light-hearted assumptions were shared right down the line of the count of all prisoners, from the bikers and white-collar criminals and the mafia men and the drug dealers and the Mexicans and the African Americans straight through to the bank robbers and the Native American cigarette smugglers and the nine-fingered Russian counterfeiter. Everyone and every group were self-assuredly able to look down upon the hacks and the caseworkers and the administrators based on these well-known facts. The accepted mythology regarding the whole penal system also encompassed all of these theories. Everyone knew that the entire prison industry in the United States, which was and is proportionally larger than that which was ever in Soviet Russia or of South Africa under apartheid, was and is a jobs and employment program for rural white Americans at the expense of the freedom of urban minorities. Only one small group of inmates did not understand their inherent superiority to the guards in this way. And that particular group personally knew the syrupy warmth of the summer and the cold-to-the-bone winter that could cover these mountains and shroud the equally hot and hard and dark and cold sources of precipitous human behavior that seemed to lurk within their brooding masses, and they knew it such a way that they only could know as neighbors, as men who need only to reflect for a second to understand the capacity that lay within each of the locals who staffed the prison.

So, when Chester the hack ambled up to me in my cell with that loose gait and those lanky limbs and his haircut that reflected a history in the military and looked at me with his odd, otherworldly eyes, I did not imagine for an instant that his wife had earned her sexual initiation at the hands of her uncle or that he and his cousin had been a bit too familiar with one another, or perhaps I did imagine that. But I certainly did not allow that to give me the impression that I might be able to dismiss him or look down upon him or to otherwise condescend to him. I too had a distant root or two in Appalachia and could never see the man without also seeing the mountains. It is not that he was not a comical figure in his own right. He was. He had what Luigi Pirandello had called the good fortune to have been born a character (from a book or a play or a movie) and his appearance had all the markings of central casting. He was of medium height and was gaunt and goofy and stoop-shouldered and had hair that was a color that one either did not notice or could not describe. His features stuck out on his thin frame like they had been drawn by a cartoonist. His larynx, his gray eyes, his big ears, his upper teeth, his elbows and knees and his very head seemed to be stuck haphazardly onto his comparatively too lean body. Looking at him made the inmates laugh with derision, even if that was almost entirely an inward laugh. In short, to me there was not a single thing about him that did not give me the same begrudging respect that I would give to a loose boulder perched over my head on a mountain climb.

As I had looked backwards into my past life, I realized that many of my problems arose from the fact that I had sweated through the fog with linguists and contenders. But I have learned that I could become happier, once I had learned the way of letting things be. I no longer have any arguments. I witness and wait. I looked upon Chester as if he were another part of these mountain forests, a crag or a bear or an oak. He was as natural as any man and for that reason he was worthy of my honest and curious apprehension and worthy of the affection I feel for all things upon which the sun and the rain may fall. I saw the world squarely and without judgment for my own sake more than for others. I also had less interest in neutral and inhibited people than I had in men and women more fully alive and dangerous, such as Chester. Those who beat the gong of revolt and renewal force me to stop and think about how it might be if I were to conspire with them. And I had found that such an approach enhanced and expanded my sense of self, which was where I now was most happy to be, to live, and from which to extend my grace.

I was also not unaware that, to the readers of this book and in particular to its most ardent believers, living in such a way was an object of wonder and emulation. I could not ignore that in so living I was both hearing and speaking with the voices of past and future generations of slaves and prostitutes and thieves and of the diseased and despairing. These beings and the stars and the grass are connected not by judgment and derision but by life and air and the positive forces of the womb and the earth and the seed of men. The voices of forbidden urges are still the call of life, and from them the veil must be removed. In my own connecting, I knew I should emulate and clarify and transfigure the way in which all of life interacts, even as I listened to Chester and especially then.

"I have a tweet," he said, "for you here."

"What is that?" I asked.

"You know how some people say they are followers of Jesus?" He continued, "Well, I actually do follow Jesus. I follow him on Twitter. So, I get these tweets. They come to me on my cell phone."

"And they come to you out of the air like that, literally over the roofs of the world?"

"Yes. Here is one right here," he said, and he read from the screen of his phone, "If God so clothe the grass of the field, which today is, and tomorrow is cast into the oven, shall he not much more clothe thee.' There you have it. What do you think?"

I was actually thinking, "Thank God for still speaking the King's English; the English of King James, specifically." But I said, "Is that all? There is not more?"

"It has to be limited to one hundred forty characters per tweet, per message. And spaces and numbers and letters and punctuation each count as a character, so it has to be short."

"That is barbaric. It yawps at you like that?"

"Yes. Whatever. So what do you think about that tweet about the grass?"

"I believe it means that all the divine mysteries of the stars in their journey are not greater than that of a leaf of grass," I said, and I could see from his face that I was finally giving him the type of answer for which he had come to me. "What is grass, anyway?" I continued. "How can anyone answer that any better than anyone else? We are all as the grass is, the handiwork of the Lord."

His smiling response elicited my customary ambivalent reaction. I was glad that I had given him that for which he had come, and that maybe he would now leave me alone. I was also concerned that I had given him what he had sought, and that maybe he would not leave me to myself. In either event, he was happy at this moment. I had done something that was good, I had supposed. I have learned to relish doing such things for the immediate return that occurs in the giving and not for what may come back to me from another person. There was a pause. It appeared as if he was about to turn to leave. I could see it in his eyes for a second. And then he looked more directly at me and in such a way that I knew that for some time in the future I was going to be asked to fill in for him all the blanks that inevitably lurked within one hundred and forty characters of any of the hermetic and mystical sayings of the peripatetic Nazarene. For this hack, I would have to be, and would be required to remain, his tweet man.

"Tell me more," he simply said.

"The grass itself is a child, as we are all God's children. We will all be cared for in the same way and need not fret beyond that fact. The grass lives in all climes and places and among all peoples. It is alive and in a way that shows the victory over death. As a matter of fact, it grows over the graves of the dead. My own old grandmother is dead now only two years, and there is grass growing over her relatively fresh cemetery plot. The grass is very dark to be coming from white hair of old grandmothers."

"You sure showed them Muslims," he said. And I could tell that this was his thanks, as he turned and walked away from me down the row of my cell block.

It is one thing to have the respect of the guards, but if a hack appears to have become your buddy you have a problem in prison. Whenever any incriminating piece of information about an inmate would become known to the administration, it always was then assumed to have been passed to a hack by an inmate. The guards are simply not a part of the prison social fabric, nor are they insightful enough to figure out things on their own. When they do learn something, every prisoner then considers which inmate might be talking to the guards about the matter. So as Chester left my cell I found myself vaguely hoping that no one would decide to tell the authorities about the liquor and drugs behind the plumbing access panel in the men's room of my cell block, or that no one would blow the whistle on Spike's jailhouse tattoo business, or that no one would reveal that the newly arrived pre-operative trans-sexual inmate was servicing Book and his followers on a regular basis. I had found that last fact curious in its own right for a few reasons, the first of which was that it raised the question of when is an inmate a man or a woman. The Bureau of Prisons and Book had reached different conclusions, the former just based on some adherence to form and the latter more spiritually based on what the inmate felt she was.

It was the very next day when Chester decided to show up again at my cell. It seemed that he was not really interested in much beyond his tweets and my interpretations. He read to me another one.

"Here," he said, "and, 'Leave thy gift before the altar, and go thy way; first be reconciled to thy brother and then come and offer thy gift,' it says. What does it mean?"

"It means that you cannot find God if you neglect your fellow man, and that you first must find God in your brother before you try to bypass your fellow man and go straight to the source. Whoever degrades another person also degrades God, and whatever is said or done goes always straight to God. In this way, it is clear that God is a democrat."

"God don't love no Democrats," he countered, "because they do not believe in him."

"But he believes in them. I think that is the point. He is as much in them as in anyone else. We are all divine, inside and out. We make holy all that we touch or all by which we are touched. Our hair or our thoughts or the smell of our body is as holy as a prayer or as a church. We piss miracles."

"Here," he said, "is another, 'Love your enemies, bless them that curse you, do good to them that hate you, and pray for them that despitefully use you, and persecute you.' What do you think of that?"

"Evil does not live alone. It is part of each of God's children and grows in us like the grass grows. It is natural. We cannot separate it from our divine selves. I know what it is to be evil, to do evil. And so do you, or anyone else. I have tied the knot of confrontation. I have lied and cheated and stolen and resented and begrudged. I have felt anger, lust, greed, guile malignance. I am the same as anyone else in that way, and in that way I am not less natural or no less divine. We are no less God's children than the wolf or the hawk or the snake or the hog."

"You're probably a Democrat too."

"As was Jesus, which is kind of the point."

"Maybe he is," he said, "because he sure dresses like one."

The sense of Jesus always being in the present tense struck me as it always has, even though here in the United States and in particular in this part of the country it is clear that he is one of the locals, one of the roughs, a world unto himself and for others, not standing above men or apart from them, no more or less modest. It was as if he had always been a neighbor here, eating and drinking and breeding, as disorderly and sensual as the locals who found him so. It is an approach that has never slipped my inward remark, but for which I have always then found I have an unavoidable sympathy.

"Basically as well, we are to be above good and evil, and withhold our judgment," I said. "I think that is called grace. We should stand apart from all the pulling and hauling, be compassionate, complacent, self-contained, and calm. We need to stay above arguments, stand tall, relax and take an interest in people but at the same time not judge them."

"You said that twice."

"I do that sometimes. Call it poetic license. The point is to approach it all with wonder and be amused. Watch what is going on, but do not get tangled up in it."

"You get all that from one hundred and forty characters?"

"I can get more than that from looking at a bean in its pod."

It happened later that day. Leaving the mess hall and turning into the first building, I went up the stairs to the landing on the second floor, where my cell block was located. There I was met by a small delegation of what could only be called the Manchester Prison Puerto Rican Debating Society. These seven or so men were part of that larger group, which seemed always to be in spirited verbal contest and in which the debate winners were apparently selected by the volume and speed of their speech. The men in this particular group were not interested in debate and they were not interested in teaching me about their culture or their music. They just wanted to punish me for having made their music go away. José, who was housed in the cell next to mine, stood in the front of them. It was his show. The others were just sort of his backup band. It seemed that the hacks had taken away his contraband digital music player. I lived next door, and the chief guard had been seen in my cell twice. It was no wonder the suspicion had fallen on me. My first advantage was that I had expected something like this to happen. Perhaps another advantage had been the expansive frame of mind in which I had often found myself as I had been playing my role of being Chester's tweet man.

José was stocky and strong and was built like a Dominican baseball player. Athletically, he had quick hands and good lateral movement. He was about twenty-five years old and had dark hair, skin and eyes. He was what my great-grandfather's generation might have called a quadroon. Despite his distinctly aquiline look, he had a certain warmth to him which was now noticeably absent. More than a couple of the members of his backup band were sporting jailhouse tattoos that had originated as drawings which I had been commissioned to make. And a few of them had a different kind of tattoo, that of a small dagger on the right hand just above the joint where the thumb meets the hand and below the wrist, or exactly to where the tip of one's own thumb would point when you might shake his hand. It was for this group the symbol of having once killed a man, a much subtler version of the teardrop below the eye favored by the bikers.

"You told them about my music," José accused me.

Few moments in my life were to have been as important as the next one. It was time for me to remain master of all of that which was in my control, which was only myself and to retain aplomb in the midst of all irrational things. I decided to feel as if I were in the ocean or in a stream, passive, receptive, silent, but not so much as to appear defiant or recalcitrant but flowing with them as part of them. I thought and perceived and reacted with a self-imposed balance and treated the affront as less meaningful than it was. I was as a tree or a raccoon in the way each such being might confront a storm or an accident or hunger or the night. I was natural. My personality was invisible. And I was sympathetic.

"They took your music? That is messed up. I am sorry that had to happen," I said. So far, the tone had not escalated. There was some shifting among the group. It was less poised for action.

"You been talking to that hack," he said.

"I know how important that music is to you. I know how much you liked to listen to it," I said.

I remembered that whoever walks a furlong without sympathy walks to his own funeral, dressed in a shroud. There was more shifting. Some of the guys with the tattoos started to look around. José was now operating outside of his plan. He began to cast about for what to do or say.

"You were friends with Little Philly Ray, and they sent him away," he said.

"I miss Philly," I said. "He was a funny guy. Wasn't he?" And then I ventured a smile. And that did it. José gave me a quick dismissive look, and they all turned to face each other and to conduct the remainder of their debate society meeting in animated Spanish. I walked to my cell. I also knew that I could not stay there as much as I had hoped to do earlier. If I was going to receive calls from Chester the hack, I would be better off doing it when I was in the company of other inmates who would witness the conversations and who would be able to vouch for me later and, more importantly, whose presence would largely deflect the scrutiny applied to a guard visiting an inmate alone in his cell. I made a point to be in the library during almost all of my free time and was often with my friend John, who was now rather preoccupied and who also was giving me some extra personal space. Or I would be with a lot of the white-collar criminals who tended to frequent the library, either to research their own appeals or to be where the books and each other were. José found me there the next day, in order to apologize. My friends from the Puerto Rican Debating Society had found their informer.

Chester also found me in the library the next day and he had to address me in front of John and in front of Georgi, the nine-fingered Russian counterfeiter. Georgi was only nominally from Russia. He had been born in Odessa, in the Ukraine. Of all the types of criminals that populated the minimum-security prison at Manchester, the counterfeiters were my favorite. They always had an air about them that was somewhat debonair and sophisticated. They had savoir faire and were a bit like fictional British secret agents, in that they were worldly wise but they also had a flair for the mechanical and the practical and the physical. I also found it interesting that the only other counterfeiter in the joint at that time was an Armenian. It was as if that part of the world along the Black Sea, because it was such ancient crossroads, was a breeding ground for men who would say, as Georgi so often did, "If some government can make it, so can I." What Georgi did after he had witnessed this particular visit from Chester was to ask me a question about how much I had charged per hour when I had consulted or advised on the outside, and when I told him it could be as much as a few hundred dollars per hour, he said, "That is not much. I could make sixteen hundred dollars every two seconds."

Georgi and John had been my cover. They were seen to have been present during the visit from the guard. And to a certain extent I had been temporarily immunized from suspicion by the positive outcome of my experience with the Puerto Rican Debating Society, that experience having been subject to much spirited and rapid debate. And there was also my association with Big Frank and the organized crime members, which prevented suspicion from too quickly settling on me. I felt a bit better about how this visit might have been seen. Chester had a question about another tweet.

"Here is one. 'He that receiveth you receiveth me, and he that receiveth me receiveth him that sent me.' What about that one?" Chester asked.

"It means that the kernel of all creation is love, and that all the men that were ever born are my brothers and all the women ever born are my sisters and lovers. Whoever degrades another degrades each of us, and whatever is said or done returns at last to one's self, and also whatever you do or say comes back to you. It is the god that is in you and in others to whom you must look first," I answered.

Some readers know that these were not really my own thoughts but have been the thoughts of all men and all women of all lands. They enclose all things. They are not a riddle. They do not need to come from a book. They have not originated with me. They spring from the sod and the sand and the springy moss in the spot where your footfall has lifted. They are as close or as distant as they always have been. I was full and complete in conveying these to this man.

"Here," he said, "is another. 'For with that judgment ye judge, ye shall be judged: and with that measure ye mete, ye shall be measured.' Is that the same?"

"Please consider," I said, "that maybe you might want to write this next part down, or memorize it. It might not hurt to hold it in your mind or hold it on a piece of paper in your pocket as you go about your life and your work here in the prison. It is as much for you personally as it is for any man: What is commonest and cheapest and nearest and easiest is me (and is you too), me taking chances in giving to life and to others generously, spending myself freely among women and men for vast returns, preparing myself to do good and to positively relate to each person I encounter, not asking any god to endorse my compassion, but scattering it freely forever."

I could see that he was taking it in but that it chafed him a little bit. It may have been that he did not like having the audience and it may have been that he did not like the backspin I was putting onto my return. It was also possible that he did not like my tone or perhaps it was the substance of what I had to say that perturbed him. It was also quite possible that he had heard of this book you are reading or had known someone who had read it and that he was resentful of how he had been portrayed in it. He sort of just turned and walked away. And I knew enough about him to know that anything about him that he took the effort to hide was not a thing that was normative even in the slightest degree.

My next notice came to me in the weight room. The weight room was not a place in which to loiter in prison, at least not for me. It was where the crudest of the vilest went to hang out and where the worst came out in them. I had ventured into the weight room early on in my bit but only because that was where the boxing speed bag was. I had boxed as an amateur in my youth and I had always loved the sound and feel of making that teardrop-shaped bag bounce to that marvelous martial rhythm between my fists and the small round ceiling that surrounds the swivel from which the bag hangs. And it had always been relaxing for me in a curiously intellectual way. I also liked that it trained my reaction time and my hand speed. I felt those to be much more important than brute strength. It was also a great aerobic workout for the upper body.

I might as well have walked into that weight room and told everyone I thought they were stinking morons. They hated the sound. Apparently, the incoherent exhortations and the inarticulate grunts and snorts that these men exchanged were as much or more important to their apparently homoerotic preening and prancing as was actually working hard to be stronger. The sound of another way to get into shape was not something for which they had much respect. I found that I had to become the personal keeper of the speed bag, taking it down and storing it in my cell, because it would regularly get shanked, stabbed, if I left it to defend itself. I once even decided that I might gain some freedom from harassment if I announced to all of them that I would quit hitting it if any one of them could make the bag sing the way I could, with what they could not know was only apparent ease. The ensuing scenes were almost so comical as to imperil my position even more. These men were tight and ponderous in their upper bodies. And my being able to make the speed bag rhythmically fly was something that only looked easy; it had been the result of much practice. Several of them tried it, and each looked like an elephant at a keyboard, and they could not avoid thinking I had embarrassed them. At one point I had tried another direct approach.

I announced that I would only continue to work the speed bag if I could lift more weight than any of them, at a weight machine of my choosing. They tittered and slapped each other on the behinds in a way that often also occurs in the Classics Department library of an Ivy League college. They were bonding over their discovery, in this case of my supposed folly. That some middle-aged college-educated inmate of moderate build would think he could challenge the each of them to a weightlifting contest struck them in exactly the spot where they were most likely to fail to reflect upon all of the facts. I chose the leg extension weight machine, the one that requires very strong quadriceps muscles. Apparently, whatever the protocols are for looking good in a prison weight room, they do not include strengthening anything below the chest and shoulders and arms and back. I easily lifted more weight with the front of my thighs than they had ever considered. Suddenly all the boys' bonding stopped and they quickly became sullen and dour. I finished my working out on the speed bag, and that was the last time I did it. I knew I had done what no inmate should ever want to do; I had appeared to win a contest. I quit because I preferred that the bag be the only thing that had a chance of getting shanked.

My unwanted and subsequent return to the weight room came at the request of Big Frank, who had been losing weight and had decided that he should build some muscle mass in order to take the opportunity of having been in prison and in order to improve his health. He selected one of the guys named Tony and me to work out with him. During that time he also recruited each of us to possibly join him in what he and his comrades always called "our thing." For this Tony, who was a made man in Boston, it merely meant a transfer to Brooklyn, New York. That would have been harder than it may have appeared. He would more or less have to start over again, but at least Tony was already part of the same general program. For me to have become a member of their organization would have required me to demonstrate that I had been committed. I would have to kill in order to prove I was willing to be a part of it all and to lock myself in as being as clearly in danger of serious prosecution as any of the rest of them. I was able to resist this attractive prospect as well as whatever the many other charms were in being a mafia man. I politely declined the offer. But what concerned me in all of this was the change that I had seen in Frank.

My own prosecution had been somewhat publicized, and it was clear that what had been one of the things that had led to my conviction had been that it had not ever even occurred to me to make a deal or to cooperate with the prosecution. In retrospect, I had been quite stupid in a way. The more sophisticated criminals were my friends who had testified against me in exchange for immunity from prosecution. But in another way, I preferred to have been the one who took the full weight of the government prosecution rather than to have been one of the ones who simply had turned on his friends. It was a curious thing. And it was not about friendship. It was about the way I saw myself.

During one of these first few sessions of lifting weights with Big Frank and one of the guys named Tony it became apparent that Frank was no longer sure that I had not cooperated with the government in some other related prosecution. At one point he said to me that he thought it would have been all right if I had provided information to the prosecution in order to help them with another case against someone else, as long as that someone else had deserved it. The irony of his statement was not lost on me, and it was just as likely for him to have been sincere as it was for him to say that the Brooklyn mafia families would begin to recruit for new members in Sweden or in Norway. My integrity had been questioned and in the context of my being offered a job. It was actually a brilliant piece of game theory. Frank had raised the stakes and had called my bet. He was much more likely in such a case to learn what he wanted to know.

My integrity had been called into question at the very place in which it had first served to preserve me in this baleful place, and at the foundation of my protection. If that had not been concern enough, Chester's next visit again occurred in my cell only this time it was after the last evening count and during lights out. It was clearly suspicious to any and every inmate and it was a violation of protocol. A night visit from a hack could only be an action to accompany a breach of security. Such visits only happened when information was sought in a way that was sensitive to time passing as in an emergency or in a disciplinary action, or when the inmate himself was being visited to be taken away. When I saw him appear in my cell after midnight I had assumed it was because I was going to be hauled off to solitary confinement on some manufactured complaint. I assumed that he felt that I had crossed him at our last meeting, and was about to make me pay for it. But he just got out his cell phone and went right back to asking me about his tweets.

"Here is one," he said, "that I will read to you. 'Naked ye clothed me: I was sick and ye visited me: I was in prison and ye came unto me.' What about that part about prison?"

"It means you might want to examine how you conduct your job here," I said as gently and as softly as possible. "It means that you are to be judged by how you treat the least among the people of your life. It is not whether you go to church or pray or whatever. What will matter in the judgment of your life will be how you have treated me and how you have treated these other men in your care at this prison. Wherever a prisoner walks, there you walk, and wherever you walk, there walks your god."

The blankness that was his most obvious characteristic faded for a bit, and he became more attentive of me, as he said, "You and me don't have any problem."

"I know," I said. "And most inmates here do not have a problem with you. But there are a few men in this prison who for some reason have an irrational fear of you. Perhaps you might want to think about that, in the context of what you have learned about this tweet."

"They can all go piss up a rope, for all I care, the bastards."

These mountains in this part of the North American continent cannot help but evoke their various bones. These peaks appear sometimes like reclining figures, and under those green ridges there seem to be spines. And the stark and unbreakable part of their stone interior sometimes peeks through the trees like a broken bone. There is also a dark spiritual rigidity that the mountains suggest. And even a casual glance at the deep hollows in the heights of the mountains reveals distant and detached and distinctly unsociable locations that positively have provided men the discretion that they personally lacked as they had dealt death to another man and had left those carcasses to bleach in the wind and sun and rain, never to be found. These mountains were surely about bones.

The hardened interior of my new good friend was about to be showing itself a bit more. There was a flash of flint in his eye as he swiftly crossed the space between us and twisted my arm behind my back, holding his leather- covered lead blackjack to my jawbone.

"I own you," he whispered harshly into the side of my head. "I fucking own you. Never forget that." Then he just as swiftly let me go. And before he left he turned quickly as he stepped out, to say one more thing, "God bless you."

The sanguine nobility of any individual can be proven by his unconstraint. Heroism can be a kind of negative capability that allows a person to walk at ease through and out of that custom or authority that suits him not. Admittedly, this poses a greater difficulty in a place where the constraints are robust and numerous and are assiduously and muscularly enforced. In a way, such buoyance is even more precious and substantial where and when it is arrived at with some difficulty and some risk. A design was being born inside of me.

My friend, John, made a point to sit next to me at lunch the next day and inquired about my previous night's visit. Every other inmate was keeping at a good distance. John told me he had expected that I would not have been among the general population in the morning and that he figured that I would likely have been thrown into the hole. The mention of solitary confinement gave me a very strong feeling that sprung not from any apprehension of the loneliness and fear that might accompany being locked for a time in a cell behind the razor wire of the larger prison next door, but from something close to the opposite. I told John that the visit had been just another Bible study class. He gave me his wry look and smiled.

"Yeah, I heard some of that in the library the other day," he said. "The two of you make an interesting pair, the moron and the savant."

"There is an indescribable freshness and unconsciousness about an illiterate person that humbles and mocks the power of even the noblest expressive genius," I said.

"In Chester's case, you would be talking about his badge and his blackjack," he said, adding, "and I have heard those words before. Why are you telling him all that stuff?"

"Mostly because I believe it," I said, "and because I try to live it. I cannot help but embrace him and anyone else as part of my celebration of myself. This approach may also have a usefulness in this situation that goes beyond its only true value, which is its value to me. In fact, it may have saved me recently when I had been invited to an impromptu meeting of a subcommittee of the Puerto Rican Debating Society. But I really just try to be that way all the time."

"Okay, Christian, but I never could get myself to grasp the embracing celebration of all that is life and the world and other people. My feelings are too mixed."

"And that is the point, I believe. A wise and witty shaman with an antique temperament once looked directly into me with his sallow eyes and told me that a celebration is also a lamentation. We must love all other men and women and life and the world for many reasons but the primary purpose might be that we really hold all these things in contempt. The true miracle of it all begins and ends with our own senses and our own heart and mind. Or at least that is where our understanding of it ends, and that is all of the world that we are able to purely cherish. All that is beyond that, beyond ourselves, is lamentable, so we must love it and celebrate it because it is dreadful. I would say that we must honor the sublimity of our contempt by rising above it, but that verb combination is far less expressive than what I really mean. Our contempt is love."

"Well, I suppose it is not indifference, at least," he said. "I am sure that your Bible study friend does not quite see it that way."

"Not that he knows," I said. "But it is there. And maybe you can call it his God."

The next time I saw Chester I was again sitting alone in the mess hall at dinner that same day, the day following his last visit. He was walking his rounds while we all ate and he had a weird gleam to his gait. It was a little too crisp and sharp to have been indicative of his normal mood. No inmate ever addressed a hack in such a setting, and something was clearly up in him. But at that moment I loved him as I loved the earth, and my judgment fell all around him not as judgment but as the sun falling around a helpless thing. In my softest and most sympathetic tone and in a *sotto voce* that only he could hear I gently addressed him.

"Chester, do you have any more tweets to show me?" I asked. And no one else heard me. But the substance of what I said stopped him in his rounds. He noted specifically that I had said that he had shown an inmate a cell phone, which was a violation of the set of regulations he had to follow. He did not want anyone to hear that.

He quickly walked right up to me and stood over me. It was his silent rejoinder and no one could be confused by what it meant. I felt compelled by compassion to speak again. The cleanest expression is that which finds no sphere worthy of itself and then makes one. In the same sympathetic tone with which I had addressed José and his friends, I again spoke.

"You shall no longer take things at second or third hand nor look through the eyes of the dead nor feed on the specters in books. There was never any more inception than there is now, nor any more youth or age than there is now; and will never be any more perfection than there is now, nor any more Heaven or Hell than there is now. You stand in the moment before, during, and after the creation and the judgment."

"Quit while you are ahead, dead man," he muttered to me under his breath.

"I also say it is good to fall," I practically whispered. "Battles are lost in the same spirit in which they are won. I sound triumphal drums for the fallen dead."

"You had better not take the Lord's name in vain," he snarled.

"Believe in the flesh and the appetites. Seeing, hearing, and feeling are the true miracles, and each part of us is a miracle. I am divine, inside and out. I make holy whatever I touch or whatever touches me. The scent from my armpits is holier than any prayers. My heart and my mind are more of a church than any building either of us has ever seen, and they are also more divine than your good book. The effusions of my body are closer to God than any of the words you have shown me," I said as I stopped, and then I finally spoke in normal speaking tone, one that could be heard by more than just the two of us. "If there is any other thing that is worthy of my worship that thing is you. You are divine, as is any other man in this room."

And that was it. He was on me suddenly and with the same savage alacrity with which he had privately penetrated the serenity of a few selected inmates previously, with the identical swift brutality with which he had once dispatched an old man who may or may not have been his father up in one of those high mountain hollows, and with the same pitiless eagerness with which he had violated his fourteen-year-old cousin who had once snuck out of her own horrible trailer home in order to express her nascent sense of independence and to attend a party and get drunk where he and his friends had been more or less waiting. I could not raise a hand to my own defense, and no other inmate would attempt to pull him off of me. I had to engage my love of humanity and above all the innermost reaches of my deepest self in order to passively withstand the blows that rained down on me for the minute and a half that it took the other hacks to arrive and to wrench him away from me. I took hard fists to my ribs and back, but mostly I felt the warmth and pain of being alive. I was being tossed in the sea surf, being buffeted against the beach and all times feeling the sea's urge and surge, the procreant power of the world. Faintly, almost as in the distance and mixed in with the sound of these particular breaking waves, I could hear the faint utterings of the same phrase over and over. It was Chester. He was saying, "God bless you," with every blow. And then it ended.

Almost every trial, hearing or appeal that I have ever witnessed has been a foregone conclusion. It is far too easy for a judge or any other person to form an impression and far too difficult for that person to then decide that he or she has been wrong. There was to be a hearing on this incident, and the outcome could never have been held to have been in doubt. Chester would have to go away. He would receive some notice in his file and on his employment record and he would be transferred to another facility and likely to a prison with a higher security level. For him in particular that would present even odds that he might become maimed or even killed. The bright glint of his hardened bones would shine through a bit too much among those men who had so little left to lose. I too would have to go away at least for a while. I had literally done nothing wrong. There was no justifiable reason for any punishment to be meted out to me. There just simply had to be a balance. If Chester had to go, some token of punishment for me also had to be given; no incident could ever simply just be considered to be, or shown to be, a self-contained malfeasance by any prison personnel. After all, we inmates all were already guilty.

I was called into the office of the warden. There with me sat the warden, his assistant, the caseworker in charge of the conduct of my incarceration, the lieutenant of the guards, who still very much had the power to assume the color of a rutabaga, and Chester. Nothing would be said in front of me about Chester's reassignment, but it was written on his face and signaled in his posture. This hearing would be about me. I looked at the whole process as if I were in the room and also as if I were watching the scene on television, with a side-curved head, curious as to what would come next.

The warden stated that we were there to decide what to do about the incident in which I had provoked one of his guards to attack me. It was made clear that they had already decided that the reason the attack had been provoked was that I had profaned the sacred, that I had in some way blasphemed. I was most interested in reaching the outcome of this meeting but on this point I could only be aware that I had the power to make every word draw blood. I pointed out that in the United States of America we are the race of races, we are the faith of all faiths, that each among us is an equable man and that we govern ourselves with a steadfast refusal to enter into arguments about God. There was a reason that the amendment to our Constitution that prevented me from being punished for such a reason was listed as the First Amendment, because it was paramount that no government entity could punish a man for his opinion on faith; not even a prison acting against a prisoner may do so.

I stopped them all for a moment with that observation. I could see that the lieutenant was not taking this well, even though he had not understood it. The warden glanced at his assistant, and she gave him a discreet look which more or less showed a concern about the truth of what I had said. The hearing had more or less been brought to a halt. Outside the prison, soaring on an updraft over the sunny southern side of an Appalachian ridge, a North American red-tailed hawk swooped on swift loop. He accused me of loitering and gabbing. I too am not tamed.

"And as to you, corpse," I said directly and gently to Chester, "I think you are good manure. But that does not offend me. I smell the roses that will grow from you."

He quickly shifted in his seat. His eyes flashed. The lieutenant looked at me and was confused. The assistant warden looked at me in a way that was more knowing. She had a sense that I was letting them all off the hook for trying to punish me on grounds that might leave an opening for me to cause trouble about it. The warden was thinking he should be relieved. And I was not quite finished.

"If you want me again," I said softly, "look for me under your boot soles. You will hardly know who I am or what I mean, but I shall be good health to you nevertheless and filter and fiber your blood. Failing to fetch me at first, keep encouraged; missing me one place, search another. I stop somewhere waiting for you."

The gavel came down on that.

Chester did not know it at that time, but he had also just received another tweet, saying, "Teaching them to observe all things whatsoever I have commanded you: and, lo, I am with you always even unto the end of the world."

The decision was rendered. I was to spend two months in the hole before I could be returned to the general population at the minimum- security prison. The lieutenant would take me directly to a solitary cell inside the bigger facility, and there I would stay. I would eat, sleep, and be awake without the company of any other inmate or guard. I could have books brought to me from the prison's limited collection. Even among those books would be a few I could happily read and re-read and from which I would distill some difficult pleasures. But the greater pleasure would be in being alone with myself, with simply being me.

There are in each of us deeper selves. When one of us has not been caught after having done something too bold or risky, we will get into the car or go to our own room and we will say to ourselves, often quite out loud, "I got away with that one." That self to whom we are speaking is not one we ever show to others, or do so only at our own peril. It is perhaps our deepest self, and it is unrestrained. We are most at home with that self.

In that place, on my first night in the hole, I was briefly visited again by my divinely striking Jesus, who asked me in her ethereal voice what I thought were the divine insights that had been part of my spiritual sojourn up to this point. I gave her my best approximation of each of the six, about the holiness of skepticism, about the sacred value of play and friendship, the blessed difficulty of living a life of faith in the world, something I was not quite sure of which related to what I knew about Hell and its inhabitants, the importance of revering the bottomless possibility that lies inside each of us, and the grace of embracing all and every one and every thing and doing so for what may seem to be counterintuitive reasons. She stopped well short of congratulating me. She told me that each of the twelve disciples of truth was much larger and more complex than I had noticed about the first six and that they were all deeper in context and that each of the revelations were linked to one another. She also said that my instinct about my possession might have been correct in that each of the dozen revelations were directly connected to her. And she said they were only understandable by coming to fully comprehend the final revelation, the twelfth one. And almost in passing she let it drop again that my very salvation was dependent upon my being able to grasp and to incorporate all of the insights. Her attitude was what might be called her "get behind me" demeanor. It was far less gentle than it had been when I had seen her previously in the video.

I noticed that she was wearing a charcoal-gray, long-sleeve, open-front sweater over a white smock top, and a pair of matching charcoal gray slacks. She was also wearing a triple strand pearl necklace and a pair of designer black sandals. There were many reasons that I would always want to see her again, and this was just another one of them, despite her firm deportment.

Then she very sternly said that the next six disciples of the divine truth would be far more difficult for me to grasp, as they would not be so direct but would depend upon my powers of observation. She also said that I would again have to confront paradox since the second half of the insights would be more about who it is we really are on the inside even though I would learn them through observation. The next one, the seventh one, in particular would only involve me peripherally, so she said I had better pay close attention. She told me that first six had set the foundation for being my able to perform the skillful analysis that would be required for me to extract each of the next six insights from their varied contexts. I was not looking forward to this prospect. I had been to Hell and back and more for these understandings and I was thinking I might like to bail out.

"And do not think to quit this journey," she commandingly intoned.

"I know I will enjoy being alone. And all this interacting is tiring. And now you are telling me that I will have to pay closer attention," I sighed.

"That is exactly what I am telling you. You will have the next two months in here to rest up and be revived, and to contemplate. Keep on the lookout when you are returned to the general population. You will have to be observant in order to succeed in the second half of your pilgrimage. I hope you do not think there is such a thing as 'halfway' when it comes to the divine or to salvation or damnation. I

am telling you this much. Do not even think to set aside this book."
And then she left me alone.

I relished those sixty days in the hole. It was enough. I was
enough ... the smoke of my own breath, my respiration and inspiration, the beating of my own heart, sound of my own voice, the
passing of blood and air through my own lungs.

BUCKEYE

The symbol of the state of Ohio is the buckeye. I have never been exactly sure what a buckeye is. Perhaps it is a nut or a seed. I do know that I have had considerable experience with them, almost entirely when I was a boy. My friends and I used to whip them at one another. One never just threw a buckeye. They had to be whipped. It was all in the arm motion. We also whipped crab apples at one another and we whipped them both in the context of the inherently martial games we played in the fields and yards and woods, whether we were playing the game we called cowboys and Indians, or if we were driving the Nazis out of the those western Pennsylvania forests, or even if we had scheduled a battle with the boys from the next neighborhood over. Buckeyes were better to whip than crab apples and they came in two different states, with husks and without husks. They flew better without the husks, as the inner nut or whatever was hard and smooth and dark brown with a beige patch and it fit perfectly in a boy's hand. They stung where they hit. There was a certain romance to the husked ones even though they did not fly as well and were not as easily held. The husks were green and rough and covered with tough spikes. Basically it was easier and better to whip the husked buckeyes and they hurt more when they hit a boy where he was clothed. But the husk had a specific effect when it happened to hit on the skin. Buckeyes, husked or not, were indestructible. They could be seen where they had fallen on the roads, uncrushed by car tires.

"You are not comparing me to the buckeye in that damn book of yours, are you?" asked Dwayne Abram, who always had a way of saying what he thought or saw or felt or was, or of simply being those things. "Man, Christian, that is just corny," he added.

I knew a man in prison whose sobriquet was Psycho and another whose nickname was Maniac. Both were my friends. Maniac's real name was Bobby Gela. Dwayne Abram was Psycho. Maniac was a working class white man in his early twenties who was loosely associated with the biker group in prison but who was really just a car thief and a young man who loved machines. His spirit and his forehead each had a slanted shine to it that just plain unsettled people. Psycho was much harder to describe. He was a man of African American descent, thirty years old, who had grown up entirely among rural white people in eastern Ohio. He was soulful and expressive but very unassuming and every inch a creature of the countryside. Maniac had once described a car chase to me, in which he had escaped from the police and he had told me about how he had gone speeding into a certain intersection in Pittsburgh with which I was familiar. I could easily picture how his car had sped down the hill on Marshall Avenue and had hit the level spot of Brighton Road as if it had been a ramp and how his car then had literally taken flight for a few dozen yards in the heart of a city neighborhood. Psycho liked to talk about deer hunting and football and fishing. Maniac had never killed a man but he had it in him to do such a thing. If he were to have ever done it, one would have a very difficult time ascribing any reason or motivation to it. Psycho was one of the men I knew in prison who actually had killed a man or so. He had done so as a practical matter as a part of his employment as a hit man for the mafia in Youngstown.

I would have let Psycho babysit my children. He was just that way. Maniac scared me. I was always wary of him. He was crazy.

I entered prison as had been required by my understanding of the best way to survive, by keeping to myself and not drawing any notice and by not forming any connections. My situation became quite different not long after that. It was true that at one point I had become a bit too high profile. My stint in solitary confinement then had lowered my visibility somewhat. I was not so much concerned about being rather well known and it has very a little to do with this story. The larger and more substantive change that occurred since I had first been incarcerated was that a significant number of inmates had learned to trust me. My efforts in helping Spike with his custody and divorce issues had become known. So men would then come to me with their legal issues and their prison paperwork and appeals. Not only had I not continued maintaining the standard of keeping to myself, others were not doing so with me. My personal image of the place had become quite detailed. I no longer had the temporary and infernal power to hear the soft undersong of prison, the sound of the crying of grown men, hard men. But I constantly felt the recondite and ineffable spiritual distress of knowing too well or perhaps knowing too much about too many of those men. It gave me a shrewd perspective from which to tell this, his story.

And somehow I knew from my dream that it seemed to have been decided that my spiritual journey through prison was about to take a turn. Events were now taking place from which I was to be required to learn more by observing than by participating. I had directly received the foundation of an understanding of the first six revelations and I was now to stand on that foundation as I was to learn the others, as if they were the parables of the New Testament. I would have to pay close attention to those around me, to those outside of prison but affected by it, to those parts of my past evoked by prison, and even to my prison dreams and visions. In this and in other ways, it was not unlike learning from life. And at this point, I was to learn from Psycho.

The deer-hunting rifle was at the core of the case against Psycho. It was the only thing that the detectives found when they came to search his house and arrest him. He had kept no guns or knives or any other weapons. There was literally no evidence of his work for the Italian mob in nearby Youngstown. The gun was for deer hunting, not for men. The prosecution had fashioned a case against him for conspiracy, based upon observation and testimony. It was a relatively flimsy case, but the presence of a gun automatically brought an additional five-year mandatory minimum to the possible sentence. As most federal crimes require mandatory sentences, there could be no room for judicial modification of the sentence at all. No judge could stop and consider that a thirty-aught-six rifle with a scope was for hunting deer and did not pertain to a conspiracy to commit any crime. It was simply considered to be a gun. And it meant five more years. Psycho entered a plea and took that five-year sentence. It was another small quirk of injustice that he had to serve a sentence for a charge that usually must be based upon another conviction and that he had pled guilty to no such conviction. It was similar to the consideration that the gun had not been used in any crime. He had simply gone to prison for five years for owning a deer-hunting rifle.

Words will wander and it is often difficult to speak an issue home. In this case the word, injustice, makes almost no sense. The five years that Psycho was to serve were small payment for the taking of life, and there can be no doubt that the prosecution would have done all it could to stretch whatever charges it might have made stick, in order to get to the point at which it felt the larger crimes were being punished. The injustice was still manifest in the sense that various prosecuting attorneys have also managed to accomplish exactly this sort of stretching in cases where their motivations were based solely on the desire to increase the total time of all the sentences that would appear on their employment and promotion records and where the defendant had been entirely innocent. None of these concerns ever troubled Psycho. He simply understood that a man went about his life and that sometimes he went to jail. He approached all of it with an equanimity that was spiritual in nature.

This must have been what had been seen in him by Gaetano Volpe, who had initially recruited him to work for the gang in Youngstown. Guy Volpe had a habit of taking his men out of town on hunting trips and other exercises that were unusual to the urban and criminal operations of his crew. Even though Youngstown is smaller than its not-too-distant neighbors of Cleveland and Pittsburgh, the organized crime of those larger cities has long been run by the mafia family in Youngstown. The Youngstown gang had to learn how to travel well early on in its development. Guy Volpe may have been a pioneer in what could be considered something along the lines of a corporate retreat for wise guys. Volpe liked to get his men out and alone as a group in order to see each of them more clearly and to judge how they responded to one another and to cement their organization as a crew within the larger family. One of the issues that would often arise on these excursions was the fact that the hunting guides and the motel operators or any of the other regular citizens with whom they might come into contact might witness something or other that they had never seen before and should not have seen but which might commonly occur within the group dynamic of his team.

The young black hunting guide had immediately drawn the attention of the observant Volpe, if only at first because it was unusual to find a person of color working at a hunting camp near the game lands east of Rogers, Ohio. The fact that Psycho had never reacted to any of the things that happened when Volpe's crew had been together was so singular that Volpe had taken the unique step of scheduling a return trip to that same camp almost solely for the purpose of observing him. Each of these mob corporate retreats was held at a different place because too often a waitress or a maid would be compromised or a comment would slip, and that person who had come into too close a contact with the crew would then have to be offered a gift which implied a threat. Usually such a gift was cash and it came with the understanding that what had been witnessed by the citizen had been important enough to garner a significant effort on the part of Volpe to keep the incident under cover. It was always understood by the civilian that this significant effort could encompass a positive result in the case where there was cooperation or a negative outcome when the assistance could not be purchased. In any event, familiarity was to be avoided at all costs since it could too often lead to a misunderstanding. Return visits had never occurred, except this once.

Psycho had clearly kept his head during that first trip. He never once took notice of any of the comments or wild stories or of the rough way in which the individuals in Volpe's crew would occasionally manifest the workings of the group's internal hierarchies. He went about his job as if he were only there to do the work. He simply guided the hunts and managed the hunting cabin. In many ways he was more like a good soldier than the soldiers in Volpe's little legion.

There is a point in the imagination of a creative man when the wrong thing is correct almost simply because it is wrong. Guy Volpe had this imaginative faculty, and everything he knew told him that working with a black man who was an outsider in any way would cause a problem for him with his superiors. It simply could not be done, and the instant that such an enterprise might go wrong he would suffer for it. Even if it were to work out well, if anyone for whom he worked were to have known about it there would have been questions. Gaetano Volpe had not become the chief of his own crew at the relatively young age of thirty-five because he refused to think outside of the box. The singularity of the question, the very fact that the qualities he was sure he had been observing had appeared in the person of a rural Ohio black man of about thirty years old, is what appealed to him most. Psycho was also an excellent deer hunter. He had patience. And he suffered the jests and jabs of the men in the Volpe crew as equably and discreetly as he accepted their failures and mistakes in the hunt. With a complete lack of effort, Psycho had held the attention of the crew's chief.

At his foundation Psycho was entirely phlegmatic, but resting upon that base was a sort of country lightness, an outward humility and almost a lack of self-consciousness that his urban cousins would have called "cracker." It was really and simply a refusal to show that he took himself seriously in a way that shallow observers could inevitably not perceive. He also had a slightly high voice that had a little bit of a crack in it, not unlike a country music singer. There was no trace of urban African American dialect in his speech. He was of medium build and height and a slightly darker than medium color, and there was a slight Asiatic look to his face that is common among American black families who were first brought to the shores of South Carolina from Angola and who are known there as Gullah. Had this been explained to Psycho, it would have been the first time he had heard of it even though he had known that his family had immigrated to Ohio from South Carolina. That slightly eccentric look of his also made his fundamental character more difficult to detect by anyone not as perceptive as Guy Volpe, which is to say every other man on the trip.

Familiarity differs from unfamiliarity the way an electrical shunt is different from a complex electrical circuit. Current flows easily in both directions through a shunt. On the second trip to the hunting camp east of Rogers, Ohio, Psycho was exactly as he had been during the first trip and exactly as he would have been if the visitors had been businessmen from Cleveland or farmers from outside of Cambridge, Ohio. But the members of Volpe's crew had seen him before. They had witnessed his lack of interest in them and in some instinctive way they must have sensed the attention that their boss had paid to him. The jests and jabs became a little more pointed. After all, such things were always intended to get a little bit of a rise out of their objects. It was hallmark of every mafia soldier not to take notice of an insult from a superior and not to ever attempt to trade an offense. This was often tested. It was a part of the fabric of their social relations, insulting downward and never in the other direc-tion. It almost never extended beyond the outside of the boundary of the group. But these men in this crew on this second trip to the same camp felt a little bit familiar with their guide the next time they had seen him. And at least one of them had decided that it should have been simple and easy to get some kind of a reaction out of this black man from the rural part of the country.

At first there were questions about whether or not he liked country music. Then they would call him the black Elvis or the colored Johnny Cash. They asked him if he slept with his own cousins, the way that they thought his white neighbors had. They called him a cracker, a black cracker. They also commented upon all that they thought would normally draw a comment from a man of color who would have grown up in neighborhoods near their own. They asked him about white women. They let slip a racial epithet here and there. They disparaged African American celebrities. To all these things he either offered a polite answer or he stayed quiet when no polite answer was available. And when the nine millimeter hand gun came out and was laid on the table during the late-night poker game, he did not leave the room as would have been the reaction of most men who had been gun trained as he had. He stayed put at the side of the room, ready to get more food or more beer or to clean up. He did not even register a reaction when the gun was picked up and aimed at him by a drunken member of Volpe's crew, who said, "Maybe I should just shoot the eggplant and see if that gets a rise out of him."

Only a look from Guy Volpe had been required to put an end to that. In fact, Guy's forbearance during the preliminaries to the gun incident had been felt by his crew as much as they had felt, and had felt challenged by, the imperturbable nature of the object of their jests. They half- expected the game to be called short and were not surprised when it had been. Guy also looked at Psycho and inherently understood that he need not say anything to him or in any way highlight what had just happened. So it was only a *pro forma* exercise later when he approached Psycho with five one-hundred-dollar bills and handed them toward him and offered them to him "for the trouble."

"Weren't no trouble at all, Mr. Volpe. You know you don't have to pay me extra for just doing my job."

"Would you at some point mind doing another job here or there for me?" Guy asked.

"A man has got to work," Psycho answered.

The silent and discreet understanding that had existed from the very beginning between these two men was to become more express and explicit from that point forward. Volpe came to him with twenty thousand dollars and a contract on a Mexican drug dealer who had once been cooperative with the Youngstown organized crime family but who had since taken steps to not only declare his independence but to also challenge the family. A soldier from the Italian mob had gone missing from one of their crews that had operated in that area. He had run afoul of this newly independent group. The Mexican boss always kept his own crew around him and there would have been some difficulty for the Youngstown family in sending one of their regular exterminators to take care of the pest.

The Mexicans lived in a part of the black ghetto in Youngstown and mixed uneasily with those inhabitants, but they were more or less accustomed to seeing darker faces among their own. The drug dealer and his band of bodyguards even liked to go to a club on the third floor of an old warehouse in town that played salsa music and rhythm and blues music and had a mix of blacks and Latinos. In fact, some of the Mexicans preferred black women because it was felt that they would be less likely than a Latina girl to want to get into a serious relationship and then try to convert these men to the life of family and the church. The Mexican gang took very little notice when an African American waiter they had not seen before came to bus the empty glasses and bottles from their table. They simply patted him down before he was permitted to enter the group. They did not pay specific attention when he dropped one of the glasses and it broke. Even though they certainly noticed it, they just as surely did not react swiftly enough when he took that broken glass and rammed it forcefully into the throat of their boss and gave it a deep grind into his carotid artery and then added a twist and turned and walked surely and swiftly toward the window. Just as they were thinking that they should draw their guns in order to fire on him he had gracefully picked up a chair and had thrown it through the glass and leaped through the window to fall two flights and land on the pavement. He was around the corner and on his motorcycle before they even got to the window.

The swiftness, the ease and the lack of effort with which this goal had been accomplished had inured strongly to the benefit of Guy Volpe and had been worth much more to his career than the twenty thousand dollars he had paid. Notice had gone up the chain to the top of his organization. Guy was seen as having an ace in the hole, a way to get things done that was outside of the channels of normal operations. There was also some understanding that this card in the hole might be an ace of spades.

There had been an accountant in Pittsburgh who began to get jumpy when his wife decided to divorce him, and her actions seemed to reveal that perhaps he had told her a bit too much about his work for his friends in Youngstown. He placed a nervous call to the head of the organization, expecting and even asking that something permanent to be done to his wife. The answer was not as he expected and it was not offered through regular channels. The big boss reached down a level or two within his organization and had consulted Guy directly. When the accountant's tire went flat on the road home the next night, he was helped by a well-spoken and polite young black man who actually changed his tire. Had the accountant not been dressed in a suit, he would not have accepted the help at all. Had the helper who pulled over to assist him been Italian or even white, or had the young man not actually changed the tire, the accountant would have never turned his back on him for an instant. And he would have never felt the curious lack of pain followed by a fading out that accompanied having his skull penetrated by a tire iron. The wife got the message as well and moved to Hawaii.

The big boss also had a more personal problem that he also had brought to Guy Volpe. There had been a contract killer whom the boss had hired many years before, who had come from another city and who had recently begun to talk to federal prosecutors. Guy's boss knew this because he had a contact in the United States Attorney's office in that town. No one else knew it. The boss asked Guy to take care of it. The potential federal witness died of radiation poisoning within a few days of the meeting between Volpe and his boss. The story of a break-in at a cancer treatment center in Dayton, Ohio, had never made it into the newspapers. Little had been stolen, and none of it had been money or valuable equipment. All that had been taken had been a couple of what are called seeds. They are very small rods of a radioactive isotope, about the size of a tack, that give off radiation. They are kept in secure lead containers and are used in a process called brachytherapy, in which the seed is placed by catheter or some other means right next to a cancerous tumor. The radiation kills the tumor cells by altering their DNA structure. The treatment is only safe for the surrounding healthy cells if the seed is used topically near the tumor and only for a very short time. If a seed or two were to remain exposed to healthy cells for any length of time they could become cancerous themselves or would suffer from radiation poisoning.

The real trouble for Psycho only came later when a wise guy within the larger Youngstown organization but not in Volpe's crew was arrested and that person was someone related by blood to the head of the family. Volpe had already just been promoted, and whatever loyalty he felt to Psycho had been coopted by that promotion. Guy did not raise too much of an issue when it was decided that in order to save the relative who had been arrested they would make a deal and would give the authorities "Volpe's eggplant." The entire set-up was a violation of the mob's ethos. Soldiers who were arrested kept their mouths shut, fought their case and did their time if they lost. No one else was ever given over to the prosecution. But the mob's honor extended no further than the clear line drawn in a circle around the family. Outsiders did not count. In the final analysis, it had also been seen as another one of Guy's brilliant contrivances to have held in reserve, and to have made use of, a disposable asset such as Psycho. That there was also a certain amount of racism in this calculation was also undeniable.

This possibility had also not been entirely unforeseen by Volpe. He had discussed with Psycho what they both already instinctively knew, the need to keep absolutely free of evidence. They never talked on the phone. Guy would simply drive out to the country and discuss the jobs. None of the weapons used were to ever be kept. And the cash was never spent on anything extravagant. In fact, it was hardly spent on anything except an occasional normal expenditure such as food or clothes. The money Psycho earned from legal sources was then simply not spent on those same certain things and was allowed to accumulate. He had some money in his bank account, and there was some cash buried in the woods. There was nothing at all at his home to incriminate Psycho. It is just that no one had thought about the deer rifle.

The deer rifle was to have become a concern of mine, though. Psycho had not come to me with his case as had other men. In fact my career, as it were, as a legal advisor had become a sort of personal Jarndyce versus Jarndyce, only composed of numerous different cases. But despite this, I had sought out the work on Psycho's case. I had been told about it by someone else who had once read about it in the papers. And I had asked him about it after we had become friends. And we became friends only with some effort on my part. He had captured my attention by the way in which he was able to stand apart.

Skin color is the primary dividing line in prison. There may have been some minimum-security federal prison somewhere in the United States of America where white men had recently still been in the majority, but it could no longer be the case. Such a composition would harken back to the time when the federal government troubled itself only with crimes of a purely federal nature, banking crimes and counterfeiting and embezzlement and fraud and treason. Once the federal government had decided to get into the business of enforcing street-corner crimes such as the sale of illegal drugs, the rapid incarceration of poor urban men of color proceeded apace. A majority or significant minority African American population would simply take over the social operation within prison, within every prison. White prisoners subdivided along economic and social lines, and the mafia and the bikers would have been recognized as reigning groups within what may have once been the white majority, but after the shift they would simply be fiefdoms that the black majority would leave alone. The remainder of the white prisoners would be on their own. Black prisoner subdivision was more geographical or tribal, and within the majority black population a particular city's citizens would hold control.

The primary Manchester constituency consisted of African American men from Washington, DC. For some reason, black men from that city had taken over various prisons. There tended to be a combination of factors behind this, most of which arose from the fact that the city itself was black majority. The men from the District of Columbia were used to being in charge and not having to compete with white criminal organizations. This was often reflected in the sophistication with which some of those African American crime organizations had operated in Washington. Many of these groups were named for their neighborhoods, such as the H Street Crew, and they were quite advanced in the way that they paid pensions to the families of their incarcerated members, the way in which they hired difficult- to-prosecute juveniles to do their killing, and the way they recruited and paid auxiliary members whom they then placed into rookie classes at the police academy. These Washington gangs also had a reputation for exceptional brutality.

The African American community in this prison accepted Psycho but never really incorporated him. This was a circumstance which really had been of his own doing, and many of the ways in which these other black inmates set him apart and which seemed to be a consequence of his personality were really the result of his guile. These other men were a colorful and diverse group, comprising almost all elements of all the neighborhoods of Washington,

DC, from the well-off segments in the northwest of the city to the hard precincts of the southeast. The same was sort of true of the black population in general but with more being from the ghetto. But my eye had from the start been fixed on Psycho, and to me this vibrant and lively group of men became more or less of a backdrop, a setting for a remarkable person who quietly and unassumingly drew my attention. It was as if all these street warriors had faded into becoming the great host of Achaeans, who were merely the audience and the setting for an Ajax or a Nestor who would rise to address them or to lead them. Psycho differed from these men in those same ways. He was cut from a different and from a finer cloth. And there was no thread in it that was not genuine.

I was simply inspired to do what I could do for him. I had heard about his case and about the deer rifle. I felt confident that I could try to help him to get out of prison. Certain judges in different places in the country had been beginning to take a less strict approach to connecting a gun to an underlying crime. They may not have been able to exercise any discretion in the sentencing but they could interpret the intent of Congress and some were saying that Congress had actually intended that there essentially had to be a closer nexus between the gun and the crime. They were also beginning to look askance at cases where the gun crime had been the conviction and the underlying charge had been dropped or had not been part of the plea. In Ohio people like to hunt, and some of those people are judges. I had always made a point of talking to Psycho and to engaging him. He always dealt with me with the same country openness and simplicity with which he approached anyone else. But he knew I could see past that and that I had a sense for his intellectual strength and his character. He also knew that we both knew that I could never really be his friend. He was as much alone as any man could ever be, and the rest of us would always be at a distance from him, not so much due to his efforts but by the same kind of barrier that prevents different species of mammals from successfully mating with one another. I could see that the consideration that he gave me was attributable to my status, to the fact that I might be someone who could one day have some significant usefulness to him. His approach appeared to be like a rural brand of deference; almost as if this were three hundred years ago and I had been a minor noble. But he knew that I knew that that most of the respect that was elemental to his demeanor was attributable to his self-respect more than to me.

"You know that I can help you with your case," I said to him at one point.

"My case is over," he said, "and I am doing my time."

"What I am talking about will not cost you anything and it can't set you back. It can only help or it can fail to help," I said. "And I will do it for you."

"Why would you want to do that?"

"It is not that I want to help you," I said, "even though I really do want to help you. It is more that I can see that you are the last person who should be in here. You simply do not fit in here. And I would feel better about the world and about myself if I could do something that might help you get back to where I know you belong."

"Heck, you put that just about right. I don't want help and I have never needed it. It always kind of doesn't help, anyway. You know what I mean? I accept your motivation as being to make yourself feel better. I can deal with that."

"Thanks. What I am talking about is a simple motion to be filed in your case. It will simply state that your public defender was not competent enough to have given you the proper legal representation that is your right under the Fourth Amendment and that her advice to you was legally and inherently flawed because she did not understand the law of federal firearms sentencing and underlying crimes. I could draw it up fairly quickly. You would owe me nothing."

"I thought we already agreed on that. This would all be done for you."

So I talked to him about his case and how it was handled. I wrote the motion. It is technically not an appeal but was a collateral attack on his conviction. Such things are often filed by prisoners and are rarely granted. Largely this is an administrative and policy decision. The government likes its convictions to remain final. And if all the prisoners who had not received effective legal counsel were to be released and tried again, the criminal trial dockets in this country would quickly double. But I had to do this for Psycho, for myself. He dutifully accepted the motion I had drafted. I doubt that he ever filed it. And if he had filed it, it would not have received any ruling before it was already too late to do any good for him. The string of his life was held firmly in the hand of one of the Fates or it may have been that his destiny had already been set by his character.

I had maintained my spot as the only white player on a prison basketball team. I worked at it. I enjoyed it. I also liked defying the normative behaviors in ways that let me feel that I was making a mark on the place more than it was making a mark on me. And even if that could never strictly be true, I at least wanted to do more in that direction than others or more than I might have thought was possible. But my two-month stint in the hole had suspended that activity for too long. The next time I walked out onto the basketball court there was a different scene. The players on the team we were supposed to play against all walked toward me and stood in front of me at half court and told me that I was no longer going to be allowed to play. Everything that I understood or knew dictated that I walk away. There was nothing to be gained except at a cost. I had already been the only white prisoner to have played. But I figured that I still had some personal capital that I could spend. So I said that I did not think that it was fair and that I had been allowed to play before and that I failed to see that anything had changed. If there had been any change, I had improved the prison by effecting the removal of Chester. Then one of them suggested that we should just agree to let my own teammates decide.

I turned to look, and every one of them was backing away. Some even spoke to me and offered an excuse. I turned back to look at the other team and I had decided that I was going to make one more suggestion before I would eventually capitulate. I was going to suggest that I be allowed to play one-on-one against the other team's best player in order to settle the question. I would have surely lost the one-on-one game but I would have played. And that would have been my point. But as I was speaking I saw a change come over the faces of the players of the other team. It was as if some unseen force or uncanny being had whispered in their ears an inaudible spell that spread through them like a small weakening virus that settled in their knees. They gradually moved from casual defiance and disregard for me to actually half paying attention to what I was saying. And their body language changed. I could sense that something was now in front of them that had not been there before. It was very curious, and I could not take my eyes off of them. And then I heard it.

"I think maybe we ought to let the man play," said a country voice that was a little high in the male register and which had a slight crack in it, "and I will play on his team too."

No one else said a thing. I looked back, and the black men who were on my team had ceased their retreat and stood somewhere between my back and the edge of the basketball court. And Psycho stood behind them, just on the court.

"Have you ever even played this game?" I asked him.

"No," he said.

The game was so uneventful as to have been very noticeable. There were no celebrations, no trash talk, no attempts at dunking the ball through the basket, no egregious fouls by the defense, no arguing over calls that the volunteer referee made. It was not at all like a prison basketball game or even a game at any playground. My team played very poorly and almost as if they had all lost a step or two, so we lost the game by a large margin, even though our opponents also played unenthusiastically. And even though it had been the very definition of an uninteresting sporting contest, it had drawn a small crowd of spectators, and an inordinately large number of them had been white. One of the more interested spectators had been Stanley, my other black friend, who was from Washington, DC, and whose wound I had once helped stitch shut with dental floss and a leather needle.

"You need to talk to your Italian friends to see if they can protect Psycho," Stanley said to me after the game.

"I will do that," I said, as I instantly knew that my involvement had something directly to do with my being exposed to the seventh revelation, while at the same time I also understood what Stanley meant and why he had said that to me.

So, I went to Big Frank and did what I normally would not have wanted to do. I put myself in a position to owe him for a favor.

"I can't help you," he said, "because your friend belongs to our friends in Youngstown. Anything I might do would necessarily involve a negotiation with them. It would end up costing money. And it would take too long. Anyway, you ought to let these people settle it among themselves, the savages."

I began my odyssey to see if I could procure any help anywhere else. I went to Darko and Dave, the heads of the bikers. They had actually been the presidents of two rival motorcycle clubs, the Infidels and the the Elect. It had been almost ten years since there had been any blood spilled between those gangs, so it was possible for them to serve jointly as heads of their amalgamated group on the inside. Dave was low key and almost completely tattooed from head to toe and more. He would not hesitate to show you the scorpion he had inked onto his penis. He had a graying brown beard and was a bit fat and always wore a bandana and a vest and was in his forties. He was very good at leatherwork and liked to talk about how nice his Harley Davidson was. Darko was in his early thirties and was wiry and had stringy black hair down his back and a black moustache and a big nose. He was utterly terrifying in his appearance and demeanor in the way a white man can only be if he also happens to be Serbian. He said that he always repainted his motorcycles with a flat black paint, and of all the very worst calumnies and vituperations I had ever heard in my life I had heard from Darko, and they were always in reference to women.

I sketched the problem for them and asked them what they might require from me in order for me to procure their help.

"You can get on your knees and start sucking," Darko said.

"He's kidding," Dave said.

"The hell I am," Darko added. "If he is going to be a bitch for that nigger, he might as well do me too."

"Maybe I should leave," I said, "and thanks. I mean it. I don't expect anything. I appreciate your listening."

239

"I think we should take it on," Dave said, looking at Darko, "and what do you think, besides that you want to humiliate our friend here?"

"It'll be goddamn race war, is what it will be. And I am all for it. I'd be the first to make them watch me bash their kids' brains out before I cut them to bits. And that fuckin' Book, the big jig? I'd love to stick a garden weasel up his ass. But in here, they got the numbers and they are cowardly bastards. We would have to have it right out now or they would just pick us off over time. It would be damn race war," Darko said as he clenched his fists and spat on the ground.

"Hell, I'd like to do it just to get rid of the boredom," Dave answered, "and to get our guys back in shape. This may be a prison, but I can sense our guys getting soft in here. If you think about it tactically, all we would really have to do would be to take out your pal, Book, and a few of his top guys from DC, like that guy, Devantay, and the other one, G-Threat. It would take a few months for a new scum to rise to the top. In the meantime, they would be disorganized and fighting among themselves. We could have some peace around here."

"Yeah, maybe" Darko said, "but they get new guys coming in here all the time. It's a goddamn pipeline. It would only get worse. Sorry."

"So, what is your angle?" Dave asked me.

"I am not sure," I said. "It's just something I feel. Thanks, anyway." And I left, to go seek help from another source.

"It will cost you in blood. You know that. And you have to go first," is what toilet paper man told me. "You take out someone for us, and we will take one of them out for you."

I had gone to him because he had once come to me with his case and I had learned from it that he was a part of the Aryan Brotherhood, which was the context in which I had hoped to get some assistance from him. He had been sentenced to a five-year bit for the interstate transport of stolen goods. It was actually quite a heavy sentence for that crime, especially since the stolen object had been a bracelet worth only a few hundred dollars and which he had sent across state lines by Federal Express. "I hate the Postal Service," he had told me. I did not have to read too deeply into the papers to find out that the bracelet had been stolen in a robbery that involved a burglary out in the desert exurbs of Las Vegas, Nevada, in which the family had been at home at the time of the break-in and had been murdered. It was also clear that this method of operation had matched several other similar home burglaries in those areas and in which the gang seemed to not care at all whether or not they found the residents at home. They would just kill the ones that were there. I could not help but conjure up the sentimental image of past Christmas Eves at the pristine home of the toilet paper man family when he was a kid, with visions of sugar plums dancing in his head and in the heads of his three brothers, all of whom my reading revealed to be the four constituent elements of this particular gang.

I had been just that desperate to help my friend, Psycho. But I declined to continue the negotiations with this gentleman. I was fully aware even at the time of the inferred irony of the similarity between the sentences and cases of these two men, the one I had just asked for help and the one for whom I asked the help, would become a constant subject of exegesis and debate among the votaries and acolytes of this book. In fact, certain tracts would be and are and have been written on the subject. I am also aware that I have been unable to clear up these questions by clearly saying that there was no similarity at all, ironic or otherwise. Inferred or perceived irony where there is none is both more and less ironic than even unintended irony often is.

The next morning Psycho woke up well before the sun. He took his time in the shower and when he dressed he put on a long-sleeve sweat shirt underneath his long-sleeved khaki shirt and he put on a pair of sweat pants under his khaki pants. He also put on a pair of fingerless gloves and a stocking cap. He did all this even though it was a relatively warm Indian summer morning. He took two extra athletic socks out of his locker, placed one inside the other, dropped the locker's combination lock into the inner sock and placed the whole finished product in his pants pocket. I showed up at his cell just as he was finishing.

"You can't go with me. You know that. You cannot be a witness," he said, "because that would put you on the spot with everyone, hacks and inmates both."

"Why did you do it?" I asked.

"It was the right thing."

"I know you did not do it for me."

"That does not even need to be said."

"Are you afraid?" I asked.

"I was scared, once," he said, "when I was younger. And from that I learned never to be afraid again. No point to it."

He walked toward the softball outfield, the furthest point from the administration building. The roseate aurora of a new dawn increased along the finger-like columns of a high cirrus cloud to the east. The starlings and sparrows and robins were responding to the light with their sweet-sounding songs. He walked almost as if he were going to work, to hunt deer, or to clean the cabin but with an ineffably high-hearted element to his demeanor. It was as if he simply had his mission for that day and he knew that we would do it and do it well. There was something in his soft-stepping gait and mostly in his serene gaze that a person never would be able to explain so much as it can just simply be felt. Along the way he met Stanley, the wide-seeing one, who handed him a shaft made of ash wood that had been smuggled out of the wood shop. It was only about eighteen inches long and of a round width to fit well in one's hand. Nothing was said between these two men or ever needed to be said. Psycho arrived at the field and waited.

Book and his assembled myrmidons had gathered early that morning as well and had planned to track down their prey and deal with him wherever they might have found him. When it had been learned that he had gone to the softball field and was waiting, there had been some surprise among them. But Book had a better understanding than that; he had half expected it, and it concerned him. Still, this throng of ten men swelled and swarmed up the walk toward the field. They had in their hearts a mixture of contempt for their adversary and the eagerness of anticipated success, joined with the pleasure of camaraderie. It was a good morning for them. They entered the field in a group and stood to face Psycho. They roughly formed two lines, and behind them was Book.

The sight of the single man standing calmly and waiting for them was not without its effect. All the qualities that were only partially concealed in Psycho found their shallow and negative reflection in the reactions of the host of men which confronted him. Some of them began to shift and to look toward one another, when they were not looking at the ground or casting glances at their singular foe. Their bravery was only collective. As each man took his own measure against the man at the other side of the field, he seemed to know himself more intimately than before. A good many of them were ready to leave, and it was beginning to become apparent. Their apprehension was augmented by the evident fact that to Psycho they all seemed invisible. He was focused only on Book, whom he addressed.

"Come on, come on straight. You will make it all the sooner to the edge of doom."

"Do you think you can frighten me with words, like I'm some baby boy?" Book asked. "I can trade disrespect with you all day. You ain't so strong. You just crazy."

There came no answer. A flicker of a mood crossed Psycho's face like a small sunbeam. He raised his ash rod and pulled out of his pocket the lock in the sock, taking hold of it by the tops of the socks and letting the lock dangle. In his heart he sounded a song whose melody was an alternative for shining iron. A slight smile began to form on his face.

"Don't be afraid of that crazy man," Book said to his supporters. "He can't beat all of us together. Stick together and fight together, and he will lose."

Psycho sprang silently into their midst. Swinging his lock and parrying his rod, he struck the first two men he encountered and broke the arm of the first and knocked he second one dizzy. He was like a fire that sweeps across a western mountainside, setting the kindling ablaze and catching the trees afire with a blustering incandescence. A third man came at him and a fourth while he was already engaged. The one struck Psycho on the shoulder with a stick before a fist to the throat dropped him to the ground gasping and the other got close enough to plant a knee in Psycho's thigh before his own face bloomed in blood from his nose being flattened by a head butt. The blows these men landed seemed to glance off of Psycho. And as he was contending with these men a brick hit him in the side. It had been thrown by Book at the perfect tactical moment. It broke at least one of Psycho's ribs, but he managed to backhand another man with the ash rod, and that man stumbled away holding onto his upper arm.

By this time, the rest of the others had armed themselves with rocks and an occasional brick and rather than approach him they began to pelt him with these projectiles. One or another of these hit him on the side of his head and almost completely severed his left ear. Yet another hit him over the right eye, and the blood from the opening blinded him in that eye. With his injured thigh and his broken ribs and these new injuries, and with his hands splattered with blood, he angled again toward Book, who stood now behind only four other men. The iron song was still strong in Psycho's heart, and he pushed his strong body to finish the job it had started. The injuries gave him no thought other than how he must then adjust his fight to accommodate his approach. He had no concern for any wound other than the way the one on his thigh might slow him down. He could still see clearly out of his left eye. He felt no anger or regret or any kind of passion. He still had a job to do, and that was his only motivation.

He reached that next group of men and dealt blows even as he took them. There was a clatter of wood on bone and wood on wood and metal on wood. A couple more of the other men fell, and Psycho's left arm fell limp from a stab wound, and he had already begun to get faint when Book reached over the top of his men and smashed another brick against his head. That last blow seemed to Psycho as if it had hit him in a dream. He hardly felt it, as he faded into unconsciousness.

"You are not comparing me to the buckeye in that damn book of yours, are you?" Dwayne Abram had once asked me. He would not ask me such questions again. He did not die that day. And had he died it would have been in dactylic hexameter. He recovered and was sent to the federal prison hospital in North Carolina. But he was never the same. The blows to his head had taken away whatever it was that made him who he had been. He moved and spoke slowly and forgot things. He was no longer the buckeye, either husked or bare. He was simply the husk.

I knew that the seventh holy lesson had to be about courage and sacrifice, but I also knew it was more than that and deeper. There was something that was at once very elemental in the heart of my friend, but it was also something at the other end of the scale at the same time, something transcendent, something immortal. He had found something or he was something, and it was beyond life and beyond understanding. I believe that a large part of this seventh revelation was that I could see in this what others might not, see what only a perceptive reader might also notice, that this item that was in Psycho was another element of the spirit of the Lord.

As I sat in my cell that night, grieving the loss of my friend, I received another visit, one that I had been expecting, from Jesus herself. And this time she was wearing a simple and elegant, short-sleeved, off-white cheongsam dress with a high neck, open at the front. She had on no stockings, and the high heels she was wearing only had a sandal front and no back. The heel of one foot kept lifting off the shoe in a provocative way that made it hard for me to concentrate on what she said to me. She was highly comforting and helpful and encouraging. She was very much a personal savior.

"There is no need to grieve," she consoled me. "Your friend is a hero, and that is holy. And most importantly, there is some of him inside of everyone. That is a good thing, maybe the best thing."

"But it does not seem such a Christian thing to me," I answered. "You know he had killed men."

"That is a separate judgment, and not one that is pertinent to this particular insight. There is nothing treacherous or deceitful about him. And this thing he did was about you, though you may not have known it, and he had even said he did not need to say it to you. He simply lived it and accepted the death it could have brought him."

"I think I begin to understand," I said, but I was still thinking.

"That is good," she said. "You can learn these insights from your own experience, and they can be revealed to you in the stories that surround you. With hope, you see that you have been given the tools to read into these stories and sense what they reveal."

I was still looking at that provocative foot, when it and its partner carried her out of the cell.

THE INMATE'S WIFE

The inmate's wife had been driving the children to visit her husband, Christian, where he was incarcerated at the Manchester, Kentucky, minimum-security prison, when a bolt of lightning struck next to the highway, and a small sliver of it ricocheted and hit the trailer hitch on her car. She had driven well into the evening and had planned to spend the night at the home of her aunt, who lived forty miles from the prison, and to make the visit the following day. The lightning caused her to swerve hard off of the road and onto the gravel of the shoulder, knocking over the box in the back of the station wagon which contained the bottle of rum she was bringing to her aunt as a gift and breaking the bottle. She brought the car back onto the road. About ten minutes later the volume on the car radio began to slowly fade. Then the indicator lights on the dashboard also slowly faded, followed by the headlights, and then the car itself turned off, and she drifted it to the side of the road.

Almost immediately a police car pulled up behind her, and the officer approached the side of the car and motioned for her to lower her window. He was a large, dark, leering, heavy-set, slovenly man, well into his fifties, balding and heavily featured. Her window was electric, so she had to open the door in order to answer him. The boy, eight years old, and the girl, six years old, watched from the back seat of the car.

"Smells like someone has been drinking," the officer snorted, "so you had better step out of the vehicle."

She did as he asked, and he told her to walk over to the other side of the car, the side off of the road, and he told her that if she knew what was good for her and if she did not want to be arrested for drunk driving and have the kids sent to some emergency foster care while she was put into a holding pen she had better be cooperative. He pushed her head and her chest down onto the hood of the car. She could see the children, looking at her from the back seat of the car as she felt rough hands fumble with her pants and pull them down and begin to violate her. She found that suddenly she was thinking of her aunt who had the face of a jackal and was laughing at her and blaming her. She tried to focus on the children, but her daughter's face began to resemble that of her aunt. There was a smell in the air which made her remember.

When she had stepped out of the shower at home that morning she had this feeling that someone else was in the room with her. She smelled it. Then it occurred to her that this smell, this completely foreign odor, was actually her own. After thirty-eight years of life, either her smell was no longer familiar to her or she had suddenly begun to have a completely different aroma. And it was unpleasant. There had been something acrid about it, as if it were mixed with blood or iron or offal. Her third or fourth thought had been that it meant she was about to die from some dread and unseen illness. Two of her first thoughts had been guilt and a foreboding that something terrible and which she eminently deserved was about to happen to her. Her feelings toward the policeman at this later point were somewhere between indifference and gratitude for not being something much worse. She felt an urge to kiss him. Much of what he was doing felt like it was happening to someone other than herself.

Her head was being pushed down onto the hood of the car but not so much that she could not see a pair of headlights of a third car pulling up behind the police car. The officer stopped whatever he had been doing and crudely tried to pull her pants back up as she heard the door of the car that had just arrived open and then close. She finished putting her pants on as a slender blond man about her own age walked up to them and he asked if he could be of assistance and said that he had seen the lightning strike and had turned around and come back because he believed that he might be able to help fix the car. He spoke in a strong West Virginia accent, which is not quite a southern accent because it had a touch of a western drawl to it. The police officer just sort of grunted, gave the man a hard look, got into his car, and drove off.

The thin blond man in his late thirties who now stood in front of her had hands and arms that moved a little too quickly and legs that seemed too skinny to hold up the rest of his body. His tone of voice was not round or full. There was something about him that was unconcerned and facile. He had an immediately ingratiating manner that was irritating. He was given to hanging his head and talking, both a little bit too much. But upon second glance there was strength to his form that was not instantly apparent and that seemed to have been both fashioned from, and designed for, getting up off of the ground. He smiled a lot, had most of his teeth, was almost clean shaven, and his features were more even than not.

"My name is Kenny Crowe," the man said to her, "and can I ask you a question?"

The wife just looked at him.

"Did the electrical go all of sudden or did it sort of go kind of gradual like?" he asked.

"Gradually."

"Then it is your alternator," he concluded, "and I can show you."

He got her to unlatch the front hood and he opened it as he explained that in late-model Japanese cars the engine always runs cool and to demonstrate that he put his hand right on the engine block without any consequence. Then he pointed out the alternator and asked her to hold her hand close to it. It was hot. He told her that nothing under the hood should be hot like that and that it meant that the alternator had burned out. He told her he could take her to an auto parts store to get a new alternator and that he could also install it and that all he wanted was thirty dollars. She thought of her two children and did not feel comfortable taking them in a car with a strange man. But he told her to come over to his car and meet his own child and the child's mother. His car was at least fifteen years old, falling apart, and resembled an old bucket more than anything. Behind the driver's wheel of it was perhaps the softest, sweetest and most obese twenty-five-year-old blonde woman the wife had ever seen. In the back seat of the car there was a six-month-old boy in a baby seat which itself had no seat belt and which was not attached to car seat by a seat belt. Kenny introduced the woman as Melissa.

As Kenny very deftly and quickly removed the alternator from her car, the wife got her children out of her station wagon, and they climbed into the back seat of the old bucket of a car. She sat in the middle and held onto the hands of each of her children very tightly. Kenny put the alternator into the trunk and then sat in the front passenger seat of the car. He put the baby seat on the floor and held the baby on his lap, picked up an open can of beer, and lit a cigarette.

"I figure there is an Auto Zone store in Winfield and a Trak Auto store in St. Albans," he said, "and I reckon we ought to go to St. Albans first because it is closer."

The wife stared at him blankly as she realized that she was the only person in the car who heard what Melissa said next, which was, "St. Albans will close first, so we should go to the Auto Zone now." It was said in a whisper that was at once submissive and resentful, and the wife was puzzled that she was the only one who was equipped to hear it. Melissa had not heard it, even though it had been she who had spoken the words. She simply and cheerfully drove to St. Albans. Along the way Kenny sunnily expounded upon automobile mechanics, his high esteem in the local communities, his own recent stints in state and county jails, the fact that he and Melissa were married but to other people, their large extended families, the man with whom his wife was living, their child, the burrows dug by groundhogs, and all the time that he had been illuminating his life for her he had been ejecting a string of empty beer cans and spent cigarette butts out the open window of the car. They arrived in St. Albans just after the Trak Auto there had closed so they turned and drove toward Winfield.

"If you do not open this god damn door, I will call the law on you," Kenny shouted as he banged violently on the front glass door of the Auto Zone store in Winfield twenty minutes later, when they had arrived there five minutes after it had closed. Melissa may or may not have then said that the law was the last thing anyone wanted to see. The wife's impression of what the law could possibly do in this part of the country and of the extensiveness of its relationship to the people in it continued to expand. The store manager just looked at Kenny menacingly from inside the store and walked to the telephone and picked it up. Kenny kept banging on the door of the store, even more violently. The wife tiredly got out of the car, still holding each of her children by the hand, and told him that it was all right and that all she wanted to do was get back to the car she had left on the side of the road. They left the store in Winfield and drove back to her car on the side of the highway, where Kenny very helpfully pushed it several yards to where it could drift down a short hill and into a parking lot next to a convenience store and a gas station. It was there that he had an idea.

"I have a good friend who runs a NAPA auto parts store in Hurricane. I can call him right here from this pay phone and get him to open up his store for us," he said. And before the wife could answer him, he had turned and walked toward the pay phone.

It was difficult for the wife to know why her children had become ghosts. They were pale and quiet and stood by the cars in the convenience store parking lot with a curious motionlessness. When she took their hands they seemed light and as if they were floating at her side. Such children would be quite easy to convey from place to place. On the road to Hurricane, they grew even more spectral. The bucket car also had merged into the flesh that was Melissa, and both just floated along and barely above the pitch black backwoods roads. A pair of headlights had been behind them for some time, and the wife knew that it was her police officer acquaintance. She could see his leering face in the lights. He had probably taken the call from the store in Winfield.

Nothing at all unusual had happened yet this night until it had been seen that the NAPA Auto Parts store in Hurricane actually had been reopened after closing hours at the phone request from Kenny. It was simply miraculous. They were greeted at the store by three individuals. Behind the counter and clearly the gent whom they had come to see was a fat man of sixty. He had a gray beard and gray hair which peeked out from under a baseball cap with the name of the store on it. He was well over six foot tall and well over three hundred pounds in weight. All of his features were abnormally small and made it seem as if he had an antiquated child's face that was surrounded by a nimbus of flesh. He wore his store uniform and it was damp from perspiration, as was his face. Thick tufts of hair protruded from under his collar and his sleeves.

What had let them in the door had been a feral creature very much resembling a man in every way. He was apparently the assistant to the man behind the counter. He was very pale and thin and had gray eyes and blond hair. He was missing a few front teeth, and his eyes were wild brown and did not rest on a single object. He was just under five feet tall, and almost all of the skin he had which could be seen was covered in tattoos. He kept his one hand at all times on his crotch. His other hand held the keys to the shop. He looked at the wife in the way that a cannibal might. This man and his huge boss were the least disconcerting of the trio.

The feral man had brought a woman who was his wife or his girlfriend or perhaps his assistant. She was a very attractive young woman with origins in the beautiful lands of the Indian subcontinent. She very compliantly did as was directed by her untamed principal, and most of those directives seemed to come from his furtive eyes. She responded as if she were receiving completely intelligible telepathic pictographs. She was serene and alert and she wore a nice blue blouse of a moderated Indian design and a pair of slender designer American black jeans. She had a perfect hourglass figure, willowy but with fullness where a man might want it. Her skin was light brown and smooth and she had all of what might make such a woman beautiful and none of what might not. She had the doe eyes and the well-formed lips and the straight black hair and vivid features. She was not too dark or masculine or heavy featured or hirsute. She wore very well-made sandals on her feet, which had toes on them that were as long and as delicate and as articulated as fingers. It was not as if she had hands where feet should have been. Her feet were normal from heel to arch. They were simply extended by toes that were three and a half inches long and which looked as if they could accomplish any task that a hand might. The wife was at once transfixed and subtly entertained and completely disconcerted. She knew what every person must know about such a thing in his or her heart of hearts. It was not the oddity of feet, but it was the small irregularity of the spirit that somehow corresponded to it, that was what was truly and sickeningly hilarious. The wife kept her eyes on those feet, not knowing what unexpected thing might be accomplished by them, as the man behind the counter began his long dissertation. Kenny, the feral man, the Indian helper, even the two diminutive ghosts floating at the wife's side, all gave the large, damp old man a kind of marked deference. The wife was mesmerized, but not by what he said.

"Now if this here car had been a Ford or a Chevy we could have you in and out of here in a jiffy," he began. "We have all manner of alternators for Fords. We can take care of a Chevy or a Dodge, for that matter. We could even help you out if you had one of them normal Japanese cars, like a Toyota or a Nissan. But what you say you got here is a Subaru Outback and that is one of those most obscure Japanese brands." And he droned on for well more than half an hour, stopping several times to deposit the spit from his chaw of tobacco into a genuine antique brass cuspidor that was at least fifty years older than

256

anything else in that store, including the old man. The wife patiently said nothing. But she thought she could hear the bucket car radio in the parking lot. A voice on it was noting only to herself that all of this conversation and meeting could have been obviated by a few words that could have been said during the phone call that had generated them. It was as if observing the courtesy had been the only important thing in setting up this meeting. The only important thing to the wife at this point was that she was not succumbing to the seemingly inescapable paroxysms of horror and apprehension that were about to beset her as she contemplated the very real prospect of those toes opening her purse, rifling through it, stealing her cell phone and dialing some long-distance number in Mumbai.

The wife thanked everyone at the store for re-opening several hours after closing and for explaining to her the exceptional circumstance which prevented them from helping her any further. The fat old damp man just smiled. The feral man stood by, looking expectantly, and his comely Indian companion began acting very agitatedly. The old man kept talking for a long while and the feral man moved closer to him as the young woman started to pant. The old man finally said his farewell to them all and then handed the cuspidor to the feral man, and the woman did a pirouette. The wife could not bring herself to look at what it might mean for such a woman to spin on tiptoe. The wife put her ghosts back into the Melissa car, and they all set off to return to the convenience store and to her obscure Japanese station wagon when Kenny suddenly had another, seemingly brand new, idea.

"You know, my brother is a mechanic and he just might be able to simply fix this old alternator. Let's just drive over there right now," he said.

The roads to this even more remote and rural place were even darker, and the conveyance had become less car and even more Melissa. The spectral children were floating and almost bumping against the fleshy ceiling of the back seat, kept down only by their hands that the wife held. The frightening headlights were again behind them. Suddenly those headlights drew close, and that car behind them was tailgating the Melissa car. Then it passed them and sped up the way and slid off the road at the turn ahead, careening through the field for a few dozen yards, rolling completely over sideways once, before coming to a stop back on its tires. The hood had popped open and the driver's door burst open. Out of the door emerged a handsome young man of only about eighteen years of age, wearing a summer sun dress. He stumbled a few times as he walked toward the road.

The Melissa car was the first to speak, but only the wife heard her say, "We are not going to stop."

"Pull over," Kenny directed.

The car pulled over, and it said, "We are not going to help that young Luke Michael. He already is on probation for drunk driving."

Turning back to the wife, Kenny said, "We gotta help young Luke here, because you just gotta help people. It's only courtesy."

"This is not going to go well," the wife heard the car say.

The wife left the ghosts in the Melissa, and Kenny left the baby in the front seat, and the wife walked up to the young driver of the wrecked car with Kenny. Kenny told the youth to be calm and to have a seat there in the field and he told them that he would return with his brother and his brother's tow truck and they would get the car and him out of there before the police came. Then they went to look at the boy's car. It was largely in decent shape, just quite banged up.

It was actually still running. Kenny switched it off. Then he looked at the wife. She looked at him. The car was a Subaru Outback, and sitting there under the open hood was a working alternator.

They quickly drove the few remaining miles to the double-wide trailer home where Kenny's brother lived. It was up in one of those remote mountain hollows at the end of a long dirt driveway and sitting next to a barn that contained a few cars and in front of which was a tow truck. Kenny got out of the Melissa. He was met by his brother, and the two of them got into the tow truck and drove off. A woman spoke to Melissa and then she told the wife that she and the small ghosts could go inside. Melissa stayed outside, idling her engine. The wife took the little ghosts into the house and quickly and quietly sat down on the couch at the end of the living room and decided to be as calm and as unobtrusive as possible.

The house was a buzz of activity. There were at least seven adults in the house, and all of them were in the kitchen, sitting around the table, drinking and playing cards while they listened to their radio scanner, which was set to the police band. The wife could hear it clearly from the next room. No one had introduced the wife to anyone, but she was getting the idea that they already must have known a thing or two about her and about her evening. There were several children in the house, and they were completely unattended and allowed to roam freely without even a hint of supervision. This scene was exactly the opposite of what the wife had remembered at the family gatherings she had witnessed at the homes of two of her former boyfriends, one who was Jewish and the other who was Italian, where the large contingents of seemingly unattended children only appeared to run wild but had been actually well observed by successive delegations of parents who would intermittently visit the children on what almost seemed to be a tacitly decided rotation by the individual parents. The scene she was witnessing in this trailer was different than those two past experiences and rather more familiar to her as well.

The wife had descended from firm *Mayflower* stock and had attended private preparatory schools in New England and an Ivy League college. Her family was entirely of English descent and Protestant and had been in the United States for at least three hundred years. Between the two of them, her parents could number six divorces and eight spouses, current or former. She had one full sister and she had a half-sister and a half-brother and an illegitimate half-sister and another half-brother, each of whom had a different combination of parents. It was also a reasonable certainty that her uncle had caused her grandfather's death after having forged the old man's signature onto a new will that left everything to the uncle. When this had practically been proven by the documents the entire family had rallied around the uncle because they realized that he now controlled the fortune and did not consider for an instant that they might successfully contest the will on fair and just grounds or that the uncle was reprehensible. The wife and her siblings and cousins and in turn her nieces and nephews and second cousins, when they had been children, had all been allowed to run loose while the adults played golf or drank or went sailing or played cards or chased one another around. Economically, life in this double-wide trailer was quite different from what the wife had known in her own family. Socially and ethnically, it was not.

When the pack of seven or eight loose children began to focus on her and on her ghosts, she was not surprised. She even knew that might be why the adults ignored her and left them alone in the living room, so that she and her phantoms could be proper diversion for the wild children. She also knew that if something were to go wrong between her and these seven or eight loose children, the presumption would go against her as the only adult. The presence of another adult would have removed that presumption. There was something else that struck the wife about these children. They all looked like Jesus, or like pictures of Jesus at various stages of his youth from church books she had seen. The first salvo was fired almost immediately. A four-year-old threw a full and unopened can of soda at the head of her ethereal son. She had anticipated it and had moved him in time. The can hit the corner of the picture frame behind him, punctured, fell, bounced off the couch, and sputtered and sprayed and spun on the floor like an artist's rendering on the Discovery Channel of some radio satellite struck by a meteorite and spinning out of control in outer space. This served to chase the band of roving Jesus children away for a while and to confirm that indeed no adult had ever intended to come into that living room.

The wandering baby Jesus children returned, though, and armed with sticks and toy guns and other remotely sharp-edged objects. They had taken a particular interest in the ghosts. The inmate's wife sat forward on the couch so that her buttocks were perched on the front edge and she was sitting with her legs forward into the room. She reached to the side and back and took each small apparition and pushed them together behind her, presenting herself as a shield. The pack of undomesticated holy children was now ravening. There was very little good that could have come from their presence in the room. The situation was only mitigated by the truth behind the appearance they each had, of being in a glassy-eyed stupor and by the occasional and fleeting interest they would show to one another or to other objects in the room. They gamboled around, unkempt and unclean and uncanny, like so many marbles in a box. The wife effectively kept various objects from penetrating either one of her small ghosts. Her efforts in doing so succeeded in drawing the attention of the wild lambs of God to her own person, and soon the ephemeral presence of the little specters had begun to evade their consideration. Then they began to poke her with their sticks and strike her with their guns and scrape her with their remotely sharp objects. They barked like dogs. They smoked cigarettes. She was gradually becoming more bruised and cut and even burned. One of the smaller ones, the one who had thrown the can, was gnawing on her ankle.

She had somewhere along the line learned she had the excellent resource with which to meet everything passively, to make herself an inert mass, to not let herself be carried away or lured into taking a single unnecessary step, to stare blankly and to feel no compunction, to ratchet down with her own hand what last vestige of liveliness that remained in her, in short to reach forward and take that final peace that comes only in the graveyard and to enlarge that within herself until it smothered everything else within her.

She was also listening intently to what she could hear from the other room in order to determine if some intervention might arrive from that quarter and because she was interested in what was coming over on the police band radio. She could tell that the level of interest of the adults in the kitchen had risen. They were commenting on what they had been hearing. The reports on the radio revealed that the police had somehow been made aware of the accident and had approached it. They had seen that there was a tow truck on the scene and had been prepared to arrest everyone there if any attempt had had been made to remove the evidence, the car or the driver, from the scene. Kenny and his brother had been at risk. But no discussion came over the radio of any arrest, other than that of the young driver. And very soon after that, Kenny returned. There was a general clamor in the kitchen when he walked in there. They were congratulating him on avoiding arrest yet another day. That racket drew the untamed youthful messiahs into the kitchen. The wife cleaned herself up.

The wife and her little spirits got back into the Melissa with Kenny and she and the ghosts were dropped off at a motel not far from the convenience store where the station wagon had been left. It had been agreed that Kenny would return at ten o'clock in the morning the next day, and they would go to an auto parts store and get the alternator. When the wife and her children woke up, they were hungry and they walked out of the motel to get some breakfast, and the first thing that they saw was that there was a Subaru dealership across from the motel. It was the only one for about two hundred miles in any direction. They ate breakfast and waited for Kenny, who had not returned by eleven o'clock in the morning. So they walked to the Subaru dealership and approached a salesman. He already knew exactly all that had happened and he sold her an alternator even though the parts shop of the dealership was not open on that weekend day, when only the sales department was open. He had to go open the parts shop specially. He sold her the last alternator they had in stock. He told her that neither of the auto parts stores which had been closed the night before when they had visited would have carried that alternator. He also told her that the police officer she had met was actually one of Kenny's cousins and that the policeman usually paid Kenny to keep him informed. He also told her that Kenny would show up and that he would just be quite late, which is what happened.

Kenny and Melissa arrived. When they drove the wife and her children to her car, which was only a few blocks away, they made several detours to buy cigarettes and to make a call at a pay phone and to mail a letter. Then they arrived at the station wagon, and Kenny put in the new alternator, and the car started up without any trouble. The wife gave him the thirty dollars, and he told her that he could get also some money on the refund deposit that is required for all environmentally hazardous auto parts such as an alternator that must be disposed of according to regulation. The wife took a picture of him with her children and got in the station wagon and rolled down the window to speak.

"You know you saved me," she said.

"I surely did not," he answered. "There is a part of you that nobody can destroy and nobody can save. A person give that part up, then you really have lost. Or you can hold out in there and never lose. You ain't gonna win. But you ain't given up either, so you can't really lose. Most people just give up."

"Or something like that," the inmate's wife answered. "I guess it's a lesson."

Christian believed that he recognized this lesson as the eighth revelation as soon as he had heard the story related to him. He had wanted to discuss this with his holy visitor to tell her that he felt he understood that the human soul is truly indestructible, but only for those with the will and the faith to believe it. But she did not show up, perhaps because he did seem to be able to see this revelation so clearly, even though he had not personally experienced it. And he felt that this story and the absence of his messiah also meant that it was time for him to recall and to discuss what he remembered about marriage and love and their relationship to the soul.

CELESTE

Being in prison has always had a way of casting my mind onto the general topic of marriage. Of course, flourishing and thriving in prison, and enjoying it as greatly as I have, has also generated numerous thoughts of my own lovely marriage. I know this is going to sound uncharitable in light of what you know about the recent travails faced by my wife, but mostly I have been reminded of a sublimely harrowing poem by Percy Bysshe Shelley that is about marriage and the most significant line of which is: ". . . shackled to a silent foe." The fact that this line never actually appears in Shelley's poem is irrelevant. It is always simply going to be the operative phrase. I am also led to this connection and observation by an inescapable and divine guidance, seeking to point me to the ninth vision.

For the vast majority of those who will feel that linking prison and marriage is a facile trick or a hackneyed metaphor, I may only suggest that they should consider themselves lucky to be able to see it that way, from the perspective of marriage and not the other way around, and never having been in prison and never being required to dwell here in this home among the dead and to hear the weary tread of the footsteps of the slaves who live here. In prison, the slants and tropes and angles that lead one's mind to marriage fecundate more quickly and thickly than the Nigerian birth rate. What may seem too obvious to the casual and erudite reader is to the man in the thick of it simply more honest. It is difficult even to know at which point to begin to elucidate; the instances are too numerous.

No matter how long the sentence, serving any term of incarceration is the dreariest and longest journey. For one thing, a man is more or less chained to his cellmate, who may be a resentful foe or even a friend, which in such a case is a difference that is at once significant and also almost pointless. My initial cellmate was utterly silent at least to the extent that he spoke no English, and some of the Spanish he had spoken at one point had reputedly been in cooperation with the authorities in the prosecutions of members of a particular Colombian cocaine cartel and had the effect of unspeaking in advance much of what he might have had to say later. He was sullen and distrusting and watchful and humorless. If that were not enough to make him some manner of a spouse, he was also actually a real magician and prone to small tricks of misdirection and prestidigitation. And he made me dread to go to bed. I am not sure what I did in my sleep that was the thing against which he would pugnaciously react, but often in the middle of the night I would be awakened in the top bunk by the bed shaking rather violently due to his strenuous efforts to make it quake. Perhaps I had moved and had awakened him or I had snored and awakened him. Whichever it was, he was getting some payback. For me, it was simply one of those banal impositions that one person inflicts upon another and occurs where the proximity is just so close that the best retort will always have been a cool lack of a response. I had learned that much from having been married.

In a way I had been and was locked into a relationship with each other person in prison, guard or inmate. The serenity of detachment was no longer physically available except in certain situations. I could no longer exuberantly separate myself from other people. Any such detachment, as is the case in such circumstances, could only be psychological. I had dozens of spouses from whom to conceal my truest feelings.

There is also the way in which I had entered this place. Judges, consultants, prosecutors, my own lawyers, bureaucrats, and many others had all made various assurances and told many ameliorative stories in order to prepare me for entering prison. Everyone had done yeoman's duty in order to make it seem like it was going to be less daunting, less alienating, less of a massive reduction of all that the world and my life had previously been. When I drove around the corner and into the driveway at Manchester, the facility that first confronted me was a massive, imposing, and windowless concrete structure that was surrounded by two tall razor-wire fences and manned gun towers. The immediate realization was not an unfamiliar one at all. It was that a hefty number of disparate people had conspired to tell me the same large and concerted lie. This notion faded somewhat when I was redirected to the minimum-security satellite facility next to the big prison which had confronted me to my surprise. But then what settled in was the realization that I was still in a place about which no one had been honest because it was something about which no person could be honest, unless they were already there. And even then those who were already there had an interest in lying about it, like just so many virtuous husbands.

Lying and not lying and the feelings I have had about each serve together to be a good starting point to this story, which is also the story of my marriage and which also must start with Celeste. There have been very few women who were ever like Celeste.

"If you want," she had said, "you may sodomize me. Then I will get up and cook you a steak."

267

I was not sure if I had heard her correctly. It was only the third or fourth time we had been together and it was one of those times when, early on in a relationship, a couple finds themselves in bed during the day, waking up several hours after already having made love. Of course, at the time I thought of the Muslims. To conceive of a holy martyr's heaven as being a place where a man would want only virgin lovers can only be imagined by a culture which sees women as so alien and threatening as to feel compelled to force them into burkas and second-class citizenship. This particular woman was a woman for a man's man. And it was not as if she needed to strive for male attention or for affection. It was simply and inevitably drawn to her. It came her way in the street, in a crowded room, over the phone, by her choice of words, by the sound of her voice, while she was still and particularly as she was gracefully moving. She may not have been the first woman many men might notice but she was the one they were to later decide they wanted. And she could cook one hell of a steak.

One time I told her that I thought that one of my strengths was that I been raised in a family with three sisters and no brothers, and that meant that I had learned how to talk to women. Her answer was that if I really had been educated by that experience I would have said that I had learned how to listen to women. I also had once said to her that I thought it was unfortunate that Sigmund Freud had been generally discredited because there was a certain usefulness to the exercise of looking at everything as having to do with sex. Her answer was that such a view left sex itself in a tenuous position and that fortunately sex was the one thing that was not about sex because it was about power. She also understood inherently the problems with apologies. First of all, they are offered for the wrong reason too often, for merely unavoidable events or mistakes. An apology is only in order when one person intends harm and then correctly repents, and even then it is a minus two on the ledger between two people. The harmed person undergoes having to offer forgiveness upon the receipt of an apology, on top of suffering the harm. Celeste never apologized for dropping something or forgetting something. And when she did something on purpose that hurt and then later realized the error, she also did not apologize. She said, "So spank me." By saying this she would offer to set the ledger between us at even, rather than set it at minus two. No one so wise should have also been so humorous and so playful.

She had a ready and natural generosity of spirit, one that never strayed far from what Juliet had told Romeo in the garden. She knew that the more she gave of herself the more she had and that her greatest desire was for the feeling of that loving and that giving which was already inside of her. I think at one point or another during our relationship that I must have gone to the refrigerator to get my own beer, but I do not remember it. It was almost a point of honor with her to take care that I never got a beer myself. She said they would taste better if she retrieved them and she would kiss me with each delivery. Many people would completely misunderstand this upon witnessing it but there was not one thing about it that was ancillary or subservient. It was commanding and brilliant, and to this day I cannot drink a beer without thinking of her. And this was merely emblematic of all of the other ways in which she took claim of things and feelings, simply with the eloquence of loving to give freely and without concern for any return other than in the joy of giving. There will always be certain places, cars, theaters, churches, restaurants, parks, hillsides, coatrooms, towers, pathways that will be forever marked in my memory by the power of the generosity of her intimacy and the sheer joy that marked her half of the experience.

Claude Lévi-Strauss, the great French structuralist, endeavored to show that many forms of human activity may be illuminated by striving to see their underlying patterns or structures. In this way I have found it instructive to view each human character as standing somewhere on a graph. The elevation, the y axis of the graph, is strength of character; a person with strong character will be located somewhere in the top half of the graph. The goodness of character is charted horizontally, along the x axis of this Cartesian plane, and those with goodness of character will be located on the right side. The vast majority of men and women may be found in the lower right quadrant, being basically good folk but often without the gumption that might have been required to help or hide a Jewish family during the Nazi occupation. The evil and the weak may be found in the lower left quadrant or in church or in your neighborhood or in your bedroom, just lacking enough strength of character as to be unable to resist the normative and healthy currents of civil society but flowing along peaceably enough with them until such time as order will break down just a little bit, and then they will accelerate that process by then thinking first and only of themselves and not really of themselves or their larger interests but of their most immediate and most selfish interests, as is evident in the lines for post-Thanksgiving sales at retail stores. You can find Hitler in the corner of the top left quadrant, with the strength and the will to promulgate unspeakable evil. Very few people are to be found in that top right quadrant with Celeste, both good and strong.

If you can appreciate the way in which punctuality is actually very sexy, then you might be able to understand the way in which the most hypnotically alluring feminine trait that a woman may possess is to have both a strong and a good character. Jane Austen's *Pride and Prejudice* should create in the discerning male reader a deeply rooted concupiscence for Elizabeth Bennet that springs not from her vivacity or from her wit but from her unerring instinct to follow the deeply moral directives of her own character even against the influences and arguments of society, of convention, of seeming necessity, and of her friends and family. Properly read, Austen should be a form of pornography for the morally and spiritually discriminating man. Merely looking at Celeste always convinced me that if we were hiking in the deep woods on some remote trail in the Cascade Range and if I had broken my leg that she would do all in her power to personally haul me out of there, or she would die trying. Nothing could have made me want her more intensely.

She was fluent in French, so much so that if I were to remain quiet in a Paris restaurant with her while she did all the ordering, the supercilious waiter would assume we were both Parisian. The ease with which she would slip between French and English was similar to the grace with which she would change to handle any social situation, from meeting grandma to attending a dinner party to managing the threat of being mugged by thugs outside of the railroad station. It was the same poise and charm with which she would negotiate all the shoals and eddies of potential injury and blame that might lie along the uncharted route of any intimate relationship, or with which her clothes might slide to the floor whenever I would take her head in my hands and kiss her face. Her sense of humor was light and insightful and inciting and she had the quality of making those around her at ease and enlivened at the same time.

Her natural grace had the effect of excellent film editing. It seamlessly fit together all the different women that she was, all the different sides that she had, into one coherent whole and it never was jarring to see any part of her personality emerge from behind another no matter how different those parts or scenes may have been. The French speaking Celeste was quite different. Her statements came more in the form of informal questions and her air was more playful. At that point she was, in a word, French, and the transition from her, say, to the analytical and determined person who was also one of the English-language versions of Celeste would pass by almost unnoticed. The woman in her who was a whimsical but observant tourist of life would easily blend into the all business and rather masculine woman who could manage the complex logistics of organizing an event or a trip in half the time it would have taken another person. The voracious and questing intellect of the woman she was when she was reading or talking to someone of interest could effortlessly transform into a woman who might laugh a little too long or too much at something that was simply silly. And from the sleepy Celeste or from the preoccupied Celeste or from the slightly injured Celeste, there could emerge the Celeste on fire, the one whose heavenly name barely did justice to the surfeit of additional life to which she gave infinite promise.

There was a subtle music to every aspect of her. She placed one foot in front of another with a simple combination of rhythms that lurked just beneath notice. Her hands moved in the air with the coordinated transitions of flocks of birds in flight. Her arguments and expositions were woven and never merely linear and contained within them themes and progressions that revealed the harmony of her intellect. She laughed with a lilt. Her voice itself was quite deep. Sometimes I would pick up a phone answering machine or voicemail message from her and if she might not have prefaced it with her name or some other reference to her and if it were a practical message and not a communication of affection I would often get a few seconds into the message before I realized that it was not from one of my male friends. And all trace of the depth of that register would simply disappear like a fog burned off in the noontime sun whenever she would speak to me in the timbre and pitch of her passion. The lilt that was in her laugh would then thread its way through the girlish tones of her most intimate songs.

There is rashness. And then there is the boldness that arises from wisdom. In an interesting twist, wisdom may also arise from having learned from rashness, making this wise boldness the grandson of rashness in certain cases. This boldness which arises from wisdom only ever appears in some women or men and even then only at a certain age. It was one of Celeste's singularities that she possessed this quality from the beginning of her adult life. She could size up a situation or a person or people and determine if it warranted even the possibility of taking a bold step. She knew not to get into a parasail at a Mexican resort or to just jump off of a pier into the water or to go grocery shopping when she was hungry. But she would climb onto the back of a motorcycle with me or she would squeeze through a break in the fence in order to get to the precipice that had the only view above the Greek Theater in Syracuse or she would break a conventional taboo when she felt there was requisite excitement and trust and mutual consent and desire.

The simplest and fastest way to describe her beauty was to say that she looked like a young Ava Gardner, the American movie actress from the middle of the twentieth century. A reader two hundred years from today will be likely to have electronic and pictorial references appurtenant to this book that will show him or her what that means, but for the readers even then who will do it the old-fashioned way or for those now who have no access to or memory regarding the look of that actress who was once regarded as the most beautiful woman in the world, I will continue to explain and describe her and at the same time describe Celeste. There was something that was at once handsome and exotic and passionate and dramatically feminine about her face. Had her features been less shapely and poignant she might have appeared merely masculine. But there was strikingly feminine clarion call to her face that overwhelmed the handsome aspects of the strength of her features. It was not a countenance that could be taken in with a glance. Pretty is always apprehended immediately. But pretty is never beautiful. Unusual may be beautiful and it takes some time to discern.

Every feature of hers was vivid, and it is difficult to say which one struck me first, except to say that it was obviously her eyes. But they were not what set her aspect apart so much as it was her magnificent nose, or more it was the way in which her nose and eyebrows and forehead combined to form a unique setting for her eyes. It was as if a Tartar had wandered well off course in the fourteenth century and had left his seed in the Ireland of Celeste's ancestors. There was a decided curved slope to her arched eyebrows, slightly inward and downward toward the center, so that the precedent set by her high and clear forehead gathered your glance and moved it almost as if down slight inclines toward her nose, which in turn rose almost directly out of that forehead as in the ancient statues of the nobility of the Roman Empire. It was a strong and direct and proportional nose. The basic line of it was quite straight from forehead to tip. But it had slight, distinctly feminine, and almost voluptuous small sharp curves around the tip and the nostrils, almost as if our ancient Tartar had taken an Arab chum with him on his imputed Celtic romp. The best of dark and bright that met in her face were also shown in her skin, which was very fair, and her eyebrows, which were very dark. Her hair was a riot of mediumbrown waves and large curls.

The theater of this upper part of her face was matched and joined to it by her prominent cheek bones, which began next to her eyes and angled inward toward the shadowed hollow of her cheeks, which lay in front of a very strong and distinctive jaw line that ran from her ears to the foundation of her aristocratic jaw before it tapered slightly to end at an equally strong and distinctive chin. The power and handsome nature of these features were also again accented by small but dramatically feminine flourishes in the curves of her cheeks and beside her mouth and on her chin. These small accents of femininity bloomed into full womanly glory in the form and shape of her lips, which had a penetrating life of their own even on her already dramatic physiognomy. Her upper lip exhibited all the inviting and subtly Levantine curves that appear in men's dreams of harem girls. A slight arc ran inward from each end of her mouth, slightly upward and then down, to begin that slope back up to each soft, round height that rose on either side of the downward peak at the philtrum, that slight bracketed depression that ran from the tip of her nose to the middle of her upper lip. They were the artful curves you might find on a violin or a vintage wooden yacht. Their counterpoint was the simple and ample curve of her nether lip, which was merely there, not as wide on her face as the upper but fuller and deeper and pouty. It was just as inviting as the upper lip but in a more direct manner.

No amount of fatigue or drink or even conscious effort could possibly obscure the pale fire of her blue/green and almond-shaped eyes, nor could anything hide what Tolstoy had once called an excess of vitality, which for her was the fuel behind that fire. Her lashes were thick and curved, and the line of her eyes had that same slight inward and downward angle that was present in her eyebrows and which most gave her the exotic look. Sometimes they appeared to be blue and other times they seemed green but they always had that force. They always flashed her most lively and deep responses and thoughts and emotions. Even when she was ruminating, the penetration and gravity of her mind was evident in those eyes. They were direct and pure and intense. It was from those eyes that I mostly gathered the certainty that she loved me. I certainly loved her.

"So what do you really think?" She turned to me and asked one day as she put down the phone. "How did I do? Did I make sense? I am so used to having the time to write. So when I give an interview I worry that my thoughts have not been fully gathered or expressed in a coherent fashion. And that interview will be broadcast on National Public Radio, so I want it to have been well done. They were asking for a follow-up and some additional insights on the piece I had written on the demonstrations in Paris."

"You did very well. They obviously love you at NPR. They keep calling back," I answered.

"Is that all?"

"You made a lot of good points that I do not think they will get anywhere else."

"Yes, but what else are you not saying? I kind of don't know how I sound when I am speaking. I just want your honesty. You know that I love that you are honest with me. It is perhaps what I love most about you."

It was late on a Saturday morning. She was wearing nothing at all but one of my dress shirts she had thrown on as a sort of a night gown. In such cases it was difficult for me to think of anything more than her legs and the rest of her miraculous body that they were holding up. Her legs were slender and shapely, and, as if that were not enough, she had two of them. Each one was vying with the other for perfection. My late father would have called them Hollywood gams. In fact, that might have become his permanent nickname for her. I knew that under that shirt the rest of her was just as slender and well formed. The bone structure of her face was built to last. She would be a handsome woman well into her later years. After the fullness of her flesh would have faded somewhat, those bones would have maintained her face as that of a woman who would always be quite attractive. Her lithe body was the same way. It would last. It was all a composition of beautiful economies, and no part of her body would fade or transform into something too different. In 1650, Diego Velázquez painted *The Toilet of Venus*, which now hangs in the British National Gallery and is known as the *Rokeby Venus*. It shows many of the elements of the genius of Velázquez, his startling realism, his command of light and space, his sense of visual irony, his ability to imbue his subjects with life and personality. But in many ways it is simply a three-hundred-and-fifty-year-old painting that is all about the beauty of the feminine posterior or the splendor of a particularly exquisite and individual feminine fundament, such as was also lurking barely concealed behind the tail of my dress shirt.

My passion for Celeste was rarely disengaged from my respect for her or from the deep spiritual regard in which I held our affection for one another, an affection that in many respects was more important than any other component of my love for her. That required that I give her my best, that I give her my honesty. I hate compromise, generally. And compromise could not be housed under the same roof with Celeste and my love for her.

"I don't know for sure," I said, "but sometimes in those interviews it has seemed like you forget to speak in complete sentences all the time. You have so many ideas and you are excited. No one actually speaks in complete sentences anymore, anyway."

"You do. And so do I, or at least I thought I did. Now I am going to have to worry that I am walking around with sentence fragments popping out of my mouth, completely unrelated to each other, it seems."

"No, no, you are taking it all wrong. I hardly noticed it at all."

"Clearly, you think I am a half-wit. It seems," she said, breaking out her arch little smile, "that upon pouring my coffee you have also decided to pour invectives in my ear."

"You know that is a mischaracterization. I can simply love you no other way but honestly and sincerely. It would be a crime to treat you any other way. I despise meaningless embraces, flattery, bland courtesies, broad compliments attributable to all and any and made worthless by the commonness of their currency. If I praise everything you do, my merited praise will become meaningless. The day that I oblige you with condescending palliatives, please take me out and shoot me."

"Why should I wait until then? Who wants you hanging around here just in order to hear me speaking in ungrammatical fragments of sentences?"

"I do not want to doom this love affair to the common courtesies of polite society. You should not want to condemn me to false and artificial intercourse. We ought to both prefer the genuine variety. Let me behave like a real man and a man who loves you and who speaks his heart honestly to you in everything I say."

She smiled to herself and then looked at me and smiled again. I looked at her legs.

What was left unsaid was that the truth can be quite uncouth and that the fabric of all social relationships is woven with white lies. They become like ghosts that inhabit the useful connections and mechanisms of a family, a love affair, a friendship. After a while you are merely feeding the ghosts. I had wanted less than that with Celeste, and more.

"You know that Callista is coming east for Christmas and she wants to visit us here," Celeste said to me several weeks later, over dinner.

"Do you mean Kate?" I asked.

"Callista was always her given name."

"Yes, but when you first met her freshman year and the two of you became friends she told you her name was Kate. And she went by the name, Kate, the whole time we were in college. She was called Kate when she married Jeff right out of school and was still Kate when she divorced him six weeks later. She was Kate for several years for us and for dozens of our friends."

"Well, she wants to be known as Callista now, so we ought to respect it."

"And I want her to call me Donkey Dick."

"How about if I am the only one who calls you that?"

"Who the hell wants to be called Callista, anyway?"

"Her parents gave her that name."

"And you saw what she did with that, right? She walked into school and told us all to call her Kate. She got it right that time. And look at it this way. Who the hell gets divorced after only forty days of being married, the animals on Noah's Ark? And what woman in her right mind would ever have married Jeff in the first place?"

"My best friend did."

The truly honest mind remains open. Out of love and self-respect, I reserved judgment and intended to be open in my approach. It was, however, going to be difficult. Although I never would have married him myself, Jeff was my friend and when he said that Kate had been the definition of "not there," it rang true to me. She always seemed to be holding back, so much so that it gave rise to the presumption that she was only appearing to be holding back because there was nothing there to restrain in the first place. My own opinion was that she had mastered the art of turning the blank stare into a kind of fashion statement, as had Jackie Kennedy Onassis. That same blank space of hers had become the perfect movie screen upon which projections could be shined by bright and imaginative college boys who then would think that they loved their own projections.

Celeste's love for her friend was very real. It had always mystified me how they might have got along, except perhaps as a puzzle and a puzzle solver. Celeste was as I have described her, rammed full of life in much the same way that Callista seemed to be emptied out. To be fair to Callista, or Kate, I had not seen her in years and I also hold a very dim view of all men and women. They are all either fools or charlatans or else they are too tolerant of the fools and charlatans in their midst.

Callista arrived, and I had cooked a gourmet meal of veal marsala and mushroom risotto and fried asparagus. I have always loved to cook. It is a passionate exercise but it requires a plan and well-timed execution. It has taught me to be a certain way about all of my passions. I learned that it is best never roll over and let passion express itself through me unmediated and as an explosion. I prefer to respect it, nurture it, suppress it, and harness it into useful energies.

"Is this veal?" Callista asked.

"No, it is chicken," I responded.

"No, it is veal," Celeste said.

"I can't eat it," Callista said.

"I am so sorry," I apologized. "How thoughtless of me and how short-sighted. I should have considered the possibility that you would not eat veal."

"It's not just veal," she added, "but also most meats and most prepared foods. I think we should only eat what has been produced by sustainable organic farming."

"If we were to do that," I said, "most people would starve, the environment would suffer even more, and people would start to get sick. It is such a California vanity to talk about sustainable farming. There is an abundance of small local farms run by hippies there that can supply a tiny percentage of food locally. But each of those farms is by definition not sustainable because California has no water. Stop the massive unsustainable publicly funded redistribution of water and those farms dry up. And so-called sustainable farms use two and a half times as much energy as conventional farms, so they are environmentally unsound. And the incidences of poor produce, diseased produce, tainted produce, and even pesticide-laced produce all go up when the food supply is so fragmented. And there will never be the infrastructure for sustainable agriculture to supply even a smaller fraction of the food that people need. The answer is not sustainable farms, but reforming our existing agriculture to provide healthier food in an environmentally safer manner."

"We have to start somewhere, because every child," she continued, "has a right to delicious and organic food from sustainable farms."

"On your ashram, maybe," I added, "but few concepts are as addle-brained as the so-called right to food."

That effectively put an end to the discussion and to dinner and to my active participation in the group. Celeste and Callista retired to the living room to renew the bonds of their friendship. I cleaned up, drank a beer that I retrieved myself, and began to re-read *The Canterbury Tales.* Soon I was called into the living room, where I continued to read and tried to keep to myself. But there was some discussion about an opinion piece that Callista had been asked to submit to the editorial page of the *New York Times.* I honestly tried to stay out of the discussion. Then Callista drew me in by handing me her draft of the piece and asking for me to give my opinion.

"It is charming and well written," Celeste had already commented. I shot her a glance, as she continued, "It is full of feeling and delightfully and gracefully expresses its positions and opinions."

Callista looked at me, and it grew a little bit colder in the room. Celeste looked at me and I could feel her eyes on my skin.

"I am really not equipped to speak on the matter from a substantive perspective. And I am also constrained by the fact that I am not really your friend, Callista, and that you and I do not share that kind of openness."

"We are friends," she said, "because Celeste loves you. So I must love you as well. You may feel free to be honest."

"Well, I am honored. But you really cannot want to extend that honor to me," I said, "since you do not know me well enough. The offering of opinions as you request would be unwise, until we have spent a lot more time with each other, and you have learned the kind of opinions that I keep."

"What you are saying makes me value your opinion all that much more," she returned, "because you clearly intend to be honest. And you are being humble about the substance. You know quite a bit about the subject. But I am mainly interested in your opinion about the writing."

Celeste looked at me and for the first time in the years I had known her as a friend and the months I had loved her as a woman she had a blank look on her face.

"It is not writing," I said. "It is clownishness. The only thing missing are those little symbols you make out of punctuation. I think you call them emoticons. It is not even journalism or even West Coast journalism. I guess it could be called West Cost digital journalism. But if you look up the word "writing" in the dictionary, I am sure that West Coast digital journalism is listed as an antonym. Your hyphens almost outnumber commas. No idea is expressed other than by disjointed ejaculation. The tone is that of a middle school social studies presentation: like, you know, maybe we would all be better off if we lived in teepees."

Celeste looked down, not knowing that at that moment I had never loved her more purely or more honestly.

Callista fired back, "I am not in need of your approval."

"And that is a good thing," I said, "because it is unlikely to be forthcoming."

A general silence ensued from that. I had shaken the bunk bed. No response was the best response. Callista left eventually, although I am not sure if it was later that day or days later. Celeste and I had the conversation a few days after that, a few silent and watchful days. Celeste started the conversation.

"You probably should not have done that to Callista," she said.

"Love should not lie," I said, "and that means she should see the two of us clearly and take all of it in the right spirit. She should be ecstatic that you are loved by a man who gives you only his heart and not his guile."

"It's unusual that being loved so well should feel like having been handled rather roughly. You have a strange way of wooing."

"It is my own way."

"I think that is an accurate and descriptive summary. I certainly have not seen it anywhere else."

"I love you, Celeste, in a way that is almost impossible to bear. Let's just run away, you and I. My sister has a place in the woods of Montana with an extra house on the ranch. We could stay there for free, at least at first. We could each write. We could find a way to get by. We would be away from all the lies and the compliments and the false praise and the hypocrisy. We would be free of all the people who speak only what is dead in their hearts. And we would be successful and then we could write our own ticket."

"If you are asking me to marry you," she said, "I will. But I have to stay here and work for the paper. I can't flee my friends and family. I need them. And I will learn to live with the way you feel about people. But I will not move in order to escape civilization."

That was about fifteen years ago. For the last dozen years or so, I have been shackled to a silent foe. But my wife was never and is not Celeste. Celeste moved separately on to a successful career and to her own marriage. I had found those two things separately as well and they lasted until I landed here. My career can no longer be said to be successful. My marriage has certainly suffered, although I do not know if it could ever be said to have been successful. I am not sure what marriage ever is. The question becomes: Successful at what?

And if you have been a careful reader, you do not need me to supply my answers. You feel them in your own mind. You may sense them as your understanding of my point of view. Or you may realize that they have always been your own.

I had come to the right decision about Celeste but I had come to it backwards or for the inverse of the right reason. I decided I would not stay with her unless she could have lived with me apart from the world and let herself be loved with total honesty and without the specters of slight pale deceptions. But I think that part of the eighth divine insight might be that it turns out that it can never have been possible to have been married and to have lived and loved with total honesty and without the ghosts of little white lies, and that somehow the true, honest self and loving attachment are at odds. So I was glad that such a thing did not happen with Celeste. In all honesty, I was very glad.

This memory had come to me when I had gone for a run. Exercise was an important element of my spiritual survival in prison and will also be when I leave it. From out of the fog of this particular late evening at the end of my run came a voice, a soft but strong and recognizable feminine voice, with more than a little transcendent authority in it.

"You know that eighth insight can be turned inside out, don't you?" said the beautiful and commanding divine savior of a woman who had more than once come into my prison cell to dispense to me the heavenly truth. Until such time as I had seen her at that moment I had not even known there was such a thing as designer exercise clothes, but apparently there is a French company, called Anatomie, and they had made her black leggings, her white scarf, her black fleece top, and the gray plaid parka she wore over it. Her deportment was playful and brisk and it was full of that enigmatic grace and mysticism that so typifies many of the parables she had told in the New Testament.

"I am not ever sure I get any of it right," I answered. "It is all rather deep and complex."

"Just keep being careful about coming to any conclusions by remembering the first revelations. And know you are heading for the final understanding and will begin to see the connectedness of all of these insights. You will always be in a state of learning and of trying to understand even at that point."

"I kind of get that, but what does that part you said about 'inside out' mean?"

"You are correct in assuming that love and affection make the most intrusive inroads into innermost and truest part of the soul and that those attachments make it necessarily less honest and pure. But if you invert that you will see that the damage also runs in the other direction, if you know what I mean."

"I think, I hope that I begin to see what you are saying," I said. "We should draw a sharp division between the self and love. That same indestructible element of soul that is shown in the eighth insight is where we should dwell and prosper, and then we may love only selflessly."

"I think you are only beginning to grasp the way in which the revelations are connected, nor is your analysis all that particularly deep. Your friend Psycho had loved you, which is what I had almost said to you at our last meeting. I am not sure you knew it or were able to admit it. It was also ingrained in him that the self and love are often at odds. He simply and elementally did what he thought was right by that feeling. There was not an ounce of self in his consideration or in his love."

I was stunned by this revelation, but mostly by the truth of it, which I had only partially realized until I had heard it spelled out for me.

"And it all may be in how you remember Celeste, or remember anything," she added, smiling. "Memory and willfulness are always in a bit of a wrestling match, and this is inherent to thinking and imagination and to who and what you are. Try to think back to your strongest and earliest memories." And she jogged away, very stylishly.

MY DRUID MOTHER

My very first memory, I believe, is of gravel and it is of gravel of exactly the same kind that can be found at the Manchester minimum-security prison comprising the running track that is around the circumference of the softball fields, where I had decided to place myself every evening at a very early point when I first found myself on the inside, and after I had determined that I should make sure that I dedicated as much of my prison time as possible to various manners of self-improvement, having planned to emerge from this place in better condition than I had entered it, and taking the added time and opportunity that I have for reading to focus only on reading those books that I feel offer me the opportunity to brush with greatness, and to a large degree also focusing on my health and physical well-being, which has been done with considerably greater ease than confronting the more difficult pleasures of Dickinson or Goethe or Joyce. Everything in prison is on a very early daily schedule, meaning that breakfast is at 6 a.m., work starts at 7.30 a.m., lunch is at 11 a.m. and dinner is at 4 p.m., leaving any European feeling that an entire evening meal was missing, and leaving no time early in the day for running or for any elective activity, requiring that I have each day gone to the running track only in the evenings, before we have to put out the lights and retire to our cells.

My divine visitor had left me again, alone on that running oval, and I knew she had somehow imparted to me that memory of

Celeste and also set me up for having this one, so I looked down at the gray gravel of the prison track, which was exactly the same as that of my life's very first memory; each stone about the size of a green pea but irregular in shape and sharp on the corners and edges with the mass of them making a distinctive crunching sound when one steps on it, a sound that is very similar to that of a car tire passing very slowly over crusted snow and ice. When one picks it up it has a remarkably sensual and enjoyable quality which illustrates the way in which that crunching sound is made, because each pea-sized nugget is covered in a thin coat of a stone powder that serves as a dry lubricant that allows each gravel grain to slide against those next to it, the stones rubbing and sliding against one another and together smoothly and sounding pleasingly, and generating even more of the dust that is the mark of their being constituent parts of a larger whole. This quality of moving easily together in a larger whole is what makes the gravel so useful, because it flattens as you walk or run on it and with a cushioning effect that is as agreeable to your step as the sound is to your ear.

I have always liked running on this gravel because the softness of that sound would have an interesting effect when it consequently had been put into a gentle rhythm by the sound of my feet jogging on the prison track, setting up a moderate tempo in which each beat would strike with that crunch that is neither sharp nor distinct, since each beat would have its own beginning, its small crescendo and its denouement, such that were it to be compared to a drum or drumming the sound would have to be that of the brush and not the drumstick. Combining those qualities with the slow rhythm of the jog, the gravel became like listening to the drummer in a smoky Harlem jazz club, laying down the languid rhythm for a classic jazz ballad, so that it was not difficult to seem to internally hear the strains of "My Funny Valentine" or "Autumn in New York" or "Willow, Weep for Me" rising above the rhythm of the soft crunch, crunch, crunch of the gravel under my feet while I was running alone in the twilight on that gravel track.

And that was often the mood with which I have confronted that exercise. The somber jazz disposition was perhaps too fitting for the baleful setting and the solitary exercise, meaning that my runs have trained my body but have also exercised my soul with that marvelous self-indulgence that is the blue mood of loss and regret and belatedness and is also a way of wallowing in that pain and elevating it to a level of both celebrating it and diminishing it. The smoke-filled jazz club in my head was generated by the gravel, and time after time such as this I have also sat by that track and held that gravel in my hand and with the same unforgettable feeling I would recall the yesterdays of my earliest youth and of what I believe was my very first memory, and that would be of this same wonderful gravel, grinding its way into the skin of my cheek and temple and forehead as my innocent toddler face had been forced down into it by the boy who was my best friend.

An entire complex vignette of memories may reside in something so unprepossessing as a handful of small stones, memories which may not have been accessible through a voluntary mental search but which may spring from the associations contained within an object or objects, remembrances so vivid and so seemingly new that they present themselves to the individual as fresh and engrossingly crammed with events and feelings that, even though they are not real or actually being witnessed with the senses, are far more sympathetic and transparent than the concrete occurrences that one may witness and that involve actual persons whose motives and thoughts are almost entirely hidden to our senses, and with the dramatic impact of these memories being enhanced and not diminished by the fact that they may not be entirely comprised of recollections and historical representations but may in part be authored by the person doing the remembering. It is for these reasons perhaps that the memory of being pushed face first into the gravel at the age of one or two years was not entirely unpleasant. What was present in this particular memory is perhaps only slightly more important than what was absent, which in the case of this specific memory would be my mother. It would make sense that the skein of my childhood remembrances would begin at the moment when I had at first been out of my mother's care or that moment when something of note actually first happened without her being there, and I assume that she was doing her housework nearby on that hot summer early weekend afternoon and was keeping an eye on me somehow from a safe distance after she had left me to play with my toy rubber truck in our gravel driveway. In some issue that arose concerning the truck, Skippy Hanrahan, who was exactly 364 days older than I and who was our nextdoor neighbor, found that the optimal way for him to diplomatically address the truck issue was to push my face into the gravel. I thought of my absent mother at that moment and I vividly remember that some of the gravel stuck to my face when he finally let me up. And now for me part of my mother's spirit resides in that gravel, along with these other memories.

Both by the freshness of these recollections, which are wholly inspired entirely and suddenly by objects, and by the possibility that they may in part be dramatic re-creations of an event, containing certain novel elements that owe more to aesthetics than to the historical truth, give the opportunities for certain surprises and revelations. So it was in the case of these memories, for stranded within this particular frame of remembrances are unexpectedly found certain characters, elements, and deeds which bear a direct relationship to events and persons that occur elsewhere in this narrative and which happened only much later than the time of the earlier remembered occurrences, giving one great cause to not only reconsider the meaning of those earlier memories, but to re-evaluate the significance of both the discovery that significant characters in the narrative may have been known earlier than was previously thought and the fact that such a discovery had, for some reasons, remained hidden for so long.

Skippy resides now in some Alaskan pipeline laborers' camp or a flat suburban tract of cinder block homes in Florida or perhaps even in a quiet grave, as well as existing in some kind of lesser pantheon of legendary figures who peopled the neighborhood of my earliest youth. Face down in the gravel, I could still see the infantile beginnings of what would later become his mercurial charm and his lively strength and the undeniable juvenile charisma that could only arise from a complete lack of self-consciousness combined with a devilish smile. Everything about him was left-handed. He was compact and athletic. I would grow to be bigger, stronger, faster and more athletic than he by the time I was only about six or seven years old, but it would be several more years after that before I actually felt those things to be true. He had that wonderful quality of being able to act and in most cases to perform effectively without thinking, a faculty that was beyond me even at the earliest age. He was blond and had brown eyes and was considered to be a cute boy whose father was a steamfitter, black Irish, had a wry sense of humor and was always wincing from the pain of a permanent back injury, and whose mother was a redheaded drunk.

Even though everything that happened to me in those first ten or twelve years of my life, living in that smalltown neighborhood, was either related to my mother or related in some way to my nascent independence from her, the map of the neighborhood was almost literally my father. It was a working class neighborhood, and he was a young lawyer with a practice in the city and by a certain point he had done legal work, most of the time for free, for almost every one of our neighbors.

There was a young girl, only three houses down on our side of the street, who clearly saw my father as a father figure of her own, which when I was six struck me as a somewhat overly broad definition of the relation but which arose naturally from the fact that I had witnessed my father when I was even younger getting dressed to make the long trip to a place with the exotic name of Grand Rapids in order to perform some legal service on behalf of this girl's family, said legal service being to procure for Debbie Reiver and her family the freedom from the financial loss they might have incurred when her own father had been killed in a traffic accident caused by a truck that had crossed the middle of a Michigan road and had run headlong into her father's car. My father had undertaken the case, as he often had with other cases involving our neighbors, with no fees being charged, and the subsequent relief felt by Debbie and her mother and her brother, Gary, had not only generated the gratitude of the younger two Reivers, but caused them to see him in a rather paternal role. My father's ersatz adoption of Debbie had not prevented her from later attempting to find in promiscuity and teenage motherhood something that she had lost in Grand Rapids that fateful day; nor had it kept Gary, who after high school had survived an army tour of duty in Viet Nam, from going off the road on a curve on that steep hill leading up to the neighborhood and taking with his own the life of Betje Koekje.

The Koekjes, seventh house down on the other side, were a large and boisterous family of Dutch immigrants, the inside of whose household I imagined as being as crowded and as lively and as earthy as the Brueghel painting of the *Wedding Dance*, long before I had ever seen the painting, and to this day I cannot look at the *Gipsy Girl* painting by Franz Hals without feeling that it is a picture of Madolen Koekje, the oldest of the six siblings. Mr. Koekje had always scared me as a child, and I gave him a wide berth partly because I do not think I ever saw him when he was not stained with the grease and grit of his automobile repair job and partly because of something about him which was summarized by my father, who would nonchalantly say simply that he was a Dutchman, pronouncing that single word as if it had been an entire closing statement at trial. I was to lose this fearful apprehension of Mr. Koekje's gruff and brusque demeanor years later when I was sixteen or seventeen and the family car I was driving had broken down on a remote country road, and Mr. Koekje showed up with an avuncular warmth that was new and surprising to me and as a result of my phone call to my parents, as he fixed the car without requiring so much as a word of thanks, since he was more or less the automobile mechanic permanently on call for our family, servicing or fixing our cars as needed and at odd times and for no cost and with all the taciturn version of cheerfulness that he could muster, simply because my father had performed some large and complicated and useful legal services for him, also at no cost.

We had a plumber such as that, who lived next door to the Koekjes, the sixth house down on the other side, Mr. O'Bryan, whom I distinctly remember fixing a broken water heater at our house at around midnight one evening during a party to which he had not been invited and cheerfully asserting when my father tried to pay him, "Your money is no good with me," and lodging in me permanently the ironies of that phrase. Throughout those first years I remember in that neighborhood that a fresh-baked strawberry pie would land on our front porch about every two months, sealed up neatly in a light white cardboard box, which would open and fill our kitchen with the scent of butter and fresh-baked dough and that sweet and tangy aroma that only strawberries may have. Perhaps I might have once seen that the box had been left there in the moments before dawn by Mrs. Granger, who owned a little bakery in our small town and who lived at the other end of the street, or, as is more likely, I had imagined it from something I had heard. My mother was always made aware in advance by Mrs. Mersereau, who lived three houses down on the other side of the street, of any important sale of large appliances that might be about to occur at the Sears, where her husband was a salesman. And Mr. Keenan would often get us free tickets and other special considerations at the ice skating rink where he worked.

There were other men and women in the neighborhood who would seem to take care to give me certain attention, such as the men who would coach me in little league baseball and who taught me that game, or the neighbor woman who took the time to show me her operation for the keeping and breeding of beagles, or the others who would variously loan me a ten-cent piece so that I could buy ice cream from the good humor man without having to run home for money or who would make calls of which I was unaware and which would track my wanderings so that when I returned home my mother would often already know quite a bit about my day. In all of this was a kind of a map of the unseen helpfulness of my father that overlay the neighborhood, and it was how I often learned many things about this emotionally distant and often absent man, indirectly or only upon later reflection of seemingly unrelated incidents, which made the neighborhood a little bit more my own and slightly safer for me than perhaps it was for the other children. But that is not what returns to me from those times now as I sit next to the track in prison with a few stones of gravel being loosely shaken in my hand. What I feel is a sort of a connection from that place to this place, one that is about the understanding of freedom and also something else, and it is a connection that is made even stronger by the fact that this new and current understanding of those events contains within it a very direct and startling personal connection to the events and persons within this prison.

Even a hurried perusal of any English dictionary will elicit a quick and vivid picture of how the Dutch have been seen by the English-speaking peoples. You will see Dutch oven, Dutch angles, Dutch auctions, and Dutch doors. There is also going Dutch, Dutching, Dutch date, and a Dutch book. One may also have a Dutch uncle or be in Dutch with someone. And of course there is Dutch courage. The portrait drawn from those words and phrases is one of a people who are ingenious when it comes to practical matters, who are not particularly generous, who can be quite brusque and poorly tempered, and who perhaps have a demon or two that may be exorcised by strong drink, and that would have been Mr. Koekje, or at least how I saw him and experienced him through what I knew of his family, particularly his son, Henry, who was part of our gang of boys from our end of the street.

Henry's sister, Ciska, was what we called a tomboy and was a year older than I was. We played a brutal boy version of backyard American tackle football with neighborhood boys of all sizes and rules that kept changing, but what did not change was that it involved full-body collisions at relatively high speeds and without any safety equipment or supervision and that were followed by scrums and wrestling struggles that concluded on the ground in a pile. In school, the Koekje girls were known by the American versions of their names, Madeleine, Betty, and Cindy, who, since we also knew them as Madolen, Betje, and Ciska, gave us a kind of intimacy that came with growing up in that neighborhood, this being additional to the intimacy we boys all felt with Cindy because she always played in those backyard football games with us, at first because she was faster and tougher and more athletic than most of us and later because she knew and welcomed the fact that in those scrums our hands would be at work doing more than trying to dislodge the football or bring her to the ground.

Betty, who later was to die in a car that Gary Reiver would drive over the side of our street that was at a bend where it descended the steep hill into town, was special in her way, and in a way that was quite similar to many of the cases of other young women in our town. By the time I had graduated from high school I knew more than a healthy share of dead young people and knew certainly more than my own children could come to know by the same time in their lives, although I am not sure if this may have been a factor of what is called socio-economics, or of later changes made in automobile safety, or just of the times, but upon reflection I saw the way in which the young women in that unfortunate group were all like Betty. Luanne Kerner also died in a car crash, and Linda Buss died on the back of a motorcycle that some boy had wrapped around a telephone pole, and Patty Comstock, who had actually been what passed for my girl-friend when we were in kindergarten, died from a drug overdose. In each case, every death had been associated with the fact that each girl had been in the company of boys who had been a few years older than the girls. And each girl had been pretty, and more than that, like Betty Koekje, each girl had been very physically attractive and sweet-tempered and feminine and had attained those developments at a relatively early stage, as in the case of Luanne Kerner, with whom it had almost been as if her soon-to-follow death had been fore-ordained by the way in which she had seemingly developed the body of a voluptuous woman in the three months of summer between eighth and ninth grades. These girls would be selected by and would be marvelously attracted to the seductive allure of these roaring boys who lived with one foot in the void, boys such as were being formed in our neighborhood. These girls fell to a kind of harvest of death simply because they were sexy.

Henry Koekje was our friend, and his presence in our little gang of pre-adolescent boys bracketed me between Skippy and him in the middle of the leadership of our little group, which was comprised of the boys from our end of the street. The boys from the other end of the street, the Grover boy and the McCain kid and the Pugh boy and their friends, may have had first names, but we did not care to remember them because we were at war with them, which was only a natural consequence of geography. Somewhere about six houses down from our end of the street was the demarcation point for our gang, ending on the other side of the street at the Koekje home, because the home on the other side of it was occupied by an older couple with no children, and on our side of the street the boundary was the Blanton home, which housed Jimmy Blanton, and he could belong to neither gang of boys. It was often said of him that he was retarded, but even in those less enlightened days we were told not to call him that, and we were merely told that as an infant he had suffered a high fever and that it had somehow affected his development. It was just that he was not at all like all of the other boys since he was stolid and indifferent and there was the hint of a threat to him at all times, as if he might break out of his apathy with some inexplicable violence. Oddly enough, he kept rabbits in a pen at the back of the Blanton property and later, when I had been forced to read *Of Mice and Men* in high school, I could only picture Jimmy Blanton in the role of Lennie Small, especially since Jimmy was also larger, stronger, and older than the rest of us but did not mix with the older boys his own age, preferring instead to show up among us, unwanted and watched carefully since none of the our boys were indifferent or stolid and in fact were the opposite, and all of our violence could be explained. So from the Koekje home on the other side of the street, and on our side from the Blanton home to my end of the street, the boys were in our gang with Skippy. We had at our end the cul de sac with a pine tree in the middle of a turnaround, and they had at their end the steep and winding hill that was the only entrance into the neighborhood.

Henry Koekje was tough, as was spoken to by the way his dad appeared, to be and he was often our designated champion, selected for the tests of single combat because of his toughness and because Skippy usually wanted to avoid getting involved himself and because I had a very vivid imagination and could too easily envision various and unwanted outcomes to my own involvement in such contests. And Henry seemed to enjoy them, even though later, in high school, Henry was to become sort of a ladies man, and this was based on a kind of sensitivity that young women saw in him and which I had overlooked, but which in retrospect had been evident in a couple of instances. One was when we were throwing rocks over the cliff behind the O'Bryan house, and young Davy Miller reached into his shorts and in a rather perfunctory manner pulled out a still warm turd that simply rested in his hand. I can still feel the pride of that moment that I had in keeping myself from regurgitating, a pride which was doubled when Henry just let go and vomited, and the combination of Davy's action and Henry's reaction caused each one of the other boys except me to follow their example. My mental composure was often my contribution to the group, and in this case I calmly suggested that Davy send the offending object the way of the rocks. At another time Henry was clearly getting the better of some kid from the other end of the street in a fist fight that the members of both gangs were watching and the outcome of which would determine some property right to some part of the middle of the neighborhood. Henry usually bested whichever boy they put forward. The fight had basically been about to be concluded in our favor when one of the boys mentioned that Henry's face was bleeding, and he put his hand to his face and touched the blood and when he looked and saw the blood on his hand he began to cry and he ran home.

At the edge of the backyards on our side of the neighborhood there was forest that sloped gently down to a creek that was at the middle of a small valley, and on the other side the forest sloped up and began that part of it that was wild, and that whole forest was our

Germania, the wilderness beyond the edge of our empire, but it was also a part of the soul of each boy and simply felt and looked and smelled different but in a way that would appeal to a part of the heart of any boy, a part of it that was atavistic and bolder and brighter and just plain better. There were so many secret spots and special trees and hiding places that it would be impossible to explain what each of them meant. In some places the ground was a soft carpet of dead pine needles while in other places the brush was so thick it could not be penetrated by sight for more than a few feet. and it was not uncommon to be surprised by a deer leaping out of that brush. Some trees were strong enough and high enough that, after climbing for many minutes to the top, a view could be secured that would take in much of the canopy of those wooded hills, stretching for miles.

For a small town there was a fairly extensive sewer system that we would roam for hundreds of yards beneath the road surface in these tunnels, in the confined spaces of which a boy of over ten would have had trouble but also in which for the several years before we reached that age we had been able create a subterranean extension of our realm, and we could even store supplies in some of the culverts that would open up into larger spaces. The sewers to me will always be like the gravel in that they remind me of my mother or of her absence, with the difference being that the gravel came to remind me of the first wonderful time of experiencing something memorable in her absence, but the sewers related to the first time when I found a way to enforce her absence internally from my concerns and my thoughts and feelings, since every one of the things we did as this group of boys, or almost every one of them, had been expressly forbidden by my mother, and this particularly applied to any sojourns which might have taken me beyond the neighborhood.

My mother was none of the things that her surviving older sisters, my aunts, were, and perhaps this was because she had been born the last and most beautiful of ten children and had for her entire life received all of the attention of her older siblings, and none of it was ever disciplinary or even critical. My aunt Rose, the oldest, had been sort of a junior mother for this entire family and was simply the most generous and warm-hearted soul I have ever known, one who never saw me or my sisters and cousins without some gift, tangible or intangible, and who was embarrassed by any gratitude that was shown her. My aunt Sue was as playful as any group of boys and would laugh at the slightest provocation and was an excellent professional chef who would occasionally enlist my cousins and sisters and me in the service of making a large batch of ravioli or other pasta or pastries, all of which would fill her house with the most inviting and memorable scents of garlic and sausage and basil and tomato sauce. My aunt Anne had been a Navy nurse and was practical and worldly and understanding to a degree that would have been surprising in any woman of her era, but in a daughter of immigrants her refusal to be judgmental was astonishing. My mother was, as I have said, none of those things her sisters were and she supervised and monitored and taught and admonished and prohibited and scrutinized and censored my sisters and me with great skill and passion, doing all of this until such time as we would walk out the door and go to play in the neighborhood, and, unlike my sisters, I went to play with the boys.

I took my very first exciting and noteworthy trip outside of the neighborhood when I was five and just before I had entered kindergarten, and it was in this episode that I now find a curious connection to this prison. It had been an excursion to the town and through the sewers, the corrugated steel tubes of about three feet in diameter which had seemed to me to be great hallways that must have been built by magical underground creatures, each step deeper into them being an entire journey into a place that had been forbidden and was also forbidding, and when we would get to a sewer grate we could be undetected witnesses to the street life above as if we had been invisible or were secret agents, the mere idea of which was magical and astonishing, the simple notion of being beneath the surface, unseen but seeing.

And it was in this instance that I saw something which at the time had only an independent significance, for its peculiarity and its noteworthiness, but which now shines forth with a radiance of new meanings which race beyond my ability to understand and which has and will have become the subject of much theological debate among the votaries and practitioners of this book, and its other devoted readers. Looking through one of these grates and into the main street of the town, in the small square in front of the general store and across from the post office, I was able to see the first person I had ever seen of what I had thought at the time was African descent, even though I had seen many African Americans from a distance on sports fields and through the car windows as we rode by them while they were waiting at bus stops downtown in the city and even though this young woman, I realized later, was clearly more of a mix of the African and Caucasian, and perhaps even Asian, races. Since this entire memory had been submerged in my consciousness until that moment in which I picked up the gravel, I can't say whether it completely surprised me or that it did not shock me in the least to see that this young woman, sitting casually on the hood of a late model American sedan next to Madolen Koekje, laughing with Madolen and touching her and sipping lukewarm beer while they were flirting with the young man in front of them both, was none other than the same alluring distaff messiah who had been visiting me in this place of incarceration for the purpose of my spiritual education.

This feeling of not being surprised by being surprised was enhanced by the freshness and by the possible novelty of this image or memory which appeared to me in the mantle of truth, since it was a vision or a remembrance that had clearly been made my own and as such had quickened my interest and held me in thrall in the way that some wonderful and lucid disclosure in a novel disturbs the reader to read directly further without delay, and which was heightened by the obvious fact that she had little changed if at all, and perhaps even that only in her clothing, between the time of this, one of my earliest memories, and the time I had just seen her jogging away from me here on this track. She was not dressed in her designer jogging wear but was clothed in a plain pink sleeveless sweater top and knee-length blue jean pants, with pink ankle socks and white flat-soled sneakers, and with her hair pulled back by a hair band, which meant that, in short, she was dressed like my teenaged older sisters or like Madolen or any of the other girls of that age and time, and none of this was so strangely familiar as the understanding that I also and only now recognized the young man whose company she and my neighbor were so clearly enjoying. He was the same age as the girls and appeared to be at least two dozen years younger in this tableau than he was the last time I had seen him, which had only been a few hours earlier in the mess hall at dinner, but what was behind those eyes had not altered or had not changed much because I could see in them clearly that same wisdom and knowing recall that they still so unmistakably had now, some thirty years later, even as they then turned to look directly at my five-year-old self, hidden in the darkness behind the sewer grate, as both he and the celestial young lady (but not Madolen) turned to look, and I found myself, or my past self, face to face, or face to grate, with her and with a young and handsome and thin version of Big Frank, and as I came face to face with their apparent and historical friendship.

When I had to return home from my sewer sojourns later that day it actually put me into a state of panic, because I had always been subject to the understanding that my mother knew everything that I ever did, a certain knowledge of mine that had been casually reinforced by the occasional comment that she had made from time to time that had revealed that she actually had known something that I had done that day and which she had undoubtedly gathered from some phone call she had received and of which I was unaware. I literally believed that she would see on me or in me all that I had done that day and that she would know I had violated her prohibition against leaving the neighborhood or doing anything even remotely dangerous or which would reflect poorly upon her if I were to have been caught doing it. The fear I felt was elemental, and I did not want to answer her questions as to where I had been.

I entered the kitchen and I was stricken, and in some manner this might have been helpful as it hit me in such a way that I fell deeper within myself and was silent and still. The kitchen would several years later be a place where my mother would smash me square in the chest with a grapefruit she had decided to throw rather than to slice, after I had made some sarcastic comment, and where she would break a wooden paddle on my posterior, or it may have been over my back, and the kitchen was also more or less her realm, and even my father seemed reduced when he was in that room, substantially her room.

I lied. I do not know what had even possessed me to consider trying such a gambit. Perhaps I had been impressed by the notion of recently having been invisible or the awareness of keeping beneath the surface had given me the idea, particularly as I had also been beneath the surface for my first ever close inspection of an exotic woman of African descent, talking to my neighbor and to a dark and handsome young man toward whom I had felt a natural affinity. Or maybe it had no import at all, since I had already taken the step of disobeying my mother by going into the sewer and out of our neighborhood, and that naturally meant that it was just as likely that a lie would follow, or maybe it was some kind of contagion I had contracted from being with the other boys, for certainly I had witnessed the indomitable Skippy lie on several occasions. I told her I had just been a few doors down the street, playing with Billy Thompson.

She believed it. She might well have also been preoccupied, because the moment passed quickly but not without giving me the feeling that I had won the lottery or that I had discovered a new continent or had made some great scientific finding or that the secrets of an entire universe had just opened up to me. She simply could not see that I had told her a lie and there was something about that which had been sublime and had been more than liberating. I remember every significant first I have ever experienced, but I remember each of them with less vividness and less intensity than I still remember that moment, and all of the boyish peregrinations and extirpations and conversions and exchanges and confrontations which I have already described only became possible after that day and as a consequence of that moment when I was no longer who I had been and

I had forever been given the key to be able to continue to make that kind of transformation.

We moved from that neighborhood later, when I was twelve and I began junior high school, to a place three miles away, across the highway at the end of another street with a cul de sac street and a turnaround, a newly constructed community in which the men who lived there were doctors and executives and my father was not the only lawyer and the houses were much bigger. Essentially my childhood had ended, and I found a girlfriend, and the original neighborhood had also been directly about my mother and about the breaking of that bond but it had also been indirectly about my father. The people of that older neighborhood had reflected for me the things about him that I did not see when I saw him at home, which was essentially at dinner in that kitchen and for a few hours afterward or on the weekends. There were other similar but metaphysical neighborhoods that indirectly reflected him after he died, and I learned to also see him in them fairly clearly but indirectly even though they existed in the intangible realm of the mind and personality of his surviving spouse, and those inner neighborhoods of hers reflected his isolation and his frustration and his losses and limits, and I came to know him better and to love him more again as a function of learning about him indirectly, just the same way as I had learned about him from the old neighborhood where I had lived from birth to adolescence. And that was just one thing that I learned there. I also learned that I could survive in this prison.

The two are inextricably linked and prison regularly brings back the memories of that neighborhood. The gravel is not the only thing. In here, I have found myself back among the boys, and it is oddly like home. And I know that the old neighborhood experience will never remotely be part of the life of my son or daughter, who grew up with play dates and organized events and with parents who did not lecture or prohibit but who were much more a part of their lives. Perhaps there is still an American neighborhood now where boys roam free and time is unstructured and safety is an afterthought and wars are fought and fist fights are brushed off as naturally occurring and some of the children do not survive to adulthood. It is not something I would want for my children, except as an abstraction. But I would not trade it for anything in my experience. I love Skippy for being my first friend and for having pushed my head into the gravel. I experience all of these memories of that past time in much the same way as I have experienced jogging on the prison track. It is like a jazz sound track in my mind, desultory and evocative, with no discernible plot line, loaded with self-indulgent feeling, with each small section containing its own story and with an occasional heightened and intense and unforgettable fragment, and about each of them there was something that showed that we boys had been given a kind of curious freedom that had been something on the order of perhaps too adult, which may be why the memories of these adventures can spring to mind from a stone of gravel in a prison exercise yard, and why there they have a deeper and spiritual meaning.

I had been exposed to the first nine disciples of truth, the visions of divine guidance, but I did not need them to know that memory can sometimes be a kind of Hell, and that it also is an integral and inseparable element of each soul. What I had gathered from my journey thus far is that while God may be transcendent what we may know of him or her is written on our inner parts. God's law is merely immanent and is at least in part composed of our memory. For instance, the very purpose of prayer is to remember. This ninth revelation only barely eluded my grasp in much the same way that it came to me clearly, as a memory or even as a vision. And now I knew that tenth element of the set of twelve divine truths was about to be shown to me in a much less inward way.

PETER SOONER

It is impossible to keep a troll locked up. This has never stopped governments from continuing to try to do it. It would be too amusing by half to say that Peter Sooner arrived in our minimum-security prison facility one summer day or that he had been incarcerated there, when it was more as if this place outside of Manchester, Kentucky, was simply the geographical spot at which he had fallen to earth from heaven or had climbed up to it from out of Hell. I believe he had been placed there, in order to convey to me the eleventh revelation. He was for one thing simply better than the rest of us. He was tall, about six feet four inches, thin but strappingly well-built, as if he were a basketball player. He was handsome with sandy blond hair and blue eyes that always had a playful shimmer in them. He was only about twenty-four years old and was fluent in Spanish, Italian, and French. He had the odd habit of breaking into song in a baritone voice that contained within in it a lower-register version of the pleasing tone of an Irish tenor. He was very bright and witty and was an amazing story teller and a liar of some accomplishment that was well beyond what could be indicated by his youth. He was charming to a fault, and his natural charisma would override any apprehension you might have that he was dealing with you falsely. Soon after he arrived fires began to break out.

There was a small forest fire that occurred just outside the prison facility and which drew fire trucks from the neighboring communities. No one knew how it started, but many of us watched it burn and watched it being put out. Peter had sidled up to me and stood there, watching with me as the tongues of lambent flame lapped against the sides of the trees, and the burning of living wood made a chorus of crackling and hissing.

"Have you ever noticed," he said, "how fire is dearer to us than food or love?"

"I have read those words somewhere," I said.

"I thought you would be the one who might."

"They are from some poem," I said, "and there is something about it sending sparks up into Heaven, or something like that."

"It is by D. H. Lawrence and it says, 'a huge blaze like a phallus into hollow space.' I guess that is the part you mean."

"It would have to be 'huge,' wouldn't it, if it were Lawrence? He also says something about fire being our brother."

"You remember the poem pretty well," he said. "It relates 'our fire' to fire in general."

"So, you are the one who set this thing?" I asked.

"I can't answer that but I will say this. The vast majority of people who set fires are males, and people who set fires for pleasure are said to be pathological. But on the other hand, it is quite prevalent and rather well accepted that young boys and adolescents will set fires rather blithely and without any signs of any kind of disorder."

"Well," I answered, "I do love a good fire."

"So you do, Christian. So you do."

There was a rather morose older man who was locked up with us. He had been a lawyer and had somehow become too close to his criminal clients. He was a bit heavy and had trouble getting around and needed a cane. His considerable intellect was often employed, planting and harvesting in the fields of cynicism. He was respected by the inmates for his ability to help them with their paperwork so he was in a sense a colleague or a rival of mine in that realm. There was something about him that was false. I am not sure what it was. Perhaps he never really engaged people. Maybe it was his beard. I had a bigoted former stepfather-in-law who used to unleash all manner of ethnic slurs on me for being half Italian, all of which would slide right off of me as being too antiquated to have any effect anymore and because I had never faced even the slightest degree of discrimination. But I always sort of adhered to one of his other biases or at least I saw some merit in it. He simply referred to any well-off or well-educated man who had a beard as a "bearded wonder," and I could never help but smile at that. There is at least the possibility of pretension in any beard.

Peter had somehow penetrated the shield this man held up that kept him from allowing himself to engage people. He and Peter were quite close, almost immediately. They both worked in the library although it was never clear how that plum job went to Peter so soon after he had arrived. One day in the mess hall, our bearded wonder suddenly stood bolt up, veered to his wounded side, careened into the next table, upset several lunch trays and glasses, convulsed several times and finally passed out and fell to the floor, clutching his hands to his throat.

"I thought that went rather well," Peter said to me. He had been sitting across from the man.

It was ruled an attempted suicide and that is in fact what it had been. The fellow had not died. He lived but in a much diminished state, lasting only a couple of more months in the federal prison hospital facility in Butner, North Carolina.

"I should have figured he would have botched it," Peter said later, when we learned that the man had lived, "you know, with him and that beard and all."

"You knew about it?" I asked.

"I helped him. He had some very serious problems at home. There were going to be some additional prosecutions, and he was going to have to be moved to a harsher facility. And worse, it was going to jeopardize what living his family had been able to maintain. He had been talking about it and about taking this way out. I sort of helped him to come to this decision. And I offered my practical assistance and directed my slaves to get some kitchen chemicals that would do the job for him. They were in his drinking glass. Apparently, he balked on drinking the proper amount. I had told him to do it with some flair, you know."

"Well, it was all rather dramatic," I offered.

"But it had the wrong ending," he answered, "which was not beautiful."

Peter's mention of "slaves" was not all that far off the mark. He was one of the small number of inmates who was a kind of a slave owner. It is one of the peculiar quirks of human nature that men and woman will want to abase themselves before some cause or some notion of the divine or some other individual and it is no less true in prison. Most of the young men who were in his slave stable put themselves there after they had heard him singing "If I Loved You," from the musical *Carousel* in the exercise yard. He was also quite obviously and strongly bisexual, so most of those boys were quite attached to him. There were only five or six that he truly seemed to own, and most of them were Puerto Rican Debating Society boys who were exiled from their community for being gay and were only reeled back in here and there as needed. They loved Peter for speaking Spanish and for being so beautiful.

They also had access to the prison microwave oven and they were magnificent at making snacks seemingly out of the very few resources available to prisoners. They all worked in the kitchen. Although the kitchen only ever produced the worst kind of bland provender, the dishes that these men could make in that microwave were an entirely different matter. They would fill the air with the scent of onion and garlic and tomato and cheeses, and for a few seconds there would be a hint of a memory of what really good cooking had been on the outside. One day, something was put in that oven that reacted to the microwaves in such a way that it exploded and started several small fires in the common room where the oven was located. I went to look at it and found Peter there.

"We meet again," I said. "I am starting to think there is a connection."

"There cannot possibly be one," he said, smiling. "Pyromania has long been associated with sexual impotence."

The reason that I know that Peter was bisexual rather than gay is that I had seen him in the visiting room. On warm summer days the visiting room was actually extended out into the yard in front of the prison and it could almost take on the relaxed atmosphere of a picnic. Whenever he had visitors, Peter's usually came in pairs, or sometimes there would be three of them. They would invariably be young women, and they would be quite friendly with each other as well as with him. Physical contact between inmates and visitors was prohibited because of the possibility of contraband being passed, but that rule was often neglected. Largely, though, there was no touching. The warmth that his visitors felt toward him was still palpable and it could be felt in the way they looked at him and talked with him. He also had the effect of drawing the attention of the female visitors who were there to see other inmates. He never discouraged this. He encouraged it. One such female visitor wandered into his little group after her inmate boyfriend had been called back into the facility for some reason or other. This prisoner's girlfriend did not leave when he had left and she then just became part of Peter's little harem that day. It was also a day when some of the prohibited touching had occurred. The calling away of the inmate and one other smaller administrative demand had left the outdoor portion of the visiting room not covered by any hack. Kissing, hugging, passionate embracing, groping, and outright sex ensued for several minutes during that short period. Some of that contact had involved Peter and the other inmate's girlfriend.

This brings us to the rather difficult-to-believe tale of the capuchin monkey. There would be times when Peter would just have this little monkey with him. It was inexplicable. The monkey only ever appeared when there were no guards to witness him. It was as if the little creature had some kind of hack radar. It was also unclear as to where the monkey was living. Capuchins do not naturally occur in North America any farther north than the southern half of Central America. It was still summer, so maybe it was able to temporarily survive in the Kentucky forests outside of the facility. It is possible that one of Peter's friends had placed the monkey in the woods outside of the prison. It certainly showed up inside the facility on occasion, usually when only a few inmates were around and off at the outer edges of the grounds, outside. Peter would be reading a book on the bench at one end of the complex or he would be talking with a group of inmates at the end of the exercise yard, and the little capuchin would be there by his side and looking every bit the part of an organ grinder monkey that so many of his species had been.

The inmate with the peregrinating girlfriend finally found the opportunity to confront Peter in just such a situation. He and a few of his friends had tracked Peter down at the field beside the bocce court. Because of his size and youth Peter did not invite personal confrontation directly. But this inmate figured that he had the drop on this big young man because he had his friends with him. He had not figured on the monkey. Just as this inmate was about to grab Peter and was counting on the assistance of his friends he saw out of the corner of his eye a furry brown and beige flash and before he knew it he was being set upon by a very quick and very resourceful *Cebus Capucinus* which landed on his head and neck and shoulders and began to shriek and pull out the inmate's hair and to pummel and to bite him about the face and ears and neck. The inmate took off on a run, flying past big Frank and the mafia guys at the bocce court, past the young black men playing basketball, past the bikers sitting on the benches. All the time, he kept trying to dislodge the simian from his person and each time he was only temporarily and barely able to get the monkey off his back, so to speak, and off his neck and shoulders. The animal would drop to the man's lower back, would clutch his shirt in his little hands and would hang on with all his might and then would return to shriek and pull and hit and bite about the man's head. It was a spectacle that only ended when the inmate ran into the administration building and the creature fled into the woods.

The ensuing administrative hearing must have been quite interesting but all we know of it is that the inmate accused Peter of owning the monkey and of having made the signal to sic the monkey on him. Peter had said such a thing was absurd. The other inmate had claimed that the monkey had been seen with Peter. Since no other inmate would allow himself to cooperate in the investigation, and each of them had said that they had seen nothing, it became merely the word of this inmate against that of Peter. Doubts were cast as to whether there had been a monkey at all, and the prison authorities certainly were required to be skeptical simply by the unlikeliness that a monkey of South and Central American habitats was lurking in the woods of Kentucky waiting to do the bidding of a particular inmate who had just arrived. Peter had played into the absurdity of the situation by claiming, "Oh, yes. I have seen that monkey. He's a good beast, he is. He will listen to reason. But we are only a passing acquaintance, he and I. He does not tell me where to live, and I do not tell him how to pick his friends." It was a statement, like so many others, that was only made more ridiculous by the likelihood that it was quite true. The inmate was sent to the hospital prison to be treated for rabies and for his injuries and was then transferred to another facility. His girlfriend continued to appear in our visitor room.

For much of the time he was with us, Peter seemed to be playing a role. This is a statement so trite as to be blandly applicable to every other prisoner in the place, but for him it was different. He inhabited the role, or roles, and they were all considerably more dramatic than the quiet and determined and guarded persona assumed by so many others. The capuchin episode also lent to him a certain bizarre air of quirky menace that he wore like a cape. The satisfaction that he got from playing the role was augmented by the pleasure he had received from courting the danger of that confrontation and from the way in which he had destroyed that other inmate. He had become Peter of the inexplicable monkey and he enjoyed it. He had said about it, "Watch me. I will fly too. I will wash myself clean in the bath of the keenest winds."

The next fire occurred in the room that was known as the chapel and that was used by most of the religious denominations for various services. It started in, and was largely contained in, the piano that was there for the purposes of accompanying the hymns. The fire was smothered by the use of the ready fire extinguishers. The piano was then rolled outside onto the pavement of the walkway leading from the administrative building to the buildings housing the cell blocks, where it promptly reignited. There was then no effort to extinguish it. Now that it was outside there was no danger. And it was quite interesting. This time the flames were accompanied by the springing of piano wires. Peter was there, and I did not wait for him to speak first this time.

"Some say the world will end in fire," I observed.

"Some in ice," he answered.

"I hold with those who favor fire."

"I know you do," he said, "but I was thinking more along the lines that it was about time that chapel had held some kind of Zoroastrian ceremony."

"You mean, the immanent and un-burning fire?"

"Yes, like that book you are un-writing."

"Yeah," I said, smiling at him, "maybe I'll see you at the next blaze."

"I think it best we part before the last remains of our friendship melt away like smoke."

The arithmetic was starting to work against Peter in a way, but either he was still very much unaware of the problems or he was actively courting them. The monkey business may have added some panache to his role but it had also created and had hardened some enemies for him. This latest incident had been a bother to big Frank and his men since the chapel was more or less their domain. And it mattered little to them whether or not they could determine for certain if Peter had been the cause of the fire. They had always been successful operating on what had been strong hunches. The ranks of his little slave coterie had also swollen, but most of the new recruits were unfortunately coming from the lineups maintained by Book and his men. Peter only became more buoyant and lively. The effect of this may have been to have delayed any action on the part of big Frank. But this was only due to Frank's excellent sense of economy. He knew Book would soon be doing his work for him.

Book and a couple of his minions had been watching Peter and had cornered him in the mess hall several minutes after the room had officially closed. They were about to move on him when he hopped onto one of the tables and began to sing a soulful and sweet rendition of "Some Enchanted Evening" from the musical *South Pacific*. The effect of this was surprising. It stopped Book and his men in their tracks long enough to draw a small crowd and the attention of one guard. The glowering of Book indicated that the next time he had Peter at his disposal he would be even rougher than he had planned for that time. Then Peter did another unexpected thing. He did a pirouette and he flung his arm in the direction of Book and his men, extended a finger and said, or rather sang, "In his pockets he has crystal methedrine. Once you have grabbed him, never let him go. Once you have grabbed him, never . . . let . . . him . . . go."

That was the last we ever saw Book in the Manchester minimum-security prison. But now the mathematics were becoming inexorable.

Peter had made an enemy of every man who wanted to keep a secret from the authorities and who had ever been informed upon. He just smiled and looked at me and he said something I cannot forget.

"Whenever you are confronted by a problem," he said as his smile grew to a great grin, "go around it."

Very soon after that, only a few days later, a posse of lawyers arrived. Apparently, Peter had been being held on a charge of contempt of court, and it turned out that he was one of those rare individuals who sort of had his own key out of the joint. All he would have had to have done was to no longer be in contempt. In other words, he could answer the questions in court that he had refused to answer and he would then go free. The lawyers had brought the court order for his release. He did not need to answer the questions. The case in which he was being asked to testify had ended in some other way. He was no longer in contempt because there was no trial. He just walked away.

Later, my friend John said to me, "It just makes so much sense that he was in contempt of court. He seemed to have such contempt for everything."

"On the contrary," I answered, "he used to always say, 'Wisdom in extremes is folly.' He was completely without judgment."

I had only some filmy and flickering insights into what was this eleventh instance of the revelation. Those were made more evident to me when I returned to my cell and found that my divine guide was there, my mixed-race movie actress messiah, wearing a very chic light gray three piece cashmere suit. The slacks fit tightly, but the long-sleeve top was loose with a large open collar, and the short-sleeve sweater over it reached to her knees and had huge pockets. Almost inexplicably but fittingly there appeared unto me a cloven tongue as of fire and it sat upon my head.

"I think I am beginning to get the picture," I said to her in French and not in the English you are reading here. "And fire may be the holiest and most spiritual . . ."

". . . part of each of us," she finished my sentence, which I heard in English.

"And even though it has nothing to do with justice or morality it is divine, maybe because it has nothing to do with those things." She then added, "And, Christian, I think you are ready for the final vision."

ΛLPHABETS

I have reached the impossible part of the story. Even when one attempts to describe the indescribable, one must use words which carry with them their own varied and limited meanings that are subject to the reference points of what each reader understands about each word or phrase from her or his own reading experience. What then might have begun as a very difficult if not impossible exercise in description or explanation becomes an experiment in literary criticism.

One night recently in my cell, during a rare time when I did not have a cellmate, I saw something very strange. Bunks are assigned by seniority, and for some reason the lower bunk in every case and without exception is always for the inmate who has been in the facility longer. It is as if whatever minority percentage of inmates with seniority who might have chosen the top bunk had been brought into complete consensus by the prison need for uniformity in its lexicon of implications. If seniority in one cell or another were to have been the top bunk then the general meaning of seniority would become uncertain for the whole facility. One can easily see that for all practical purposes that every cell was really the cell of the lower bunk man. The other fellow was just a visitor, which will put into perspective how and why I was encouraged to stay silent about the whole bunk-shaking episode of my earliest incarceration. When the top bunk cellmate had garnered enough time to be assigned to a lower bunk in another cell, he would take it. And for however many days before a new man came in or was assigned, the lower bunk man would have the cell to himself. It was at one of these rare times when I had my cell to myself that I saw this strange thing in the unexpected dark.

It can never really be dark anywhere in a prison. There will always be enough areas that simply must be lighted so that, even after lights out, and even within an unlit cell, there will always be some ambient light. This night it was dark. There may have been a power outage, but even that would have kicked on the emergency generators and would have supplied the prison with its normal nighttime lighting requirement. For some unknown reason there was just no light. In that dark I thought I saw an iridescent flicker in the mortar of the cinder block above my locker on the wall across from the bed. I looked more closely and I could not see it again. I got up and stared at the spot and I could not see it. I flicked on my cigarette lighter and focused again on the same spot in the light of that small flame and I could see nothing unusual. So I got back in my bunk and I closed my eyes. When I opened them I saw it again. So I concentrated on it until it again disappeared. Then I closed my eyes and recalled what I had just seen. In the image in my mind, I counted down the blocks from the top of the cell and the blocks over from the wall and I was able to locate where the shining had been as if on a map or a grid. I got up and went to stare again at the spot but still could see nothing. I drew a circle around where I remembered it had been.

That morning I woke up and I looked closely at the circle, and surely enough within the middle of it was a slight deviation in the paint over the mortar in the spot between the blocks where I had marked the circle. I opened up my nail clipper and with the emery board extension I scraped the paint just enough to get down to the mortar and saw that the irregularity was covering something that was encased in the course between the blocks. It was about half an inch long and as thin as a small paper clip and it was the color of the cement filling, only it also seemed to be clear. I worked at it for a while and loosened it. Then I covered it with a drawing that I taped over it and went about my day's work and meals and my workout and my running. I thought about it all day and I wondered if it would also glow that following night.

There was the uncustomary darkness again that night. When in the darkness I removed the drawing from the wall, the sliver or whatever it had been was clearly glowing with a pale light. I took the nail clipper again and with it I grabbed a corner of the thing and without cutting into it I gently extracted it from the wall. It was a half an inch by a half an inch square, roughly the size of a postage stamp. You may think or decide what you will about what happened next. I will do my best within the limits of words to explain it. I placed it on the desk, and it became the color of the desk, as if it were transparent. Then it began to unfold. It unfolded to the point where it was just a book, in my hands. But what I could read in that book was larger than the desk, larger than the prison, larger than the state of Kentucky. In fact, the text of the book encompassed all of the universe and all of time within it, all the while I was reading it at my desk.

I literally read everything in it. It was a literary mirror of a sort, and I was able to look at my selves in it. Only, some of what I had read then is now incomprehensible to me. My mind at the time was able to comprehend all that it read and felt and saw. I know that much, with certainty. At that point I could not have said or written anything about the experience. It exceeded expression. It filled me too full for words. But time and memory have diminished it to the point that I can find words for it now. But I even know now that I knew at that first instant that at least part of the twelfth revelation was about reading. I was certain that reading is central to the final revelation.

I read the entire lives of all my friends, family members, and former lovers. I read the history and the future of the world's great civilizations and the individual dramas of each of the persons who ever lived. I leafed through the motivations and even the dreams of my friends and strangers. I read about you, reading this book, and I read your questions. I read about the origins and the endings of all things and what is in between. I read of what has been called the alpha and the omega and what others have called the face of God. Perhaps importantly, I read and understood the meaning of all of the dozen divine revelations and I saw what they meant, how they fit together, and I grasped all of their paradoxes. I browsed articles and treatises about this book and about myself, in every way that is possible. And I read about myself in the very act of reading this thing that was about all things in one.

Then I heard a sound, one that did not come from my reading but which came from the hall of the cell block. Someone was walking. The cadence and timbre of the tread of the steps told me there were two guards approaching my cell. It could only be the hacks anyway. It was night, and the inmates were in their cells. My cell had been and was still filled with the iridescent light from the alpha and omega book. So I did what any other prisoner would have had to have done. I folded it back up to its original small size. And I ate it.

It was dark in my cell then, and I was back in my bed when the hacks arrived. They turned their flashlights on me and entered the cell and looked at me and asked me why had there been a light in my cell. I told them that I did not know and that I thought it was very weird. I also told them that I thought it was also very strange that the whole rest of the prison was dark. This halted their aggressiveness for a moment. Whatever had put out the lights in this place had been a mystery and a concern to them. In their minds, I had just placed the light from my cell into the same mystery. They turned and left me alone for the time being. Early the next morning my cell was tossed. They took the entire thing apart looking for contraband. They found none. Oddly, they never took down the drawing I had taped to the wall above my locker even though they emptied the locker and the desk beside it and took apart the bed. They might have seen the circle I had drawn or the slot the size of a postage stamp in the mortar between the blocks, where there had been the folded book in which I had read literally everything and which I had eaten and that had provided me all the answers, including the answers to the questions I had read that you have regarding this book and the dozen disciples of truth.

I had read your all of your questions. I am not willing to answer all of them, but I will give you an idea of what I had read by relating only a few illuminating elements.

This interest in Fabrizio never surprises me and it always delights me even though my own inclination is to consider and to discuss the issues that have more meat on their bones. Perhaps that is why you are the one reading and I am the one writing this book. I am ponderous and do not move without creating friction. You can always put down this book or turn off the computer screen and you do know better than I do what you like. And most people sincerely like Little Philly Ray Sanchez and they felt even more affectionately toward him as he transformed into Fabrizio. I believe perhaps that he may have learned as much from me as he had taught me and maybe he was better off for it. It is hard to tell. It is also quite possible that this seemingly elevating exposure to the world beyond his own may have had a deleterious effect on him. He has simply been that successful, and success is a great smoke screen.

I read that he had been sent to a medium-security prison but from there he was able to get that little piece of doggerel I had written for him published under his own name in the *New Yorker* magazine, and when I say it was published under his own name I do not just mean he thankfully did not credit the poem to me but that he published it simply as Fabrizio, one name. He then was able to publish a short volume of a number of other sincerely terrible poems that were liberally sprinkled with Spanish and which were based on his experiences in prison, his role as Belinda's lover or perhaps the better phrase is as her governor and on his short sojourns with me. The volume was entitled *Out From Deliteracy* and it was again published under his new *nom de plume*. I was able to read all of those poems in the alpha and omega on that second dark night, and each was more deadly than the next. I was also able to read that he had taken pains to explain each one of his poems in letters to television shows and magazines and internet outlets with prose that was only slightly less droll than it was affected.

Here is one poetic example:

When time is gray and
With it you

Come above the song
And into view.
In the morning
World of my lost
Loving fire,
No first is first
Until the sound
Of you has gone,
And into dark
Love is found
And with it
The dawn.

He explained to Oprah Winfrey, the television talk show hostess, in his letter, that the "juxtaposition of the two 'firsts' had an ironic depth that was counterpoised by the Homeric dawn reference," and that the "morning theme that runs throughout is tantamount to mourning for lost love." I have no doubt that his insistent explaining played a significant and contributory role in the events that followed and which are almost so obvious and expected as to not bear my reporting. This volume of his poetry was able to win for him the National Book Award for Poetry and to also garner a second place finish in the voting for the Pulitzer Prize for Poetry. He was, at the urging of several liberal publications and luminaries, transferred from behind the razor wire at the Manchester medium-security facility to the Duluth, Minnesota Federal Prison Camp, which was minimum-security and was known as the least punitive spot in the entire federal system since it was not appurtenant to any higher security prison and was free standing.

Belinda followed him to rent a house in Duluth and to allow herself to be developed as a photographic model for the illustrated version of his volume of poetry, which was released after he had won the awards and which was graphically designed quite tastefully along a bondage and discipline theme with each poem juxtaposed, as it were, with a photograph of the lovely Ms. Hahner in various poses of abject submission and which languished on the *New York Times* bestseller list for only thirty-one weeks.

The foreword to that illustrated version was written by none other than our friend Mr. Benyamin Hamete, and part of it went like this: "Belinda and Fabrizio will be inseparable in time and in the hearts of men and women for having understood two important things. In confronting the world, with its institutionalized injustices, its hypocritical orthodoxies, its consensus of mediocrity, its calamities, and all the other of its many tyrannies, it is often the best thing to approach it inside out as it were and to impose upon it a different order, a vision of one's own, and one that is playful or heroic or loving or beautiful or just plain strikingly mad. And nothing succeeds so much as two individuals being able to share this play with one another as two characters and as two co-authors who hear, see and feel each other first and the world second, if at all."

Your questions about the issues raised by the Rabbi and big Frank are answered in a dream, but not just any dream. The dream I had read is about a woman whose story is so large and significant that it will be the main part of that sequel to this book, the one that Big Frank had mentioned. This woman is one of the most significant figures of what will be our future history. She will have been a religious, social, and political leader unlike any other and she will have brought about much of that future in much the same way you are considering it as you read this passage.

Melinda Sherman of London, Kentucky, joined the United States Navy at the urging of that crucified Jesus we were told she saw on the telephone pole. All that you will read from this point is what I read that night and it is what will have happened years from now. She entered the Navy and was tested and sent to officer candidate school and then to flight school, where she became a helicopter pilot. She was wounded several times in action serving in one of the many small wars her country initiated in the Middle East and South Central Asia, including once quite grievously while extracting a Navy Seal team from a successful covert mission deep inside of a dangerous and hostile region. It had been her courage and fortitude that had kept that mission a success. As enemy forces had been closing in on that special forces team, she sustained several wounds landing her craft and picking them up. She stoically maintained consciousness only until the very moment she had landed her helicopter on the deck of her ship. She then lay in a coma for two weeks and recovered, having lost her spleen, some of her liver, and the ability to have children. She went on to fly Navy helicopters for a total of twelve years and then served the rest of her time as an officer in Naval Intelligence. For her efforts, she emerged from the Navy as a captain after twenty five years, with the Purple Heart, the Bronze Star, the Navy and Marine Corps Medal for heroism, the Joint Service Commendation Medal, and the Congressional Medal of Honor, just to name a few.

All of this did not escape the attention of the leaders of the political parties, and soon after her discharge she was recruited to run for the United States House of Representatives. She won election to the United States House of Representatives; where she earned a reputation for speaking the truths that most politicians are too emasculated to ever speak. She criticized the kind of wars in which she herself had been decorated. She railed against their cost and their failings. She hit home and won some concessions with her argument that the United States was paying to provide military defense for countries which paid little or no contribution toward that defense. She derided the war on drugs and government intervention into the family and the failure of the United States to realize that many of its foreign policy goals, its environmental issues and its fiscal short-comings could be addressed eloquently and simply by a large federal tax on gasoline. Her failure to be cowed by polls or the press or the attacks of her opponents was surprisingly viewed by the people of Kentucky to be leadership, and she was later elected to the United States Senate from that state.

All her life she had been strong and athletic. During most of her time in the Navy she had also been a triathlete, swimming and cycling and running many dozens of miles in each triathalon. She was five foot nine inches tall, and her shape was womanly, with a narrow waist, strong athletic legs, and a medium-size chest. But all of this was on a muscular frame and not at all soft, and her shoulders and arms were a little broad and solid for a woman. Her face was handsome and strong-boned but still very attractive in a feminine way, with soft but piercing green eyes and sandy blonde hair, which she kept short.

Senator Sherman had dreamed an idea that she then implemented and that would propel her to international prominence and into the White House. She decided to take a trip, with only two assistants and one reporter, who was also a videographer for an internet news outlet, to the most conservative mosque in Dearborn, Michigan, which is the largest community that is majority Muslim in America. Upon arrival in Dearborn, she and her small entourage dressed in proper conservative dress and entered the mosque. The Senator then attempted to enter the part of the mosque which is reserved only for men. She was stopped at the door by the guard. With the same quiet but adamantine determination with which she had placed a wounded and embattled team of Navy Seals safely onto the deck of an aircraft carrier, she quietly walked past the guard and into the men-only section of the mosque. What happened then was a kind of a modern American version of a good old Middle Eastern stoning of the type that has been going on for over a millennium and continues to this day over there. A group of men surrounded her, screaming at her and punching her and kicking her. She was even stabbed two or three times. And all the while, she kept her calm. Then she finally fell bloody to the floor. Her two assistants had once been Navy Seals. They stood over her and protected her and pulled her to safety.

The entire event had been captured on digital film. The Greek chorus for this drama had been a handful of American Muslim women who had followed her outside, partly out of curiosity and partly out of sympathy. They punctuated the event with cries and ululations and screams of surprise. Several of them prostrated themselves. The video was on the internet within minutes and was picked up shortly after that by every major news outlet in the world. And within minutes after that she was in a television station news studio in Detroit, Michigan, discussing what had happened.

"The intersection of life in faith and life in the world," she began her televised address to the public, "is a very dangerous place at which to stand. Faith in itself, and religion at its most personal, pose no danger. But the instant that religion takes a stand within the world, it is nothing more than a political party and in many cases an extremist political party. If you look at what happened to me at the mosque, you have to ask in what way the faith of each of the individuals there could possibly have been affected by my entry into their place of worship. Is their personal faith so fragile that it would suffer by my presence? And could their God have been damaged by the actions of one middle-aged American woman? One would have to answer, 'No,' if one had an abiding faith and one that was deeply personal. The problem is not what you believe but what you impose upon the rest of us. And in many cases the desire to impose upon others is stronger than any personal faith.

"We may not judge another person's faith," she continued, "but we must judge its actions and the effect it has on the rest of us. Perhaps America is a faith. I must say that it is my faith. I have an independent right to find my own way to God and I believe that each one of us has it as well. And, like everything else in America, it must be democratic. We each have the right to be free of each other's faiths. The actions of each faith may be judged by the way it treats its members and non-members, by the way it treats women, by the way it treats the least among us, by the way it treats those who are its neighbors, and by the way it respects itself in the face of differing beliefs. It is one thing to live your own life in faith, it is another thing entirely to say that your God gives you certain sanctions within the world, such as the right to bomb innocents, or to take and command a land, or to oppress women."

She was later elected President. It turned out that Senator Sherman had read this very book you are reading and was in fact one of the *Gospel Prism* devout, a true believer. She had paid particular attention to the third revelation. And she firmly believed that she had the power to dream the future into existence, but that is another story for another book, the sequel that Big Frank had mentioned.

I will also relate the story I had read in the all-encompassing book of what became of Chester. He was sent to work in the medium-security prison in Bradford, Pennsylvania. He was detailed to the yard and to the mess hall and as such he was regularly among the prisoners in groups and not when they were alone or in small numbers. He did not come to have too much personal interaction with any of them as individuals. His more deeply personal idiosyncrasies or what this narrative referred to as his "shines" were not given the opportunity to be particularly and individually observed. What were noticed were his lanky country gait, his often blank or quizzical expressions, his more general inexpressiveness, and the odd glint in his eye that was the spiritual equivalent of being cross-eyed. These were noticed by the assemblage of inmates and as a group. To this convocation of hardened men looking at twenty or more years on the inside, Chester was a character out of some mean streets version of the *Commedia dell'arte*. More specifically, he was the harlequin servant. His entry into the yard or the mess hall would be met with a kind of heightened combination of what is the substitute in prison for mirth mixed with actual contempt. He invited a lack of respect. In a prison this is the equivalent of a loose ratchet on a machine gearbox. Occasionally there would be a shake and a shudder within the group of inmates. And always there was a slight looseness that could almost be heard in the workings. It was accompanied by the implication that the next shake and shudder would be a precipitous one.

The Drug Enforcement Administration of the United States at one point had an extensive detail of agents assigned to follow the Grateful Dead rock and roll band from concert to concert. After the Grateful Dead ceased touring, this detail followed the concerts of a group call Phish. Essentially, each of these bands had attracted legions of young fans who liked to enhance their concert experience by taking hallucinogenic drugs such as LSD. They were "acid" bands. The acronym DEA is widely referred to in prison as the Degenerate Entertainment Agency, because entertainment was clearly one of the primary charters of this government agency. Their agents on this detail were surely hearing more decent music than was being heard by their counterparts who might be listening instead to the sound of automatic weapons being fired at them as they came upon surprised members of armed Mexican drug cartels at night border crossings in the deserts of the American Southwest. And few things could be more entertaining than simply the notion that these acid band agents were keeping America safe from the unbounded menace of a few incredibly fey and wan teenagers who would otherwise be threatening everyone else and the American way of life by their spaced-out stares, their swaying to the music they often heard only in their heads, and the way in which they tended to drool onto the tops of their shoes.

Prisoners in minimum-security prisons such as this one would certainly be entertained when one of these individuals landed in our midst. And there would be the vastly more entertaining spectacle of what would assuredly happen to one of these children if he were to find himself suddenly inside of one of the big houses, the maximum-security prisons, or even inside a medium-security prison such as the one that then employed Chester. There can be no doubt that the authorities were aware that, for the majority of both prisoners and hacks, being able to observe the consequences of such an eventful individual incarceration would be like a trip to the Colosseum of Rome in the reign of Vespasian.

These inmates who had been harvested by the DEA were indeed children. The fans and concert-goers for those two bands were habitual and followed the bands to almost every concert like a gypsy caravan. That majority were experienced and knew to avoid the DEA agents among them. So the only criminals being charged and convicted were the unsophisticated ones, the callow kids like Chickenhead, who one day in high school had decided to become a Phish fan and who had shown up and had been arrested at his first concert. He was not with us at Manchester for very long.

I had read in the alpha and omega volume what had happened to Chickenhead after the he left us at the Manchester minimum-security facility and coincidentally had followed Chester to the Bradford medium- security prison. I am certain no one ever knew Chickenhead's real name. Nicknames are minor and obscure arguments in favor of the notion of Plato's ideals. This young man's prison nickname was something much closer to his real and true and Platonically ideal name than his given name ever could have been. He was tall and thin and very pale, with even paler blue eyes. His head was larger than the proportion of his body would specify. And his medium-length black hair never did what hair should, choosing instead to fly off in swatches indicating a differing set and only three of the four major directions of the compass. This east-south-north or west-south-east look of his hair and the dramatic way it offset the rest of his coloring is what had given someone the first insight into his ideal name.

The rest of him only served to confirm the insight. He had a superficial kinetic quality to his movements, and to stand next to him was like being in the woods when the leaves are falling off of the trees. You were likely to get hit but you would be unlikely to feel it. He alternated between moments of very focused behavior and long intervals of inattentiveness. These second moments were really periods of absorbed attention only to his own thoughts, from which he could not be distracted by what might be observed in the world around him. He had an odd susceptibility to extremities of expressions of emotion. Things were either the worst or the best for him. Even incidental physical contact could surprise him to the extent that he would start or jump. And his long, thin fingers never seemed to work in concert or to contain much grace. They were often splayed or akimbo or they failed at some simple task, and this gave him the impression of being younger than his nineteen years. To an informed reader, this description indicates the actual truth of the diagnosis; Chickenhead had the version of attention deficit disorder which does not include symptoms of hyperactivity.

This is what had caused him to be moved from the relative insecurity of our minimum-security facility to the outright jeopardy of the medium- security prison. He had simply jumped and had run the wrong way when he had been startled by guards who had been running in his direction in order to apprehend a pair of inmates who had been jogging past him in order to try to hide their contraband alcoholic beverage, their prison hooch which had been brewed from the anaerobic fermentation of sports drinks. He was rounded up with them and sent off. We never knew what happened after that, but I was able to read in the book that had unfolded on my desk that coincidentally he had followed Chester, who had also been sent to

Bradford. These two men recognized each other uneasily, as is only possible for a hack and a convict, but they recognized each other.

Chester's particular appearance and demeanor had caused a lack of respect that the group of inmates must have for a guard, and this was like the described loose ratchet on a machine gearbox. Chickenhead's look, demeanor, youth, and inattentiveness were more than that. They were like blood in the water to sharks. In that prison he was basically traveling like a diminishing and detached and passive wraith from one assault to another gang rape to being robbed and intimidated to sleepless nights of sobbing in his bunk. It very soon came to a head only a few weeks after his arrival, in the far corner of the exercise yard, in a scene reminiscent of Nathanael West. Pursued and hounded through this mental and emotional maze and like a cornered prey, Chickenhead had finally let out a cry of frail defiance and stood to fight his tormentors, his chin quivering, his odd fingers shaking, tears running down his face. It was a harbinger of his doom. The group of inmates had flexed like a single muscle, and now they were poised.

In such a situation there were two protocols for Chester. As a prison guard he was supposed to intervene and prevent any violence. The more informal procedure for a hack would have been to let it happen and to steer clear of any personal danger while calling for some help. But perhaps Chester had been in some way contaminated by his tweeting episode at Manchester. What is more likely is something conceivably more universal. Maybe Chester had within him more than one self. The detached self, who he thought he really was, could observe and participate at the same time. It could roughly accommodate what he was seeing happen and would think first to be restrained. But perhaps there was a deeper self within him that was unfathomable and bottomless and which was destined to move and react. He knew that for Chickenhead he largely felt only a kind of disdain, the natural contempt that he felt for all criminal convicts and a particular disapproval that he felt for the weaknesses of this particular one. There was also a connection from them having had been together at Manchester which was a familiarity that Chester resented. It is likely that this derision was swept aside by that immeasurable self within Chester but it is even more likely that his contempt was actually its motivation. He decided to follow neither protocol. Chester simply looked upon the suffering of Chickenhead with restless and drooping eyes. He understood that the other man was himself. He dropped the badge and radio and the other insignia of his official status. And he went and stood with the boy, fought, and perished by his side.

More than a thousand years from now there will be a history of the future written. And I have already read it in that remarkable book, which I also ate. A thousand years from now most people will look back upon us the same way that we look back upon those peoples of over two thousand years ago. We view the devout faiths of those people and we call those sincerely followed religions (Greek or Roman or Egyptian) mythology. A thousand years from now, they look at us and see our religions as mythology.

And the primary myth they will see is that there was any such thing as certainty about the divine. They find it quaint that any man or woman, Muslim, Christian, or Jew could ever say with certainty that he or she knew God. In the faiths of the Greeks and Romans men such as Icarus or Phaeton who had tried to appropriate the divine for their own use were struck down by the gods for violating the order of the universe, which kept men below the gods. A thousand years into the future, statements of certainty about the will or the mind of God will be seen as the same cosmic overreaching. It will be as if Ovid again is the most important writer.

This part of the story ends necessarily where the entire story began, with toilet paper and in prison. Ingesting the alpha and omega volume concerned me at least as much as it must have been considered by you. For three days afterward, I was meticulous in examining everything that came out of me, every particle and speck. I have since come to be skeptical about the book entirely and all that I had read in it. It was what was. It had conveyed to me all that I have said. But perhaps it was not a true version of what it purported to be. I wonder about this because I never saw it again.

I did see my guiding Christ again, one more time, a week later. Seeing her again was of great concern to me because she had indicated that my salvation was hanging in the balance. I had now completed my journey and believed at that moment, even though the complete understanding that I had gathered from reading the alpha and omega book had fled me, that I had maintained a fairly good, if gentle and caring, grasp on her twelve disciples of truth, the dozen divine insights.

Jesus came to me in the visiting room with my mother, who said she was quite upset with me "about some of things in that book of yours." I looked at my mother with one of those silently conveying looks that are inherent to our ethnic heritage, and we both knew that my look said, "You do know who this person really is, don't you?" And my mother gave me another Sicilian look in return that said that she was unimpressed. My beautiful female Christ was wearing a simple pair of blue jeans and a pale blue blouse as she spoke to me, in a familiar and almost sisterly manner.

"So, pilgrim, Happy Judgment Day to you. Do you have a report to give to me?"

"I will give it a very brief try," I answered tentatively. "Each of us contains within our deepest self an immanent and indestructible soul. It is fiery and full of its own music and is capable of the most outrageous originality and self-sacrificing love. It is limitless and bottomless and able to fill any and all others with the power of its findings. It is best served and preserved from danger and manipulation by drawing a hard line around it, over which we should not impose the self on love or impose our faith and beliefs on others. This boundary should only be crossed with the buffering provided by distance, irony and playfulness and with the intent to embrace all others not only if they are different but because they are."

"That is not a bad little catechism. It is hardly everything. But you seem to have learned something. Every expression is a reduction and a mistaken reading of the truth. Yours is not a particularly bad misreading. Don't worry that you might have been judged. Your salvation is still hanging in the balance. We are never fully formed, and our comprehension of divine wisdom will always be something at which we must labor and of which we may never be assured."

"That is reassuring," I said.

"You also always have to be very careful," my divine visitor said. "Our humanity sees the divine as a mystery and cannot know it. It has no attraction or repulsion. But the demon in us wants to appropriate the divine. If we feel we have been visited by the Lord or that the Holy Spirit has entered us, the proper reaction is merely awe. As soon as we decide to make use of it in our dealings with others, we are responding to something in ourselves which is not divine."

"Which is what I had done with my attempt at evangelism," I confessed. "But I think I see it now. Our skepticism should contain within it all of the weight and import of knowing that the downside of a possible mistake in our supposed certainty could have the worst possible negative consequence."

"That would truly be God's will, and it should be clear to us through knowing the only part of creation which is truly available to us. I will tell you something funny," she added. "Some people who will accuse you of blasphemy because I am in your book."

"I fail to see what's so funny about that. It is actually very . . ."

". . . ironic," she interrupted. "These will be people who have found God in a book. They essentially will be saying that it is all right to find the Lord in one book but not in any other."

"Oh, that makes it much better," I said.

"The mystical book which you read in your cell last week and the book you are now writing and the holy books of those other people and any book in general are all a crucial part of this final revelation. You personally experienced a few revelations and then you had to read meaning in the rest of revelations in the stories around you. Part of this final insight is that reading is a key element to your salvation. Only by reading do you quickly and easily reach beyond the souls of your family and circle of friends and acquaintances. Reading is your opportunity to brush with the minds of other people, great women and men who have also been visited by divine inspiration. Reading deeply of the great books is your best opportunity to find the divine."

"And there is more to it than that, I know."

Then she said, in French, "But of course. And you will have to keep reading in order to figure it out. The other holy irony is that this

341

book of yours attempts to state something that itself acknowledges cannot be fully stated. So don't step away from this book just yet. Au revoir, my Christian," and she and my mother left the visiting room.

I have since spoken at length about this entire spiritual journey with my attorney. I have my own lengthy interpretation of the progress made throughout my prison pilgrimage to the twelve revelations of divine truth. But since I actually am the pilgrim, it is not my place to give you my full and direct interpretation. The last person anyone wants to hear discuss a book is the person who wrote it. For one thing, you may make the horrible mistake of assuming that my interpretation is the definitive one. It is always best to read the book through the prism of your own mind. Besides, I have already taken a few hundred pages to give my story to you. My legal representative knows my mind and he has read this book through his own prism, and perhaps that makes it a better example for you than my own. He is as likely to be as correct or incorrect as any one of us. His somewhat extreme and illuminating interpretation will only encourage you to discover your own.

AFTERWORD

I have represented the author of this book for a period of time constituting many years before his current incarceration. His opinions and insights are as familiar to me as my own. Many years ago he referred to something that he called the war between the page and the screen, a war that he had said that the page of written words was doomed to lose, and which it waged against the various versions of the screen: the television, the computer, the cellular phone, and that curious oxymoron, the electronic book. His favorite adage many years ago was to say, "We will all know that the final bugle call in the last stand of the written page will have been sounded when Hollywood will make *Paradise Lost, The Movie.*" That day has arrived.

He had also been able to predict that when books will have been reduced to digital form their substance too will be forever altered. This is nowhere more evident than it has been in what is the wild popularity of the electronic book *Blades of Grass*. It was inevitable that once Walt Whitman's *Leaves of Grass* had become available in digital form that some enterprising soul would have done a cut-and-paste job on the text and would then have set about to edit and rewrite it, taking out the endless cataloging, changing the archaic syntax, filling in the numerous ellipses, adding several acronyms and emoticons, and generally streamlining the text for a digital age audience. In fact, *Blades of Grass* replaced almost every ellipse that had been in *Leaves of Grass* with "lol," which is internet shorthand for laugh out loud, generating: "I am large, lol, I contain multitudes," which has become one of the favorite lines for the multitudes of new readers, who, along with the person who had amended the original, all reminded the critics that Whitman himself was throughout his life a tireless reviser. The unintended irony, of course, is that for Whitman's generation a leaf was also a page of written words and a blade something else entirely.

Our inmate author also anticipated that this very same thing would happen to his own book, as indeed it has. But *Gospel Prison* and *God Awful Prism* and the other reflections and inversions of his original book have not come close to matching the popularity and profound impact of *Gospel Prism*, largely because our author had anticipated them. This book has been conceived and designed with holes in the narrative and with the capacity to assume other books, so that it may be unwritten and rewritten and so that it may live and breathe in a way that makes it the first book and the last book. What the author may or may not have been able to anticipate is exactly what that profound impact might have been. The book accommodates this, though, so what he may or may not have meant is secondary to the text. You must make your own judgment. But from this point on, I will relate to you what I believe he told me.

That God is in this book and that this book indicates a way in which the divine may be found in other books is a belief that is held by a growing number of very devout followers of this book, some of whom have actually read it in one or another of its forms. And in fact this is part of the twelfth and final revelation of this book. Christ may visit each of us, and each of us may be inhabited by the spirit of the Lord. And such a thing has indeed happened to others, that is, to authors, and specifically each one of the twelve divinely inspired writers reflected in each of the twelve insights. The Lord has spoken to us from the books of those twelve writers, and also from many other books, dozens of which are also referenced in this book. Seek God in what you read and you will know the divine when you see it. If a child reads any book he is looking in its pages at a very spare road map showing him a way toward the Lord.

As stated, this particular book is a book in which a reader may detect holy truths and it shares this quality with the books of faith and with other books. The leap from the pages of this book to faith may or may not be made by the reader. This is much the situation with most books. That leap may be institutionalized in an organized religion, in which case what is written in the stories on the page becomes secondary to the religion. *Gospel Prism* and the other books it reflects have yet to reach this stage, and this book was conceived and designed in such a way as to resist and to assimilate that seemingly inevitable development. It is simply both too mercurial and encompassing, which of course is something that may also have been said about the New Testament. Part of the faith which most believers currently have in this particular book is that it also encompasses other books, and that part of this detective story is the specific road map it lays out for finding the way that those books are also vessels in which one may search for the traces and suggestions of God.

The Boy Scouts of America have an international system for marking trails that is understandable to the initiated and which uses stones and blazes and sticks to show which way the path through the forest goes and also does not go. Each reader of this book may find in it the spiritual equivalents of these markings. And he or she may also find the blazes within all other books. My own reading of this book is perhaps less meaningful than your own, and each of our interpretations are subsumed by and contained in this book.

The first revelation seems to me to be that when Christ, distaff or otherwise, visits any of us, or that when the spirit of whatever God in whom we believe enters us, the most important part of each phrase is its object, the word "us." Each one of us is all that we each actually have and all that we truly know of the whole of God's sacred creation. Any holy visitation or even any mundane understanding may only be devoutly understood on our own terms and subject to our own God-given uncertainty, temperaments, and vapors. The true study of the divine is the study of ourselves, and we must understand ourselves first and best. Uncertainty is one of our truly divine hallmarks, and we must hold anything that strikes us as the most sublime truth with the most gentle and delicate care. This uncertainty may actually be the most holy element that is within us. It is irony and is the very basis of our thinking. It is the way in which the Lord made us different from his other creatures. Humanity was able to harness the value of fire because one person first had a strong and divine doubt that a forest fire was entirely something terrible and something only to fear and to flee. If one is certain of receiving the love of one's spouse or children, or is certain of one's continued health, or is certain of one's faith, then the truest devotion to our understanding of ourselves as the pinnacle of creation is to be devoutly skeptical of all such certainty. Holding each belief only gingerly is not only more delicate and beautiful and more likely to preserve each belief, it is also God's will.

And what the twelfth revelation shows is that the expansion of the truths of this first insight was once a divine disclosure made to a Gallic man who kept to himself in his tower with his kidney stones.

After all, if the spirit of the Lord may enter Carl Cartright while he is kneeling on the floor and if it may enter any one of us at any time, it most certainly must have entered the writer of those divinely wise essays four hundred years ago. To read what he has written will point to the larger holy truths of this book's first insight. And he himself is also the insight or the disciple. Each revelation is as it appears to us in this book. It is also in each of the authors reflected by each insight. And it is in his or her writings. So each holy revelation is tripartite, a type of holy trinity.

The second vision indicates a central truth of the way that the world or life may be best approached, while it is also a reflection upon the first revelation. The piously gentle and devoutly delicate care with which we should apply divine or absolute truths or any other beliefs to life may be most sacred if that approach is also ironic or playful. And it will be more holy and meaningful if that playing is shared with a friend or a loved one. A playful and ironic application of anything that you believe can never be a harmful application, and avoiding such harm is part of God's directive to us in the second insight. And when it is shared with an individual loved one it is more personal and immediate and is necessarily leavened and lightened and made less harmful and even more poignant by that sharing. This merely scratches the surface of the way in which this insight is more fully apprehended in the writings of the disciple of the second truth, who like our author spent some time in prison once, and who like our first disciple wrote over four centuries ago. And he also happened to have written in the original language of our Little Philly Ray Sanchez.

That there is a terrible danger in ignoring these first two understandings is what God shows us in the third revelation, which she expressed through writings of an actor and director who was divinely inspired at roughly the time of the first two revelations. The dogmatic application of faith to a life in the world is dangerous to those affected by it, as it has been to all the casualties of wars of faith. Deaths and loss caused in the name of faith are anathema to God. And the rigid and aggressive application of faith to the world is also potentially harmful to those who would apply it, in the way it was used against the Rabbi by Big Frank. Communism is a kind of faith or a belief. The criminal Communist regimes were not created by criminals but by true and honest believers. All such applications of that belief to the real world have been bloody failures even for their believers. They have also been oppressive in the same way that the Inquisition was tyrannical or in the same way in which innocents have been murdered by the faithful who wear bombs or fly planes into buildings. Most importantly, when we look at what we believe are the dangers of other people's faiths, our negative reaction is God's interior roadmap in our own souls, showing the perils of applying our own faith to worldly circumstances.

Without taking worldly action based upon our beliefs, in other words in the safety of our own minds, we may have the utmost and godly reliance in them, no matter how startling or individual or original they are. In other words, Hell is populated by exactly the persons you are certain are there. You may be divinely assured of your trust in your understanding of who is in Hell, so long as you also have faith that there is no need to actively give this believe some material expression, so long as you take no steps to hurry anyone's admission to that infernal place. Just simply and internally and ironically be sure of what you believe. This fourth divine revelation reflected by this book was shown by Christ to a visionary who lived and wrote in a very refined Renaissance city state some seven hundred years past and who expressed it through his poem more fully than it can be stated here or anywhere else.

This heartfelt confidence is utterly holy and it is at the core of the ability God has given to each of us to resist the influence of convention, to inwardly rely upon our own best judgment, to privately maintain a protest against the dogma and doctrine of the majority or of authority. Each and every great movement began as the idea of an individual who simply posed that awareness against all authority. This is a kind of devil we each contain, and there is nothing wrong with it. It is merely the personal strength that God grants each of us. And central to each individual is a soul which is also a question, a mind which is also possibility, a substance which is also a void. The fifth chapter and revelation of this book points to a person who may be considered the greatest Protestant poet of all time, who more fully expressed his divine revelation of the iconoclastic power each one of us possesses through God, as well as the power of each individual idea to subvert the dominant paradigm in the way that any strong or true idea may take root in the spaces that are the questions and the souls of other men, and where that idea may flourish and spread. And so it is beginning to be with this very book and the poem it reflects in its fifth insight.

And in America only several generations past, God spoke to us through a rough man's rambling words and presented the world with a more full understanding of the sixth insight, which is only palely reflected in this book, that all celebration is also a lamentation, that every laugh contains a tear, that the greatest sorrow is also a very powerful affirmation of life. Through this person's writing,

Christ has shown that each feeling of every person is the feeling of each other person. You divinely contain all the elements of every person who ever lived and who will ever live, even and especially the elements and persons you feel you should hate. This paradox requires each person to lovingly embrace all others, as Chester was embraced and as he later embraced, in spite of and because of what might be your contempt.

The *Gospel Prism* devout know to return to the readings that are reflected in it, in order to gain more divine understanding.

There is piece of God that is in us that also seems to be an ancient divinity who predates the notions we may have gained from any of the great faiths. God was in every human before any of the holy books were written. She was and is a part of us that is atavistic and ineffable and deep within each of us. God spoke to us of this through a troubling and thoughtful Slavic aristocrat who wrote of it well over a hundred years ago. It is hinted at by the seventh insight from this book, which also reflects the original writing of the ancient Greeks. It is a recondite part of each of us that knows no creed. As it was in Psycho, it is simply bolder and brighter and perhaps better and it sends us into burning buildings without thinking and with a psychological depth, strength and purity that we may never fully understand. This holy element lies beneath and contained within that part of each of us that is a blank or a question or a soul. It strives to be known through our daring, our love, and our sacrifice. We must never be unaware of its existence.

The world is a strange and dangerous place, as our author inmate's wife had experienced. Time scorns us. Loved ones may betray. Power and authority oppress. Illness and violence and loss arrive at our door on wings. The unworthy succeed, and justice is elusive. A man who also had Kenny's last name, but as spoken in another language, shared with us his expansion of the holy insight he received from the Lord, and that is the eighth insight related in this book, which is that the deepest part of us is unreachable by the world and by life. We may faithlessly surrender it up, and for that we will suffer more greatly than if we devoutly resist life's intrusions into this citadel of the soul. We do God's will in the case where we hold on tightly to what is deepest inside. Then it is indestructible. And it is a holy source of a patience which is also strength.

This deep and internal and indestructible solitude is a divine territory to be celebrated and defended. It is also not to be squandered. God came to an individual who shared the professions of the human source of our third revelation and who shared the nationality of the human source of the first one and he then illuminated his divine revelation more clearly than did the lover of Celeste in this book. Sometimes the most dangerous incursions against this divine potential indestructibility might be made by love and by attachment, and not only by yielding to danger and calamity. We sacrifice some of our holy inward foundation when we love. This is the ninth revelation of this book. But like each other divine insight, it contains many ironies and may be seen inside out or viewed as in a mirror. If love may be destructive of the self, then love should also be selfless. The self (or you may call it selfishness) may damage holy love, as was also explained in Saint Paul's letter to the Corinthians. Think of it this way. Upon falling in love, it would not make sense to turn to the loved one and say, "I love you so much and you are so precious to me that I want you to see me when I am at my worst and I want to exalt you by requiring you to take care of me when I am sick and to forgive me when I behave poorly." Yet in effect this is what we do by seeking attachment. When we are angered by a loved one's betrayal we are expressing the self and not our love. God has shown us that love and the self are at odds. Whether we preserve the self from love, or the other way around, is our choice.

I believe that the tenth holy understanding of this book is that God shows that all of what we think and all of who we are is woven through with the fabric of memory, as it was shown in the memory of our author the prisoner. Divine revelation has no prejudice and is blind to all else but the soul, so it is not to be surprising to us to know that God visited a half-Jewish gay man who then bound this revelation up into no less than seven volumes for us to explore. Within our cognitive faculty, memory is the lord. The Lord himself is also one who remembers, as was shown in Genesis 8:1 and 19:29 and 30:20. And we learn from the tenth insight of this book and from those seven volumes more than one other thing about our memory and its relation to our thoughts. God has shown us that one of those things is that memory will sometimes lie to us. And it always embellishes. Not only are we subject to tempers, we are made of the very stuff of vapors.

We contain in us a dangerous and preternatural destructive fire, as did Peter Sooner. That is what the eleventh divine understanding of this book seems to be. In some ways, this force simply stands against all that is. It is not the protester of the fifth revelation, nor is it the heroic element of the seventh insight. It is simply fire. And it may be the part of us that is closest to God, is the most in his image, and is at one with his law of the universe. And this eleventh revelation can be found more in the words of a cantankerous Scandinavian who received it from the Lord and then dramatized it. We ignore it at our peril.

What we know at this point of the twelfth holy vision is that all of what we have found to be insights in this book are merely hints of greater and holier versions that may be found in other written works, which were written by, and are personified in, other individuals who received divine visits in some form, as did our author. These writings have all become the expansion of this particular gospel, to the believers of this book. Those greater works are themselves also only hints from the Lord. And they are in fact a part of an even larger testament, of many other words that have come to us from the many other books of men and women and through them from the divine. How they fit together, and what they all are together, is a constant exercise of studious worship by the sect of believers spawned by this book, or it may be their worshipful study.

This final sacred understanding reflected in this book was first visited by God upon a South American visionary in the previous century, and the Lord has shown that his writing actually was also reading. God is often so paradoxical, as she is when she shows we should be confident of our beliefs but skeptical of their application. And the startling second half of this twelfth revelation is that what you are reading as beginning to happen here is what will be entirely the case in the future. Men and women will believe that each book has something in it of God and some books more than others. The Bible is a book. A book is the Bible.

The current state of affairs that confronts the pages of written words as they exist in actual books presents a paradox for the religion which will spring from the legions of believers who already accept *Gospel Prism* as an article of faith. One of the characters in this book has been attributed with saying that religion is like democracy in that it is base and must appeal to the most common human denominator. This may not actually be true except to the extent that it may apply somewhat to the major world religions. The religious cult of this book may remain just that, an elite and arcane faith that is small in number and strong in belief and dedicated to holy study and in which the lay members are also the priesthood. They may become something like a gang of Poggio Bracciolinis, scouring the countryside, this time not for monasteries that may contain the lost manuscripts of Ancient Rome and Greece, but for the ruins of public libraries and book stores and private collections that may hold the books that contain the divine spirit.

This legion of the faithful will eventually merge with the much larger but ever shrinking group of non-believers simply known as readers or as deep readers. The religion of *Gospel Prism* will become one with the sect of the book, or the cult of books. And actual books will become very rare. And to the extent that they remain in virtual form they will be ephemeral and changing and not all that credible. The vast majority of all the other people who are members of the major world religions may no longer find themselves in the odd literarily critical position of worshipping a character to be found in a book. They will simply find that they and millions like them worship a character that they have heard or have been told was once in a book, if that is not already happening.

Two final things might at this point be said. No matter which type of prison to which you have been consigned, the search for God in many ways and in one important way is in your hands right now. And the aforementioned cult of this book and the cult of the book may very well be a sect of one, and that may also be in your hands right now.

ACKNOWLEDGEMENTS

Saying that none of this could have happened without my wife, Lily Chu, is correct but far less accurate than to admit that, absent her confidence, support, and love at various points in time over the course of our marriage, I would have been squashed like a bug. Her part in all of this is far too pervasive to describe, and is far more fundamental than my own role.

A more specific debt is owed to the late Marie Colvin, who told me to write the novel. Then she edited it, inspired and encouraged it, and eventually carried the original manuscript in her knapsack over barbed wire fences and through sewers to her untimely and tragic demise in Homs, Syria. We first became close over forty years ago and the next forty will be impaired by her absence.

Part of Marie's genius was to see through me, as when she said that we both knew that everything I ever do, I really do for my daughter, Harriet, who is also the main reason I get up in the morning, as is her brother, Simon.

Thanks also go to this book's first professional editor, Tim Binding, to Caroline Michel, who assigned him to me, to Cathleen Colvin, who sent that macabre manuscript to Caroline, to Anna Faktorovich at Anaphora Books, who first agreed to publish, and to John Bond at Whitefox, who undertook this final project, to Tim Inman, his assistant, to Fiona Marsh, Tony Mulliken, and especially

Fiona Livesy at Midas Public Relations, and to Kristen Harrison at Curved House. To Gordon Lish, who taught me that fiction should try to be poetry, I give my belated thanks.

And to Harold Bloom, who is a voice in my head, a friend, a hero, a professor, and a bright cynosure for all things literary, goes my most humble gratitude.